"SILAS . . . REALLY . . . WE SHOULDN'T."

He smiled wickedly.

Turning sharply from him, she stumbled . . . and fell right into the fountain.

When she surfaced, Silas was laughing heartily. Before she could catch her breath enough to tell him he was a disgusting, loathsome, subhuman slug, he kicked off his shoes and climbed in beside her. "I've caught me a water nymph," he said, with a gleam in his eye.

That did it. Something inside her snapped and laughter tumbled out. "Silas—" Her protest died when he placed a gentle finger over her wet lips.

Drawing her close, he murmured, "You're safe with me." His finger trailed slowly down from her lips. "I swear it."

His hands were gentle, his eyes were tender. He wrapped her in his surety and strength and carried her away with him . . .

CARRIED AWAY

SUE CIVIL-BROWN

AVON BOOKS ◆ NEW YORK

CARRIED AWAY is an original publication of Avon Books. This work has never before appeared in book form. This work is a novel. Any similarity to actual persons or events is purely coincidental.

AVON BOOKS
A division of
The Hearst Corporation
1350 Avenue of the Americas
New York, New York 10019

First Avon Books Printing: January 1997

AVON TRADEMARK REG. U.S. PAT. OFF. AND IN OTHER COUNTRIES, MARCA REGISTRADA, HECHO EN U.S.A.

Printed in the U.S.A.

RA   10 9 8 7 6 5 4 3 2 1

Prologue

—◦◦◦—

Dying was the nicest prospect Morris Feldman had faced in many years. He hugged the knowledge of his impending demise to himself like a priceless secret, sharing it with no one.

Instead, he locked himself away in the laundry room, hiding from his ex-wives and their various friends and progeny, and gave his attention to writing down the few ideas and memories he wanted to survive him.

Marrying six times had not been one of his brighter moves but he excused himself for it. After all, there'd been a damn good reason every time. But inviting all of his ex-wives to live with him . . . well, that was definitely *not* his brightest move. Now he had to hide in the laundry room and use the folding table as a desk if he wanted to do the simplest thing. He thought of bringing his laptop down here, then dismissed the notion. He'd been writing with pen and paper since Teddy Roosevelt was president and he'd bowed to modern inventions only because they were necessary. For personal communications, a pen and a notebook would be fine.

And these communications were very personal. Odd, but when he thought of leaving his last words to someone, he didn't think of the people with whom he spent the most time—his plethora of wives for example. No, he thought about two dear friends with whom he spent very little time.

And maybe that was the thing. Maybe they'd understand because he *had* spent so little time with them. Lord knows the more time he spent with his exes, the less they understood him—and vice versa.

Besides, by leaving these notebooks to them, he could drive every one of his relatives and ex-relatives crazy, one last time. The thought made him cackle with glee. What a hoot! He only wished he could be around to see the uproar.

It wasn't that he wasn't leaving something to everyone. Far from it. But it would drive them nuts to know he'd left something like this to people they didn't even know. The idea appealed to him.

So he hid in the laundry room, writing as quickly as he could, dreaming of days past and gone. When he emerged he felt better somehow, as if he had purged his soul.

And when he died, he was going to die smiling because he had managed to play one last trick on everyone who knew him. He'd be dead, and they'd all be tearing their hair and wishing they could kill him.

Oh, the joy of it!

1

―――∞∞∞――――

Oh, please, don't let it be him!

Danika Hilliard's stomach tightened into a painful knot the instant she heard the growl of an approaching car. For the last two months she'd been trying to convince herself that she could handle this, but now that the moment was at hand, she was absolutely certain that there was no way on earth she could share the same roof with Silas Northrop for the next six months. Setting her book aside, she hurried out to look, hoping against hope it was merely the gardener come to cut the grass.

The humid heat of the September afternoon settled over her like a wet, suffocating blanket as she stepped out onto the balcony that overlooked the driveway. Below her a camouflage-painted Jeep rolled to a halt. Moments later, the engine died, leaving the afternoon quiet except for the soft clatter of palm fronds in the breeze.

Camouflage. The Jeep looked awful down there, parked on the paved circular drive, surrounded by lush green lawns and a riot of tropical blooms.

Just as out of place as did the man who climbed out and began tugging a large, heavy box out of the back. He seemed to dwarf everything around him, dominating in his mere presence.

3

It was him. It was Northrop. Her stomach sank sickeningly.

Just as he was turning with the box, he caught sight of her on the balcony. Startled, he lost his grip and the box slipped from his arms and landed right on his foot. His mouth opened on a foul oath but he caught himself in the nick of time.

"Oh, *fu*—udge. . . ."

A wild and totally inappropriate urge to laugh nearly overcame her, but she stifled it. "The door's open," she called down to him stiffly. "You can take the south end of the house."

Then she turned and fled, needing escape as desperately as she suddenly seemed to need air. She was behaving like an abject coward and she knew it. There was an awful lot riding on the outcome of the next six months. Her entire future, for one thing. Well, her entire future if she ever wanted to be anything except a high school English teacher and, foolishly enough, she did.

But six months with Silas Northrop? The thought terrified her. Oh, she supposed he was a decent enough man . . . at least she hoped he was, because she really didn't know him at all. But he was so . . . so *male*. His very presence was powerful. Overwhelming. She wanted to believe that he unnerved her only because she was used to dealing with ninth- and tenth-grade boys who were all swagger and no substance, but she had the uneasy suspicion that just wasn't true.

At least in a house like this, they wouldn't have to talk much. The place was constructed with shameful extravagance in three stories around a central atrium where a huge fountain played and palms reached upward to a glass skylight. Surrounding the second and third floors were the galleries, covered and railed walkways onto which all rooms opened in a Moorish style.

It was certainly a magnificent house, nearly big enough for a small hotel. Whoever had built it must have been fond of entertaining, for the large number of bedrooms and sitting rooms could have no other purpose. Her benefactor, Morris Feldman, had written his last six bestsellers here, claiming that it was a wonderful writer's retreat. His only complaint had been that he was "ceaselessly surrounded by a sea of sycophants" to whom he didn't seem to know how to be quite rude enough.

The memory of those tart words, spoken roughly over the telephone only a few months ago, brought a faint smile to her mouth. Morris was gone now, dead of a heart attack in his sleep. His legacy to Danika had been the gift of six months without interruption in which to write her novel.

And Silas Northrop. Somehow she could well imagine a wicked sparkle in Morris's eye as he thought up this benighted scheme. Yes, he would have seen the humor in it; she just wished *she* could!

She was hoping that if she ran fast enough, she could get down the stairs and out the back door toward the beach before Silas retrieved his box and carried it in the front door.

She failed.

When she was almost down the stairs, he suddenly materialized at the foot of them like a conjured ghost, blocking her way. No box was in sight.

"Going somewhere, Ms. Hilliard?" he asked pleasantly. Too pleasantly.

Her heart was hammering, and she was dragging in air with painful little gulps. All of a sudden she was miserably aware of her short-shorts and halter top. The bright pink and turquoise outfit had seemed so daring and adventurous when she had bought it in Ohio. Now it only seemed skimpy and silly. Fancy feathers for a little sparrow. "I, um, I'm going to feed the birds. I always do at this time of day."

"A creature of habit?" He smiled, showing rows of even, white teeth. "How can you develop a habit so fast? You only just got here."

She drew herself up to her full five-foot-four. "I've been here two weeks, and it's time to feed the birds!"

"I'm sure they can wait a minute while you explain what you meant when you said I have the south side of the house."

"Oh!" She blinked, and despite her determination not to feel intimidated, she backed up a step, at last bringing her eyes level with his. "I, um, I divided the house in half. I thought we'd both be more comfortable that way. I mean . . . if we aren't running into each other . . . all . . . the . . . time . . ." Her words started to trail away as cat-green eyes bored into her. Good God, Morris had saddled her with a housemate who was a lunatic! The look in those eyes was nearly enough to curdle her blood.

"I see." He smiled again, but it didn't seem to reach the bleak depths of his eyes. "I gather it didn't occur to you that I might have a preference as to *which* half of the house is to be my prison?"

For an instant, she was utterly nonplussed, uncertain whether to reply to his accusation that she was imprisoning him, or to his suggestion that she had been rude not to consult his wishes. Both, she realized with sudden embarrassment, could certainly appear to be true. "I . . . didn't mean—"

"I'm sure you didn't," he interrupted ruthlessly. "Maybe you'd better just tell me why you gave me the south half of the house."

"Because . . . because it's nearly identical with the north half! At least on the second and third floors!"

He nodded slowly, never taking his eyes from her. "What about this floor?"

"Um . . . we have to share the kitchen and laundry, of course."

"Of course. I suppose you divided the refrigerator in half?"

She wanted to crawl into a hole somewhere, recalling the sight of her groceries all very neatly placed as if there were indeed a dividing line. Her cheeks felt hot enough to blister.

"I hope you didn't try to divide the washing machine."

That did it. In an instant her temper flared to white heat, banishing all her uneasiness and timidity. Her temper had always been her most serious flaw, one she had struggled to overcome, but now she was grateful for its rescue. Drawing herself up stiffly, she glared at him. "I was merely trying to make this as easy as possible for both of us! Neither one of us can be happy about sharing a roof with a complete stranger, and it seemed to me we'd both be more comfortable with some ground rules! If there's something you don't like about what I did, it's open to discussion. It is *not,* however, open to browbeating and intimidation!"

"Browbeating and intimidation?" His scowl seemed to deepen and he stepped back from the stairway. "Go feed your birds, Ms. Hilliard. We'll discuss arrangements after I've had a chance to look around."

With her temper still hot, she had plenty she could have said, but innate caution sealed her lips. She had no idea, after all, of just what this man might be capable. Giving him one last measuring look, she darted past him toward the kitchen.

Every few days she bought day-old bread from a bakery outlet and ripped it into chunks to scatter for the gulls. She had shredded today's batch earlier, and now all she needed to do was take the bowl out into the backyard.

That was when adrenaline deserted her, leaving her limp against the edge of the counter. Good Lord, how could she have argued with him that way? He might be any kind of person, and he was nearly twice her size!

But even as she clung weakly to the counter, some voice in her head scolded her for being overly dramatic. Morris Feldman would *not* have expected her to share the house with just any kind of person. Morris wouldn't be so careless of her safety. No,

whatever else the man might be, it was safe to
assume that Silas Northrop was neither a rapist nor
an ax murderer. In fact, he was probably a model
citizen.

And quite justified in thinking that her pro-
nouncement about the division of the house was a
little high-handed. Oh, heck, be honest, Dani. It was
obnoxious. How would she have felt in his position?

Ready to do battle, she admitted. On principle
alone she'd have found it necessary to raise a fuss.
Just to let him know he couldn't order her around
any way he chose.

"Grrr." She growled at herself and decided she
owed the man a sincere apology. But that could wait.
First she had to feed the birds and gather a little
backbone so she could face him. As she had discovered on the stairs, he wasn't an easy man to face.

In fact he was downright intimidating. She had
thought so at the reading of the will two months
ago—her presence kindly paid for by Morris's
estate—and nothing so far had changed her mind.
He was big, he was powerful, and he was aggressive.

Still not very happy with herself or the progress of
events, she left the kitchen with her huge stainless
steel bowl of bread, walked through the atrium with
its quietly gurgling fountain, and stepped out
through the heavy double doors into the backyard.
Here the grass was as green as out front, but it
quickly gave way to a rising dune that was covered in
sea oats and crowned with a scattering of palms.
After a short climb up a well-beaten path, one could
cross the dune to the pristine white sands of the
beach.

The place was idyllic, and she could well understand why Morris thought there was no better place
on earth than this to write a book. What she couldn't
understand is why Morris insisted that both she and
Silas Northrop occupy the premises at the same
time.

Sighing again, she tossed some bread chunks out

onto the lawn. In just a few minutes, a huge flock of gulls would begin to make their appearance. She had never expected to find the birds here so tame. Even now, a snowy egret watched her from further down the dune, his head cocked a little as he took measure of her. And just last night she had seen a roseate spoonbill. The birds alone could make her want to spend the rest of her days here.

She had met Morris five or six years ago when he had come to give a lecture at a local college. As a hopeful novelist, she had naturally gone to hear what the master of the bestselling family saga had to say. She had asked a couple of questions, and something about one of them must have struck Morris, because he asked her to stay after the lecture.

That evening had begun a wonderful friendship that had continued largely through correspondence. His letters had been eagerly awaited treasures, and he had also seemed to enjoy hers.

And he had never stopped encouraging her to write her novel. Amazing how many excuses she had managed to come up with. So, Morris-like, he had evidently decided to put an end to her excuses by giving her six months with all expenses paid in which to write it. And at the end of that six months, if she managed to complete her novel and get it into a form that his agent deemed acceptable, she stood to inherit half of this fabulous house and all its contents.

Well, she'd inherit it if Silas also managed to finish his book. That was the clincher she really couldn't understand. Why had Morris tied the two of them together in this way? They'd both inherit, but only if they both completed their books. And he had stipulated that in order to be eligible for the inheritance and the six months of expenses, they had to live here. At the same time.

She'd have wondered if he wasn't up to a little matchmaking, except that never was a man so down on marriage as Morris Feldman. He'd tried it six times, he said, which was testimony to his foolishness, and he could swear beyond any shadow of a doubt that he'd rather go to the stake than marry again.

So he couldn't have planned this as a matchmaking thing. No, he really had intended her to write the book she had often talked over with him, and he must really have intended for Silas to do the same. That left the presumption that he had thought they would somehow goad each other to success, for there could certainly be no other reason to put the two of them together.

Six months with Silas Northrop. Lord, could she survive it?

The first gull darted down and grabbed a piece of bread. Moments later he was followed by another, and another, until the yard was covered with birds, and the air was full of their cries. Some of them even flew right in front of her, beaks open, nearly hovering in their desire to grab a piece.

Everything else seemed to slip away, and she heard herself laughing. All of a sudden, the irritating presence of Silas Northrop seemed like such an unimportant thing.

"Are you rehearsing for an Alfred Hitchcock movie?"

The sound of Silas's voice startled her so much that she dropped her bowl and scattered bread everywhere. The gulls didn't appear to mind; after an instant during which they must have decided that Silas was no threat, they fell ravenously on the bread.

Danika turned slowly, not wishing to startle the birds the way he had startled her. "Do you always creep up on people? You scared me half to death."

"Are you always so inattentive?" He was leaning against the frame of the open door. "Never mind. There's an oily individual out front asking for you. Says he's Morris's nephew."

"You don't know?"

"Don't know what?"

"If he's Morris's nephew!" She scowled at him. "Was he at the reading of the will?"

Silas shook his head slowly. "Believe me, if this one had been there, I'd've remembered. On the other hand, there's the possibility that he wasn't mentioned in the will. Somebody told me a whole passel of Morris's relatives wasn't mentioned."

"That's true." A seagull hopped almost close enough to peck the toe of her white sneaker and stood looking up at her. "Morris told me once that he had more relatives than an army has soldiers, and that a lot of them weren't going to be happy with his will."

"Sounds like Morris, all right." He shook his head, and for the merest instant a smile seemed to tug at the corners of his mouth. "Well, this character may or may not be related to Morris, but he wants to talk with you."

"He asked for me by name?"

"Sure did."

She didn't like that. She couldn't have said exactly why, because it wasn't as if nobody in the world knew she was here, and besides, if nothing else, salesmen came looking for her all the time by name . . . especially since she'd been placed on the textbook committee. Of course, that was Ohio and this was Florida, and she couldn't imagine why anybody would want to see her. But that wasn't sufficient reason to feel uneasy, was it?

Nevertheless, she *did* feel uneasy, and couldn't quite prevent herself from glancing at Silas as if he afforded some kind of reassurance. The instant her gaze touched him, she grew annoyed with herself. Here she was acting like some helpless Victorian female when she was a modern woman of thirty who was perfectly capable of taking care of herself! She ought to be ashamed.

She spared a glance for the birds, who didn't seem to mind eating from the tipped bowl, then strode past Silas as if she had forgotten his existence. Whether the visitor was nephew or salesman, she could deal with him—just the way she had been dealing with such things throughout her entire adult life.

Silas had been right, she thought when she saw the man who was waiting in the atrium. If he had been at the reading of the will, she would never have forgotten. He wore a dark gray suit and a black shirt that was buttoned to the neck, attire far too warm for the hot, humid day. His black hair was slicked straight back from his pointed face, and caught into a short ponytail at his neck. He was, she thought, trying to look like some movie star whose name escaped her at the moment—except that this man was far too short and broad. He couldn't have been any taller than her five-foot-four, and he was built with a solidity that made her think of a cinder block.

He was pacing briskly back and forth when she first saw him, and when she spoke he paused only the merest instant before resuming his restless walk.

"You wanted to see me?" she asked him.

"You're Danika Hilliard, right?" He hardly waited for her affirmative before plunging ahead as he paced. "I'm Ernie Hazlett, Gert Plum's nephew." He glanced at her again, and she must have looked blank because he elucidated. "You know, *Gert*. Morris's second wife."

"Oh!" The syllable managed to sound as if she were suddenly enlightened, which she wasn't at all. Morris had never mentioned his wives by name to her, and even if he had she still wouldn't understand what any of that had to do with her.

"Yeah." He paused, flashed her a quick smile that was almost charming, and resumed his pacing. "Anyway, she was living here before the old man died. Damn lawyers threw her out, you know."

"No, I didn't know." She was at once astonished

by the idea of one of Morris's ex-wives living here with him, and horrified by the thought that the woman had been coldly thrown from her home upon his death. "I'm sorry." She shifted uneasily, feeling guilty, although she wasn't quite sure why.

"It's terrible. Truly terrible." Ernie shook his head. "She's not as young as she used to be, Ms. Hilliard. Morris always promised he'd see she was taken care of and then, bam!" He slammed his fist into his palm. "Out on the street with nowhere to go." He paused in his pacing and shrugged modestly. "I took her in, of course. And I really don't mind sleeping on the couch." Another modest smile.

"I'm sorry." And she truly was. It would be terrible for anyone to lose their home, but she rather thought that if Morris had promised to take care of his ex-wife, then he had. Somehow.

Ernie's smile grew broader. "You're very kind, Ms. Hilliard. Anyway, Aunt Gert and I are pretty crowded, you know? And she's not at all happy to be away from the home she loves, and she was wondering if—"

"No."

Danika jumped and spun around to find that Silas had silently joined them and was standing there with his arms folded over his powerful chest, looking as fierce as a pagan warrior and as immovable as the Rock of Gibraltar. "Why don't you wear a bell?" she heard herself snap irritably.

"Silence is golden," he told her, grinning, before he fixed his gaze on Ernie. "Ms. Hilliard and I stand to inherit this house at the end of six months, Mr. Hazlett, and your aunt would just have to move out again because neither Ms. Hilliard nor I can afford the upkeep. We'll have to sell this place."

Too true, Dani thought. The upkeep was probably more than her entire salary. Just to think about having to hire a gardener. . . .

"But that would give my aunt time to move more

gracefully," Ernie argued pleasantly. "Time to adjust to the changes, find a place she likes—"

"She's already had two months to do that, Mr. Hazlett," Silas said implacably.

Dani turned, wishing she had the nerve to argue with him. Silas's answers struck her as hard and unfeeling, yet she knew he was correct. On the other hand . . . Dani found herself envisioning an elderly woman in failing health who had been cast onto the mercy of relatives. "Silas, I think—"

"Don't," Silas interrupted. "Hazlett, I won't allow your aunt to move in here. The current situation is the one Morris wanted. If he had wanted your aunt to be living here, he would have said so, just as he wrote into his will that Ms. Hilliard and I should share the premises for six months. And since your aunt and others are conspicuously missing in Morris's list of desired occupants for this place, it may be that we'd be violating the will if we let anyone else move in here."

Dani blinked, feeling a little astonished. She hadn't even thought of that. Such a simple thing would probably put them in violation, and then they'd *all* be thrown out.

Ernie Hazlett's smile dimmed about a hundred watts, but he nodded. "You're right. I didn't even think about that. I'll give Morris's attorney a call in the morning and see about that. If he says it's all right—"

"I still won't," Silas said flatly. "Ms. Hilliard and I are here to write books. We can't be having a lot of distractions."

"I assure you, my aunt wouldn't be a distraction!"

"No?" Silas smiled cynically. "Then why are you so eager to get her out of *your* apartment?"

"Was that really necessary?" Dani demanded a few minutes later, once the door had closed behind Ernie. "You were insufferably rude to that man!"

"Don't you think he was a little rude to be

throwing his elderly aunt on the mercy of two total strangers?"

Mouth agape, Dani stared after him as he marched away, leaving her alone in the atrium with only the bubbling fountain for companionship.

Well, yes, she found herself admitting. It had been rude of Ernie Hazlett even to suggest such a thing. Had she been in her own home, she never would have entertained the notion. On the other hand . . . On the other hand, what she really wanted was to meet one of Morris's former wives, one of the famous bevy who had caused him to swear off marriage forever.

Of course, Morris had liked to think of himself as something of a rake, a dashing but ever-elusive ladies man. He had adopted a studied pose of misogynism when it came to women as potential mates, yet he had treated Dani with all the affection and understanding of an uncle. A pose, pure and simple.

Glancing up, she felt her heart stop beating and her breath lock in her throat. There, smiling down at her from the third floor gallery, was Morris.

Silas heard the bloodcurdling scream and his reaction was as instinctive as breathing. He dropped the Marine Corps marksmanship trophy he was setting on the windowsill and dove for the 9mm Browning he always kept close at hand. Because he hadn't yet found a place to stash it, it was on the bedside table. An instant later he was dashing through his bedroom door, rolling across the walkway and ending in a crouched position near the rail, gun leveled downward.

All he saw was Dani, frozen on the far side of the atrium, staring upward as if she had just glimpsed a demon from hell.

"Dani? What the hell . . . ?"

"He's gone!" she said dazedly. "Just like that he's gone!"

"Who's gone? Dani, what the hell is going on?"

She turned her head jerkily to look at him, then abruptly let out another shriek.

"Dani?" Convinced that she was having some kind of breakdown, he slowly straightened and lowered his gun. "Dani?"

"You have a gun!"

"Of course I have a gun!"

"You can't keep a gun here! No way! They're dangerous! And you were pointing it at me!"

"Oh, for Pete's sake!" Disgusted, he flipped the safety back on and leaned over the rail, glaring down at her. "You were screaming. I was going to protect you. And a gun is only dangerous when handled by a fool! What the hell were you screaming about?"

She turned her head swiftly, and looked up, scanning the topmost gallery. "I saw him," she said. "I *know* I saw him!"

"Who? Hazlett? Did he come back?"

She shook her head and turned in a circle, looking everywhere. "Morris. I saw Morris."

"You couldn't have seen Morris! Dani, the man's been dead for months!"

"I know that!" she snapped, turning to glare up at him. "I *know* he's dead! But I saw him! Right up there!" She pointed to the gallery above and to the right of his head. "He was smiling down at me like he was about ready to laugh. I screamed and . . . poof! He was gone. Just like that." She snapped her fingers for emphasis.

Tense seconds ticked by before he spoke. "Are you sure you didn't see something else?" he asked carefully. "A shadow or a reflection—something you mistook for Morris?"

Because the question wasn't accusatory, she chewed her lip and thought about it. "No, it was Morris. I'm sure of it. And he looked as if he thought this was all very funny."

"That's Morris all right," Silas said, his patience beginning to evaporate. The woman wouldn't even consider the possibility that she'd been mistaken and he had never suffered fools gladly. "And if he were around, I'm sure he'd be laughing his damn fool head off. But, Dani, his ashes were scattered over the Gulf of Mexico. There's absolutely no way Morris could be here!"

"I *know* that," she said sharply. "But I saw him anyway. Either I've gone completely off the deep end, or we have a ghost!"

2

"Ghosts!"

Silas muttered the word as if it were an epithet, and shook his head. Crouched down behind a table in a sitting room on the south end of the house, he was connecting the cables of his computer. He'd managed to skin his knuckles on something or other today, and they twinged now as he screwed the parallel cable into place.

Despite the air conditioning, he had opened the window to let in the sultry air. The hollow drumbeat of thunder was marching closer, and the palm just outside the window clattered in the strengthening wind.

"Ghosts!" He muttered the word again. Six months with a woman who saw ghosts. Hell. But why should it surprise him? Morris had always had a warped sense of humor.

The air was humid enough to wring as if it were a wet towel. He was soaked with sweat, but he hardly noticed. What he noticed was the uneasy tension of the air, an electric edginess that was like a foreboding. The light was turning faintly green as it dimmed, until it was as if he were looking through bottle glass.

"Ghosts." He shook his head yet again as he stood up.

The last of the blue sky had long since vanished, and gray-green pillow clouds covered the heavens. The gulf tossed restlessly, black waters and white-caps beneath the churning sky. It was going to be a bad storm, he thought. He'd better wait until later to plug in his computer.

A gust of wind slapped him in the face as he closed the window. Thunder growled like distant artillery fire and a crazy tracer of red lightning zipped from cloud to cloud.

He ought to close up his car, and while he was at it, it wouldn't hurt to look around and make sure all the house windows were closed and that nothing had been left outside that might get damaged by the storm.

Downstairs in the atrium, he paused to look up at the galleries, particularly in the direction Dani had seen the ghost. Not that he believed in ghosts, but he'd have liked to have seen what it was that made her think Morris was standing up there. A plant, a confluence of shadows—just about anything could have been mistaken for a person.

The only alternative explanations he could think of were unpalatable: that someone was playing some kind of joke on them, or that Dani had in fact seen a ghost. He didn't believe in ghosts, but he never for a moment doubted that she had seen *something*.

The storm had darkened the atrium, too. The dim green light that came through the skylight only seemed to enhance the shadows, deepening them until the corners were hidden and the depths of the galleries were shrouded in darkness. A drum roll of thunder, suddenly loud, shook the very ground and made the trees near the fountain shudder.

Something at the back of his mind flickered darkly and, for the space of a heartbeat, reality slipped its moorings. *Beirut.* He tensed, expecting the godawful screams.

They never came. Another heartbeat and he was back in the atrium, listening to the grumble of a late summer thunderstorm. The shadows had deepened, and were twisting like dark wraiths. Shaking himself free of the coldness that seemed to be trying to grip his mind, he headed for the front entrance, sure there had to be a switch to turn on lights somewhere in this atrium.

"Who's down there?"

Dani's uncertain question from above caused him to pause. "Just me. Do you know where the light switch is?"

"No, I never needed to find it. Morris has the atrium lights on some kind of timer. But it wouldn't matter anyway. The power's out." She gave a nervous little laugh. "I was reading and my lamp went out. So did my computer."

"Hell." It was getting seriously dark in here. He could see Dani only as a ghostly blur on the gallery. "Can you see well enough to get down the stairs?"

He was a little astonished at the alacrity with which she joined him. Given her actions earlier he'd assumed she had hated him on sight. It would have been better if she had. She was a cute armful, and he was going to have trouble as it was keeping his thoughts from wandering. He wondered if Morris had realized what a distraction this woman's presence was going to be. Yeah, he decided grimly. Yeah, Morris probably had. It'd be just like him.

"There's got to be a switch somewhere," he told Dani when she reached his side. "It's ridiculous to think the householder would be at the mercy of a timer, and I want to set the lights to come on as soon as the power does."

"I couldn't agree more. It's just that I never needed to look for it before."

She was breathing quickly, he noticed, probably from the exertion of her dash down the stairs. And maybe a little from something else.

"I was reading a book on ghosts," she told him

with another nervous laugh. "You can imagine how I felt when the lights went out."

He looked thoughtfully down at her. "Do you read a lot of books about ghosts?" Even in the dimness he could see her jaw drop a little.

"Actually no," she said sharply. "It's the first one I've ever looked at. I pulled it out because of what I . . . saw earlier." Her voice hushed a little, as if she had become once again aware of the darkness of the atrium, of the long shadows that hovered around them.

He wasn't a fanciful man by nature, but he had an adequate amount of imagination, and he wasn't entirely immune to the spookiness that was permeating the atrium. If ever there had been a perfect place and a perfect time for a ghost to put in an appearance, this was it. "I didn't really get a chance to look around down here yet. I wouldn't be surprised if we find the circuit breakers and probably a timer for these lights in some kind of laundry or utility room, though."

"The breakers are in the laundry room," she told him. "I remember noticing them."

"Well, that'd be the logical place to put the timer, I'd think. Of course, if Morris had it put in—"

"Then it could be anywhere," she said, surprising him with a gurgle of laughter. "Maybe all the way up on the third floor."

"In the bathroom," he added, joining her willingly enough in the humor of the moment. "Under the bathtub."

"So nobody could fuss with it." She laughed again.

"Right. Well, we'd better check the breakers," he said, his voice suddenly firm. "The storm might have caused a surge that threw the main."

She nodded and turned. "It's this way. I never realized it could get so dark in the middle of the day."

"Didn't you get storms like this in Nebraska?"

"Ohio. Yes, sure, we had plenty of storms. It's

just . . ." She trailed off as if she didn't know quite how to explain.

"I think it's this atrium," he said. "Light from above, but no side windows."

"That must be it."

But she didn't believe it, he realized. Nor was he quite certain he did. There was something about the atmosphere . . .

The breaker box and the timer were on the wall beside the folding table. Unfortunately, none of the breakers had been thrown, so they were out of power for the duration. As for the timer, it was a simple matter to turn it off and throw the switch that manually controlled the atrium lights. "Now we ought to have plenty of light whenever the power comes back on," he told her. "Listen, I'm going outside to look around and make sure everything's battened down for the storm."

"I'll come with you," she said swiftly. "You might need an extra pair of hands."

He managed to suppress the smile before it reached his lips. He'd willingly bet that she'd read too many ghost stories just before the lights went out, and was feeling jumpy.

The atrium was still shrouded in deep shadows, and the light improved only minimally when they stepped out the front door. The wind snatched at them with strong fingers and an occasional solitary raindrop splattered against them.

"It's so wild!" Dani exclaimed as they tromped around the house.

"This is my favorite time of year here," he told her. "One whopper storm after another."

"Just tell me there aren't a lot of tornadoes."

He glanced down at her. "I can't do that. We have quite a few. Waterspouts, too."

"I knew it was too good to be paradise."

A chuckle escaped him. "Every rose has a thorn."

As they came around the southwest corner of the house, the wind hit them like a hammer blow. Dani staggered and he instinctively reached out to steady her. Lightning flickered blindingly and thunder rolled with a force that made the ground tremble.

"We need to get inside," Dani said, raising her voice to be heard over the noise of the storm. "This lightning is dangerous."

"You go on in. I want to finish checking things out."

Evidently lightning didn't scare her as much as being alone in the house, because she continued to follow him. Great, he thought. Just what he needed for a housemate—a woman who was more scared of shadows than of lightning. This was going to be a wonderful six months.

The patio furniture was heavy wrought iron, probably safe from anything except a tornado. There were some large potted plants lining the covered patio, but nothing that looked as if it needed to be protected from wind and rain. He decided not to move them.

Just then, a bolt of lightning struck a palm not twenty yards away. A fireball of blinding brilliance seared his eyes, followed by a crack of thunder so loud it rattled his bones.

And somehow, Dani was in his arms, pressed shiveringly to his strength. She was so small, so delicate, so feminine—the embodiment of a soft dream that wasn't meant for him. For a long aching instant, the storm seemed to be raging in his head, consuming him with a need to hold this woman closer . . . closer . . .

He dropped his arms and stepped back as quickly as if he had found himself holding a burning brand. No way. Absolutely *no way!* "You okay?" he asked gruffly, turning away before he even had her answer.

"Yes, fine . . ." She found herself speaking to his back and felt somehow rejected—which was ridiculous, considering they were near-strangers who had no business being in each other's arms. Stepping away had been the gentlemanly thing for him to do.

Telling herself it was absurd to feel disappointed and rejected, she followed him on leaden feet—and felt absurdly disappointed anyway.

The wind was pounding mercilessly at them, and the lightning seemed never to stop. Spatters of rain grew more frequent, big, stinging drops.

They made it back to the front door just in time. Seconds later it began to rain in earnest, almost in sheets it was so heavy. They stood in the archway watching it for a little while, but finally the sheer stickiness of the day urged them indoors.

The power still hadn't come back on, and the air was beginning to feel warm and stale.

"Well, isn't this the pits," Silas grumbled. "Almost too dark to see your hand in front of your face and no lights. I guess I could keep on unpacking, but it's damn near too dark to see what I'm doing."

"Certainly too dark to read or write," Dani agreed. All of a sudden that seemed like a serious liability. At home she would have shrugged it off and curled up with her cat to watch the storm's fury. But her cat was staying with a friend and something was making her very reluctant to be alone. She needed to be busy so she didn't think. Didn't feel the thickening atmosphere in the house. Her mind sought desperately for an excuse to keep Silas from leaving her.

"I could make us some sandwiches," she offered in a breathless rush. "It's late and I didn't have lunch . . ." She trailed off, wondering what it was about this man that made her feel like a gawky teenager.

"Sounds good," he said. "I probably should have gone shopping on my way here."

"Don't worry about it. I've got plenty for now. You can take care of that later."

What a different tune this was from the one she'd been singing when he showed up, he thought with amusement. Her inconsistency was turning out to be surprisingly intriguing.

The kitchen was shadowy in the dark green light

that came through the windows. Like being under water. Her idea of a sandwich turned out to be alfalfa sprouts, sunflower seeds, and olives on mustard-slathered bread. If he hadn't been so hungry, he probably would have choked on it, but as it was he managed to be reasonably polite while promising himself that he'd get some real food later.

"I'm really uneasy about that Hazlett guy," he told Dani as they sat on opposites sides of the center island and ate. "There was something sneaky about the way he wanted to dump his aunt on us. And he couldn't really have expected we'd take her! Hell, we don't even know the woman."

"I don't know *you*," Dani reminded him.

"That's different. We're both here because Morris was crazy and he wrote a crazy will and is probably laughing himself sick from here to eternity over it."

The corners of Dani's mouth quirked upward. "Maybe. But I don't think Morris was crazy, Silas."

"Then you didn't know him the way I did. I met him in Beirut, you know. I mean, the guy was *insane!* He didn't have to be there. He'd retired from being a war correspondent just after Vietnam. He was making enough money from his novels to afford more than one place like this. Why the hell did he suddenly get a wild hair to come to Beirut?"

"What were *you* doing there?"

"I didn't have a choice—I was on active duty. USMC."

So he was a marine. She figured that probably explained a lot about him. "And that's where you met him."

"That's right. Damn fool was acting like he couldn't get killed. When I told him nobody was immune to bullets and mortar shells, he just laughed and said that nobody was immune to the one with his name on it."

"I can believe *that*," Dani agreed with a nod. "He was quite a fatalist in some ways."

"He was *crazy*." Silas shook his head. "Flat out

crazy. I saw proof enough of it. And that's what this is, this whole setup. His brand of craziness."

"He sure had his moments."

"And this is one of them. The thing is, Morris could be absolutely insane in spur-of-the-moment ways that would curdle your blood, but this thing is far from spur-of-the-moment. This took thought and planning."

"At least enough thought to get it written into his will. I wonder what the attorneys are getting paid to administer this?" She shook her head again. "It doesn't matter, I guess. What matters is that I don't think Morris did this just for the hell of it."

"We agree on that much." He took another bite of the sandwich and gave thanks for the green olives which took the edge off the alfalfa sprouts. "The burning question is, what did he hope to accomplish?"

"Besides getting the two of us to write books? I haven't a clue. And I really can't understand why he was so determined to get me to write my novel anyway. I mean . . . I don't even have a track record. There must be hundreds of other people he knew who are more qualified and more likely to succeed."

"What do you do ordinarily?" he asked her. "Before you came here, I mean."

"I'm an English teacher. High school."

"I should have known."

For some reason, she didn't like the way he said that, and she bristled. "Why? Do I have green spots? The bubonic plague?"

"No. What you have is a prissy, precise way of speaking. Like you're acutely aware of grammar." He wagged a finger when she opened her mouth to retort. "I admit the prissiness isn't from being a teacher, but the precision is."

"I am *not* prissy!"

He infuriated her by laughing heartily. "Sweetheart," he said in an appalling imitation of Bogart, "if you can say that, you don't know the meaning of the word!"

Prissy!

She considered boiling him in oil, but the logistics defeated her. First, she'd have to find a pot big enough to hold him, and then she'd have to wrestle him into it. No, it was out of the question, but the mental images were enough to make her chuckle despite the sting of his words.

She wasn't prissy. Not at all. He was stereotyping because she took care with the English language and with her diction. She didn't slur her words, and drop the g's off endings all the time, the way most people did. It was her belief that the letter was there for a purpose, so she enunciated accordingly. Silas Northrop wasn't the first person to tease her about it.

But prissy! She really didn't like knowing that Silas was characterizing her that way.

The lights still hadn't come on, and finally Silas had grown impatient and tried to phone the power company. The phone was also dead, which led to the inescapable conclusion that somewhere lines must be down.

Without the air conditioning to keep it moving, the air was growing stale and warm. The rain rattling fiercely against the mullioned kitchen windows was the only thing that kept Dani from flinging one of them open to let in some air.

Silas sat on the other side of the center island, watching the storm with brooding eyes and drumming his fingers on the countertop. "If we don't get power back soon, we might as well drive into town and find some place to get dinner."

"How long has it been?"

He lifted his arm and peered at his watch. "Over two hours."

Over two hours and the storm only seemed to be getting stronger. She shivered a little and tried not to think about the echoing silence in the atrium or about having seen Morris on the third-floor gallery. It wasn't that she feared Morris, but . . . well, a ghost wasn't quite the same thing as Morris in the flesh.

The kitchen was so dark that it was difficult to see anything at all. They'd hunted around in drawers for candles and had failed to find any.

"I can't believe there aren't any candles," Silas groused for the fourth or fifth time. "This is hurricane country. People keep candles and oil lamps on hand as a matter of routine!"

"Maybe we haven't looked in the right place."

"Where would you put them?"

The utility room, probably, but there were none there. They'd checked that out, too. "I don't know. I haven't really explored everything in the house. I mean . . . I felt as if I was being nosy and trespassing, you know?"

He turned his head, apparently to stare at her, but she couldn't really tell in the stormy dusk. Finally he spoke.

"We've been invited to *live* here for six months, and we may inherit the whole kit and caboodle if we finish our books. I think we've got a right to poke our noses into everything."

"Maybe." She shrugged. "It still feels like Morris's house, and I still feel like a guest." *Prissy.* She could almost hear him thinking it, and her temper flared briefly.

"That'll wear off," he said after a moment, and returned his attention to the storm.

She was getting tired of his heavy silence, tired of the heaviness of the air, tired of sitting here unproductively watching a storm that appeared to have no end. Tired of being aware of his masculinity in a way that was leaving her strangely edgy. She couldn't quite seem to force from her mind those brief moments outside when he had held her, and had the most disgraceful yearning to feel those strong arms again. Which was utterly ridiculous—and possibly insane—because she didn't even know the man.

Unable to hold still another minute, she slipped off the stool and began to pace aimlessly. If the lights would just go on, she could go work or something. Going into town with Silas to have dinner somehow seemed like a dangerous prospect. Much better to stay here with her nose in her computer or in a book.

Silas spoke suddenly. "Did you hear that?"

"What?"

"Kind of a banging." She shook her head and he shrugged. "Probably just the storm," he said, and resumed his brooding.

She wanted to groan with frustration. It wasn't that she wanted to be friends with this oaf—heaven forbid!—but he could at least make some kind of casual conversation to help pass the time. It was the courteous thing to do!

She was still glaring at his profile when he abruptly cocked his head. This time she heard it too—a definite, distant banging.

"Sounds like something has broken loose," she said. "I didn't see any shutters. Did you?"

He shook his head and rose from his stool. "I'm going out into the atrium to listen. I might get a better idea of where it's coming from."

The thought of going into the shadowy atrium was scary, but not, somehow, quite as scary as staying here in the nearly dark kitchen while the storm pummeled the windows. At least in the atrium she wouldn't be alone. Silas would be there. She knew that in the broad daylight she was going to feel like a fool for even thinking this way, but right now she didn't care. She absolutely, positively didn't want to be *alone*.

When Silas realized she was following him, she thought he made a disgusted sound, but just then the rain rattled bony fingers against the glass and drowned whatever he may have muttered. Nor did she bother to ask him to repeat himself. No point in asking for insults.

In the almost-dark, the atrium seemed huge. An echoing cavern that was slowly surrendering to night. Shadows were creeping forth from every corner, and the rain drummed on the skylight as if it wanted to batter its way in. Danika's eyes kept trying to stray to the third-floor gallery, but she refused to let them. She didn't think she could survive the shock of seeing Morris up there again. Not that she would, she argued with herself. No way. It had been some kind of aberration, some strange blending of light and shadow, not Morris at all. But she didn't dare look anyway.

They stood there a few minutes listening, trying to hear the banging noise again. The fountain was silent now, without power, so only the storm sounds reached them, a steady background of hammering rain and growling thunder. Lightning flickered, causing the shadows to dance eerily for an instant.

Just as Danika was concluding the sound wouldn't recur, they heard it again. This time there was no mistaking it: someone was pounding on the door.

There were a great many obstacles in the atrium—benches and chairs mostly, and a stone statue which looked like a replica of the Mayan god Chacmool, the chunky figure that reclined and held a bowl on its belly to receive sacrifices, usually of the human variety. It was utterly out of place, and she had more than once wondered what it was doing there. Right now, however, she merely wanted to be sure not to break one of her toes on it.

The back of her neck prickled uncomfortably with the sense that she was being watched, but she steadfastly refused to look up at the galleries. If there was something up there, she most definitely didn't want to know it.

Silas muttered something as they felt their way to the door.

"Pardon me, but I didn't hear you."

He raised his voice. "I said I hope it's somebody from the phone or power company. I need something more substantial than alfalfa sprouts for dinner, and I don't want to drive through this storm if I can avoid it."

"Alfalfa sprouts are good for you!"

"They're poison. A man needs meat to survive."

"Hah. I should have guessed you were a carnivore," she said tartly, glad for even this momentary distraction from the certainty that they were being watched.

"I'm an omnivore," he grumbled, "and I chew up and spit out little ladies like you if they get too uppity."

"Uppity!" Uppity and prissy. Gee, didn't he have a flattering view of her?

She nearly stumbled on a step, having forgotten that the center part of the atrium was several steps below the landing where the front door opened. At least she managed to stifle an exclamation, and hoped Silas hadn't noticed her clumsiness.

He reached the door and opened it a few inches. Into the stale interior wafted the softer sea air, fresh with ozone and rain, loud with the storm. A man stood out there, little more than a shadow.

"Can I help you?" Silas asked. Danika had to bite her tongue to keep from correcting his use of "can" to "may."

"I'm Lester Carmichael," the man said, and then waited as if his name should have opened the doors and drawn forth a fanfare.

Silas took a few seconds to digest this information. "I see. I'm sorry about that. It must be really tough."

Dani nearly choked as she forced unexpected laughter down her throat. How could he?

Lester Carmichael missed the point entirely. "I beg your pardon? What must be tough?"

But Silas chose not to tease him any further.

"Wrong person," he said shortly. "Am I supposed to know who you are?"

"Oh, I'm sorry. It never occurred to me Morris might not have mentioned me."

Morris, you bum, Dani found herself thinking. What did you set us up for?

"No, he never mentioned you," Silas said flatly. "Should he have?"

The wind gusted sharply, and Lester's raincoat whipped around him. "Well, I'm kind of surprised he didn't," he said. "I'm his stepson."

A rivulet of ice seemed to snake down Dani's spine, and despite herself she turned to look up at the third-floor gallery. She almost thought she could see Morris there, in the deep shadows. A shiver slithered through her.

"What do you want me to do about that?" Silas asked Lester.

"About me being Morris's stepson?" Lester seemed stumped. "I don't know. I didn't think it was a problem."

Dani turned her back quickly on the gallery, not wanting to see any more. As it was, the Alice-in-Wonderland quality of Silas's conversation with Lester was far more interesting.

"I guess it's not a problem unless you make it one," Silas told Lester. "Are you planning to?"

"Planning to what?" Impatience edged his voice. "I think you're as crazy as the old man was!"

"Morris?"

"Yes, Morris! Damn it, I just stopped by to introduce myself, see if I could help you get settled, and pick up some stuff my mother and I left here."

"Ahh . . ." said Silas, as if greatly illuminated. "You and your mother left stuff here."

"That's right." Lester shifted impatiently. "Do you mind if I come in out of the rain and get it?"

"Actually, I do. I have no way of knowing what's yours and what isn't. I suggest you come back here with Morris's attorney."

He pointedly slammed the door, then turned to Dani with an impatient growl. "I've only been here a couple of hours but it already feels like Grand Central Station! How many relatives do you suppose Morris has?"

"I don't know. I never really thought of him as having any. I mean, yes, once he told me he had more relatives than an army has soldiers, and he was married six times, but he never talked about any of them. I guess I never thought that any of them might still be a part of his life."

"Neither did I, but I'm beginning to wonder. Six wives and God knows how many stepchildren, nieces, nephews . . ." He shook his head. "Are we going to have to deal with all of them?"

"I used to date a lawyer. He said money brings out the worst in people when someone dies."

"Well, Morris's estate was plump, all right. More than enough to bring people crawling out of the woodwork." He sighed. "Damn it, I wish the lights would come on."

"Me, too." At any moment she was going to have to turn around. When she did, she was going to have to look up at the gallery, and if Morris was still there . . . She shivered and wrapped her arms tightly around herself.

"Let's get out of here," Silas said abruptly. "Let's just go and find a place to have dinner."

"My hair . . ."

"You look fine, Dani. Windblown is in style."

"I need my purse." But she didn't want to go upstairs to get it. Not into those dark shadows.

"Forget it. Dinner's my treat. You don't need a damn thing. Let's just get out of here."

There was nothing she wanted to do more at the moment, so she nodded.

Silas flung open the door and swore sharply. "Damn it! What the hell are you still doing here?"

Lester Carmichael was leaning nonchalantly against the wall of the entryway, arms folded. "The weather's treacherous. I nearly got killed getting here, so if you don't mind I'll just wait until the rain lightens."

Dani looked swiftly at Silas. "Maybe we shouldn't go into town. I mean, if the conditions are that bad . . ."

"I'm going to starve to death," Silas groused. "Hell, I *am* starving to death."

"Well, I'd offer you some more alfalfa sprouts . . ." She trailed off and swallowed a giggle as he glared at her.

"Don't even suggest it! It isn't that far to town. We'll just drive slowly."

Lester shook his head. "Trust me. You don't even want to try it."

Silas scowled at him. "You just want to get inside the house."

"What for? With you breathing down my neck every second, I wouldn't be able to get Mom's stuff anyway."

"Silas—" Dani started to say, but shut her mouth abruptly when he frowned at her.

"Don't *you* start," he said.

Her chin lifted sharply as anger came to her rescue. "I was just going to point out that since we don't have any lights, Mr. Carmichael wouldn't be able to see his mother's stuff anyway. In fact, he probably couldn't even find his way to her room!"

"That's not the point!"

"Then what is the point? To go out on these roads and get ourselves killed while this man stands in the archway trying to stay dry? Really, Silas! If the roads are as bad as Mr. Carmichael says, then I think we'd be wise to stay right here and wait it out."

As if to punctuate her words, lightning flared brilliantly, turning the world beyond the archway almost white with its intensity. Thunder rumbled endlessly.

"The important thing," Dani continued to say, "is

for us all to get inside before one or all of us gets struck by lightning!"

Silas was clearly unconvinced, but after a moment he nodded. "All right. But you stay with me," he said to Lester.

Lester raised his hands, palms open. "You got it."

Dani didn't want to go back in. The atrium seemed bigger and more threatening than before, and although she tried hard, she couldn't recapture her initial delight in this room. If Morris had been there just then, she probably would have scolded him, fright notwithstanding.

Since Lester was going to be with them for a while, Silas evidently decided to make the best of it. "You wouldn't happen to know where there are some candles or oil lamps, would you?"

"Actually, yes. In the hurricane room."

"The hurricane room? What the hell is that?"

"That's just what Morris called it. It's at the back of the house, just off the back archway."

Dani knew immediately what he was referring to. Both the front and back archways were about twelve feet deep, and the back one had a door in the wall.

"It's just a storage room, really," Lester continued, leading the way cautiously. "That's where Morris stashed the storm shutters, bottled water, and things like that. He was dead set against leaving oil lamps out, or candles, because he figured folks wouldn't be able to resist lighting them and he didn't want a fire."

"Sounds like Morris," Silas muttered. "No fear of bullets and bombs, but a worrywart about fire."

Lester laughed. "He nearly drove my mother crazy with some of that stuff. But I guess that's okay because she nearly drove *him* crazy. You could say she's a little eccentric."

"Which wife was your mother?" Dani asked.

"Number five. Tilly."

Dani found herself liking Lester Carmichael a

whole lot. He wasn't greasy or slick like Ernie Hazlett.

Silas might have been reading her mind. "Do you know Ernie Hazlett?"

"That sleaze? Yeah, unfortunately. I think the guy would sell his own mother if he thought he could make a dime."

The storage room was unlocked, but it had no windows and the little bit of light that remained in the day hardly penetrated past the door.

"Like looking into the jaws of hell," Silas remarked.

"It's not going to be easy to find candles or lamps in there," Dani said doubtfully. If possible, the darkness beyond the threshold seemed even more threatening than the shadows in the atrium, and all of it because she thought she had seen Morris earlier. If only the lights would come on and put her out of her misery!

"The power goes out here all the time when there's a storm," Lester said. "I'd be willing to bet the lamps are right inside the door."

"Makes sense," Silas agreed.

But Dani noticed that neither man hurried forward to check it out. Lester understandably looked indifferent to the whole thing. Silas looked as if he didn't want to turn his back on the other man— probably a comprehensible concern for a marine, but ridiculous nonetheless, Dani thought.

Or maybe Silas didn't want to enter that yawning darkness either. Glancing at him, she found it impossible to believe he was as cowardly as she was. No, he was worrying about Lester.

Looking into the darkness again, she squared her shoulders. Not since childhood had she allowed herself to be intimidated by something as ridiculous as the lack of light.

There was nothing in that storeroom except the lamps they needed, and there were two men here with her, either of whom was capable of coming to her rescue if there *was* something in there. Although what could there possibly be other than a few spiders . . .

She shook her head, drew a deep breath, and stepped forward into the darkness.

3

Both men reacted immediately, becoming instantly protective in the knee-jerk way of men, reluctant to let anyone think that they didn't have as much gumption as one diminutive high school English teacher. She had to hide her smile.

"No way you're going in there," Silas said gruffly. "I'll do it."

"I've got a lighter," Lester volunteered, patting at his raincoat pockets. "That'll give us some light."

Dani felt a little thrill of admiration when Silas stepped unhesitatingly into the yawning darkness of the storeroom with only a butane lighter to illuminate his way. Despite her announced intention to go in there, she'd have seriously hesitated when it actually came to crossing the threshold. Of course, Silas hadn't seen Morris earlier. If he had, he might not be quite so eager to go into dark places either.

But wasn't that ridiculous? She suddenly realized that she had seen Morris while the atrium was fully illuminated.

Silas's sudden oath yanked her thoughts back from their wanderings.

"Who the hell put a brick on the floor?" he demanded irritably. "Are you sure you don't have any idea exactly where the lamps would be?"

Lester sighed. "I was a *kid* when I lived here. I remember the stuff was kept in there, but I wasn't allowed inside, for obvious reasons."

Silas barked another oath, and there was a thud as something fell. At least it didn't sound as if anything had shattered. "I swear," he growled, "that I'm going to get into the car and go into town for a leisurely steak dinner, and you two can sit out here in the dark! Damn it, why don't they get the power on? It's been over two hours!"

"I seem to remember long outages happen quite a bit here," Lester remarked.

"Wonderful." Silas couldn't have sounded more sarcastic if he had tried. "Make a note of that, Dani. Numerous extended power outages. You better save your work often when you're writing."

"I always do."

Silas's answering growl emerged from the dark beyond the storeroom door. "I should have guessed. Not anal retentive, are you?"

Dani snapped her teeth together with an audible crack. Boiling in oil was simply too good for this man! Drawing and quartering was becoming a distinct possibility. "No, I am *not* anal retentive," she said between clenched teeth. "I am *sensible,* a quality with which I'm sure you have absolutely no familiarity!"

Lester gaped at her and then turned swiftly away, emitting a cough that sounded suspiciously like stifled laughter. Dani tossed a glare at his back for good measure. "Can you see anything at all, Silas?" she demanded.

"My thumb and about two inches around it. My thumb, by the way, is blistering from this damn lighter." He swore again. "Lester, there's no way those lamps are near the door. I've checked both——"

A crash that sounded very much like shattering glass caused him to bite off the word. A few moments of silence followed, and then Silas's voice issued forth from the dark. "I think I've found them. Don't anybody light a match. There's lamp oil all over everything in here now."

"Congratulations," Dani said sourly. "Next the house burns down."

"Wouldn't surprise me." Silas appeared in the doorway holding two lamps by their necks. He set them on the pavement, then disappeared back inside. Moments later he returned with two more lamps. "How many do we need?"

"Just a few, I'd think," Dani managed to say civilly enough. She didn't want him to guess that she was still smarting over the "anal retentive" remark. "We ought to get power back before too much longer."

"I wouldn't bank on it," Lester said bluntly. "A storm like this one can cause an awful lot of damage to lines and transformers."

Going all night without power was something Dani hadn't even considered until this very moment. The mere thought of it made her hair want to stand on end.

Standing there with a lamp in each hand, Silas looked intently at her, then glanced at Lester. "If we don't get power back soon, I'm not only going into town to get dinner, I'm going to spend the night there." His look dared Dani to argue. "And you're going with me if I do."

Ordinarily she would have bristled at being ordered around like that, but for once her quick temper didn't cause her to cut off her own nose to spite her face. If Silas took a room in town tonight, she certainly wasn't going to stay here alone.

She bent to pick up the two lamps from the pavement, but Lester beat her to them.

Silas kicked the door of the storage room shut and led the way back into the house. "That's going to be one hell of a cleanup job," he remarked. "Lamp oil and glass everywhere. It sounded as if the damn thing exploded."

"Tell Rosario to clean it up," Lester suggested.

"Who's Rosario?"

"Morris's jack of all trades. I'm surprised you haven't met him."

"I just got here."

"I've met him," Dani said. "I thought he only did the gardening."

"He'll do anything else you ask him to," Lester told her. "Morris relied on him for everything. Repairs, heavy cleaning . . . you name it. He's what you writer guys used to like to call a general factotum."

"I'll clean it up myself," Silas said shortly. "A grown man ought to clean up after himself."

"Not in most of the households I've been in," Dani couldn't resist saying. Silas favored her with a scowl.

The oil lamps helped a great deal in the kitchen. Dani hunted up a brick of cheese and some whole grain crackers, which seemed to meet with considerably more approval from Silas than the alfalfa sprouts.

"I wonder what happened to Edna," Lester remarked, his mouth full of cracker. "She used to be Morris's cook. A damn good one."

"I don't know." Dani glanced at Silas, but he shook his head. "I didn't know Morris had a cook. I didn't really know him all that well. We corresponded but . . ." She gave a small shrug.

"I may have met her," Silas said. "A tall, chunky, dark-haired woman? But I don't know what became of her."

"I think Edna was the only woman who could stand Morris for very long," Lester said. "He wasn't easy to live with."

"Morris was crazier than a loon," Silas said bluntly. "Talented beyond belief, a damn fine reporter and novelist, but crazy. Nobody could have lived with him for very long."

Lester laughed, a sharp crack of sound. "He was

crazy, all right. But I worshiped him when I lived here. I was the right age to think he was the neatest thing since bubble gum, and I had every intention of growing up to be just like him."

"Did you?" Dani asked curiously.

Lester shook his head. "I came to my senses."

That drew a belly laugh from Silas. Dani felt laughter twitch her own lips, but managed to restrain it. It didn't seem proper somehow to laugh about Morris when he was so recently dead. On the other hand, Morris himself would probably have been the first to join in if he had been here.

And that was when she realized her real reluctance came from the fact that she believed Morris *was* here. Morris, the man, had been her friend. Morris, the ghost, was something else altogether.

"How is it your mother left things here?" Silas suddenly asked Lester. "Was she living here recently?"

Lester looked startled. "You mean Dracula didn't tell you?" An unexpected laugh rolled out of him. "Oh, this is rich!"

"Dracula?" Dani repeated uneasily, acutely aware of the shifting shadows that surrounded them. She didn't believe in vampires. Absolutely not.

"Oh, sorry!" Lester's smile was wicked. "Dracula is the family nickname for Morris's attorney."

"It fits," Silas conceded. "What didn't Dracula tell us?"

"That all of Morris's ex-wives were living here when he died. Dracula gave them until three days after the funeral to clear out."

It was nearly seven by the time the storm eased enough for Lester to leave. Silas and Dani saw him off, then climbed into the camouflaged Jeep and headed for town.

"Can you imagine sharing your roof with six ex-wives?" Silas asked with a doubtful shake of his head. The windshield wipers slapped rhythmically as scattered rain drops splattered against the car. He leaned forward, gripping the steering wheel tightly, as if he could will them to make it safely.

"I never would have believed it possible," Dani conceded. "I can't imagine it was peaceful."

"Correct me if I'm wrong, but I thought the entire reason people got divorced was because they couldn't stand living together. Why the hell anyone would want to share a roof with all his exes . . ." He shook his head and scowled into the stormy night.

"What's equally interesting," Dani said, "was that he was apparently solicitous enough of them to support them, but when he died they were all thrown out. Does that make sense? Why didn't he leave the house to them?"

"Maybe because he left them something else. Or maybe it was just a big oversight."

"An enormous oversight. But . . . if Morris had just forgotten to deal with it, wouldn't his attorney have given them a little more time to move out?"

"Are you suggesting *Morris* stipulated that they had to clear out within a couple of days of his funeral?"

"I guess not," she said hesitantly. "It doesn't seem like Morris, does it?"

"Actually it does. I think you've got an idealized notion of our benefactor, Dani. He was perfectly capable of being ruthless when he wanted to be."

"But . . . why have his wives live with him and then be ruthless after he died?"

He shook his head. "You got me there. I think I'll call Dracula in the morning and ask him what the story is. Besides, if all those women were moved out that quickly, I imagine we'll be hearing from some others who left things behind."

"Maybe." She turned her head and looked out through the rain-streaked side window at passing buildings. The night always had a strange glitter to it when it rained. The sound of tires on wet pavement carried her back to her childhood when her family had driven overnight to Grandma's house for holidays. She had felt so safe then, sure of her father's care. With her arms wrapped snugly around her now, to combat the chill of the Jeep's air conditioning, she wished she could feel that safe again.

"How about Japanese?" Silas asked her when they neared town.

"I've never had any."

"How'd you ever miss it? It's perfect for a health food freak like you."

"I'm not a health food freak!"

"Anybody who eats alfalfa sprouts by choice is a freak. That stuff is for cows!"

The temptation to respond scathingly almost overwhelmed her, but she restrained it. On no account was she going to let this man turn her into a shrew. "Japanese sounds fine. I'd like to try it."

He glanced her way, as if suspicious, then shrugged and wheeled them into a nearly full parking lot. "The sushi here is fabulous."

Raw fish? She felt her stomach roll uneasily. "Have you heard about the stomach worms you can get from raw fish?"

He switched off the ignition and leaned toward her, grinning. "Live dangerously. Take a chance, schoolmarm."

She clenched her teeth so hard her jaw hurt. Drawing and quartering, she decided. Definitely.

She was still seething inwardly by the time they returned home that evening. Throughout dinner she had refused to let him see just how much his calling her a schoolmarm had angered her. She had also refused to let his dare provoke her into an unsafe act—namely, eating raw fish. Not that the sushi hadn't looked a lot more tempting than she had anticipated, but she had stuck to her guns and was proud of the fact.

Backbone. That's what she had.

It was small consolation.

Whatever backbone she had, though, had nearly disappeared by the time they turned onto the street that led to Morris's house. She was almost on the edge of her seat, wondering if the lights would be on at last, or if she'd have to face the dark, echoing cavern of the atrium with nothing but an oil lamp.

"You said you met Morris in Beirut," she heard herself say. Well, any distraction was better than digging her fingernails into the palms of her hands so hard it hurt.

"That's right."

"When the marine barracks was bombed?"

The car suddenly swerved, just a little. Seemingly endless moments of silence passed before Silas answered. "Yeah." One syllable, bitten off sharply.

She looked at him, trying unsuccessfully to read his face in the dim interior lighting. Had he, perhaps, been in the barracks? All of a sudden she lacked the nerve to question him further. She dropped the subject as abruptly as she had broached it.

Just then they wheeled into the wide, sweeping driveway.

"Well, hot damn!" said Silas. "The lights are on."

She turned to look, a murmur of relief escaping her as she saw the light blazing from the lamps at the entry and along the edge of the drive. Above the entry, light from the atrium spilled through the glass of the balcony doors. "Thank God!"

Her relief was short-lived, however. As they drove up to the door, she saw another vehicle parked out front. Awaiting them.

"Well, hell," Silas muttered. "I wonder which relative this is."

"Maybe we'll actually get one of the wives this time, instead of an emissary."

He glanced over at her with a slight smile. "I'm developing a real curiosity about these exes of Morris's."

"You, too? I keep having visions of these really

eccentric women in turbans, jewels, and flowing robes."

"Probably not too far from the truth. If this keeps up, I think we ought to invite them all to a tea party or something."

He braked behind the waiting car. As he did so, a blond woman climbed out and walked back to meet them.

Well, Dani amended, "walk" wasn't exactly the right word. She sort of . . . swayed. Or . . . snaked. That was it. What the boys in her classes called a snake walk, a sinuous swaying of hips and breast that was guaranteed to get a man's attention.

Dani glanced at Silas and didn't know whether to laugh or snort. He was watching the woman approach with his eyes slightly narrowed and his mouth open.

"Wipe your chin, Silas," she said tartly. "Only infants drool."

He tossed her a scowl then pushed open his door. "Something we can do for you?" he asked the woman as she drew near.

"You must be Silas Northrop," she said with a warm smile. She looked past him. "And Danika Hilliard? Hi, I'm Morris's agent, Max Fuller."

At both the east and west sides of the second floor there were large alcoves which overlooked the atrium and opened through french doors onto the balconies above the front and back entrances to the house. These alcoves had been decorated with chairs and sofas and small tables to make cozy conversational groupings and it was to the western one that the three of them carried frosty mugs of iced tea.

"I happened to be in Tampa on business," Maxine Fuller told them, "and I thought it would be a great time for all of us to meet. I hadn't counted on the storm making me so late though. Sorry about that."

"No problem," Silas told her.

Of course it was no problem, Dani thought with

an errant, inward sigh. Max Fuller was the kind of woman who would make men take notice, and who would make every other woman within visual range seethe with jealousy. She was tall and slender, elegant in a white silk pantsuit. Probably in her early to mid thirties, she was not only beautiful, she was successful. Quite enough to intimidate Dani, who by comparison looked and felt like a country mouse.

And if Max Fuller was any indication of Morris's taste in women, then Dani no longer felt any pressing urge to meet Morris's exes. Not that Max didn't seem to be perfectly nice. It was just that . . . just that women like Max made her feel jealous and inadequate.

"Morris thought very highly of the two of you," Max was saying. "He was absolutely convinced that you could both write great books. Did he ever see anything you'd written?"

Danika felt heat creep into her cheeks. "Only my letters to him," she confessed when Max looked at her.

"I write a column that's syndicated with the Hargrove Service," Silas said. "I know he read a lot of those."

Dani wanted to sink as she realized her pigeonholing of Silas Northrop as a macho meathead couldn't have been further from the truth. He, at least, was *published,* which was far more than *she* could say.

"I understand both of you are writing novels? But neither of you has any other fiction-writing experience?"

Silas and Dani glanced at each other before nodding.

"Well," said Max, "Morris usually knew what he was doing when it came to writing, so I'm not going to second-guess him." She gave them each a smile. "The important thing is that you both get to work and finish those books for me. I presume you both know what you're going to be working on?"

Again Silas and Dani exchanged glances. With a

sense of astonishment, Dani realized that Silas was as uncomfortable with the idea of discussing his book in front of her as she was about discussing hers in front of him. And he must be awfully used to criticism, since he was a columnist.

Max picked up on their uneasiness instantly. "I'd like to meet with you individually in the morning to discuss your ideas. That way if there seem to be any glaring problems we can catch them before you get too far. I also want to see what you have after you've written fifty or sixty pages. The thing you have to keep in mind, though, is that I'm not an editor. I'm not going to nurse you through these books."

"Then why do you want to know all this now?" Dani asked her. "Why not wait until we're done?"

"Ordinarily I would. Neither of you has a track record as a novelist, and my usual policy is not to look at first-timers until they've at least finished the property. Maybe your ideas will sound good to me in the morning, but that still doesn't prove you can produce a successful novel . . . or that you can even finish one. However, since Morris seemed to think you had something special, I'm curious." She shrugged, smiling almost whimsically. "I want to see if I can get an inkling of what he saw in the two of you, and since I was in the area I decided not to wait." Putting her glass aside, she rose.

"And now I need to get back to Tampa. Ordinarily when I visited Morris I spent the night but . . ."

"There's plenty of room," Silas said. "No need for you to drive back tonight."

Dani's reaction to that invitation shocked her. It was merely the courteous thing to do, even if Max *had* fished for the offer, but she felt angry. Furious. Invaded. Her future might well hinge on this woman's opinion of her, but Dani wanted to throw her out into the stormy night anyway. Wanted to tell her to "drive back to Tampa and don't come back unannounced." But because Max's opinion was going to be very important, she bit her tongue and fumed.

"I couldn't possibly impose," Max said, giving Silas a dazzling smile.

Like hell, Dani thought. Impose is *exactly* what this woman wanted to do. Look at her, measuring Silas as if he were a racehorse on the auction block. Silas was the real reason Max wanted to stay. The drive back to Tampa wasn't *that* long.

But there was nothing she could do about it, so she rose, too, and smiled sweetly at them. "I'll just head off to bed then," she said. "See you two in the morning." Let Silas find sheets for the bed. Let *him* settle her in. Manlike, he'd probably made the offer without thinking of who was going to make Max's bed, or find towels and soap for her, or make her breakfast in the morning!

Unfortunately, in her haste to escape, she had been uncharacteristically rude. Realization struck her just as she reached her room and she plopped down on her bed with an explosive sigh. Darn it! What must Max be thinking of the way she had taken off without even offering to help make her feel at home?

But what did it matter? Max wasn't a paragon of manners either, showing up unannounced and then fishing for an invitation to stay. Not that nearly anyone wouldn't have done exactly the same thing in Max's position. This house was big enough to stash a dozen guests in without much trouble. It was unfair of her to be annoyed at Max for doing what she herself would probably have done in the same circumstances.

No, Dani acknowledged uncomfortably, her entire reaction was nothing more than a jealous snit because she wished some man, *any* man, would look at her the way Silas had looked at Max. The way Morris had probably looked at Max.

Good grief, how could she have forgotten about

Morris? Or rather Morris's ghost. Oh, why had she
been so quick to run off by herself?

The warm pools of light spilling from the lamps
on the night table and on the dresser suddenly didn't
seem so bright. In an instant she became conscious
of the shadows in the corner, under the dressing
table, out in the hallway, and in all the empty rooms
of this vast house.

Good grief, she'd done it again, allowing her
temper to overrule her common sense and get her
into a position she wasn't happy about. When, oh
when was she going to learn to think first?

She sat up slowly, trying to ignore the uneasy
feeling that made the back of her neck prickle. It was
just her imagination, she told herself. She'd been
living here for two weeks without any discomfort at
all. Living here *all alone* for two weeks. In all that
time she hadn't seen or heard one thing to make her
feel uncomfortable in this house.

As for what she had seen on the gallery earlier—
that *had* to have been some trick of the shadows as
the day grew stormy. What else could it have been?
She'd been thinking an awful lot about Morris since
arriving here, and her imagination had simply taken
a pattern of light and shadow and filled it with the
friend she was missing.

There was no reason to think the shadows which
had been so benevolent all this time had suddenly
become threatening. No reason at all. Whatever she
had seen on the gallery certainly hadn't hurt anyone
or anything.

But threat seemed to inhabit the shadows anyway.
A draft from the air conditioning trickled down her
neck, raising goosebumps on her arms.

Maybe what she needed to do was go up onto the
third floor and look around. Reassure herself that
there was nothing up there. And when she didn't run
into Morris's ghost anywhere, maybe she could
finally dismiss it.

First thing tomorrow, she promised herself. In the

early morning before the day's heat raised the temperature up there to a suffocating level. It was a
simple equation she'd learned a long time ago: face
your fears and vanquish them.

But for now . . . for now the shadows in her room
still loomed ominously, and her heart was beating at
an uncomfortable rate. Probably the best thing to do
would be to go work on her book until she felt sleepy
again.

A roll of thunder made the bed tremble, and the
lights flickered.

"Oh, no," she groaned. She had a flashlight in her
purse, but that was in her office. Whatever happened, she didn't want to be all alone in the darkness.

Jumping out of bed, she hurried across her bedroom and threw open the door leading onto the
gallery. The atrium was still brightly lit by the
dozens of lamps scattered around the fountain and
along the galleries. The soothing sound of rushing
water still rose from the fountain. A laugh caught her
attention and she turned her head to see Silas and
Max walking along the gallery on his side of the
house. When they saw her, they paused and both
looked expectantly at her.

Another rumble of thunder, even louder, was
followed by the flickering of lights.

"Damn," said Silas, his voice echoing in the
atrium. "Not again!"

But after interminable seconds, the lights
steadied.

"Something wrong?" he called across the atrium
to Dani.

In spite of herself, she was touched that he had
even asked. "Just . . . edgy. Must be the storm."

Silas looked at Max. "Dani thought she saw Morris this morning."

"Morris! But he's dead!"

"Just a trick of the light, I'm sure," Dani said
between her teeth.

"But Dani," Max said, "you must have been terrified! Good God, I'd be looking for some other place to stay if I'd seen that." She looked around nervously and backed up a step, forcing Silas to do the same. "Maybe I will go back to Tampa tonight."

The grip of Dani's anger at Silas eased a shade. "It was probably nothing, Max," she managed to say, sounding as if she really meant it.

"Besides, we have to stay here," Silas said. "Terms of the bequest. This whole exercise will be pointless if we violate the will."

"Maybe for you," Dani snapped. "I'm not here to inherit this dang house, I'm here to write my book. At home I'd have to keep working to pay the bills. This sabbatical is a godsend to *me*."

"I think she's mad because I told you about Morris," Silas said to Max.

"Don't be mad," Max said to Dani. "I've got all the respect in the world for ghosts. I used to share a house with one, and if you'll pardon me, I have no desire to do it again. I'll be back in the morning."

Dani would have liked to go with her, but would have felt like a fool for doing so. The trouble with being strong-minded and independent was that you couldn't indulge sheer cowardice even when your knees were quaking. Not that hers were. No, certainly not.

Max was walking briskly toward the head of the wrought iron staircase, calling out as she did so, "Come with me, Dani. I'd enjoy the company and I'll bring you back in the morning."

Oh, how she longed to say yes, but a glance at Silas kept her from doing so. He didn't say anything, but his posture was expectant, sort of like a panther about to pounce. "Thanks, Max," she said. "But I'll stay. Ghost or no ghost I have to live here for six months."

"Have it your way." Max waved casually over her shoulder. "I'll see you both tomorrow."

Silas suddenly moved, as if abruptly jerked awake. "I'll walk you to your car, Max."

"Thanks."

Realizing she was about to be left alone in the echoing atrium, Dani hesitated a moment, uncertain whether to dive back into the relative comfort of her bedroom, or follow them out front.

"Dani," Silas said as he followed Max down the stairs, "come with us."

It was as if someone had stroked her fur the wrong way. Before she could even weigh the consequences, she responded contrarily. "I think I'll stay here."

Silas kept descending the stairs, and didn't glance back. "Dani, I'd appreciate your coming outside with me."

It was a polite request, so polite she didn't feel comfortable refusing it. But she refused it anyway. "I don't think—"

He abruptly halted on the stairs and turned around to glare at her across the width of the atrium. "Damn it, woman, come down here now!"

He couldn't have guaranteed her noncompliance any better. She stiffened, drawing herself up to her full height, and glared right back at him. "Silas, I—"

Max interrupted her. "Dani, come down here now. Please." She had paused on the stairs and was looking back up at Dani, too, but instead of Silas's glare, Max appeared genuinely concerned. "Please, Dani," she repeated.

Max's tone alerted Dani to the fact that something was wrong, that this wasn't some arbitrary request. "I'll be right down," she said to Max, and took care not to look at Silas.

There were two wrought iron staircases, one on each side of the atrium. She descended the one on her side and joined the other two at the fountain. "Okay, what's all this about?"

"There was someone standing in the doorway behind you," Max said flatly. "A man. And it wasn't Morris."

4

≈≈≈

Every drop of blood in Dani's body turned to ice. The back of her neck prickled violently and a shudder ripped through her. There suddenly wasn't enough air in the entire universe.

"Dani . . . Dani, it's okay," Silas said. "He's gone now. Max, you and Dani go out and lock yourselves in your car. I'm going to check this out."

But as quickly as she had frozen, adrenaline came rushing to Dani's rescue, replacing fright with fury. She whirled around and glared up at the gallery. The first words out of her mouth were, "How dare he!"

"Oh for heaven's sake, Dani!" Silas said disgustedly. "Don't go all macho on me."

"That's reserved for marines, I suppose," she retorted acidly. "The rest of us just have to cower. Well, I won't! That man was up there, near my room . . ." The realization sank home yet again, making her knees feel suddenly weak.

"Stop it, you two," Max said sharply. "Dani, come with me. Silas, just call the police. Don't try to be a hero."

"If we wait for the police," Silas argued with inescapable logic, "he'll be long gone. You two just get out of here while I go look for him."

"I'm not leaving you to face him alone," Dani

protested. "He'll be less likely to hurt you if there's a witness!"

"A dead witness can't tell any tales," Silas growled. "Will you just get out of here now? Damn intruder is going to get away while we stand here and argue . . ." Muttering to himself, he turned and loped up the stairs with an ease Dani would have admired at almost any other time. Right now it just added to her annoyance. The man was a born showoff.

"This is incredible," she said to Max. "First some crook has the audacity to break in here, and now Silas is acting like some movie hero when it would be far wiser to just let the police handle it! Men! I swear!"

"Actually," Max said reasonably, "Silas will be a lot safer dealing with the intruder if he doesn't have to worry about us. We really ought to do as he said and wait in my car."

"Right. And be carjacked by a desperate thief who's trying to escape Silas. Do you know he has a gun?"

"The thief?"

"No, *Silas*. He scared me half to death with it earlier when he was waving it at me."

"Waving it at you?" Max looked shocked. "Why in the world was he waving a gun at you?"

"Because I screamed when I saw Morris." She flushed a little at the memory, and glanced up toward the gallery where Silas was now peering into rooms. "I guess we ought to at least go some place where we aren't such obvious targets if someone starts shooting. But *not* the car. If the thief needs to escape in a hurry, he's going to want one of our cars." Setting her chin, she took Max's arm and led her toward the laundry room. "There's a stout lock on the laundry room door. We'll wait in there."

Max was still looking vaguely poleaxed. "Dani . . . Dani, do you mean to tell me Silas threatened you because you screamed when you saw a ghost? And I thought he was such a nice man!"

Startled, Dani looked at her. "Do you always jump to wild conclusions? Of course he wasn't threatening me because I saw a ghost! Really, Max, Silas may be maddening, but I don't think he's that crazy."

"But you said—"

Dani shook her head vehemently. "You misinterpreted me. He was waving a gun because he thought I was in danger, not because he was mad at me for screaming." Drawing Max into the laundry room with her, she turned and threw the deadbolt on the inside of the door. It seemed like an odd place to have a deadbolt, but there had never been any explaining some of Morris's notions.

"Morris used to hide in here," Max whispered suddenly, as they stood there in the dark, listening for any terrible sound from without.

"He did? Why?"

"He felt besieged."

"By whom?"

Max gave a little chuckle, strangely out of place under the circumstances, yet somehow very appropriate. "Those wives of his. Have you met them?"

"Not yet."

"Then it's kind of hard to explain. Morris's taste in women was . . . unusual."

"I always kind of wondered about his being married so many times."

They were silent for several seconds, listening for any sounds from the rest of the house. "I guess," Dani said finally, "it's going to take Silas a long time to check out so many rooms."

"Yeah. And the guy's probably long gone anyway. He'd be crazy to hang around once he knew he'd been spotted."

Dani nodded, forgetting that Max couldn't see her in the dark. "Tell me about Morris's wives."

"Oh, hell, that's a job that would need a whole

book!" Once again, Max laughed softly. "His first wife, a woman named Roxy Resnick, is a psychic. I mean, just imagine every derogatory stereotype you've ever heard about psychics and fortune-tellers, and that's Roxy. As far as I know, the woman doesn't own a single piece of clothing that isn't purple. Says her 'guide' prefers it. She's nice enough, I guess, but ditzy. Extremely ditzy."

"I'd like to meet her." Dani was almost embarrassed to admit it. "She must be interesting." More interesting than a mousy high school English teacher.

"Oh, she's interesting, all right. Morris collected unusual characters the way other people collect dust bunnies under the bed, but I sure can't figure out why he married them all."

"Sexual attraction," Dani suggested, her cheeks flaming at her boldness.

"Probably." Max laughed. "Yeah. Raging hormones. I'll buy that one. Morris had a lot of hormones."

"Really? I never noticed." She flushed again, grateful for the dark. "Of course, we didn't meet face-to-face very often."

"Trust me on this one. Morris had a healthy appetite for women. He was also monogamous. Or to put it more accurately, he practiced serial monogamy. One woman at a time. He didn't believe in cheating."

"That's a rare trait."

"Yeah." Max gave another quiet chuckle. "He had a tendency to focus in a single-minded way on a woman. A woman he loved would probably have felt like the center of the universe."

"But his interest doesn't seem to have lasted for very long."

"Nope. My predecessor said Morris appeared to throw himself wholeheartedly into relationships, but what he was really doing was running away. She told me to take care he didn't try to run away into *my* arms."

Dani could have sworn she heard Max sigh. "Do you wish he had?"

"Not really. Morris was an incredibly attractive man, even at seventy. Amazingly magnetic. It would have been easy to fall under his spell except that . . . well . . ."

Dani waited impatiently, certain she was about to learn something very important about Morris.

"Morris only *appeared* to give himself to a woman," Max said presently. "The truth is, for him, women were a distraction from something he couldn't handle. But don't ask me what his demon was."

The idea that Morris had been pursued by demons was a new one for Dani. She had always thought of him as being amazingly well-balanced, a very together sort of person. Although, upon reflection, perhaps any man who'd been married six times couldn't truly be "together."

There were still no sounds from without to give them any clue as to what was happening with Silas. Only the steady rushing and gurgling of the fountain could be heard from beyond the door. "Does it seem to you that Silas is taking an awfully long time?"

"It sure does. But considering there are nearly forty rooms in this place . . ." Max's voice trailed off.

After a few moments, Dani spoke. "Morris used to call me occasionally just to chat, and every single time he called he complained about all the people who were living here with him, and how he couldn't get away from them. I guess having a big place like this would make it awfully hard to tell someone they couldn't stay with you."

"Morris's biggest problem wasn't that he had so many bedrooms," Max said drily. "His problem was that he felt guilty about all his divorces. Why else would he let all his ex-wives move in with him?"

"I can't understand that."

"Well, it's the only explanation *I* can think of for it. He used to bellyache to me about it, too, and then tell me he was locking himself up in the laundry room so he could have some peace and quiet. A couple of times when I came to visit him, we held our conferences in here."

"That's ridiculous! He could have put a good lock on *any* room."

"That's what I thought, but you know Morris. It must have tickled his sense of humor to hide in the laundry room."

"His sense of humor was warped."

Max chuckled again. "Warped hardly begins to cover it. Maybe he let all his wives live with him because he thought it was amusing."

Dani thought about that for a minute. "You know, I could almost believe that."

"Me, too. And that's scary."

"Why?"

"The thought that I could actually connect with Morris's sense of humor is terrifying."

Dani was growing to like Max more and more. Max was, in fact, exactly the kind of woman Dani had always wanted to grow up to be: confident, successful, beautiful, witty, intelligent . . .

She sighed and strained her ears, trying to hear something to indicate it was safe to leave this laundry room. "Max, I'm getting worried about Silas."

"This is an awfully big house, Dani."

"But if something has happened to him . . . How long are we supposed to cower here?"

"Good question."

"I'm going out there." Before Max could stop her, Dani was on her feet and out the door. She didn't have a clear plan of action, only a need to be sure that Silas hadn't been hurt by the intruder. What if he had been shot? Good grief, they might not have even heard the sound and Silas could be lying in one of the rooms above, bleeding to death . . .

Stepping from the darkness of the laundry room into the well-lighted atrium made her eyes hurt. She blinked rapidly, trying to adjust, and scanned the galleries for any sign of Silas. Nothing moved up there. Nothing.

"I don't know about you," Max said from right behind her, "but I don't feel any overwhelming urge to go up there. It's not like I have a black belt in karate, or a gun in my purse. If some guy were to jump me, I'd just screech and collapse in terror."

"Me, too, probably," Dani admitted. "But I'm so worried about Silas!"

"Well, that's easy." Max cupped her hands around her mouth, tilted her head back, and shouted Silas's name. The word ricocheted around the atrium, bouncing from ceiling to floor it seemed. No answer.

"That's not good," Max said.

"See, he's been hurt. I knew it! We have to go up there!" Instinctively she started looking for something she could use for a weapon.

"Go up there?" Max repeated. "Why the hell don't we just call the cops? This is supposed to be their job, not ours! *They* have guns."

"I know but—" Before she could finish the sentence, Max interrupted her by shouting yet again for Silas.

Silence mocked them, softened only by the burbling of the fountain. Frantic with worry, Dani grabbed the first weapon that came to hand—a rock from the landscaping around a palm tree—and started toward the stairway.

Just then, an annoyed voice hollered down at them from above. "Damn it, didn't I tell you two to stay in the car?"

Dani dropped the rock with a thud on the tile floor. "Silas! I was getting so worried! Are you all right?"

She saw him then, leaning over the third-floor gallery rail.

"I'm fine," he said. He loped down the two flights of stairs with surprising speed and came to a halt in front of them. "As near as I can tell, the thief is gone. I'd just like to know how the hell he got out of here so fast from an upper floor!"

"Maybe there's a secret passage." Dani wished the words unsaid as soon as they escaped her mouth. It seemed like such a wild idea, but on a day that had already been filled with ghosts and strange characters, somehow a secret passage seemed, well, apropos.

"Good God," Silas muttered. "Ghosts and secret passages! Let me guess—you're writing a Gothic romance, right?"

Dani glared at him, but didn't dignify his attitude with a response. Max was kinder.

"I don't know, Dani. Wouldn't Morris have crowed about it if he'd had a secret passage? It seems like the kind of thing he would have delighted in dragging people through."

"Yeah," Silas muttered. "He'd probably have thrown in a skeleton or two and some implements of torture for atmosphere."

"It was just an idea," Dani said defensively. "Somehow this guy got out of here without Silas catching sight of him."

"It wouldn't be that hard, really," Silas said grudgingly. "Every time I stepped into one of the rooms to look around he had a chance to slip out."

"But nobody can close the front or back doors without making a racket," Dani reminded him. "Those heavy doors bang no matter what you do, and they're closed just the way they were earlier. If he slipped out through one of them without making a sound, he'd have had to leave it open behind him."

"That's true," Max agreed, looking unhappy.

Silas enumerated possibilities with evident distaste. "Then he's a ghost. Or he didn't get out. Or there's a secret passage."

Dani shivered, and unconsciously drew closer to Silas. "I don't like the idea that he could still be here."

"I vote we go to a hotel for the night," Max said. "We have no idea how he got in, or what he wanted, or whether he might come back . . . or even if he's really gone. It'd be better to wait until morning and check this place out again."

Dani nodded. While she didn't really want to spend any of her limited funds on a hotel room, she certainly didn't want to stay in her own bed tonight. There was no way she would be able to sleep, and no way she wanted to spend the entire night in a state of nerve-screaming tension.

"That's a good idea," Silas said. "You two find a place to stay tonight."

"What about you?" Dani asked.

"I'm going to stay here. If that sucker's around somewhere, I want to get my hands on him."

"But, Silas, that's not safe! You can't stay here alone." Dani was more annoyed than concerned for him. What a typically male thing to do! He ought to pound his chest and let out a gorilla yell. "I'm sure your marine training made you feel invincible, but you're not! What if he's armed and comes upon you unexpectedly? What if you fall asleep?"

"A marine never sleeps at his post."

There was a sparkle in Silas's cat-green eyes. Dani peered at him suspiciously, wondering if he was taunting her. "Silas, you're only human."

"Too true." He turned to Max. "I can handle things here. You two just find yourselves a place to stay tonight."

Max shrugged. "It's your head. Me, I want to sleep tonight. Come on, Dani. There's no point in all of us sitting up all night."

Dani hated to leave Silas alone here. Every instinct rebelled against it. She felt like a deserter. On the other hand, Silas kept telling them to go, and kept insisting he would remain here alone. What was she supposed to do? Remove him bodily? She could hardly fling him over her shoulder!

"Very well," she said shortly. "Let's go, Max. There's never anything to be accomplished by arguing with a man in the grip of machismo. Their brain cells are too involved in stupidity to hear reason."

Max stifled a laugh, revealing it only in the dancing of her blue eyes. Silas scowled at Dani, but the expression somehow lacked its usual ferocity. Perhaps he was having second thoughts about his foolhardiness.

Dani turned and marched toward the door, aware that Max was right on her heels. All of a sudden, she drew up short. "My purse! I can't check into a hotel without my credit card!"

"Where is it?" Silas asked.

Dani turned and looked up at the second floor, in the direction of her bedroom door. As one, Silas and Max's gazes followed hers.

"I'll get it," Silas said. "Where exactly is it?"

What a dilemma! She didn't want to go up there herself, or let him go for her. But without her purse she couldn't stay at a hotel . . .

"Tell you what," Max said. "I'll pay for the rooms. You can reimburse me. Forget your purse. Let's just get out of here." She faced Silas. "You really ought to come with us. Or call the police."

"What are the police going to do that I didn't already do?" Silas shook his head. "The thing is, I don't want to abandon ship in case the guy comes back. Don't worry, I'll be fine."

Just as Max and Dani were turning to leave, the knocker rapped sharply on the front door. For an instant, none of them moved.

"I wonder what relative this is," Silas grumbled. "If it's Lester again, I may pop him in the nose. This is getting ridiculous!"

His grousing helped shatter the tension that had

been so thick, but neither Max nor Dani entirely relaxed. At this point, Dani thought a little crazily, she wouldn't have been surprised if Silas found the Headless Horseman on the other side of that door. Lord, why didn't she just go back to Ohio and forget all this nonsense? How she yearned for her snug little house, and her cat, and her orderly routine!

Silas opened the door more cautiously than was his wont. Stepping back a little, he revealed to Max and Dani a pleasant-looking, plump, middle-aged woman, who was dressed in a no-nonsense gray business suit and pumps.

"Mr. Northrop?" she asked.

"Yes."

"My name is Moonglow. Dawn Moonglow. I've come to warn you that your life is in danger."

With an introduction like that, they could hardly leave the woman standing on the doorstep. Silas asked her in and they adjourned to the library, a spacious room off the atrium where books lined the walls, and deep chairs offered comfort.

"Maybe you'd better tell me what you mean by that," Silas said. Instead of taking a seat, he stood by one of the curtained windows, thumbs hooked into his jeans pockets, hips canted to one side in a way that Dani found completely distracting despite the circumstances.

"I hate to do this," Dawn Moonglow said. She pursed her lips tightly, and pushed her glasses up her nose. "I have the greatest respect for my mother and her abilities, but I absolutely *loathe* having to be her emissary."

Dani, Max, and Silas exchanged dubious glances. Silas spoke. "Who is your mother, what does she have to do with this, and why the hell is my life in danger?"

He sounded so impatient, Dani thought, that it was a wonder Dawn Moonglow didn't just shrivel. Instead the woman thrust out her chin and scowled at him. "Don't try to browbeat me. I'll explain everything. Of course I will. It would be pointless otherwise!" She cocked her head to one side. "May I have a glass of water? I had pizza for dinner, and now my mouth is as dry as cotton."

None of them moved, all equally reluctant to chance missing anything Dawn Moonglow said. It was Dani, finally, who yielded to the role of hostess . . . though she promised herself that she would have a few words with Silas on that score later.

Dawn drained an entire sixteen-ounce glass of water in one long draft, then set the glass down with a thump on the wooden table beside her chair. "Much better," she said with obvious satisfaction. "My tongue was sticking to my teeth."

"So," Silas said, "what is this threat?"

"First I have to explain about my mother."

Silas sighed. "Let me guess. You're related to Morris Feldman."

"Hardly." Dawn shook her head emphatically, causing her jowls to quiver, but displacing not a single hair on her heavily lacquered head. "I came along *after* that. My mother is Roxy Resnick. She was married to Morris for a couple of years before *I* saw the light of day. She was his first wife, actually."

"Was she living here with him before he died, too?" Dani asked.

"Briefly. It was more of a vacation, actually, while her house was being remodeled. She and Morris stayed good friends despite their divorce. My mother was always trying to protect Morris from another of his follies, but without much success to judge by the fact that Morris married five more times. Mama always said Morris should never have married anyone, that he wasn't suited to it at all."

Silas made an impatient gesture, but Max and Dani ignored him. "Why?" Max asked.

"She said his heart was never in it, not with any of his marriages."

"I fail," said Silas, "to see what this has to do with a threat to my life."

"Absolutely nothing," said Dawn, "Whyever would you think it does?" She looked at Dani and Max. "Is he always this egocentric?"

"Apparently so," Dani couldn't resist saying. Really, this was getting to be amusing. Silas glowered balefully at the three women. "But if there's a threat to Silas . . ."

"Indeed there is," Dawn interrupted. "One would be wise not to ignore it."

"And how is it," Silas asked too politely, "that your Mama has reached this startling and obscure conclusion?"

Dawn looked at him. "Through her crystals."

For several moments, no one said anything. At last it was Silas who spoke, as if measuring his words very carefully. "Through her crystals?"

Dawn nodded. "I know. It sounds strange. You'll have to let me explain."

"Please. We're all ears." Silas's words were laden with sarcasm, but either Dawn failed to hear it or she chose to ignore it.

"You have to understand, Mama is psychic. She gets messages from beyond all the time, and they're almost always right. It is *never* wise to ignore Roxy Resnick."

The faces of her listeners must have mirrored disbelief, because she nodded and said, "I know, I know. It's hard to believe. That's why I absolutely *hate* being the one she sends to deliver her messages. It's a wonder I haven't been shot or committed to an institution!"

Dani felt a surge of sympathy toward the older woman. Whether she believed in psychic powers or not—and on this subject Dani was so far withholding a decision—it was impossible not to feel commiseration for Dawn Moonglow's position. "Why doesn't your mother deliver the messages herself?"

"Because she's seventy and doesn't get around as

well as she used to. It took me nearly five hours to drive up here from Fort Myers, and now I have to turn around and drive back. Mama couldn't handle that."

"That's certainly understandable."

Dawn sighed. "Believe me, if I thought Mama was just crazy, I wouldn't do this. Unfortunately, she's *not* crazy. She gets the straight dope, and she's right about things far more often than she's wrong."

"How does she get the information?" Dani asked. She could feel Silas's impatience growing, but she ignored it. Let him get impatient; there was no way they could evaluate the message Dawn had brought unless they knew how it had been obtained.

"She channels," Dawn explained. "The spirits speak through her. Well, actually through her crystals."

"You mean the crystals talk?"

"Of course not. Mama says it's as if the crystals tune her to a frequency that makes it possible for her to channel her guides. Sort of like a radio."

Silas made a muffled sound to which no one paid any attention.

"So then Roxy can hear her guides?" Dani was valiantly trying to understand the process involved because it might be important, but so far the waters only seemed to be growing muddier.

"Mama doesn't hear them at all," Dawn said with a shake of her head. "Mama doesn't hear anything. The guides speak *through* her. Mama is merely a channel for the communication."

"Oh." It was clear as mud, but she was beginning to get an inkling that the crystals somehow tuned Roxy Resnick to a frequency on which a disembodied spirit was able to speak through her. "So how does she get the messages if she doesn't hear them?"

"I record everything her guides say." She spoke as if Dani were learning impaired.

"That must be quite a task." This from Silas, who sounded utterly bored.

"Nothing I can't handle," Dawn said with evident pride. "I make my living as a stenographer."

"Oh," said Max. "Do you work in a courtroom? I've always thought that must be fascinating."

"It's more exciting outside court," Dawn explained. "I take pretrial depositions for attorneys, and that's a great deal more interesting than the goings-on in a courtroom, I can tell you. When there's a divorce case, it can get downright lively. Just last week the husband crawled across the conference table and tried to strangle his wife over something she said. It took both lawyers to get him off her."

"I'd love to hear all about this," Silas said, "but some other time, Ms. Moonglow. You came here for a reason, I believe."

"Well, I did." Dawn nodded and reached into her purse, pulling out a thin stack of steno tape. "It was at her last session—she holds one a week, usually, and rarely more than that. It's just too fatiguing for her, poor dear."

Silas rolled his eyes. Dani shot him a glare, then smiled at Dawn. "Was this her regular session, then?"

"Yes, it was, just this afternoon. We always hold a session on Saturday afternoon because it's more convenient for some people. It doesn't interfere with anyone's work, you see."

"How many people are involved in these sessions?" Max asked.

"Well, it varies according to how many people want a reading. We sometimes have as many as ten or twelve there. This afternoon we had only five, though." As she spoke she was flipping over the pages of her steno tape. "I want to get to the part where you were mentioned so that I tell you precisely what was said." She glanced up, her eyes looking small through the thick lenses of her glasses. "Sometimes the exact wording can be critical to the understanding of the message."

"How did Silas even come up?" Dani asked. "Was someone asking about him?"

"You know, that was really interesting. Usually we only get messages for people who are present at the sessions, or for their close relatives. We didn't know at first even who Silas Northrop or Danika Hilliard were."

Dani shifted uneasily. "I was mentioned?"

"Indeed you were. Didn't I already tell you? The guide says your life is in danger, too."

5

―――≈≈≈―――

Her life was in danger, too.

Dani felt stunned. She didn't believe this psychic hokum at all—good heavens, she never even scanned the horoscopes in the newspaper—but it was still disturbing to be warned you were in danger by someone who believed it to be true.

"It's so unusual, too," Dawn was saying as she continued to flip through her steno tape. "As I was saying, the guides generally address only people who are present at the sitting. At first we couldn't imagine who Mustafa was talking about."

"Mustafa?"

"One of Mama's guides. He's the one who sent the message about the two of you. Oh, where is it? I know it's here . . ."

She flipped through several more pages, her scowl creasing her forehead between her eyes. Then, with a smile of evident satisfaction, she looked up. "Here it is. The sequence of events is different from what I was remembering. Memory is a funny thing, isn't it?

"Anyway, Mama was fully in a trance at this point. Elroy—that's another one of her guides—had been giving some information to one of our clients when Mustafa suddenly pushed through. He's always been a little rude, you know. We think that's because he was raised in a culture that doesn't respect women. Mama is convinced that Mustafa hates having to speak through a woman. Once she wanted me to suggest he go find himself a male medium, but I couldn't quite bring myself to do it." She smiled again. "It's a little scary dealing with spirits. I mean, just the fact that they're there at all . . . well, you're never quite sure just what they might be capable of."

Silas cleared his throat impatiently, and asked, "Could we get to the point here?"

Dawn continued as if he'd never spoken. "Anyway, Mustafa pushed through, right in the middle of Mama's reading for a client, and insisted that we take immediate action. He kept saying Morris was worried about his friends, that his friends were going to be hurt. Initially we didn't even know who Morris was. We thought it was a message for one of the other clients who were there.

"Finally we managed to pin down that Morris was Morris Feldman, and that he was worried about Dani Hilliard and Silas Northrop. I can read you the exact words, if you like."

"No thanks," Silas said swiftly. "Did he say what kind of danger?"

"That part was a little confusing. Let me see . . . Here. 'There's a treasure, but the only treasure is one of the heart.' "

"Oh, for Pete's sake," Silas muttered under his breath.

Dawn either didn't hear him or chose to ignore him. Unruffled, she continued reading from her notes. " 'Some think it will make them wealthy . . . tell Dani and Si to beware. Tell them to leave before it's too late.' " She flipped a page. "He goes on a little here about one of our clients who was in the room at the time. I can't read it to you for reasons of confidentiality."

"Obviously," Silas said sarcastically.

"But here," Dawn continued, apparently impervious, "he comes back to the subject. 'Morris is worried . . . tell Dani . . . tell Si . . . harm. Someone intends harm . . .'" She looked up. "And that was it. It was emphatic enough that Mama and I decided we couldn't sleep a single night if we didn't warn you immediately."

"Well, that's real helpful, I'm sure," Silas grumbled. "We've got a treasure that isn't a treasure that someone thinks will make him or her wealthy, and that someone—possibly not even the same someone—intends some unspecified harm. Why didn't you fish around for something more specific?"

For the first time, Dawn took umbrage. "It doesn't work that way, Mr. Northrop! The spirits tell us what they can. It doesn't always seem clear because there are so many difficulties in the communication. It's not a telephone call, you know! There's a great deal of static, and the difficulty of having to use another person as a mouthpiece . . . haven't you ever played Rumors? That game where someone says something and it's passed from person to person down a line? Things get garbled. This is no different."

"But what use is it?" Silas demanded. "You drove all the way up here from Fort Myers to tell us we're in danger, but you have no specifics. Danger from whom? From where? What kind? Over what? You should have saved yourself the trouble and just called on the telephone! It would have done as much good."

Dani wasn't much for this psychic business either, but Silas was being unpardonably rude and she couldn't refrain from telling him so. "You know, Silas, when someone has gone so far out of her way to help you—even if the help is no help at all—you could at least be polite enough to thank her and refrain from telling her that her efforts are useless!"

Silas snorted angrily. "Why should I be polite? Was it polite for this woman to drive up here in an attempt to terrify us with nothing more than a vague threat from a spirit who is probably the invention of her mother's sick mind?"

"Good God, Silas," Dani said, shocked by his bluntness in front of Dawn Moonglow.

But Dawn was unfazed. She rose to her feet and faced Silas down. "My mother is not sick, Mr. Northrop. She is a channeler, someone with a gift that makes her a conduit between the earthly world and the spirit world. She accepts not a dime for the work she does, and she finds it a heavy burden. I'm sure there were countless times when she wished she had never been born with this gift!"

"It isn't much of a gift when the information it provides is worthless."

"Worthless? It is worthless to know that there is something in this house that someone wants badly enough to threaten your lives?"

"We had already figured that out this evening when someone broke in!" Silas towered over the woman, glaring down at her.

"My God," Dani said. "My God! Silas, do you realize what this means?"

He turned his head almost reluctantly to look at her. "What? What does what mean?"

"Think about it, Silas! Someone broke in here this evening. At the same time Dawn Moonglow was driving up here to warn us our lives are in danger."

"So?"

"So obviously her mother got an accurate message from somewhere!"

Silas was being utterly unreasonable, so Dani and Max took Dawn into the kitchen for a cup of tea and a little snack before she left.

"Men," Max remarked, "can be so pigheaded sometimes."

"Silas in particular from what I've seen," Dani agreed.

"No, no," Dawn said. "Really, it has nothing to do

with his being a man. I'm quite accustomed to this kind of reaction from nonbelievers. Their minds are so closed that they can't allow even the merest possibility that psychic abilities can exist. And if they're faced with evidence they can't ignore, they become quite angry. It's perfectly normal."

"Well, I must say you handle it very well," Dani told her warmly. "I was getting very angry myself, and it wasn't me he was attacking."

"He wasn't attacking me either. He was attacking a concept he finds threatening. Having Roxy Resnick for a mother, I've met an awful lot of people who react just as Silas does."

"And it doesn't bother you?"

"I've had a lot of time to get used to it. More than forty years to be precise." She pulled a pack of cigarettes from her purse and waved them at Dani and Max. "Do you mind?"

Neither of them did, so she lit one. "The thing is, what my mother does is real. It's hard to be a skeptic when you see someone like Mama who is right so often. Just today with the two of you she was right, wasn't she? How could she know that someone was going to break into this house?"

"But does that mean the threat is past?" Dani wanted to know. "Was the intruder the threat she was talking about?"

"I don't know." Dawn shrugged and blew a cloud of smoke. "I'm inclined to think Mustafa wouldn't have broken into the session this afternoon if a one-time break-in was all that Morris was concerned about. On the other hand, we're dealing with spirits here. Who can say for sure?"

Max, who had spoken only a couple of words since Dawn's arrival, leaned forward with a question of her own. "You really think Morris sent this warning?"

Dawn nodded emphatically.

"But how would he find this . . . guide to pass the message along?"

"Spirits aren't bound by space and time as we are. Even if he hadn't already known Mustafa, Morris could have done this."

Dani's head was beginning to whirl. "Morris knows Mustafa? How?"

"Mustafa was Morris's informant in Beirut, when Morris was working as a reporter there. He was killed by the same bomb that nearly killed Morris. You heard about that, surely?"

Max nodded. "I certainly did. Morris called me to tell me all about it right after it happened."

"Well, when Mustafa first channeled through my mother, he kept insisting he wanted to speak to Morris. We figured he'd go away once he told Morris whatever it was he needed to, so we got Morris to come to a sitting. Morris was convinced that this was definitely the Mustafa he had known in Beirut. We figured that would be it, but it wasn't. Mustafa never did go away, and Morris came to the occasional sitting to chat with him. In fact, Mustafa told Morris he was going to have a fatal heart attack just three days before it happened."

A chill crept along Dani's spine and prickled her scalp. "Mustafa predicted Morris's death? Morris knew that?"

"Of course. He was there when Mustafa predicted his heart attack."

"I don't think I'd like that," Dani said, looking at Max, who shook her head in agreement.

"Morris didn't seem upset at all by it," Dawn said. "That was the really odd thing. He seemed glad to hear it."

"That sounds like Morris," Max said. "Exactly like him. His reactions *never* were normal."

Dawn left a short time later, insisting that she had to return to Fort Myers by morning so she wouldn't miss church. Dani turned from closing the door behind her to find Silas standing in the atrium, arms folded across his chest, a scowl darkening his brow.

"Did you get your fill of garbage for the evening?" he asked.

"You know, Silas, a closed mind is the hallmark of a fool."

Max stepped between them. "This is pointless, folks. Absolutely pointless. You two have to live together, and it'll be a lot easier if you avoid skinning each other alive."

Dani was instantly mortified. Hadn't she vowed she wasn't going to permit this man to turn her into a fishwife? "You're right, Max. I'm sorry. It's been a long day and my temper is frayed to ribbons."

"Let's get going and find a motel then," Max replied. "I'm pooped and I need a bed."

"No."

"No?" Silas and Max repeated the word in unison.

"I'm not leaving. Doesn't this strike you as a little strange, the way Dawn turned up with a warning the same evening we had someone break in? Maybe it *was* a warning from the spirit world. Anything's possible I guess, and she *was* convincing. But I can't escape the feeling that someone is trying to scare us out of here, and I'll be darned if I'm going to let them do it!"

Silas stared at her in astonishment, and then a warm, appreciative smile spread across his rugged features. "You're something else, lady. I thought you'd swallowed that horse manure hook, line, and sinker."

"You're mixing your metaphors, Silas. If you mean that I'm not accepting her statements uncritically, you're correct. She's persuasive, and she makes her point compellingly, but the coincidence is just too much. Only a fool would dismiss the possibility that she's engaging in an attempt to get us to leave the premises."

Silas flashed a grin in Max's direction. "Doesn't she sound like a schoolmarm? Okay. I'm impressed. I was beginning to wonder if your brain had disengaged. I'm glad to know you haven't swallowed all this spook stuff."

"Well, if the two of you are staying the night, I guess I will, too," Max said. "It's late, I'm exhausted, and I'm damned if I want to try to drive anywhere in this rain. However, I don't think we ought to separate."

"I agree," Dani said. "If someone *is* trying to scare us off, they're hardly going to stop at this point."

Max had fallen asleep ages ago, or so it seemed to Dani. The two women had curled up with blankets and pillows on the couches in the library, and Silas kept guard by the partially opened door, his Browning pistol in his lap.

The rain continued to fall dismally outside, accompanied by an occasional mournful howl of the wind. Even through the closed windows it was possible to hear the clatter of the palm fronds as they tossed restlessly.

A thin strip of yellow light fell through the door from the atrium across Silas's lap and onto the floor of the library. From time to time, the lights flickered and Dani caught her breath, terrified they would go out again. But each time they recovered and burned steadily, gradually easing her fright.

She didn't want to be in the dark in this house, not tonight. Not after Morris's apparition, and the intruder. She hardly dared to let herself think about the fact that she had been alone in her room earlier, and that an unknown man had also been up there nearby.

She opened her eyes and looked at Silas. He could have taken a comfortable easy chair, but instead he sat in an unpadded, straight-backed chair. Probably to make it harder to fall asleep. How could he sit there like that, alone in the quiet of the night with nothing to occupy him? He must be bored to tears. Which made it silly for her to lie here awake and afraid, and him to sit there awake and bored. They might as well keep each other company.

Wrapping the blanket around herself, she sat up and hobbled across the library to an armchair facing Silas. He watched her approach through eyes that were little more than black holes in the faint light.

"Can't sleep?" he asked quietly.

She'd always prided herself on her independence and ability to handle things, so it hurt to admit the truth. "I'm scared."

He astonished her by not dismissing her for silliness. "Hardly surprising," he said in a voice that was a quiet, deep rumble, sort of like the purr of a very big cat. "Only a fool wouldn't be scared, Dani. Something crazy is going on here. Otherwise I wouldn't be sitting up all night with a gun in my lap."

He had a good point. She felt a smile spread across her face. "Thanks."

"Forget it. It's just the truth."

"How can we live here if we have to stand guard all the time against people breaking in?"

"I've been thinking about that. I'm not sure that we really have to worry about being hurt."

"Why not? Dawn said—"

"Keep in mind that Dawn was either repeating a psychic message which could mean absolutely nothing at all, or she was trying to scare us out of here. Either way, it's not a threat I can take seriously."

"Why not?"

"Because warning us off is a stupid thing to do if they want to kill us. What's the first thing we're going to do tomorrow?"

"I don't know. What?"

"We're going to call Morris's lawyer and ask him what the hell is going on here. And Max has already heard this malarkey. Anyone who hurts us now is going to be taking a big risk because people will be aware of what's going on. So . . . I'm convinced they just want to scare us off."

"But if we refused to be scared away . . ."

"I don't think that'll change much. They'll probably try harder to frighten us, but I don't think they're willing to kill in order to get what they want. Seriously, Dani. If they were, they wouldn't have bothered with the warnings."

"That's assuming Dawn was part of the play."

"True. But consider that we've also had two other people trying to worm their way in here, and an apparition on the gallery . . . No, I get the definite sense that we're not in any direct physical danger."

She wanted to believe him. It also struck her that he was attributing Morris's apparition to a scare tactic. How would someone do that?

"If you want my prediction," Silas continued, "I'm willing to bet we get overrun by relatives over the next week or so as everyone who suspects there's something valuable here tries to get in to look for it. And if we refuse to be run off by ghosts, by intruders who make sure we see them, and by psychic predictions, they'll probably get even more persistent about getting in here."

"That's assuming there really is something valuable hidden here, as Dawn suggested."

"Give me one other reason why we should be enjoying all this attention. Nobody could possibly want this house. It's the biggest white elephant I've ever seen."

"But what could it be? I can't imagine that Morris overlooked anything of importance in his will. Good heavens, he even made sure that a cut-glass vase went to the housekeeper!"

"It does seem funny." Silas rubbed his chin. "Well, I'll beard the lawyer in the morning and see what we can learn. In the meantime, Dani, I honestly don't think we're in any real danger."

"Then why are you sitting there with that awful gun?"

"Because it turns Max on."

Dani didn't know whether to be mortified or

furious. Max had been patently admiring earlier when Silas took up his post with the gun, while Dani had been openly disturbed by the weapon. "Guns are terrible things," she whispered firmly. "Just awful. They're good for nothing except hurting people!"

"Actually, darlin', they're damn useful for protection."

"And for impressing people who think brute force is admirable."

He smiled unexpectedly, showing a row of even, white teeth. "Why do I get the feeling that you don't think very highly of men in general?"

"I don't see the connection." It was getting hard to keep her voice down when he was being so irritating, but she really didn't want to wake Max. "I didn't say a word about men, only about a stupid gun."

"No, you said something about brute force, which is a term generally used in reference to men."

"That's a leap to a faulty conclusion."

"Is it?"

"Do you two ever let up?" Max inquired sleepily from across the room. "You remind me of my younger sister and brother." She pushed herself up on one elbow, hardly more than a shadow.

"Sorry," Dani said, her cheeks burning with embarrassment.

"Is something wrong?"

"Not a thing," Silas said. "Dani was just casting aspersions on my gun."

Max flopped back onto her pillow. "I like guns," she muttered drowsily. "They make me feel safe." In a little while, a soft snore indicated she was sound asleep.

"I'm hungry," Silas whispered a few minutes later.

Dani tugged the blanket closer around her shoulders as a trickle of uneasiness poured down her back. "The kitchen is all the way on the far side of the atrium," she reminded him.

"Do you really think someone is going to pop out of the woodwork *now?* Dani, it's nearly five a.m. Whoever broke in must have left hours ago."

"Probably." She clutched the blanket tighter. "It's not exactly *him* I'm worried about."

"The ghost? You're worried about seeing the *ghost?* Dani, for heaven's sake, it was just a trick designed to scare us. And even if it wasn't, what harm can a *ghost* possibly do? He's not solid. He couldn't even punch you!"

"He could give me a heart attack!" she replied furiously.

Silas fell silent, looking astonished. A few moments later he murmured with surprising gentleness, "It really scares you that much?"

"Well . . . yes," she admitted, wiggling unhappily in her chair.

"Then come with me to the kitchen."

"I don't want to leave Max alone here. Good grief, Silas, she's sound asleep and can't protect herself!"

"Oh yes, I can," groaned Max from the couch. "I'm not asleep anymore. You two are whispering until this place sounds like it's full of angry bees. Come on, we'll *all* go to the kitchen and you can tell me about your books."

Max departed at dawn, having approved their sketchy synopses. Just as the sunrise was casting an orange glow through the fronds of the Washingtonia palms, Silas and Dani watched her roar down the drive. The sound of her car engine gradually faded away until only the birds and the soft morning breeze made any sound at all. It was going to be a beautiful day.

At least as far as the weather was concerned.

"Why do I feel as if I've been had?" Silas asked the world in general.

"Because we probably have been," Dani said sourly. "The only way we're going to get any peace and quiet in this place is to figure out what this treasure is supposed to be and find it so they'll all leave us alone."

"It'd be a hell of a lot easier if we had any idea what it is. We don't have any idea if it's a book, a piece of art, a chair, or bankbook hidden in some cranny. We could spend all our time looking and never even figure it out. No, the best thing to do is try to ignore all this hoopla and just get on with our books. That's what *we* came here to do."

"Easier said than done. One day of this stuff and I'm exhausted." She sighed and pushed her hair back from her face. "I think I'll go for a walk on the beach and see if I can't unwind enough to take a nap. If I don't get some sleep, I'll never manage to write a word today."

"Mind if I trot along?"

It astonished her that he wanted to spend any more time with her. They seemed to get on each other's nerves with amazing regularity. On the other hand, it didn't seem to bother Silas that they squabbled so much, and when she thought about it now, she realized that the mild irritation he caused her was more challenging than annoying. How curious!

The rain had left the beach heavily dimpled, covered with tiny craters left by the larger raindrops. Here and there the delicate prints of seagulls' feet left lacy traceries in the sand. A pelican perched on a piling at the end of the seawall that cut across the south end of the beach and ended about ten feet into the water.

"Those sea walls don't work," Silas remarked.

"You sound as if that amuses you."

"It does. It always tickles me when we're forced to admit that Mother Nature knows best. This entire state is a study in the catastrophes man causes when he thinks he can do it better."

Above them on the dune, an egret paused in its search for food among the sea oats to watch them cautiously as they approached. Moments later, having decided they weren't a serious threat, it took a couple of steps and ducked its long neck to seize an insect.

"I can't get over the birds," Dani said. "It's incredible. There are so many of them. So many big ones. And they don't seem to be afraid of us, either."

"They aren't. The big ones, like that egret, could do some serious damage to you if you got too close and scared them, and they know it. Besides, most folks here like the birds. Or at least treat them with respect. As for the gulls and terns . . . they're used to being fed."

"They sure seemed to know the drill when I did it the first time."

"Probably a number of the people living around here toss them scraps."

The air was so clear that even the most distant of the palms were etched sharply against the sky. The waves which yesterday had crashed restlessly against the shore now lapped gently in a lullaby of sound. Sleepiness began to steal up on her, beckoning quietly.

She yawned, and without a word Silas turned them around and headed them back toward the house.

"What do you write your column about?" Dani asked him.

"Boats and boating."

"Whatever got you into that?"

"My dad was a shrimp fisherman on the coast here. I grew up surrounded by boats, the sea, and all the lore. When I got out of the Marine Corps, I bought a boatyard and after a bit started writing about it for a local paper."

"Do you still have the boatyard?"

"Sure do. We mostly do drydock work on fishing boats, but occasionally we handle some pleasure craft." He shook his head, giving a quiet chuckle. "It can be mind bending to see what some people can afford just for fun."

"I know. This villa still blows my mind. I just

can't imagine actually owning a place like this. Actually being able to maintain it. I have enough trouble with my little place in Ohio."

"You own a place?"

Dani smiled. "Sort of a place. Not much more than a cottage, actually. A bedroom, a living room, a kitchen, a mud porch . . . and a postage stamp yard that I can mow with a manual mower. Just enough room for my cats and me."

"Cats. I should have known you'd like cats."

She bristled a little at the implied criticism. "I suppose you like dogs?"

"Big dogs. St. Bernards, golden retrievers, elk-hounds."

"It figures." They had reached the back porch, and she suddenly found it difficult to curb her irritation. She was tired, and what could be less important than whether she liked cats and he preferred dogs?

He laughed outright. "Your goat is so easy to get, schoolmarm. Go on up to bed. I'll make sure the ghoulies and goblins don't get you."

She hated him, she decided as she headed upstairs. Yes, she really did. With just a couple of words he had made her feel foolish, and that infuriated her. Somebody should feed him to the army ants.

But she was tired, and her room was cool and dimly lit, the curtains still drawn from last night. Fear seemed far away, and anger swiftly followed it. She was so tired she could hardly keep her eyes open while she washed at the sink and pulled on a white cotton nightgown. The percale sheets felt crisp beneath her as she slipped beneath the coverlet.

Sleep. At long last she was going to sleep.

At least, that was what she thought until she saw Morris standing at the foot of her bed.

6

"I tell you, he was standing there smiling at me!"

Dani stood shivering in her thin cotton night-gown, shaking as if the temperature were below freezing. For a few moments it had been—during the time she had seen Morris. But Morris was gone and the temperature was back to normal. She shivered anyway.

Silas, she thought, was staring at her as if he couldn't quite decide whether or not she was sane. A variety of emotions had skittered across his craggy face, everything from impatience to disbelief. None of what Dani read there made her feel any better.

"It couldn't have been Morris," he said finally. The Browning automatic hung at his side, held in a relaxed grip.

"I almost think I'd prefer a ghost to the other options." She shivered again.

He didn't answer for a moment. When he did, it was in another direction entirely. "This isn't going to work. How can I write if you're always shrieking your head off?"

At that she lost her temper. "Always? *Always?* I do *not* always shriek my head off! Once before. Just *once* I screamed. How dare you insinuate that I'm shrieking all the time? I'm telling you, I saw Morris standing at the foot of my bed! What the *hell* would you have done? Shot him?"

"It would have done a hell of a lot more good," he growled back. "We'd at least know if this apparition is flesh and blood!"

She vowed then and there that she was going to take her revenge on this man if it took the rest of her life. What about flaying him? Yes, that was it. She'd flay him, slowly, and then fillet him.

"Damn it, woman," he groused, "will you at least put on something decent so I can discuss this with half a brain?"

Automatically, she looked down at herself and felt heat rush into her cheeks. She wanted to sink! The cotton of her gown was so fine that the dusky shadows of her areolas were visible through it. If he could see that . . .

Nearly choking on her embarrassment she took a quick step toward the door of her room . . . then halted again, caught between Scylla and Charybdis, to use a classical metaphor. Or, to be colloquial, between "a rock and a hard place."

"Just grab a robe," he said in a tone that might have been strained . . . or disgusted.

"I—can't."

"Why not?" Desperation. That was definitely desperation she heard in his voice. Somewhere deep inside her it registered pleasurably, but her mind and emotions were too busy dealing with another reality to take note.

"I . . . what if it's still in there?" she asked weakly.

He swore viciously. "Okay. Just tell me where to find your robe. I'll get it."

"It's on the chest at the foot of the bed."

Wrapping her arms tightly around herself, she watched him stride into her room and envied his apparent fearlessness. That's how she ought to be, she told herself. Why in the world should she be afraid of Morris's ghost? After all, in life he had treated her with unfailing kindness. Death shouldn't have changed that.

When Silas returned in a moment, she snatched at the satin robe gratefully. "Thank you."

"Morris wouldn't hurt you," he said gruffly, awkwardly helping her to settle the robe on her shoulders.

"I know." She knotted the belt snugly. "It's not Morris I'm worried about. Well, actually, I am a little, but that's not my main concern. It's . . . well, you remember we were talking about somebody faking the ghost by means of projection or some such?"

"I remember. And frankly, I'm more inclined to believe that's what's going on."

"Maybe." She couldn't make up her own mind one way or the other, probably because neither possibility was palatable. "Is that supposed to make me feel safer?"

He shook his head. "Hardly."

"Have you considered what that means?"

"That we might be in danger?"

She waved a dismissing hand. "That goes without saying. What I'm talking about is . . . how did somebody know to make that apparition happen? How did they know I was in bed? Was someone watching me? Maybe that man you and Max saw last night? *Was he watching me when I undressed?*"

He suddenly looked as unsettled as she felt. His jaw worked tensely as he glanced back into the room. "I think I prefer the idea of a ghost."

"Me, too." She shuddered. "God, I feel so violated!"

His hand lifted, hesitated, finally reached out to grip her shoulder gently. "I'll check it out, Dani. So help me, if there's a peephole in that room, I'm going to find it."

"Wouldn't it just be easier for me to move?"

His grip on her shoulder tightened in a gentle

squeeze. "How do we know every room isn't wired? No, I want you to feel safe in at least one room."

In that moment she felt more kindly toward him than she would have dreamed possible. "Thank you," she managed to say. Cancel the idea of flaying him.

At least for now.

Two hours later they weren't much happier than when they had started the hunt. Nowhere did they find a sign of anything that could possibly have been a peephole. Nor was there evidence of any equipment that could have been used to project an image of Morris.

"I'm telling you," Dani said as they went downstairs to make some lunch, "he looked as solid as you do. That's what scared me, Silas. He didn't look like a wisp of smoke that vaguely resembled Morris, or even like a one-dimensional image. He looked fully three-dimensional. I could have reached out and touched him." But what if she had reached out, and her hand had gone right through him? She shivered, wondering if the shock would have turned her into a gibbering idiot.

"No, you sit while I make the sandwiches," Silas said when she started to open the refrigerator. "Well, if Morris looked solid enough to touch I don't think it likely it was some kind of projection."

"Why not?"

"I'm not sure the ordinary person could afford the kind of technology that would do that . . . if it's even possible."

"So he's a ghost." Her stomach did an uneasy flip-flop as she wondered what that might mean.

"I'm not exactly ready to commit to that. I mean, it's possible somebody's figured out a way to do this. I can't guarantee that no one has. It's just that there should have been some sign of equipment, or a hole in a wall or behind a mirror . . ."

"So it's Morris."

He nearly glared at her. "I can't accept that."

"Why not?" She scowled right back. "Why is it harder to believe in a ghost than it is to believe that someone has spent a small fortune and created an elaborate scheme to scare me out of this place?"

"It just is."

"It would be a whole lot easier for me to believe if they just tried to kill us. For heaven's sake, Silas, just think what would be involved in a scheme like this! Why wouldn't they pick a more certain and cheaper way of scaring us out of here? I mean, I'd skedaddle fast if someone smashed my compu—"

She was abruptly silenced by his hand over her mouth. "Don't give anyone any ideas," he muttered.

She nipped his palm and watched with satisfaction as he jerked his hand back. "And don't manhandle *me*."

"I wasn't manhandling you. It was just the fastest way to shut you up."

"You need some training in manners and common courtesy, Northrop. Just don't do that again!"

"All right. All right." He looked more amused than cowed, however, which did little to improve her temper. "I don't particularly care whether you think it's a ghost," he told her. "Believe what you want. Just don't try to make a believer of me."

"If you want to waste your efforts looking at all the wrong things—"

"Hold it right there," he growled, slapping a loaf of bread and a brick of cheese on the counter. "I will *not* be wasting my efforts. It strikes me that there isn't a whole lot a ghost can do to hurt you except scare you. A human being is a whole different ball of wax. I'd rather be prepared for the worst case, *if* you don't mind." He bent to the refrigerator again, rummaging noisily. "Damn it, we need some cold cuts."

"There's plenty a ghost can do to hurt us," Dani said stubbornly. "I was reading about poltergeists that start fires."

Silas snorted and dumped a couple of tomatoes next to the cheese and bread. "We don't have a poltergeist. We have a Morris. Does it strike you that Morris would want to burn this place down around our ears?"

Dani chewed her lip a moment before reluctantly admitting, "No. He wasn't that crazy."

"Agreed. If it really *is* Morris—and by no means do I agree that it is—then his presence is benign. It may be that he wants to communicate something to you, but he wouldn't harm a hair on your head and you damn well know it." He scowled at the food-stuffs on the counter. "I guess it's grilled cheese sandwiches or nothing. After lunch we're going grocery shopping. This is ridiculous!"

It was a relief to leave the house behind. Dani dozed all the way into town, waking only when they pulled into a parking place at the supermarket.

The day had turned sweltering. The merciless midday sun hadn't yet finished drying out yesterday's downpour and the air was thick with humidity. Just the short stroll across the parking lot made Dani feel as if she were going to melt.

In sharp contrast, the air in the store was frigid. Just five minutes after stepping inside, she wished she had brought a sweater.

Only half awake, she followed Silas up and down the aisles, trying not to shudder over the quantity of red meat and junk foods he heaped into the basket. He was a coronary waiting to happen.

The brisk air inside the store slowly began to increase her alertness. In the cereal aisle she grabbed a box of oatmeal, and later picked up a bag of brown rice. A vegetable stir-fry sounded good, she found herself thinking, and began to look forward to the produce section.

A sorry commentary on the state of her life, she thought—looking forward to the produce section. Good grief. What she wanted was romance and high adventure, right? Only she seemed to be caught up in the middle of an adventure of some sort and all she could think about was how very much she needed to catch up on her sleep. Hah. Some heroine she made.

Of course, Silas didn't make much of a hero. He was distinctly annoying and irritating and didn't at all understand the meaning of gallantry. She doubted very much that he owned a tuxedo or even knew how to knot a bow tie. He probably drank beer from the bottle or can, watched football with his feet propped on the coffee table, and belched noisily.

You're something of a snob, you know. Morris's words from a few months ago suddenly floated back to her. She couldn't now remember what they had been discussing, just that it had been a cold winter evening with sleet rattling against the windows of her little cottage, and Morris had called unexpectedly. Even now his words stung. He had said them gently, almost tenderly, but they had disturbed Dani then and they made her cheeks burn now. She didn't want to think of herself as a snob, and it bothered her to realize that Morris may have been right.

What did it matter, after all, if Silas owned a tux? She was simply looking for reasons not to be attracted to him.

Because she was *very* attracted to him. A little sigh escaped her. Never in her life had she experienced true romance. Her relationship with Thomas Rivett, a divorce attorney, had been so prosaic and low-key as to have nearly put her to sleep. Thomas owned a tuxedo, and knotted a perfect bow tie, and had taken her to the theater, ballet, and symphony. He had ordered vintage wines for dinner, spoke flawless French, and owned an original Matisse.

But not once had he struck a spark in her heart. Or her body, for that matter. A peck to the cheek or a cool kiss to the lips might be elegant, but it wasn't designed to ignite the fires of desire.

Silas, on the other hand, made her exquisitely aware of her anatomy nearly every time he entered the room. He was the stuff of which erotic dreams were made.

Not that she was interested in such things. No, she would far prefer to enjoy a meeting of minds, a close nurturing friendship of the mind and soul. The physical portion of a relationship mattered little next to the spiritual mating.

Except that when she watched Silas's denim-clad buns moving down the aisle ahead of her, her body argued strenuously against being relegated to last place. She sighed again and forced her gaze to fix elsewhere.

Men like Silas shouldn't be allowed to wear tight jeans.

They reached the produce section at last, and Dani turned her attention to picking out a small stalk of bok choy and some fresh broccoli.

"You know," she said to Silas as she regarded the bok choy, "it would be nice if supermarkets would take single people into account once in a while. Every one of those stalks of bok choy are big enough to feed a family of four."

"Or you and me," he returned with a wicked waggle of his eyebrows. "You could invite me to dinner."

"I told you I wasn't going to do all the cooking! Besides, you don't like my taste in food."

"But I love stir-fried veggies. Tell you what, Dani. I'll wash and chop if you'll fry."

Finding herself tempted, Dani hesitated. She hated to chop the vegetables. "Well . . . I guess it would be silly to duplicate efforts."

"Of course it would," he said, beaming at her as if she had just given the correct answer to a complex problem. Why did that make her feel that she had just been had? "In fact, I'll just pick up the tab, so get whatever you want and don't worry about the cost."

For an instant some evil imp tempted her to take

him at his word, but sanity saved her. She didn't want to be indebted to this man for anything. "I'll pay my own way, thank you."

He looked as if he was about to argue, but she forestalled him by heading for the broccoli. Before she had taken two steps, she saw something that caused her to draw up sharply and turn quickly back to Silas.

"Don't look," she said in an undertone, "but Ernie Hazlett is over by the endive."

Naturally Silas did exactly what she told him not to do. "I don't see anybody."

Dani whirled around and saw that he was right: Ernie was nowhere to be seen. "I saw him. I know I saw him."

"The way you saw Morris?"

She spun around, horrified, but before she could respond in any way, Silas was apologizing and looking rather shamefaced. "I'm sorry," he said. "Really. That was uncalled for. I don't doubt you saw Morris, or something that looked like Morris."

But. She could hear the unspoken qualifier. Even she had to admit that the current incident undermined her credibility. But she *had* seen Ernie. "I know I saw him, Silas," she said quietly. A note of despair crept into her voice. "I know he was there."

"You're also very tired. No, don't get all ruffled," he objected when she got ready to argue. "I'm not saying you imagined anything. I'm saying that perhaps someone who looks a lot like Ernie was over there and you mistook him. Or maybe Ernie *was* there. I don't know. Does it really matter?"

"Only if it was Ernie and he was following us."

"Now wait a minute here. Let's not get *too* paranoid."

"Too paranoid?" She couldn't believe her ears. "What's 'too paranoid' when you consider what's been going on?"

"Just what exactly *has* been going on?" Silas asked

her. She started to open her mouth, but he fore-stalled her. "No, wait a minute before you argue. I've been giving this some serious thought, and it strikes me we don't really have a whole lot to get bent about."

"You're kidding!" All she could see was Morris standing at the foot of her bed. Not a whole lot to get bent about?

Silas gently drew her over to the oranges, so they were out of the way of what appeared to be a flotilla of gray-haired ladies in muumuus, all of them push-ing shopping carts and talking noisily to one an-other.

"Not a whole lot," he repeated. "I'm not kidding. What have we got that is actually tangible? Two appearances by a ghost, a psychic who claims we're in danger and that there's some kind of treasure at the house, and a glimpse of someone in your door-way last night. That last item is the only one that deserves genuine concern."

"Wait until *you* see Morris at the foot of your bed," she said sourly.

"My point is, would *you* go to the cops with what we've got right now?"

Dani hesitated, shifting uneasily from one foot to the other. Finally she shook her head. "I guess not."

"Exactly. Something's going on, but to conclude that everyone we happen to see is somehow involved would be a big mistake. First let's get some evi-dence."

"But doesn't it strike you as odd that we'd see Ernie Hazlett here?"

"He could just live right around here, Dani. Besides, we can't really be sure you saw him. It might have been someone who looks a lot like him."

Dani seriously doubted that the world was over-populated by short, stocky men with greased-back hair and pointed-toe shoes, but she could be wrong. This was Florida, after all, and she'd already noticed that no one in Ohio would be caught dead dressing the way so many people here did. Those muumuus for example . . .

She sighed. "Okay. Maybe it wasn't Ernie. Maybe it was. I still think we need to be paranoid."

"Moderately paranoid I can agree with. We'd be fools not to be alert. I'm just not sure how much of a threat we're really facing, though. There's a world of difference between someone just wanting to scare us out of there, and someone wanting to hurt us."

She thought she saw Ernie once more when they were checking out, just a glimpse of him through the big front windows as he walked out of view. This time she didn't say a word about it.

At breakfast several days later, they heard the unmistakable sound of the door knocker. Their eyes met in surprise and trepidation.

"Another relative," Silas said. Even after three days of comparative peace, he was sure they hadn't seen the last of Morris's family.

"But it's so early!" Dani knew the protest was silly even as she made it, but Silas, naturally, couldn't let it pass.

"I've never known a nuisance that chose to wait for a more convenient time of day."

"But most people have better manners than to knock on someone's door at six-thirty in the morning. We could be asleep!"

"I guess they want to make sure they don't miss us."

Neither of them moved, however, probably in the vain hope the nuisance would go away. Instead, the hammering renewed, louder this time.

Silas sighed and rose reluctantly. "I'll get rid of whoever it is."

"At least be polite about it."

He gave a toothy grin. "What, and take all the fun out of it?"

She followed, not in any vain hope that she might keep him in line—she knew him better than that by now—but because she was curious to see who was at the door. Besides, some naughty little part of her didn't want to miss whatever outrageousness Silas perpetrated this time.

Silas flung the door open with a flair, almost gleefully. Dani imagined that he was mentally rubbing his hands together in anticipation. She half expected to see another version of Ernie Hazlett in the entry. So apparently, had Silas. He stared, dumbfounded.

"Hallo," said a lilting voice with just a suggestion of breathiness. "I jam looking for Señor Nortrope."

Oh my, Dani thought, astonished. Oh my! The woman was about as curvaceous as it was possible to be, her ample breasts nearly spilling out of the scoop-necked sweater she wore, her skirt doing little more than to cover her rounded hips and show a shocking length of thigh—gorgeous thigh. All this pulchritude was further topped off by a mane of absolutely perfect blond hair and a pair of celestial blue eyes. It was no wonder Silas was dumbstruck. Any red-blooded male worth his Y chromosome would be, Dani thought.

But Silas hadn't been a marine for nothing. He recovered swiftly. "I'm Señor Nortrope," he said with a positively evil grin. "Who are joo?"

The woman giggled and waggled a finger at him. "Joo are making fun of my accent, señor. That is no polite."

"My apologies," Silas replied gallantly. "So who are you?"

"My name is Pepita Mayo. Moreese, poor dear sweet Moreese, was *mi esposo.*"

"*Esposo?*" Dani repeated, hanging on every word.

"Husband," Silas clarified. "Pepita here was one of Morris's wives."

Pepita got inside the door. Dani found herself thinking that with Pepita's amazing talents the woman ought to rent herself out to terrorist organizations that wanted to get past security guards. One glance of that lush Latin body apparently deprived men of their wits. At least to judge by Silas Northrop, former marine.

If Pepita was the next wave in the move to get Silas and Dani out of the house, Dani figured she might as well start packing right now.

It didn't take Silas long to get the newcomer comfortably established on a kitchen stool—where her crossed thighs were even more perfectly displayed—with a cup of coffee and the croissant Dani had been saving for her lunch. Dani was beginning to think that she might toss Pepita into the pot with Silas.

"What can we do for you, Pepita?" Silas asked.

Pepita put the croissant down and drew a hanky from her tiny purse, lifting it to the corner of her eye where she dabbed gently, taking care not to disturb her makeup. "I was so very much in love with Moreese," she said sorrowfully. "Even after we divorce we stay close. I live here until his poor heart attacks heem. Did joo know that?"

"That his heart attacked him? No, I didn't know."

That was the first inkling Dani had that Silas might have retained a modicum of sense. Y chromosome notwithstanding, it appeared he was very much on the alert.

"Joo must know," Pepita said. "He leave you the house, don' he?"

"Not exactly. We're just using it temporarily."

"Yoosin' it?" She dabbed prettily at her eyes again, and quivered her lower lip. "If Moreese don' give you thees house, then how come I get thrown out?"

Dani was suddenly convinced that this woman was exaggerating both her accent and her stupidity. Morris, even in his most hormonally driven moments, hadn't been tolerant of stupidity. "Because he didn't give the house to you," Dani said. "I'm sure the lawyers explained everything, but if you still have questions you should talk to them, not us."

"I know," Pepita said, but turned her pleading face to Silas as if Dani were of no consequence. "But the lawyers, they talk so fancy, I can't tell what they say. I just get thrown out of my house."

Silas sent a look to Dani as if to say, Here we go again. And with each word she spoke, Pepita's accent was softening—as one would expect, Dani thought sourly, of a woman who must have been a resident of this country for at least twenty years. So this was all a put-on.

"I'm sure," she said to Pepita, "that if you ask Mr. Cheatham to explain he will. Most of the lawyers I've known are very conscientious about that."

"Most of the lawyers you've known?" Silas repeated. "Just how many lawyers *have* you known? And how well?"

She scowled at him. "Mind your own business."

"I'm just wondering about your lifestyle," he explained. "Most people have very little contact with the legal profession. At least those of us who stay on the *right* side of the law."

"I have never to my knowledge been on the *wrong* side of the law. I am blessed, however, with friends from a wide variety of professions."

"Including the oldest one?"

He was grinning evilly, and she refused to dignify the question with a response. Since he'd called her a prude, he knew better anyway.

"Look," Silas said to Pepita when he abandoned hope of a scorching retort from Dani, "Ms. Hilliard is right. You need to talk to Irving Cheatham."

Pepita sniffled and sent him an appealing look.

"But when they make me leave in such a hurry, I forget to find my family Bible."

Silas looked at Dani. Dani looked at Silas. Both of them groaned inwardly.

"Your family Bible," Silas repeated. "Really?"

"It is in my family for almost two hundred years!" She blinked away a tear. "I have to find it!"

"Certainly you do," Silas agreed. "But—forgive me, I'm not trying to be difficult, but I have to wonder—just how is it you left such a valuable item behind?"

"I thought . . . I think it is in the boxes I never have unpack. I only need a few minutes to look for it," Pepita said with an imploring look at both of them. Her English seemed to be improving with every sentence she spoke. "I won't even ask you to help, and I promise not to disturb you. I'll be out of here in no time at all."

"Sorry," Silas said, smiling like a piranha that smelled blood. "The lawyers have a detailed inventory of every single item in this house. If there *is* a two-hundred-year-old Bible in this house, then it's on the inventory, and I certainly don't want to have to explain its absence."

"But—"

Dani interrupted her. "Nor do I want to have to pay for it. You're absolutely right, Silas. Miss Mayo needs to call Mr. Cheatham at once."

Pepita was not without her own resources. Her tears miraculously dried, and now she simply looked like a whipped puppy. "I don't need to call him. It's not on the inventory."

"Ah," said Silas. "Then it's not in the house!"

"But it must be! Where else could it be?" Her lower lip trembled.

"That's an excellent question! I think you need to take better care of such valuable personal items, Ms. Mayo."

"But please, you have to help me find it!"

"And so we shall." Silas rose from his chair. "Rest assured that if we find a two-hundred-year-old Bible, or anything that might possibly be one, we'll call Irving Cheatham immediately. Just keep in touch with him, ma'am. If it turns up, he'll be notified."

A minute later, Silas had ushered her through the door and closed it behind her with finality. He turned to Dani who was frankly grinning.

"You were magnificent, Silas!"

"Thank you." Smiling, he took a bow. "Good God, wasn't she something? I can't imagine what Morris ever saw in that woman! She'd drive me nuts in twenty-four hours flat."

"Boobs," said Dani.

"Huh?"

"Boobs. Bazoombas. Whatever the current male slang is for breasts. That's what Morris saw in her. Frankly, I think he must have been temporarily insane."

Silas laughed. "That's what he said he was every time he married—temporarily insane!"

Dani giggled, but her innate fairness reared its head. "But we're being unkind. This may have all been an act in an attempt to deceive us. I never thought Morris had much patience with stupidity."

"He didn't. Well, if that was an act, deliver Hollywood from Pepita Mayo."

Still chuckling, Dani glanced casually upward, then gave a little shriek.

Once again, Morris was standing on the third-floor gallery, looking down at them.

7

—∾—

"You know," Silas said grimly, "this is getting just a bit tiresome!"

As soon as Dani had shrieked, Morris had vanished, so when she pointed with a trembling hand, Silas saw nothing at all.

She was shaking as violently as a young sapling in an earthquake. "I'm sorry," she said through chattering teeth. "I'm sorry. It's just that it scares me . . ."

"Hey," he said with surprising kindness. "Hey. It's okay. I wasn't growling at you, I was growling at him. Of course it scares you."

Gently, as if she were made of spun glass, he folded her into his arms and hugged her against his broad, hard chest. "It's all right, Dani. It's okay to be scared."

For a breathless instant, Dani was aware of nothing except how good it felt to be held by Silas. His arms were warm, strong, and comforting, and his chest felt so good beneath her cheek. She could hear the strong, steady beat of his heart and found it reassuring. It was wonderful to feel so secure. Like a little mouse, she wanted to burrow into the safety of his embrace as far as she could go.

He stroked her hair and massaged the nape of her neck, easing the tension that held her taut as a bowstring. Little by little she relaxed against him. "I'm sorry."

"Don't be. It's been nerve wracking. I may not be seeing this apparition, but I can certainly sympathize with what it must be like for you."

She hadn't expected him to be so understanding. Nor had she expected him to smell so good, like laundry soap and bath soap and man. The cotton of his white shirt felt crisp beneath her cheek, like a freshly laundered and line-dried sheet . . .

Astonished by the sudden erotic turn of her thoughts, she started to pull away from Silas. This couldn't be allowed! The two of them had to share a roof for another six months, and it was going to be positively miserable if she started mooning over the man. Besides, she had had quite enough of men. Thomas's desertion had been extremely painful, and she was never going to risk that kind of hurt again. Never.

But instead of letting her go, Silas tightened his arms just enough to tell her that he wanted her to stay right where she was. "You feel a lot softer than you look," he told her almost gruffly.

It was an outrageous comment, but she didn't mind it in the least. A pleasurable little shiver trickled through her, driving out all thought of Morris and attendant problems.

"We'll get to the bottom of this somehow, Dani. I swear we will. As for Morris . . . I really don't think that an apparition can hurt you."

He was, she thought wistfully, a surprisingly comforting man when he wasn't being generally difficult, as was his wont. Part of her just wanted to cuddle closer, but common sense was frantically warning her to put things back on a more businesslike footing before it was too late. She eased backward, and this time he let her go.

"People get used to living with ghosts," she said as

she turned reluctantly to look up at the shadowy gallery. "I was reading about it. It seems unimaginable right now, but I believe I'm as adaptable as the next person."

"Well, don't get too comfortable with it. I don't want you missing that apparition once I get rid of it." He meant to be amusing, but she gave him only the faintest of smiles.

"If it really is Morris," she said quietly, "you won't be *able* to get rid of him."

He still wasn't comfortable with that possibility, and didn't attempt to hide his distaste for it. "I seriously doubt Morris has nothing better to do right now than make personal appearances on the gallery."

"Maybe he doesn't," she argued quietly. "Maybe he's desperately trying to tell us something."

"What could possibly be that important?" His cat-green eyes looked down at her, compelling in their intensity. "Think about it, Dani. If there *is* life after death, wouldn't matters here look kind of trivial by comparison?"

"That would depend on the matter, I think."

He sighed and shifted his weight to one leg, placing his hands on his hips. Something about the way his powerful hands looked on his narrow hips made Dani feel breathless. She dragged her gaze up to his face, seeking equilibrium.

"Are we talking about treasure?" he asked her. "Because if we are, we're wasting our breath. Morris's will was minutely detailed. Ask Irving Cheatham if you don't believe me. Any will that accounts for the disposition of a piece of dimestore pottery—and his did—is hardly likely to overlook anything of monetary value."

"If you recall, I said exactly the same thing just the other day. But this could be something he acquired after the will was drawn. Or it could have no monetary value at all, but simply be of sentimental importance."

"Morris was a sentimental fool. He'd never have overlooked an item of that nature."

"Unless it was something he didn't want anybody else to know about."

"Oh, right!" he said. "Morris didn't want anybody to know about it, but after he's dead he suddenly has a terrible compulsion to make sure we find out about it?"

"Do you have to be sarcastic?" She glared at him, while privately admitting he was right. It sounded awfully thin. Instead of backing down, however—she had learned as a teacher of adolescent boys *never* to back down—she changed tack. "Silas, something is going on here, and it's not a two-hundred-year-old Bible!"

He threw up a hand. "Agreed. But the problem here is that we don't *know* what's going on. Suppose there *is* something. How can we look for it if we don't know what we're looking for?"

"Somebody thinks it's a book."

He paused. "True," he said finally. "Pepita was going to look for a book. So maybe there's some really old and expensive Bible that Morris didn't put in his will."

"Could be."

"How would we know which book? I think we need to talk to Irving about this, Dani. Maybe we can persuade him to give us a copy of the inventory. After all, we might be inheriting all of it anyway."

She nodded. "Good idea. Then we can tell if we run across something that isn't in the inventory."

"I just want to know what could be so all-fired important that Morris needs to keep popping up."

Could he actually be starting to think that Morris's apparition was really Morris? Dani wondered in amazement. She hadn't considered Silas to be that flexible. On the other hand, having him be absolutely convinced that the apparition was either a hoax or an hallucination had been distinctly comforting. If Silas started believing, she wouldn't be able to talk herself into doubting what she saw.

"Well," Silas said, "I'm going to hook up my stereo. I can't work worth a damn without music."

"You're not seriously proposing to put your stereo in the atrium!" Dani looked over the railing, aghast at what she was seeing down below. Speakers the size of refrigerators were scattered around the fountain, tilted at an upward angle.

"Sure," said Silas. "We'll be able to have music everywhere this way. And the acoustics will be fantastic. It'll sound like a concert hall."

"Maybe I don't want to work in a concert hall."

"Then just close your door."

She did precisely that, returning to her computer and wondering if she was going to have to stage a raid to put those speakers out of commission. The sheer size of them—well, there was no way anything that big could sound good at a low volume. What if he liked to listen to some horrible kind of rock music? Before the day was out, she'd better get to the drugstore and buy some earplugs.

Her novel seemed to have hit a blank wall, probably because of all that had happened this morning. Between Morris and Pepita Mayo, she didn't seem to be able to concentrate on the trials and travails of her heroine. A heroine who was beginning to seem annoyingly insipid anyway. But then so did her hero. Both were too darn nice and too darn agreeable. The hero should be a little more opinionated, more definite. Kind of like Silas.

Silas Northrop as hero. She almost snickered at the thought. Most women probably wanted to dump a bucket of icy water over his head. She certainly did. Or had. All right, she could admit that he was kind of growing on her, but there was no denying he was abrasive. She wouldn't *choose* to live with him.

Would she?

The phone rang—that was another thing about this place. There was a phone in nearly every room, and when a call came in, the ringing reached a startling decibel level. They needed to wander around one of these afternoons and turn at least some of them off.

The caller was Irving Cheatham, Morris's attorney. "I had a message that Mr. Northrop needs to speak with me, Ms. Hilliard. How are the two of you getting on, by the way?"

"About as well as can probably be expected when two total strangers are turned into unwilling housemates. Are you sure you don't know why Morris concocted this dreadful scheme?"

He chuckled drily. "Afraid not. I asked him at the time, since it was so unusual, and he merely smiled. I didn't get the feeling that it was meant to be some kind of joke, however, but beyond that it's a mystery to me."

"Well, we're as much in the dark as you are. I'll get Silas for you."

"Thank you."

Silas was still in the atrium, amidst snaking lines of speaker wire and power cords. "Mr. Cheatham is on the phone," she called down to him. "Good grief, Silas, tell me you're not going to leave those cables running everywhere! It looks awful."

"You won't see a single one of them when I'm done. Promise."

"What are you going to do? Tear up the tile floor and bury them?"

He grinned up at her. "Hardly. Stay on the extension, Dani. You may as well be in on this conversation."

She had intended to all along, but she didn't tell him that. No point depriving him of his moment of magnanimity.

Silas's voice was loud in her ear when she picked up the extension. "We're being overrun by ex-relatives of Morris's, Cheatham. What the hell is going on?"

"What do you mean by overrun?"

"In four days we've had Ernie Hazlett, Lester Carmichael, and Pepita Mayo here trying to get permission to go through the house. Hazlett said his aunt left some stuff here . . . hell, he wanted us to let her move back into the house."

"Don't do that," Irving said. "Under no circumstances let that woman move back in. Morris was specific about everyone leaving the house. Moreover, he left all his ex-wives with tidy little annuities . . . more than most of them deserve in my opinion."

"A very unlawyerly comment," Silas said.

"They're not my clients. I can say anything I like about them, short of actionable slander." Irving Cheatham sniffed. "A damn bunch of money-grubbing hangers-on for the most part. I'll never understand why he put up with it. Be that as it may, there is nothing in that house that wasn't on the inventory we prepared at the time the will was drawn. Which means none of their possessions are in there. They were *all* present when that inventory was created, and they all acknowledged its correctness. None of their personal items are on it, and none of the items that remain in the house now were *not* on it."

"Well, well, well. Pepita Mayo was saying she left a two-hundred-year-old family Bible here."

"If she ever had such a thing." Irving sniffed again. "That woman's background is nothing if not obscure. It was an absolute scandal when Morris returned from an assignment married to her. Good heavens, she was hardly more than a child! Nor did it last very long. I suspect he married her only to get her U.S. citizenship."

"Well, that would explain it," Silas said. "She doesn't seem his type."

"Did Morris have a type?" Irving asked.

Silas laughed, but Dani interrupted. "I'm beginning to think he did," she said. "Damsel in distress."

There was a pause, then Irving said, "You may just have hit the nail on the head, Ms. Hilliard. His second wife, Gert Plum, was a circus acrobat who had developed an inner ear problem that ruined her sense of balance. I'm not sure about the others, but that would certainly explain some very strange choices in marital partners."

"None of this is going to help us deal with the onslaught of relatives," Silas reminded them.

"I'm not sure I have any solutions to offer," Irving said. "I can't prevent them from knocking on your door. Just send them away, Mr. Northrop."

"That's what we've been doing. What's concerning us, Mr. Cheatham, is that they all appear to be after something in this house."

Silence hummed over the wire for several moments. "You're implying that these people are . . . coordinating with one another?"

"The thought is becoming more and more inescapable," Silas replied. "We no sooner send one relative away than we have another one here making the same claim of having left something in the house."

"It *is* rather suspicious. But it really doesn't matter, you see, because everything in the house will belong to you and Ms. Hilliard as soon as you complete the terms of the will."

"If whatever they're looking for is still in the house," Silas pointed out drily.

"True."

"So we're wondering what they could possibly be looking for. What if something from the inventory turned up missing?"

"It would be theft, and I'd naturally have the police investigate it."

Dani spoke. "So it has to be something that isn't on the inventory. Do you have any idea what that might be—if such a thing existed?"

"No idea whatsoever. Nor would I be absolutely certain that just because a few people want to get into the house that there really is something to be looked for. It wouldn't surprise me at all if Morris somehow left some of them with an impression that there was something valuable here as a practical joke."

Dani thought about that. So, apparently, did Silas. "Yeah," he said heavily after a moment, "I can well imagine Morris doing precisely that and then laughing himself sick at the thought of them climbing all over this place looking for something that doesn't exist."

"Exactly," said Cheatham. "My late client was a wonderful man, an admirable novelist, and a great adventurer, but his sense of humor was positively *strange.*"

Even Dani couldn't argue with that. Despite the fact that her acquaintance with Morris had been limited to letters and the telephone, she had come to learn that there was no anticipating what would amuse him.

"Well," said Cheatham, "if they keep on troubling you, just send them to me. They have no further claim whatever on the estate, and so I will tell them."

After Cheatham hung up, Dani went out onto the balcony and looked down at Silas, who was back to fussing with his cables.

Silas looked up at her. "Not a whole lot of help, was he?"

"No. And while I can imagine Morris thinking up some practical joke that would happen after he died, that wouldn't explain his appearances to me, or what Dawn Moonglow reported her mother said."

"It doesn't explain it if you want to accept apparitions and channeling as real."

Dani sighed exasperatedly. "Darn it, Silas, something is going on that's a little bit bigger than a practical joke—unless you're suggesting that Morris

set up something before he died to make it appear
that his ghost had returned."

Silas shook his head. "No, that's pushing it even
for Morris. He might have dropped a tantalizing
hint or two, but he wouldn't have arranged for
ghostly appearances."

"And another thing. What if Morris was working
on something before he died? The people who lived
with him would know about it, wouldn't they? But
Cheatham might not have heard about it."

"One problem. If Morris was working on something, the wives would have taken it as soon as he
died. No reason for them to turn up months later
trying to look for it."

"Unless," Dani said, "for some reason Morris hid
it and they couldn't find it before they were evicted."

Silas apparently couldn't argue against that possibility. He stood for several long moments, hands on
his hips, then tilted his head back and looked up at
the heavens. "Morris, you son of a gun, what kind of
mess did you get us into?"

The heavy silence offered no answers.

Dani was going to scream. She was absolutely,
positively, going to skin Silas alive, a square inch at a
time, and then turn him into dog food. The strains
of the *1812 Overture* were filling the atrium with
their deafening roar and the amplified thunder of
cannons—"Real cannons" Silas had told her with
genuine delight the first time he had assaulted her
with the recording—and she honestly didn't know if
she could endure it another day.

For the last week he had played music loud enough
to shake the walls, claiming it helped him concentrate. In consequence, Dani had to close the door of
her study, stuff a towel into the crack beneath it, and
put on the headphones of her Walkman in an
attempt to isolate herself from the noise. While she
couldn't exactly hear the music, she could still hear

the vibrations of the deep bass, and feel the concussion of the cannon shots.

It was driving her batty.

At first she had told herself that she could learn to ignore it. After all, she had gotten through college while studying in a dorm room with her roommate's stereo blasting and virtual mayhem in the hallways outside. She could even concentrate on reading a good book in a cafeteria full of noisy teenagers. For a few hours each day—and in all fairness to Silas, it *was* only a few hours—she could handle this nuisance.

Unfortunately, with time it was beginning to irritate her more and more. Of course, again in fairness to Silas, she had to admit that she had never asked him to turn the music down. She had simply asked once if he really needed it to concentrate. Perhaps he hadn't understood what she was really trying to say. Perhaps she ought to just come right out and tell him she couldn't work with all that racket.

Why hadn't she told him? Had she somehow lost her backbone? It wasn't like her to remain silent on a matter of this importance.

She turned up the volume on her Walkman just a little more, filling her head with the soft music of Dan Fogelberg, and wondered if she was going to go deaf. What if she had the volume turned high enough to do damage and she just didn't realize it because of the racket in the atrium?

All of a sudden, the pounding roar of Tchaikovsky filled her head, drowning poor Mr. Fogelberg in the roar of cannon and the clamor of bells. Startled, she turned in time to see Silas throw the door open and storm into the room. He glared at her, his mouth working, but she couldn't hear what he was saying.

Leaning over, he plucked the earphones from her head. The *1812 Overture* reached a deafening crescendo. Silas's nose was now only inches from hers, and he didn't look at all happy. "Just what do you think you're doing?" he demanded loudly, barely audible above the music.

"What's wrong?" she asked, feeling as if she had stumbled into the middle of someone's play and hadn't been given any lines to speak.

"If you want to talk to me, just talk!" He had to shout to be heard over the music, and she winced.

"Don't shout!"

"You won't hear me if I don't!"

"Then turn off your damn music!"

"It'll be over in a minute!"

"So wait for it to be over!"

To her surprise, he obliged, straightening and standing over her with folded arms. He looked, she thought, like an executioner waiting to take up his ax.

The joyous strains of the music faded away finally, and silence reigned. Blessed silence. Dani could have snatched it into her arms and hugged it close in appreciation.

Unfortunately, Silas spoke. "If you want to talk to me, don't hover in the damn doorway like that. Just come in and talk to me."

"I didn't hover in any doorway!"

"Yes, you did, damn it! I saw you. It drives me nuts to have someone standing off to the side that way watching me. Just come into the damn room and talk to me!"

"I did no such thing. If I wanted to talk with you, I'd not only come into the room, I'd tap your shoulder!"

"Don't lie to me, Dani. I saw you! That's the third time this week you've stood there!"

"I'm not lying! How dare you suggest any such thing! I have *never* stood in the doorway watching you like that." She shook her head. "Sheesh, what an ego! As if I would have any reason to want to watch you!"

"I saw you!"

"You saw something else because *I* wasn't there! A reflection, a shadow, whatever, but it wasn't me!"

He scowled at her, his eyebrows nearly meeting above his nose. "Prove it. Come stand in the doorway."

"Oh, for heaven's sake, Silas! I'm trying to work. First you deafen me with your damn music, then you barge in here and disrupt my train of thought, and now you're demanding I come stand in your doorway to prove I wasn't there when I was actually here trying to work? Have you lost your marbles?"

"Maybe. Just come stand in my damn doorway."

Sighing, she rose from her desk and traipsed along beside him to the other side of the house. "Maybe you saw Morris."

"You think I couldn't distinguish between the two of you?" He snorted.

"But from the corner of your eye—"

"Nope, it was you."

"Then I must have projected my astral body because I sure as heck wasn't standing in your doorway!"

"Astral body!" He snorted again. "What kind of crap are you reading these days?"

"Anything that might help explain why I'm seeing Morris."

They reached the door of his office, and he stationed her right on the threshold. Then he sat at his desk and faced his monitor. Dani waited impatiently, suppressing an urge to tap her toe. "Well?" she asked finally.

"Did you change your clothes?"

She looked down at her blue chambray shirt and blue jeans. "No. I've been wearing this since I got up this morning. Why?"

"Because I thought you were wearing pink."

"Pink? Not today. I only have one pink item in my wardrobe and I wore it the day you arrived here."

Why was she being so reasonable about this, she wondered. She ought to give him a piece of her mind. But then she recalled his patience the last time she had seen Morris, and she felt petty and small for thinking this way.

She stepped into the room and faced the doorway. "It must have been a trick of the light, Silas. Maybe a sunbeam coming through the window reflected off something, or refracted in such a way as to look pink. Or did you actually turn and look at it?"

He shook his head. "I said I'd be with you in just a second, but when I turned you were gone. It was gone. Whatever it was."

Something about his description made goose bumps prickle along Dani's arms. "I don't like this, Silas."

"*You* don't like it? Something has interrupted my work three times this week and *you* don't like it?" He rose and stalked over to the doorway, then faced back into the room, looking from window to window as if trying to determine how an errant light beam could have created the impression that Dani was standing in the doorway.

Dani's gaze wandered from Silas to the words glowing on his computer screen. *Tangerine dawns and watermelon sunsets splashed across a turquoise sky . . . the breeze soft with the smell of the sea . . . the gentle lapping of waves, nature's lullaby . . .*

These were the memories Sam clung to as he lay in the heap of smoking rubble, unable to move, with his best friend's bodiless head resting on his chest. Asleep. Jones looked as if he were just taking a nap. But he wasn't, and because he wasn't, Sam clung to memories of tangerine mornings and watermelon evenings, and the clean, fresh scent of salt water.

Dani started guiltily as she realized she had been reading Silas's book. It was tantamount to eavesdropping and she turned quickly away, hoping he hadn't noticed.

But he had. He hadn't moved from where he was

standing near the doorway, but he was watching her closely. "What do you think?" he asked.

"It's . . . grim." Which wasn't at all adequate, but she was feeling embarrassed and disturbed by what she had just read.

"War is grim."

"Are you writing a war story?"

"Not exactly. It's mostly about dealing with it afterwards. For some people that's the hardest part."

Dani nodded, resisting an urge to look at the screen again. "I guess you've had to do some of that yourself."

"My share, sure. We all do."

The question she most wanted to ask was whether the scene he had just described had happened to him. She didn't dare, in part because she felt she would be trespassing where she hadn't been invited, and partly because she was afraid to know.

"That—that part about tangerine mornings and watermelon evenings was beautiful," she told him, wanting to avoid any discussion of the severed head. "It's a perfect description of this place."

"Thanks. Well, I guess we're not going to solve the mystery of what I saw, Dani. But I will tell you this—if I didn't see you, then I saw something that looked an awful lot *like* you. I honestly don't think it was just a trick of the light."

"You said it's happened three times, so it would be safe to assume that it'll happen again. When it does—"

"When it does," he interrupted, "I'm going to look straight at it and settle this issue. I'm getting tired of being interrupted that way."

"Maybe you should move your desk."

He shook his head. "Once I know what it is, I won't be bothered by it anymore. Sorry I interrupted you."

"No problem." There was actually a bigger problem, and she screwed up her courage to say, "Do you have to put the music on again?"

"Hmm? Oh, no. No, I'll leave it off for now. Maybe what I need to do is take a nap."

Tomorrow, she promised herself, if he put the music on again she was going to ask him to lower the volume. For now she was content to just have the next few hours of peace and quiet.

A couple of hours later, Silas stuck his head into her study. "Dani, when you have a minute, let's go check out the hurricane room."

As it happened, she was about to put her work away for the day, but she didn't want to make it that easy on him. Not after his accusations earlier, which were still smarting. "Why?"

"Well, I got to thinking about Pepita's Bible, and where would be a good place to hide something. Dollars to doughnuts whoever inventoried the hurricane room didn't open every single box and count every single item. Would you?"

"Actually yes, I would. However, I'm prepared to admit the possibility that others might not."

Silas flashed a sudden grin. "Magnanimous of you, m'dear. So let's check it out."

Dani really didn't want to go into the hurricane room. She couldn't explain her aversion to it. It was just a windowless room, after all, and when the power was on it was even a brightly lit windowless room, with panels of fluorescent lights hanging overhead.

Rosario, the man Lester Carmichael had described as a general factotum, had long since helped Silas clean up the spilled lamp oil, a process that had somehow involved kitty litter. The room still had a faint kerosene odor to it, probably from the lamps that stood neatly on their shelves.

"Plastic water bottles to be filled," Silas remarked from the far side of the room. "Enough for a small army. And a box full of flashlight batteries. I wonder where the flashlights are."

"Over here," Dani told him. In her corner she had

found a dozen flashlights and two camp stoves beside fourteen small cylinders of bottled propane.

"I guess Morris planned on riding it out if there was a storm," Silas said after they'd taken inventory. "All he'd need to do is lay in some nonperishable food and he'd be ready for a siege."

Dani straightened and looked at him. "Would it be wise to remain here?"

"Probably. This house has survived more than seventy years. On the other hand, if we were directly in the line of a major storm, I'd evacuate anyway. Even if this house can withstand the wind, it might not withstand a storm surge."

Just then, the door slammed shut and the lights went out. In the windowless room, the silence was suddenly absolute. Not a ray of light or a whisper of wind penetrated from the world outside.

"Silas?" Dani's voice sounded quavery in the pitch-black gloom.

"I'm right here, Dani." His voice was soothing. "I'm just trying to find some of those damn flashlight batteries. You stay where you are."

"W-what are you going to do with the batteries?"

"Bring them over to you. You have all the flashlights, don't you? Damn, I wish I smoked. My kingdom for a lighter or a match."

Dani looked over her shoulder toward the door, wondering how it was that the door had slammed and the lights had gone out at the same moment. It seemed a little bit much for a coincidence. "I thought the marine motto was *Semper paratus,* always prepared."

"That's the Coast Guard. Nope, for us it's *Semper fidelis.* Always faithful."

"Sounds like a dog." She meant it jokingly, but as soon as the words were out it struck her how they could sound.

"Watch it, Hilliard," he growled. "Teasing a marine could be a dangerous pastime."

There was a quiet bang, followed by Silas's curse.

"I thought I'd gotten a good mental picture of where everything is in this place. Not good enough I guess. Keep talking so I don't get turned around."

"Great. When someone orders me to talk the last thing I can do is think of something to say."

"You're doing okay. Try giving me a list of five reasons why that door could have slammed at the same time the lights went out."

Dani felt an uncomfortable chill run down her spine. "Well, a wind could have suddenly come up and blown the door shut and blown the power line down all at once."

"Remote but possible. Reason number two?"

"A tornado just blew through."

"I could almost count that under the wind explanation you already gave, but I'll make an exception this time." He stumbled against something and swore softly. "Okay. That's two. But don't try any variety of wind for reason number three. I want some creative thinking here."

"Morris is playing a practical joke?"

"I was afraid you were going to say that."

Suddenly he was there beside her, big and warm, a stalwart island of safety in a world of threatening blackness. His arm snaked around her and hugged her close to his chest. She could almost swear she felt his lips brush the top of her head, but it must have been her imagination.

"Okay," he said quietly. "Don't give me reason number four. Neither of us wants to hear it right now." The only thing that occurred to him was that someone had done this to them. "Do you remember where those flashlights are?"

"Right behind me."

"Turn slowly and get one, will you?"

She had been afraid that he would let go of her, but instead his hand remained on her, palm pressed to her as she turned. It was reassuring, but it was also deliciously sensual the way it trailed over her side and hip as she turned. What a thing to notice at a time like this!

His hand remained on her waist as she bent and felt around for the box containing the flashlights. In the process, her bottom bumped up against him in a way that made color flame in her cheeks. This was ridiculous!

At last her hand closed around one of the flashlights, and she straightened swiftly, feeling all flustered and hot. Of course, it was getting warm in here since the door had blown closed . . .

"Thanks," Silas said when she placed the light in his hand. He unscrewed the bottom, dumped the batteries in, and moments later the bright white beam illuminated the floor around their feet. "Ta-da! There's the door. Let's get the hell out of here and find out what's going on."

Dani followed right on his heels, eager to be out of this room, vowing never to set foot in here again. Why in the world didn't this room have even a single window?

Silas reached out and gripped the doorknob, rattling it. He paused, rattled it again. Dani felt her stomach sinking.

Silas shone the light around the knob, as if looking for something. He ran his hand up the door and back down, then shook the knob again.

"Damn it!" He swore loudly. "Damn it! Dani, we're locked in."

8

Just like Beirut, he thought when the door slammed.

Only not like Beirut. It was dark as pitch, but Silas could move, he wasn't trapped. There were no sobs, groans or screams from the darkness around him. There was just Dani, who made a single, soft whimper.

He could smell her. Not just the faint, spicy fragrance of her bath soap, but the woman-scent, musky and enticing. She drew him like a moth to flame, and yet darkness held him back.

Just what every woman needed, he thought bitterly, a claustrophobic, broken-down ex-grunt who was afraid of the dark. The perfect companion to provide a safe harbor from life's storms. How could he tell her he was afraid? No woman could possibly want a man who was afraid of the dark. There was no choice then, except to keep his emotional distance and ruck up, suck up, and press on. He felt his way toward Dani.

When he slipped his arm around her, he hugged her gently and then brushed an errant kiss on the top of her head. "We need a flashlight," he said. It wasn't an admission, he reasoned, just a solution to a problem. Let it lie.

Dani found the flashlight and the beam drove the

darkness back, and with it the nightmare. Once again he was firmly established in the present, and the past was firmly in the past.

And they were still locked in. The doorknob wouldn't turn in his hand, and there was no sign elsewhere of a latch or a bolt. Dani clutched at him, her fingers grabbing his belt.

"You're sure?" she asked.

"Positive."

"But how could that happen?"

"Not by accident, I can tell you."

"What do you mean, Silas?" Her fingers tensed around his belt; he could feel it at the small of his back.

"I mean this door can only be locked with a key."

"It was . . . it was in the lock?"

"That's where I left it. Damn!" It wouldn't do much good to smash something, but smashing something was exactly what he felt like doing. *Trapped.* Not even the flashlight could hold that feeling at bay.

"Silas . . . Silas, why would someone lock us in here?"

"Probably to search the house." It was the only reason he could think of. "Rob the place . . . I don't know, Dani, but I'm sure it's for no good reason."

She fell silent, and while she was silent he began to consider what he needed to do. Get all the flashlights working, for one thing. Whatever they did from here on out, they were going to need light.

"Let's get all the flashlights functioning," he told Dani, "and then hunt for a crowbar, or a screwdriver that I can use to pry the door handle off this damn door."

Dani let go of his belt and caught his arm. "If they're still out there—Silas, maybe we should wait. Interrupting a thief can be a dangerous thing to do."

"I know what I'm doing, Dani." Marine training had its uses. "And if I can, I'm going to catch the sumbitch who did this."

"What if we can't find a screwdriver or something?"

"It could be a hell of a long time before Rosario decides to get something out of this room."

Without another word, she helped him put the flashlights together. Even with a dozen flashlights ready to burn, they still had a big box full of batteries. No chance they'd run out of light soon.

Silas would have been ashamed to admit it, but that was important to him. His trouble with darkness was the primary reason he'd left the Marine Corps, retiring early with a disability. Just a small disability, but one that would have made him useless to the corps.

Taking a chance that he'd be able to get them out of here soon, he turned on most of the flashlights, filling the dark room with dim light. Anything that improved their chances for escape was reasonable risk.

Morris had evidently planned on a siege. Apart from the lamps and flashlights, there were several battery-operated radios, boxes of flares, two shotguns . . .

"Why on earth would Morris have guns stashed in here?" Dani asked when they found them.

"Beats me." No ammunition was in sight, however, nor was he interested in these guns. If he needed a firearm, he had his own arsenal.

The most amusing find, however, was the supply of surplus military rations. Silas laughed out loud. "I wonder how all his exes would have reacted to these."

Dani smiled up at him, her soft brown eyes sparkling in the dim light. "Are they that awful?"

"Trust me, you have to be hungry to want one. *Very* hungry."

The room was getting warmer, the air was getting stale. No light had come in around the edges of the door after it had slammed closed, and no air was being exchanged with the outside world. How long would it take to suffocate? Silas wondered. He kept the question to himself, not wanting to alarm Dani, as he continued to shift boxes around and began to sweat heavily.

Finally he swore in exasperation. "There has to be a toolbox here somewhere! Damn it, I can't believe he could have stashed everything under the sun in here and neglected to include some tools!"

"Maybe there aren't any because they're elsewhere in the house," Dani said quietly.

"Don't even suggest it. I refuse to entertain that possibility."

"Okay."

He heard the faint tremor of a suppressed laugh in her voice and was suddenly struck by how absolutely wonderful she was being about all this. She could have cried, but she hadn't. She could have given him hell for leaving the key in the lock, but she hadn't. Not once had she railed against him or against their unknown imprisoner, nor had she given way to the fear she certainly must be feeling.

"You're a real scout," he told her gruffly.

"Thanks."

"I mean it. I wouldn't blame you if you were huddled in a corner crying your eyes out."

"What possible good would that do?" She gave him a gently amused smile. "We need to keep our heads if we're going to get out of this."

It was then that the urge overwhelmed him. Like a storm surge, or a tsunami, it picked him up and swept him before it. Since the moment he had first set eyes on those full, lush lips of hers, he had wanted to feel them against his, to test their softness and—he admitted freely—erase that pursed, prim expression she too often adopted. Maybe it was because she wasn't pursing those lips right now, but because they were soft and inviting, framing the kind of smile a man would cross deserts barefoot for.

Whatever, he lost his head and reached for her.

His hands were big, and powerful, able to crush without meaning to. Aware of it, he took her shoulders with the utmost gentleness, and drew her against him.

He wouldn't have been astonished if she had objected. If she had tried to pull back, or had uttered a protest, he would have let her go. But the strangest thing happened when he touched her, and even as he saw it happen he couldn't quite trust his senses. Instead of stiffening, she softened, as if she were melting. Her eyelids drooped, her lips parted, and she sank against him, her curves molding to his angles as if they were made for each other.

His lips touched hers. An electric thrill pierced him, a sense of tasting forbidden fruit, then he was lost in the warm, sweet wonder of her. Her mouth was shy, quiescent beneath his, but generous. He made his mouth soft, shaping it to hers, and felt the slight quiver of response that rippled through her.

She was going to be angry with him later; he hadn't the least doubt of that. He was taking a liberty with her that he shouldn't be taking given their relationship. She could possibly make him live to regret these moments for the rest of the time they were together.

He didn't care. Right now all he could think of was her warm, moist mouth and the way it welcomed his tongue. His senses were whirling in soul deep awareness of her breasts, pressed tightly to his chest so that he could feel their lovely fullness in exquisite detail. His arms tightened, as if they needed to feel the slender curve of her back even more fully.

Did she even guess what a sexy woman she was? In a moment she was going to know just exactly how much he wanted her.

That uneasy realization snapped him back to his senses. He turned a little, preserving his modesty and hers, and eased his mouth away from her succulent lips. It was the hardest thing he'd ever done. Given an option, he'd have held her closer yet, and run his hands all over her, acquainting himself with every one of her soft little curves.

But he restrained himself, instead tucking her head into the curve of his shoulder and waiting for the world to settle down.

Waiting for her dander to rise. He figured he was in for a royal tongue-lashing about being fresh, forward, unconscionable, or whatever other critical words might spring to the mind of a prim, prudish schoolteacher. It was no consolation to realize he deserved every one of them, and more.

Was he out of his ever-loving mind? This was the last woman on earth he should have kissed and held. Good Lord, they had to share a roof for the next six months, and it would be a whole lot easier to endure if he didn't have the memory of how she felt in his arms to haunt him.

After a few moments, Dani eased away from him. "I think we'd better get back to finding a way out of here."

Just that. No lectures on impropriety, no references to Neanderthal manners, no comment at all on his ill-considered action. She must have been as shaken by that kiss as he had been.

For some reason, that didn't comfort him at all.

At least a half hour, or possibly longer, passed before they finally found a toolbox hidden away behind boxes of emergency supplies. A ten-inch flathead screwdriver succeeded in freeing them from the unbearably stuffy room. Silas simply pried the doorknob plate off and manually unlocked the door.

Outside, the weather had begun to change dramatically. High wide arcs of clouds had given way to darker bands, and the wind had increased noticeably. The first gust of wind felt blessedly cool after the hurricane room's heat.

The key lay on the pavement right outside, as if it

had fallen out of the doorknob. Silas and Dani exchanged looks.

"I don't believe it," Silas said. "It was unlocked so I could open the door. Someone had to have turned it to lock us in."

She nodded. "They could still be in the house."

"I know."

Just then Rosario came around the corner of the house, carrying a ladder. He regarded them a moment before leaning the ladder against the side of the house. "I'm trimmin' the palms. Gotta get rid of dead branches afore the wind blows 'em down."

Dani and Silas exchanged looks once again. The question occurred to both of them: Could Rosario have locked them in?

Rosario's dark gaze drifted down to the pieces of hardware in Silas's hand. "You got a problem, Mr. Northrop?"

Silas gestured with the doorknob. "The wind blew the door shut and we got locked in."

Rosario came toward them. "That couldn't happen. That door needs a key to lock."

"Well, it happened somehow."

The handyman shook his head. "Musta been kids or somethin'. I'll fix it soon as I got a minute."

Once inside, Silas spoke. "I don't think it was him."

"Me neither. There was something too natural about the way he reacted."

They were whispering, standing just inside the door, both of them conscious that whoever had locked them in had probably done so in order to gain access to the house, and there was a good possibility that person was still inside.

"What do we do now?" Dani asked.

"Search the place." He looked around, considering options. "You wait outside. Annoy Rosario to death, but stay with him until I make sure this place is clear."

"You're crazy!" It was almost impossible for her

to keep her voice to a whisper. "Wouldn't it make more sense to call the cops, tell them someone locked us in the hurricane room and ask them to come out and clear the house? Darn it, Silas, whoever it was probably came in here!"

"That's a distinct possibility, which is why I want you to stay with Rosario."

"No! If you search this place, I'm going with you. If you get your damn fool head shot off, you might need somebody to apply a tourniquet!"

"If I get my damn fool head shot off, I'll need more than a tourniquet. Don't be ridiculous, Dani."

"I'm not the one being ridiculous here. Just call the cops, tell them we've had a prowler and we think he may have come into the house!"

"By the time they get here, he'll be long gone!"

"Fine! At least you'll be in one piece. You call or I'll call!"

They were glaring at one another, their noses inches apart, the kiss of such a short time before forgotten—until they both suddenly realized how close they were . . .

He straightened as suddenly as if she had struck him, putting a safe distance between them. "Call them if you want, but I'm checking the place out."

Dani stared after his rigid, retreating back, thinking that maybe she ought to run over him with a steamroller. After all, that was how he'd left her feeling, with that kiss in the darkened hurricane room. Now he apparently wanted to act as if nothing at all had happened between them. Worse, he was acting like a pigheaded fool, marching off to deal with an unknown and potentially deadly threat.

Cement overshoes, she decided. She'd put him in cement overshoes and get a crane to hoist him out over the edge of the highest point of the Sunshine Skyway bridge, and she'd hold him there until he promised to behave like a normal, intelligent human being instead of a hormonally impaired model of machismo!

But first she was going to call the police before something dreadful happened.

Except that to get to the nearest telephone, she'd have to go through the atrium and into one of the rooms where someone could be hiding. Damn, if that wasn't just like Morris to put a phone in every room of this ridiculous hotel of a house, but neglect to put one in a really convenient place—such as right beside the door.

There was no sound from within the house, so Dani assumed that for the moment at least Silas was safe. She certainly didn't want to step further inside.

Minutes ticked by in stark silence. Nothing within the house seemed to stir. The atrium was growing dimmer, however, as clouds conquered the sun.

That was when she thought about Morris. She hadn't seen him in a while, nor did she want to see him right now. Unease began to crawl along her nerve endings, and she shivered with apprehension.

Rosario. He was outside trimming the trees. Perhaps he would know where she could find a phone to call for help. Maybe he even had a cellular phone in his car. So many people did nowadays . . .

Trying not to make a loud noise, she opened the door just enough to ease herself through, then closed it gently behind her.

The palm trees were rustling and clattering in the wind, and the sea oats rippled like a storm-tossed ocean. Rosario was nowhere in sight, though the ladder still stood against the side of the building.

Maybe he'd gone to get something. She raced around the side of the house, hoping against hope that his little red truck would still be out front. It was gone.

That left the neighbors. It also left her with the uneasy suspicion that Rosario might have been responsible for locking them in the hurricane room. Maybe he, too, wanted to look for the supposed treasure in the house. A strong gust of wind snatched at her, whipping her hair around into her face. She reached up and grabbed as much of it as she could to hold it out of the way.

What now? It would take too long to drive to a pay phone. If anything was going to happen to Silas, it would have happened by then. Running to the neighbors offered little better. They might or might not be home—these were mostly vacation homes, not primary dwellings. She might run down the beach to one of them in a matter of five or ten minutes and find she had wasted the time.

No, she'd better go back inside and risk getting to a phone.

Good heavens, this was ridiculous! Why did that man have to go haring off this way, taking ridiculous risks? Why couldn't he be at least a little sensible and call in some reinforcements before he charged again?

Furious at Silas, scared half to death, and ready to do battle with just about anything, Dani squared her shoulders and marched toward the front door. *She* was going to call the police, and she was going to do it with one of the phones in the house, and if she got herself killed in the process, Silas could blame himself for being such an ass!

Just as she was reaching for the door handle, the sound of a small engine coming up the drive diverted her. Turning, she saw Rosario's little red truck. He pulled up in the circular drive and gave her one of his shy smiles.

"Where were you?" she demanded. "I thought you'd left!"

He looked startled, then annoyed. "What's the hurry? I needed a pack of smokes."

"Silas thinks somebody may have broken into the house, and I was looking for you to see if you can help me call the police . . ."

It all sounded so confused. She stopped herself and began again. "I'm sorry I yelled at you. But Silas is inside, and I'm worried that there might be somebody in there who'll hurt him . . ."

He nodded briskly. "We go in together and call the damn police. What's that man doin' goin' in there all by hisself?"

"He's a marine. He thinks he's invincible."

"Hell, I was in the army. Them marines ain't any more invincible than the next guy."

"Tell that to them."

He flashed her an unexpected grin. "They don' listen so good, huh?"

"*They* don't listen at all!"

Inside, the only sound was the rushing of the fountain. Whatever Silas was doing, he was being quiet about it. Presumably he wasn't in the process of being murdered. She shivered, and kept close to Rosario as they hurried across the atrium and into the kitchen.

Rosario, carrying a hammer for a weapon, looked around behind the island and into the cabinets, pronouncing the coast clear. Dani reached for the phone and dialed 911.

"Nine-one-one Emergency Services."

"We think there's somebody in the house." Dani tried to sound as calm as she could. "Could you please send an officer out here?"

"Please state your name and address."

Dani stumbled, almost giving the woman her Ohio address, but caught herself in time, taking care to enunciate clearly as she gave Morris's address.

"We show that house belongs to a Morris Feldman."

"That's correct."

"Who are *you*?"

"I told you. Danika Hilliard."

"What are you doing there?"

"I'm visiting."

"Is Mr. Feldman there?"

"He's dead."

The dispatcher paused for the merest instant. "Mr. Feldman is dead? Was he shot?"

"No . . . no, he had a heart attack!"

"Are you a nurse?"

"No, I'm a schoolteacher. What does that have to do with anything! We think there's someone in the house—"

"If you're a teacher how do you know that Mr. Feldman had a heart attack?"

"Because his doctor said so!"

"His doctor is there right now?"

"No!" Dani shook her head, gripping the receiver so tightly that her fingers ached. "Will you please listen to me? Morris doesn't have anything to do with this. At least I don't think he does, because he's dead. But we think someone might be in the house!"

"You and Mr. Feldman both think there's a prowler?"

"Mr. Feldman is dead!"

"I thought that's what you said. Just who is in the house with you?"

"Silas and Rosario."

"Who are they?"

"My roommate and Mr. Feldman's gardener."

"I thought Mr. Feldman was dead."

"He is, but he still has a gardener." Dani was beginning to feel desperate. "He also still owns this house! Will you get someone out here, please."

"There are three of you in the house, but you actually think there's someone else in the house with you?"

"It's a possibility."

"You're not sure? Did you see someone?"

"Not this time. But we think—"

"Why do you think someone is in the house if you haven't seen anyone?"

"Because someone locked Silas and me in the hurricane room! We think it's because they wanted to search the house."

"You're locked in a room?"

"Not anymore. We got out. But we were only in there a half hour, and this is a big house. Nobody could search it in half an hour. Whoever locked us up—unless it was Morris—couldn't possibly have done everything they wanted to."

"I thought Morris was dead."

"He is, but we've been seeing him around—or at least I have—and it wouldn't really surprise me if he was the one who locked us up. It would be just like Morris!"

"You've been seeing a dead man?"

"Well, actually, I think I've been seeing his ghost. But that's neither here nor there. Someone may be in the house and I want an officer out here to make sure no one gets hurt." She was beginning to wonder who was more obtuse, the dispatcher or herself.

"So someone locked you in a room more than half an hour ago, but you got out, but you still think someone may be in the house?"

"That's right." Good grief, it sounded insane. She was beginning to wish she had never made this call.

"Are all three of you still in the house?"

"Yes."

"There's a patrol car pulling up in front of the house right now, Ms. Hilliard. You and your two companions will have to step out the front door now, with your hands up so the officer can see you. And please bring the ghost with you."

Dani gaped, uncertain whether the woman on the other end of the phone was treating her like a madwoman or was just being scrupulous about details. "I can't bring the ghost out! I don't know where he is. As for Silas, he's somewhere in the house looking for the prowler."

"Then you and the other party step out front, Ms. Hilliard. Now."

Dani wanted desperately to argue with that command. She didn't like its tone at all. It would have accomplished nothing however, so she simply said, "Okay" and hung up.

She turned to Rosario. "She says the cops are out front and we need to go out there now with our hands up."

"But what about Mr. Northrop?"

"I guess he's on his own."

Rosario shrugged one shoulder and started toward the front door. "Let's go then."

Dani hesitated. "Uh, Rosario?"

"Yeah?"

"I think you'd better leave that hammer in here. You never know what the cops might think."

He glanced down at the claw hammer held so tightly in his hand. "You're right." He set it on the island.

Outside, two patrol cars were waiting. Behind them crouched armed police officers. The sight of guns being pointed at her made Dani more than a little nervous, but she managed to keep her hands up as she followed directions to move away from the house.

"You're the woman who sees ghosts?" one officer asked.

Dani wanted to sink in humiliation. Her cheeks grew hot. "I guess that's me."

"And the man?"

"Rosario, the gardener. My housemate is still inside looking for the prowler, Officer." She wished they'd tell her to put her hands down. She couldn't ever remember feeling as vulnerable as she did right now with her hands in the air and guns pointing at her.

"He's uncooperative, huh?" asked the officer. "Shoulda waited for us to get here."

"That's exactly what I told him," Dani said in heartfelt agreement. "He was afraid the prowler would get away."

"But you're sure there's a prowler."

Dani gave an exasperated sigh. "I don't know," she said emphatically. "We had reason to believe there was one, but by now he might be gone! And probably is for all I know."

"Calm down, lady. Calm down." The cops rose from their crouched position behind the vehicle and came around the cars. "We'll go in and check things out. The two of you stay out here. Oh. You can put your hands down now."

That young man, Dani thought as she lowered her hands, had a bit of an attitude. Someone needed to shake a finger at him. Rotating her shoulders to ease the ache that had come from holding her hands up, she gave the officer her best teacher's glare. "My housemate is in there looking for the prowler. You be careful not to shoot him by mistake!"

The officer sighed. "Ma'am, we aren't planning to shoot anyone. Now stand aside."

She did so only with great reluctance, because it had occurred to her that Silas could be in more danger from these police officers with their nasty-looking guns than from a burglar who might not even exist. The sight of the two uniformed police-men walking into Morris's house with their guns drawn was enough to turn her hair white.

"Rosario, I think I made a mistake."

"Huh? What mistake?"

"Calling the police. What if they shoot Silas?"

Rosario cracked a smile. "You always worry this much?"

Dani released a sigh. "I guess I do. But if they think Silas is the prowler . . ."

Rosario shook his head. "They know Silas is inside. They'll be extra careful."

Of course they would, but that hardly alleviated her anxiety. Oh, would she never learn to leave well enough alone?

The minutes stretched endlessly. Dani wondered how long it could take for the two police officers to go through the entire house.

"What the hell is going on here?"

Dani whirled around at the sound of the familiar voice and sagged in relief as she saw Silas coming around the corner of the house.

"What are the cops doing here?" he demanded. "I

thought you were going to wait for me by the back door!"

"They're here because I called them! You should never have gone looking for a prowler on your own! What if he'd had a gun? You might have been shot!"

"So to protect me you send in two armed men who might well mistake me for the prowler? For the love of God, woman, use your brain!"

"Use *my* brain? What about you using *your* brain? You could have gotten yourself killed by going in there alone, looking for some desperate criminal! If you were so worried about the person getting away, we could have watched the doors, but you should never, *never* have risked your neck that way, you idiot!"

"I am not an idiot!" His eyes were mere inches from hers as he bent down and glared at her. "*I* knew what I was doing, which is more than I can say for you! Calling the cops and sending them into the house after me was not the brightest thing you could have done, teach! I wasn't expecting them! I could have pointed a gun at them and they'd have shot me for sure! Cripes, what does it take to convince you that I'm not one of your asinine high school students?"

"Then don't act like one! You could have— Mmmph!"

She was cut off abruptly by the hard pressure of his mouth on hers as he scooped her up off her feet and crushed her to his chest.

"My God," he whispered shakily moments later. "My God. Do you know what I thought when you weren't waiting for me by the door?"

Her mind was just beginning to formulate the gruesome pictures that must have filled his earlier, when a hard-as-steel voice said from behind, "Let go of the woman now, or I'll shoot."

9

~~~

Silas stiffened, moving not a muscle. Dani also froze, her nose pressed tightly to his chest. The hairs on the back of her neck stood on end.

"It's okay," Silas said quietly. "I'm not hurting her. We're friends."

"Let her go now!"

Muscle by muscle Silas relaxed his grip on Dani. "I'd step back slowly if I were you," he told her softly. "The man is wired."

She managed a jerky little nod and slowly—very slowly—turned around. The two young police officers she had sent into the house were both crouched, holding their pistols in a two-handed grip, both barrels aimed at her and Silas. Rosario stood to one side, looking concerned.

"I'm all right," Dani said. "Honestly. This man is Silas Northrop, my housemate. He was just hugging me."

After several seconds' hesitation, the officers lowered their guns and straightened up. "The way you had her grabbed, man," said the younger of the two, "it looked like you were hurting her."

"Just a bear hug," Silas said. "I think her ribs are still intact." He gave Dani a questioning look.

"My ribs are fine, but I've had about all I can take

of machismo for one day!" Her tart tone, much to her surprise, drew a grin from Silas, as if he were enjoying her irritation. "Did anyone find anything?" she asked. "Was this all a waste of manpower and worry time, or was someone in the house?"

"No one," said both officers promptly.

"Someone had been there," Silas said.

"How do you know?" asked the officer.

"My screen saver on my computer comes on if the system has been inactive for fifteen minutes. By my reckoning it should have been inactive for over an hour, given the time Dani and I spent doing other things and getting locked in the hurricane room. Only it wasn't on when I got to my office."

"And that means?" asked the other cop.

"That within fifteen minutes of my entering there, someone had touched the keyboard or the mouse, or bumped up against the desk."

The cops exchanged looks. Finally the older one looked at Silas. "Maybe it was the ghost." At that, both police officers laughed.

Rosario looked uneasy. Silas looked wooden. Dani fumed. Tapping her toe, she waited for the policemen to begin behaving like civilized human beings. When they continued to chuckle, she decided enough was enough and shook her finger at them.

"You ought to be ashamed of yourselves," she told them sharply. "Whether or not you believe in ghosts is irrelevant. You're both being unforgivably rude. I'm sure your mothers brought you up better than that!"

The laughter died instantly, but neither cop had the common courtesy to apologize. Instead, one of them made a big production of taking a notebook and pen from his breast pocket. "Okay," he said briskly. "Was anything missing from the house when you went through it, Mr. Northrop?"

"Not that I could see, but I'm not all that familiar with the contents of the place yet."

"But nothing obvious was missing or out of place?"

"No."

The officer flipped his pad closed. "Then there's no point in us investigating any further. Give us a call if you find that something is gone or has been tampered with. In the meantime, keep your doors and windows locked."

Dani watched the two cruisers disappear down the driveway and shook her head in annoyance. "They didn't believe us."

"No, they didn't," Silas said heavily. "It doesn't matter anyway. They can't do a thing without some kind of evidence, and we didn't even *see* the prowler."

"But we were locked in the hurricane room!"

Silas looked down at her. "It could have been a result of our own carelessness. We certainly can't prove that it wasn't. Nor is our credibility very high, apparently."

"There's no reason it shouldn't be!"

"No reason except a ghost."

Dani felt her cheeks flame, but Silas had already turned to Rosario and was offering to help the gardener with the pruning. Moments later she was all alone on the tiled front steps with a darkening sky overhead.

No reason except a ghost. Why did that give her the awful feeling that the police would probably never again respond quickly to a call out here?

Looking up at the dark squares of the house's windows, she felt a chill steal along her nerves. She should have had the sense to stay in Ohio.

"I need to check my business," Silas told her an hour later. "I haven't been there in days and I want to make sure everything is okay there."

Dani nodded, but felt a sudden attack of nervous butterflies in her stomach. After all that had happened, she didn't want to stay in this house alone.

"If you want," Silas continued, "you can ride along."

She leapt at the chance, pausing just long enough to grab her shoulder bag. She tried to tell herself that it would be interesting and possibly informative to see Silas's business, but the truth was—and even she realized it—that anything was better than risking another encounter with whatever was going on in this house.

Silas's boatyard was on a wide saltwater estuary only a half hour from Morris's house. The first thing that Dani noticed was the immense size of the steel building around which clustered smaller buildings standing on concrete stilts. It was at least as big as a large airplane hangar, but the doors opening onto the water were taller. Tall enough, she realized, to allow a reasonably large sailboat's mast to pass. The building was virtually empty, however, now sheltering only a single shrimp boat which was suspended in a frame and surrounded by scaffolding.

"I was able to finish up everything else and get it out of here, Si," said a young man named Robert Fischer. Silas had introduced him to Dani as his "right hand."

"Good going," Silas told him. Then he turned to Dani, explaining, "We're in hurricane season now. I like to keep the number of boats here at an absolute minimum from now through the end of October. I'd sure hate to see a dozen boats run aground by a storm surge."

Robert grinned. "So would your insurance agent. *Paloma* here is going to have to stay here awhile, though, boss. She's got a bunch of major problems with her hull."

"It can't be helped. What does next week look like?"

"We've got two more coming in on Monday for scraping. Should have 'em out of here by Wednesday, when we've got a yacht due in."

The concrete buildings proved to be workshops

and offices where just about any kind of fitting a ship could need was manufactured or modified to suit. Teak and mahogany filled a storeroom, waiting to be shaped to repair wood-hulled vessels. Other buildings held items used on fiberglass and steel hulls. Silas told her he vastly preferred working on wooden hulls, that laboring with planks and beams to make them fit snugly into their assigned place gave him far more satisfaction than working on a steel hull ever would. More and more of his work was with steel and fiberglass hulls, though, and it was getting so that only older pleasure vessels turned up in his yard with wooden hulls.

By the time they left the yard, Dani's impression of Silas had altered dramatically. Somewhere inside that obtuse head of his lurked the brain of a very able businessman. Even though he had mentioned his boatyard to her before, she hadn't connected him with an operation on this scale. She decided that she couldn't consider him a bonehead any longer. It simply wasn't true. Which made him all the more frustrating, actually. It was easier to forgive a stupid man for being obtuse than to forgive an astute one. And Silas was plainly a *very* astute man.

By the time they returned home, the wind was blowing mightily, tossing the palm fronds in a rush of sound, heralding the arrival of yet another summer storm. Inside the house, the sound was reduced to a quieter cataract, occasionally punctuated by a creak from one of the storm shutters.

"I think," said Silas as they stood within the atrium, "that we might be wise to set up camp together until the storm is past. We're apt to lose power again."

Dani, more frightened of being alone in the dark than of any storm, agreed. A couple of the bedrooms had twin beds in them, and Dani and Silas selected one of them to be what Silas called their "storm headquarters." In short order they had made up the beds and stocked the room with flashlights, oil lamps, and good books.

The Gulf of Mexico roared its disturbance with the thunder of pounding surf. Dani and Silas ventured out just before dark and stood on the dune, looking down at the raging waters. The tide was high, covering the entire beach and pounding at the dune itself. Wind-driven spray stung their cheeks fiercely and when Dani licked her lips she tasted salt.

Silas had to bend to her ear to be heard. "Fantastic, isn't it?"

She desperately wanted to agree. The tremendous power of the pounding gulf exhilarated her, but the wind—the wind was something else altogether.

She tried to tell herself it was wild and wonderful. For years she had made a practice of stepping outside just before a thunderstorm struck in order to feel the wind and taste the ozone, to battle down the icy tendrils of her childhood terror. The air here smelled different than an Ohio thunderstorm. Here the smell of the sea was unmistakable. That might have helped except that the wind was stronger now. Not the sharp gusts of a thunderstorm, but a steady gale-force wind that she had to lean into to maintain her balance.

A steady wind like the one that had terrorized her so long ago.

All of a sudden she was unable to breathe. Terror clawed at her and she turned wildly, seeking refuge.

Silas caught her arm. "Dani? Dani, what's wrong?"

She struggled to break free of his grip, gasping and nearly blind with fear, heedless of everything except her need to reach shelter.

Strong arms gripped her beneath her shoulders and knees and lifted her, ignoring her struggles as if they were child's play.

But almost as soon as Silas's arms closed about

her, the fear began draining away. His arms were a harbor against the wind, holding her close and safe. Nearly limp with relief, all she could do was bury her face against his shoulder and hope she didn't die from humiliation.

He carried her into the relative quiet of the house, murmuring deep in his throat. "It's okay, Dani. It's all right . . . hush . . ."

A long, shuddery breath escaped her and she squeezed her eyes tightly closed to hold back tears of reaction. She'd thought, after all these years, that she'd gotten the better of her fear. Now it seemed she had merely put the genie in a bottle. One good shake and out it came.

Silas settled into a deep leather armchair in the library with Dani on his lap. He held her snugly, stroking her upper arm gently with the palm of his hand.

"Tell me about it," he said.

"About what?" She really didn't want to admit that something that had happened to her when she was five years old could have haunted her for this long.

"About what happened that caused you to get terrified out there. I'm not blind, Dani. I've known plenty of people who've been traumatized. What scared you?"

She couldn't even bring herself to look at him, but kept her head on his shoulder. He had a thin scar under his chin, and she fixed on it, glad to have something to think about besides herself. She wondered what had caused it.

"Dani?"

He wasn't going to let it go, but she had recovered enough finally to toss it out as if it didn't matter. "Just the wind. No big deal."

"Are you kidding yourself? Because you're sure as hell not kidding me."

A spark of anger ignited, driving away the last of

her fear and embarrassment. "All right!" she snapped. "I was caught in a tornado when I was a kid. The wind gives me the heebie-jeebies sometimes!"

"Hell, is that all? Cripes, I'd be shocked if it didn't. A tornado! How badly were you hurt?"

At first when he asked, "Is that all?" she had wanted to scream at him, but then she realized he was expressing understanding, not criticism. He honestly felt her reaction wasn't at all out of the ordinary for someone who had been through a tornado.

She relaxed then, allowing herself to soften against him until she felt like a purring kitten. His gentle stroking of her arm resumed.

"So tell me about your tornado."

"When I was five, I was upstairs in my bedroom playing with my dolls. I remember there was this loud roaring noise, and I thought I heard my mother calling for me from the stairs. I learned later she tried to get upstairs to me but before she got halfway up the tornado ripped the roof off the house. A beam fell and pinned her."

"And you," he prompted when she hesitated. "What happened to you?"

"I . . . the roof was just gone. The roaring sound got really loud, and then there was this popping like gun fire—I guess that was nails being pulled loose—and then the roof just vanished, almost as if it exploded. I was looking up into the funnel. It was the weirdest thing, Silas." The memory still had the power to make her skin turn cold.

"I don't imagine too many people have looked right up into a funnel cloud and lived to tell about it."

She gave a little shrug. "I don't know. I *do* know I'm very lucky to be alive."

"What did it look like?"

"A stack of concentric rings of debris that were all moving. The strangest dirty yellow . . . and there was lightning. Lots of it shooting around the rings. All kinds of stuff . . . I saw boards and tree limbs and a chair. It petrified me. I've never been so scared in my life."

"Were you hurt at all?"

"I was darn lucky. I don't remember what happened after I looked into the funnel. They found me bruised and battered more than a hundred yards away in a mud puddle."

Silas gave a low whistle. "You were carried by a tornado?"

"It happens."

He hugged her close, dropping a kiss on her forehead. "I'm not surprised the wind was bothering you. What does surprise me is that you can stand it at all when the wind blows."

"Lots of people have to do that, Silas. I'm not the only person on earth who has survived a natural catastrophe. Actually, I'm embarrassed. I thought I'd gotten better at handling it than that."

"There wasn't a damn thing wrong with the way you handled it. Don't start putting yourself down. That wind out there is gusting at close to sixty miles an hour. That's not something anybody feels comfortable with."

It was amazing how sweet this annoying man could be when he wanted to. Unconsciously, as if she were the contented kitten he made her feel like, she stretched a little and wiggled closer.

"Uh . . . don't do that." His voice turned rough and soft all at once.

"Don't do what?" She wiggled around so she could see his face better.

"Damn it, Dani," he said between his teeth, "haven't you ever sat on a man's lap before?"

In a flash she understood and was embarrassed beyond description. How could she have been so stupid and thoughtless? She might not sit on men's laps as a rule, but she knew . . . oh yes, she knew.

Her cheeks heated painfully, and she started to wiggle again, this time to escape.

But Silas's hold on her tightened, preventing her flight. "You must be the last woman on earth who can still blush," he muttered. "Do you have any idea what an enticement that is?"

Enticement? Dazed, she stopped wiggling and stared at him.

"No," he said, "I have this strange feeling that you're also the last woman on earth who has no idea of her charms."

Charms? Now she was sure she must be losing her mind. "Silas, don't turn ridiculous on me." But her words lacked force, stifled as they seemed to be somewhere in her breast.

"I've been ridiculous before," he grumbled. "I'm sure my ego can stand the embarrassment. Quit changing the subject."

"What subject?"

"You. You and your campaign to drive me out of my ever-loving mind."

"I'm doing nothing of the sort!"

"Wanna bet?" He lowered his brows and scowled at her. "Prancing around here in those skimpy shorts and tops. Wiggling your butt when you walk. Legs like . . . Damn it, woman, you have the most gorgeous legs I've ever seen."

Instinctively Dani looked down at her legs, wondering what was gorgeous about them. They were actually very ordinary legs, perhaps somewhat muscular because she was in the habit of riding her bike to and from school every day. They certainly weren't quite as firm now as they had been at eighteen.

"Cut it out," Silas growled. "I know what's running through that severe little mind of yours. Quit putting yourself down. Your legs are driving me nuts! I want to run my palm up them just like this . . ."

The feeling of his rough palm running up the

smooth skin of her outer leg all the way to the hem of her very short shorts deprived her of breath. Had anything ever felt so . . . so *exquisite*? Her heart was suddenly hammering wildly, and her very center seemed to be melting into a soft warm puddle like chocolate in the sun.

"I shouldn't be doing this," he muttered. "Damn, I need my head examined . . ." But his hand stroked her thigh again, causing her to catch her breath and hold it.

"You like that, don't you?" he said, his voice gentling. "You feel like satin, Dani . . . so smooth . . ." He bent his head and captured her mouth with his, plunging her into a heated pool of sensation. His hand on her thigh never stopped moving. It stroked her and kneaded gently while his mouth claimed hers, his tongue sweeping over nerve endings on her lips and tongue that she had never noticed before.

"So sweet," he whispered, dropping a soft patter of kisses on her cheeks, nose, eyes, chin. "So sweet . . ."

The fire in her cheeks was now burning in her very center, a heavy kind of heat that made her feel so weak and soft. Somewhere in the back of her mind she heard a warning, but ignored it. Not once in her life, not even for one fleeting little moment, had she ever felt what Silas was making her feel with the gentle brush of his hand on her thigh, and the tender rain of kisses on her face.

She felt safer than she ever had, though she knew full well she was poised on the brink of a dangerous precipice. But the danger seemed meaningless beside the incredible possibilities that seemed to be opening for her in Silas's arms. At her age she had enough experience to realize that she might never feel this way again in a man's arms.

"Let me," he whispered. "Ah, sweetie, let me . . ."

His hoarse voice sent shivers of arousal rippling through her, banishing any last, lingering doubt she might have felt.

Silas felt the surrender pass through her. It was unmistakable in the way her face turned into his shoulder while her body relaxed and remained open to his touches. A fierce sense of victory gripped him, silencing for the moment the squawking of his insistent conscience.

Her response to him was sweet and eager . . . too eager. Some part of him realized that she was succumbing too easily and too rapidly for the prim prude she was, which meant she didn't have a whole lot of experience with the power of true arousal and how quickly it could override sense and inhibition. His conscience stabbed him again but he ignored it. The lady was willing and he was hungry for her. As hungry as he'd ever been in his entire misspent life.

He loved the way her breath caught and held when his hand slipped upward toward her breast. God, she was responsive, giving herself utterly to the moment and his touches as if nothing else mattered. Letting him see and share her response without coyness or the power games that sickened him so. She was opening herself to his possession as naturally as a rose blooming.

"Let me," he whispered again, barely getting the words out of a throat that was locking up with his own desire. He could have sworn that he hadn't been this eager since his high school days. Each time Dani stirred on his lap another shaft of passion speared through him.

One layer of tricot and one layer of cotton stood between his hand and her breast, but they were little barrier to sensitivities heightened by growing sexual hunger. She gasped when his hand closed over her, and arched as if needing to press herself even more tightly to him. Against the palm of his hand, despite her clothing, he could feel the hardening bud of her nipple. The sensation thrilled him.

She was firm, full, an exciting handful of tender flesh. Needing more, he slipped his hand up beneath her T-shirt, and then beneath her bra. He felt her stiffen, heard her sharply indrawn breath, heard the moan that escaped her as her hand found his shoulder and clung for dear life.

She was his! He knew it with the certainty of a predator moving in for the kill.

As soon as he had the thought, his conscience stabbed him with a spear he couldn't ignore. He wasn't a predator and he damn well better stop acting like one. Damn it, how could he have even let himself think such a thing?

Because he was a man, and because Dani was as enticing a bit of femininity as he'd ever seen. Even the way she insisted on pulling her shiny brown hair onto the back of her head was sexy. His fingers were always itching to pull out that barrette and let her hair down.

Now here he was with her lying across his lap, his hand under her blouse and her hair still in a disheveled knot on the back of her head. Something was wrong here, very seriously out of step.

He closed his eyes, willing his mind back into the driver's seat, battering his passion back with determination. Never, he found himself thinking, had it been so difficult to regain his self-control. He didn't like it. This woman was danger in a pair of white tennis shoes and he needed to remember that.

But he would humiliate her if he pulled away too suddenly, and he didn't want to do that. He might be a cad but he wasn't heartless.

Gently, gently, he squeezed her breast and felt a fresh spear of need slice through him. But no, he wasn't going to give in to that even if he had to chew furniture to maintain his control. "So sweet," he told her yet again, and meant it. Carefully he withdrew his hand from beneath her bra, feeling as if her imprint were burned forever on his palm.

Her eyelids fluttered open. She must have realized that his mood had changed because she abruptly pressed her face into his shoulder, trying to hide.

Then, a moment later, she slid from his lap and started hurrying toward the door.

He didn't want it to end like this. Right then he would have given anything to take back the last five minutes, to be able to prevent what she was probably feeling right now.

"Dani, wait!"

"Go climb a tree, Northrop!" She kept walking.

"Dani, please . . ."

She whirled, pointing a finger at him. "It's a real good routine, Silas. Play the knight in shining armor, rescue the damsel in distress, and then seduce her. Too bad I fell for it!"

"Now wait one minute——"

"I don't hold you responsible," she said with a wag of her finger. "After all, you're just a man. No, it was my fault for being stupid enough to think you found me attractive. I can't believe I was that easy a mark!"

"Mark?" He erupted from the chair. "You weren't a mark, Dani. For heaven's sake, calm down! You *are* attractive, and I got so damn turned on that I got out of line! I apologize for that, but I'm not going to apologize for recovering my senses before we did something we'd both probably wind up regretting."

She stood staring at him for a moment, appearing to waver, but then she stiffened. "Stuff a sock in it, Silas. I'm not buying it."

"Not buying what? That you turn me on enough to forget my good sense?"

"You got it."

"Will you listen to yourself, woman?" He nearly thundered the words. "You think you're so unattractive that I couldn't possibly have been overwhelmed by passion, and yet I'm supposed to want you enough to have schemed and pretended to be a knight in shining armor in order to get you into my bed. Does that make any sense at all? Damn it, if you were unattractive, I wouldn't want you in my bed in the first place! I certainly wouldn't scheme to get you there!"

She sniffed and averted her face, but he could tell she was hearing what he said despite disbelieving it.

"Think about it, Dani. Either I want you or I don't, but I can't do both at the same time. Who the hell gave you such a low opinion of yourself, anyway?"

"Nobody."

"Nobody? I don't believe it. Somebody made you feel as if you're sexually unappealing." He crossed the room and stood in front of her, grabbing her hand and pressing it to the bulge in the front of his pants. "Feel that, Dani? That's real, and you made it happen."

She looked up at him with wide startled eyes, then she turned and fled.

He stared after her and took one step to follow before he decided that he really wasn't worried about it. She wasn't going anywhere. Once she remembered the storm outside, she'd be back.

Until then he could just stand here and kick himself in the butt for being such an ass. Women were more trouble than they were worth, and Dani was more trouble than most. Hell, it'd be better for both of them if she continued to think he was an unprincipled jerk. Maybe this would convince her to stay out of his hair.

If only it would be so easy to get her out from under his skin.

10

Dani didn't make it very far at all. The atrium was dark, and the sound of the wind from outside was magnified in the cavernous space. Almost as soon as she slammed the library door behind herself, she regretted her impulsiveness.

Silas may have behaved like a cad, but at least he'd been a reasonably honorable one, calling things off before they went too far. And she *would* have let them go too far. It made her feel miserable to admit it, but she tried never to deceive herself. She had been putty in the man's hands, to use a shopworn cliche.

Darn it! She wanted to stomp her foot and have a good old-fashioned temper tantrum, but she knew it would only make her feel foolish later, so she reined it in. She didn't want to face him again. Couldn't stand the thought, actually. He had to realize how easily she had succumbed to his touches, and must think she was a . . . a . . . *roundheels*! Ridiculously old-fashioned term, of course, but the modern ones wouldn't pass her lips. Yes, a roundheels, or a trollop. Cheap. He certainly must think her cheap.

Oh, she wanted to die! Right there and then she wanted to be struck from a bolt of blue and crumble instantly into a lifeless heap.

Just then, as if answering her wish, something hit the skylight with a bang loud enough to leave her ears ringing. She looked up, hoping the skylight still held, wondering if she were to be deaf for the remainder of her days. She also quickly rescinded her wish for instant death.

"Where did it come from?" Silas asked, suddenly there beside her.

"Something hit the skylight."

He looked up, but in the dimness it was almost impossible to see anything. "It looks all right."

Dani stared upward too, feeling an almost fatalistic expectation that the glass would cave inward and fall right on her hapless head. Which, now that she thought about it, she really didn't want to have happen at all.

The atrium was getting darker, it seemed to Dani, and the air was growing chillier as if, without the sunlight to battle it, the air conditioning was running amok. "Maybe we ought to get set up for the night."

Silas glanced down at her, his shadowed face unreadable. "Good idea. It's getting late anyway."

Dani glanced at her watch, astonished to realize it was almost seven-thirty. The sun must be nearly setting behind the storm clouds. Darkness wouldn't be far behind.

"What we need now," Silas said, "is another one of Morris's relatives to show up."

"We'd have to let them in. We couldn't ask them to leave in this storm."

"Maybe you couldn't, but I sure could. I'd probably even enjoy doing it. I haven't much liked what I've seen of that crew so far."

"Well, Dawn Moonglow was okay."

"I guess, if you like intelligent twits."

Intelligent twits? She gazed after him, not sure whether to be amused. She didn't want to be amused by him. She wanted to be angry, but her anger seemed to have fled with that hammer blow to the skylight over her head. Now she was just feeling limp and somehow sad.

The atrium lights snapped on suddenly as the timer kicked in. Everything looked normal now. Everything was the same. Why then was a certain foreboding beginning to crawl along the back of her neck?

They made a simple dinner in the kitchen then headed up to the room they had chosen for the siege. The wind was howling now, sounding mournful as it whistled around the house.

"Actually," Dani said when they were comfortably settled with books to read, "what we need right now is Morris."

"He'd sure take our minds off the storm." Silas laughed. "Course, he'd probably blow away in this gale."

All night in this room with Silas, Dani thought as he returned his attention to his book. Help! She'd rather have one of the crazy relatives turn up. Ernie Hazlett for example. Or Pepita. Pepita had been . . . well . . . something else altogether. Between her and Roxy Resnick, the psychic—oh yes, and Gert Plum, the acrobat with the inner ear problem—she was beginning to develop an idea that Morris's taste in wives was unconventional.

And that seemed so odd to her. Apart from a bizarre sense of humor, Dani had always found Morris to be a generous, warm-hearted, very intelligent man. Could he possibly have collected wives as strays like cats and dogs?

Well, it would explain six marriages and divorces, and Morris's vow never to marry again. But whatever had started him down such a path? Useless to speculate, she decided. Morris wasn't around to ask, and no one else would know.

Rain drummed a staccato rhythm on the roof and windows, filling the house with a loud rush of sound

that made it seem so cozy in their little fortress. Her
eyelids grew heavy and the words on the page before
her became fuzzier and fuzzier . . .

Silas awoke in the dark. Every light in the room
was out, including the green glow from the digital
clock radio. Power outage, he thought groggily. He
was tempted to roll over and go right back to sleep,
but then he remembered Dani. He'd better light an
oil lamp so she didn't wake in the dark and become
frightened.

Besides, as he grew more and more alert, he began
to find the darkness oppressive. Some things never
left you, no matter how deeply you buried them, and
Beirut was one of those things for him. The experience had latched onto him at a level far below
conscious thought, and had taken root in a place
beyond the reach of reason. He was reacting like one
of Pavlov's conditioned dogs, and that bothered the
hell out of him.

It bothered him enough that he closed his eyes and
forced himself to lie still in the darkness, to ignore
the crushing sense of claustrophobia that was growing stronger by the minute. With the air conditioning off, the air in the room was heavy and stale, too
warm. Suffocating. It felt like a weight bearing down
on his chest, like the concrete beam that had lain
across him that endless night in Beirut. No, he told
himself, that was his imagination. What he needed
to do was get up and open the window, let the air stir
and cool off the room. He and Dani would both
sleep better that way.

But dread seemed to have taken control. No
matter how hard he tried to open them, his eyes
remained glued shut. Ridiculous. Intellectually he
knew that it was all many years in the past, but that
scarred part of him had never really climbed out
from beneath the concrete and the bodies of his
comrades.

Angry at himself for being trapped in unfounded

terror, he squeezed his hands into fists and directed every ounce of his will to opening his eyes.

Dani was standing beside his bed looking down at him. Bathed in moonlight, she seemed to glow softly as she bent toward him. There was such a look of appeal on her face, as if she desperately needed him to understand something. Instinctively he lifted a hand toward her.

A murmur came from the far side of the room and a creak of bed springs. Silas's breath locked in his throat as he instantly recognized that there was no moonlight in the room. No light at all. And Dani was still in bed.

As if a switch had been thrown, the apparition beside his bed winked out and was gone, leaving only a chilly breath of air to signify its passing.

Galvanized, Silas threw back the sheet and leapt to his feet. Feeling around the night table, he found the matches and struck one. Moments later he had an oil lamp lighted. It drove the dark back a little bit, but the corners of the room were still locked in the night, holding their secrets safe.

There had to be a projector somewhere, Silas thought angrily. That image had been projected somehow. Maybe on vapor from dry ice, which would explain the chilliness he had felt.

But even as his mind concocted logical explanations, he knew they were wrong. How would anyone have gotten the dry ice into the room? Why couldn't he still see the vapor rising from it? Why hadn't he seen the beam of a projector reflecting off the dust motes in the air? Even in a still room, the air wasn't clear enough to conceal a beam of light in perfect darkness.

So it hadn't been a projection. Then what was it?

He no longer wanted to open the window to let in the cool night air. The temperature in here seemed to have dropped ten degrees in an instant . . . or perhaps it was just the earliness of the hour. Four a.m. The time when the body was at its lowest ebb.

He refused to admit the apparition might have had anything to do with it.

He lit several more oil lamps, driving the shadows back into the deepest corners, filling the room with a golden glow. Outside, the storm seemed to have calmed somewhat, for the deafening hammer of rain against the metal shutters had subsided to a slow, irregular drumbeat. Like a heartbeat gradually running down.

Now why had he thought of that simile?

Hell! Swearing silently at himself, he shoved his feet into his shoes and checked the Browning he had stuffed under his pillow when Dani wasn't looking. It troubled him to realize that after years of using firearms only on the target range he was now stashing one with an eye to self-defense. Dani would probably throw a hissy fit if she knew it was there.

Settling into an armchair near the bed, he tried to recall every single detail of what he had seen standing beside his bed.

It had looked very much like Dani, but Dani was sleeping soundly in her bed with covers tucked up under her chin. Every so often she whimpered softly, as if her dream disturbed her.

He would have liked to step outside and judge the storm, but he didn't want to leave Dani alone, especially after that apparition.

The word sounded a sour note in his mind. He didn't believe in apparitions, and he didn't like the way chilly fingers seemed to march up and down his spine each time he thought of what he had seen.

Telepathy? he asked himself. Perhaps he had picked up on something out of Dani's dream and had imagined her standing beside his bed. That idea, oddly enough, was far more palatable to him than the more obvious one: that he had seen a ghost.

When people died they were supposed to stay dead. Dead and buried. All his buddies damn well had! None of them had shown up beside his bed looking as if they needed something. Nor should they. Either there was oblivion after death, or there was heaven, but in neither case should ghosts be wandering around on earth disturbing the living.

Which left him with the unhappy conclusion that he had just seen something that didn't exist, and that people beyond the grave could indeed be worrying about things on earth. Because that woman was worried about something. Reaching for something. Begging someone to hear her.

What Silas would have liked to do was forget the whole thing, but the face he had seen had been too eloquent of yearning and loss. Whatever she needed, maybe he ought to see if he couldn't help in some way.

"Oh!" All of a sudden Dani sat up, looking like a startled deer. "Oh!"

"Bad dream?" Silas asked, wondering if she was even awake.

Slowly she turned to look at him. "Silas?"

"Right here. Are you awake?"

She shuddered visibly and pulled the covers around her shoulders before she nodded. "I'm awake."

Her voice still had the huskiness of sleep, the sexiest damn sound he had ever heard. Sharing a room with this woman may have been a serious tactical error. "Bad dream?" he asked again, refusing to let his mind explore the sensual possibilities that suddenly occurred to it.

"I—I don't know," she said hesitantly. "I was dreaming about Morris."

"That, m'dear, is by definition a bad dream."

She gave a little laugh, and brushed her long, dark hair back from her face. That was sexy, too, Silas thought, the way she forked her fingers into her hair and combed it back. As a writer he ought to note the gesture and his reaction to it. Instead he just reacted. Crossing his legs, he thanked God he was wearing baggy khaki shorts.

"It was strange," Dani said. "I had the strongest

feeling that Morris was desperately trying to tell me something, only I couldn't hear him."

"It boggles the mind to imagine Morris desperate about anything."

Another laugh escaped her. "Yes, doesn't it? He was always so debonair, so . . . so . . . amused by everything, as if life were a circus held for his benefit."

"For Morris it was. Is there a word for an 'amused cynic'?"

"Probably, but I'm darned if I can think of it. Satirical is as close as I can get."

"Ah, but he kept it to himself most of the time. You just knew he was amused by the way his eyebrow would lift, or a certain tone he got in his voice. I always figured that attitude was what made him such a damn good writer, the way he saw right through things. The way he actually enjoyed human foibles."

"Well, he wasn't enjoying anything in my dream. Actually, it was a nightmare, one of those things where you're trying madly to do something but can't? Only Morris was the one who was trying to be heard and couldn't get through." She shivered again and pulled the blanket closer. "You know what scares me, Silas? That it wasn't just a dream. That Morris really *is* caught in some kind of nightmare and can't make himself be heard."

"Yeah." He studied her in the golden lamplight, wishing she didn't look so adorable with her sleep-puffy eyes and tousled hair. Six months with this woman were going to test his willpower to the utmost limits. "Well, that does it."

"What does it?" She cocked her head inquisitively.

"We've got relatives determined to search for something in this house and you're seeing and dreaming about Morris and getting the feeling that he's desperately trying to communicate something. . . ."

She nodded vigorously. "Don't you dare say I'm going insane!"

"I wasn't about to. I just figured it was time to try to get to the bottom of this."

"Bottom of what?"

"I figure if the relatives really are looking for something, and Morris is trying to tell us something, then maybe we ought to get on the stick and find whatever it is."

"I thought we already agreed it would be hard to find something when we don't even know what it is. Or if there *is* something. Besides, you don't believe in ghosts!"

"I don't. At this point, though, I'm willing to keep an open mind. Short of having you committed, I kind of have to believe you're experiencing *something* real."

"Well thank you very much," she said acidly, with an annoyed toss of her head. "I'm not in the habit of hallucinating, you know."

"Actually, I *don't* know. We only just met. But I'm willing to act under the assumption that you wouldn't be allowed to teach school if you hallucinate all the time."

Dani glared at him, uncertain whether to be offended by his blunt assessment, or relieved that he didn't think she was insane.

Silas ignored her reaction. "Given that you're experiencing something, there are a couple of different interpretations we can put on it. We could say Morris's ghost is trying to tell us something."

"We could." She agreed emphatically to make a point, but inwardly quailed at what it sounded like. If word of this ever got back to Ohio, the school board would hang her out to dry.

"Or we could think that you're picking up on something telepathically or psychically, either from the greedy relatives, or from concerns that Morris had just before he died. There's a hare-brained theory that the walls of a house can store up emotional imprints that sensitive people can pick up on later."

"Where did you come across that?"

He shrugged. "I glanced through your ghost book."

The one she had stopped reading because she had feared it was fueling her imagination. Feeling disgruntled that Silas may have gleaned some useful tidbits from a book she had cast aside, she desperately wished she could argue with him. Unfortunately, it sounded like a good enough theory to her.

"Either way," Silas continued, oblivious to her reaction, "it's probably worth paying attention to. Add it to Dawn Moonglow's insistence that there's some kind of treasure here, and the rather insistent appearances of Ernie Hazlett, Lester Carmichael, and Pepita Mayo, and I'm a convert. We need to search this place from stem to stern."

"That's a daunting task."

"Admittedly. I figure we can break it down into sections and work at it a couple of hours a day until we've been over every inch of this place."

"It'll take forever!"

"Think of it as a hobby." He sighed and passed a hand over his eyes, trying not to think of the ghost that looked like Dani. That apparition had made a believer of him. Something was going on in this place and he was damn well going to get to the bottom of it, whatever it took. He was tired of having his peace invaded by loco relatives and now restless ghosts.

He shook his head, clearing away the memory of the ghost, and looked at Dani. "To tell you the truth, Teach, if it was just the relatives looking for something, I wouldn't really worry about it. I'm not so greedy that I'd begrudge them some bauble from this place."

"Me either."

"But this Morris business—" And the woman ghost business. "Well, that makes it different somehow. Laugh if you want, but it concerns me that there may be something going on here that was truly important to Morris. He can't do anything about it now, so I kind of feel obligated."

His words had a strange effect on Dani. She suddenly looked all soft and cuddly, and not at all prickly as she had been. If he were given eternal life, it wouldn't be time enough to figure out the female mind.

"Morris had a good friend in you, Silas," she said gently. Then, as if everything had been settled, she curled up against her pillow and fell back to sleep.

Dani was of the opinion that whatever the "treasure" might be, it wasn't an object with intrinsic value.

"Why?" Silas asked over breakfast.

"Look at this place. Morris inventoried every single item here and put it all in his will. I seriously doubt he'd have hidden a Ming vase or a stash of jewelry somewhere."

The worst of the storm was over, and power had been restored before dawn. The wind still gusted, though not as strongly. The strength of the storm was reflected only in the number of palm fronds and tree limbs that littered the yard . . . and in the flowering plants, now virtually stripped of their blooms.

"Okay," Silas agreed. "Makes sense to me . . . except for one little thing—Morris's weird sense of humor."

A smile tugged at Dani's lips. For some reason she was feeling absolutely wonderful this morning. "I guess it's possible he hid a diamond necklace in a secret drawer somewhere and then forgot all about it."

Silas thought about it a minute, then shook his head. "Nah. He was nuts, but not that nuts. In fact, he was damn careful about his money. Generous but never careless."

"So scratch the diamond necklace idea." Which was exactly what she had been trying to say from the outset. Instead of being irritated by that, however, she let it go. No point in destroying a perfectly good mood.

"So what would we be looking for?"

Dani cocked her head thoughtfully. "Something that Morris wouldn't immediately think of including in his inventory of the house contents."

"Something *he* could overlook."

No light bulbs suddenly switched on in Dani's mind. She didn't know Morris well enough to have an idea about what he would consider important or unimportant, or what he might overlook.

"Papers," Silas said after a moment. "Papers are easy to overlook when you're thinking of valuable things, with the exception of stock certificates and bonds."

"A diary, you mean? But would that be valuable to anyone at all?"

Silas shrugged. "Probably. Morris was a big-name novelist. Somebody would probably be able to make money out of a diary, particularly if it were revealing."

"But would he have hidden it?"

Silas made a frustrated sound and jumped up from the table. "This is insane! We don't know a damn thing about what's going on, so we have to make all kinds of assumptions. Would he have hidden it? Hell, I don't know. Maybe this thing, whatever it is, is lying out in plain sight somewhere and we just don't know it because we don't know what we're looking for."

"But Morris's relatives would have taken it when they left here, if it weren't hidden."

He shook his head. "No. Bad assumption. It's just as possible they didn't even think about it in the rush of moving out of here. Papers. I'm going to go with the assumption we're looking for papers. Maybe deeds or titles to some kind of property that wasn't mentioned in the will."

"Now that's stretching it."

He shrugged. "Bank books? If I remember from the will, he seemed to have a whole lot of bank accounts scattered around the globe. He could have forgotten some of them."

"Or an insurance policy," Dani suggested, her imagination getting stirred up.

"Now that's a good one," Silas agreed. "I could see Morris forgetting about something like that. Problem is, most policies already have a named beneficiary, or pass by law. A policy would be useless to anyone else."

She felt deflated. "True."

"Besides, Morris carried six life insurance policies, each one payable to a different one of his exes."

"I didn't know that."

"The guy was generous. I don't know how many people would have done that. Believe me, Dani, his exes are well cared for. Every single one of them."

"And they were all living with him." She shook her head. "It doesn't make sense, Silas."

"It does if you think of him as a soft-hearted sucker—at least when it comes to a handful of women."

"It still boggles my mind. I just can't begin to imagine sharing your house with six ex-wives."

"Mostly just five, I understand. Roxy Resnick lives in Fort Myers. She just came to visit."

"Most divorced couples I know can hardly stand to speak to each other."

Silas leaned back against the counter and crossed his legs at the ankle. "It would be my guess that his marriages weren't the typical garden variety either. Divorce doesn't seem to have generated the usual amount of vitriol."

"Well, this isn't helping us get to the bottom of the mess. Maybe we should just flat-out ask Lester or Ernie what it is they're after."

Silas gave her a pitying look. "And be deliberately misdirected?"

Dani felt her cheeks flame. It seemed to her that no matter how determined she was to maintain her good mood, Silas was equally determined to irritate her. "I was being facetious," she said sharply. "You *have* heard the word?"

His brows drew together. "What's eating *you* this morning?"

"Not a damned thing except you! You know, Silas, it's generally considered rude to make other people feel like fools."

"It's always been my belief that no one else can make a fool of you. You have to do that yourself."

That did it! Now he was saying she was making a fool of herself. The man was beyond bearing. "You are insufferable!"

"Oh, spare me the theatrics," he said drily. "You're just mad because I kissed you last night."

Rendered speechless by his absolute gall, she could only gape helplessly at him, doing what some corner of her mind decided was a passable imitation of a gasping fish.

"Look," he said, "I'm sorry I kissed you. I must have been temporarily insane. There's no other explanation for it. And I can damn well promise you it won't happen again. But I can't do any more than apologize, Dani, and I've already done that. So why don't we just call a truce and get back to things that really matter."

She still couldn't speak. He must have been insane to kiss her. He would never do it again. Why did it feel as if her heart had just been crushed? She wasn't actually growing fond of this cretin, was she? "Why would you have to be insane to kiss me?"

An absolute flood of heat washed over her face and she wished it was possible to die from humiliation. She hadn't asked that had she? Oh, please, let her have only thought the question, not actually said it out loud.

But she had spoken the words. She could see it in the way Silas's face suddenly relaxed, and in the faint smile that tickled the corners of his mouth, as if he were exercising great restraint.

"I just meant," he said after a couple of moments' reflection, "that it wasn't a wise move. We have to share this house for months, after all, and it would be a whole lot easier if we didn't, uh, become sexually involved."

"Oh." It sounded like a coverup to her. He was weaseling out of the question, but before she could embarrass herself by pressing him with any more questions, she compressed her lips.

His smile broadened a shade, as if he knew what she was thinking. "I don't mean that you're not attractive, Dani. Because you are. Very. I mean . . ." He stumbled to a halt, reddening a little as he realized that he was treading on some dangerous ground now. The best way to ignore sexual attraction was to pretend it didn't exist. The fact that this woman turned him on like a switch was not something he wanted her to know.

Hell, if he could have stopped responding to her, he'd have done it in an instant. He didn't want to get tangled up with some prissy schoolmarm from Ohio. God, what a recipe for disaster! He wasn't the type to get involved for long. His interests in women waxed and waned like the phases of the moon and had ever since the corps had determined he was unfit for duty. Being an honorable man, he fooled around only with women who played by the same rules. Not innocent little schoolteachers from Ohio who probably thought that love and sex were indistinguishable.

"It's okay, Silas," she said with a wave of her hand and a tiny laugh that sounded more hurt than amused. "I realize I'm no Sharon Stone or Kathleen Turner. You don't have to pretend you find me attractive."

He should have been relieved that she was suddenly so willing to dismiss the matter, but instead he wanted to scoop her up into his arms and make the hurt go away. He wanted to sweep her away with him on wings of passion so that she would never again wonder if she was attractive.

Oh, cripes, the White Knight reaction. It was time to clear out, before he started concocting schemes to rescue Rapunzel here from her tower. Rescuing damsels in distress always wound up getting him into more trouble than it was worth.

She looked at him as if hoping for him to contradict her, but his caution won out over the impulse to rescue. He maintained a steadfast silence.

"Okay," she said after a brief hesitation. "Now that that's out of the way, let's get back to this treasure business. I think all we can do is proceed on the assumption that we'll know what we're looking for when we find it."

And that was how they proceeded, mainly because neither of them wanted to stay in the same room with the other for one minute longer than necessary. Sectioning the house for the search was a piece of cake.

Silas was deep in his novel, writing a nervewracking scene that brought back a few too many memories. Distantly he was aware that Dani was searching her section of the house. From time to time he heard furniture being dragged across tile floors, and drawers and doors being slammed. He ought to put on some music, nice and loud.

More than a week had passed since they had embarked on this fruitless endeavor. Each day they individually spent a couple of hours searching their assigned sections. Dani preferred to write in the morning and search in the afternoon. Silas was just the opposite. He'd done his banging and clanging and door slamming this morning while she'd been writing. He envied her typing speed; she had really been going at it.

They hadn't been bothered by any of the relatives, though, and that was beginning to trouble Silas. He doubted that they would have given up this easily, so why weren't they poking around? Had someone managed to find the treasure during the brief time that he and Dani had been locked in the hurricane room?

Out of the corner of his eye, he saw movement, and glanced up long enough to see Dani hovering in the doorway. Damn, he hated it when she did that.

"Just a second," he told her. "Just let me finish this paragraph." He both wanted and didn't want to be dragged out of his story. The vision was so strong right now that it was painful. He didn't want to lose it, but he also wanted very much to escape it.

When he looked up, Dani was gone. Jeez, it annoyed him when she did that. Well, if she still wanted him, she knew where to find him. Reaching over, he flicked on the stereo and filled the house with the thunder of the *1812 Overture*.

It kept the silence at bay.

Then, the power went out. In the midst of a bright, clear, calm afternoon, the power cut out. Silas watched the image on his monitor shrink to nothing as static crackled. He swore savagely, realizing that he hadn't saved a single word that he had written that day. Not one.

Furious, he leapt up from his chair and stormed out onto the gallery, planning to go down to check the breakers. Maybe his stereo had sucked up too much power . . .

Dani emerged on the other side of the atrium, brushing her hair back from her face, looking hot and flushed from her search. "What happened?"

A voice from below answered her. "I did."

The two of them looked down over the railing to see Irving Cheatham standing in the atrium.

"What do you mean?" Silas demanded.

"I threw the breaker." Cheatham looked utterly

unrepentant. "I'd been ringing the bell for ten minutes and you couldn't even hear it. I wanted to get your attention. I did."

Silas looked across the atrium at Dani. "I may kill him."

"Not now, I'd be a witness."

Irving clucked disapprovingly. "You shouldn't say things like that even in jest! If something were to happen to me, those words could come back to haunt you."

Silas grinned evilly down at him. "Who said I was jesting?"

Irving shifted uncomfortably, uncertain how to take that. A tall, thin man, he was bald, bespectacled, and severe-looking. He did not at all look like someone who understood fun.

"It's okay, Irving," Dani said. "I'll protect you."

"Do you listen to that racket at this volume all the time?" Cheatham demanded.

"It helps me work," Silas replied. Dani rolled her eyes but he ignored it.

The lawyer stabbed a finger at Silas. "If that racket does any structural damage to this house, I'm going to bill you for it."

Silas, far from being outraged, broke into laughter. The sound seemed to mollify Cheatham, who dropped his finger and relaxed.

"What can we do for you?" Silas asked him.

"I came out to pay Edna. Do you know where she's at?"

"Edna? We haven't seen her," Silas replied.

"Well, for heaven's sake," Cheatham exclaimed. "Edna has been housekeeper here for over twenty years! I can't imagine that she'd just take off without giving notice."

"Maybe she's just taking an unannounced vacation," Silas said. "Point is, neither of us have seen hide nor hair of her since we got here. Any housework that's been done, we've done."

"Hmm." Cheatham did not look pleased. "Well, I suppose I'll need to hire someone else then."

"No, really," Silas said hastily. "Don't bother. We don't want a housekeeper, do we, Dani?"

She glanced at him, wondering why he was objecting. Surely he didn't think the two of them were going to dust all the rooms of this monstrous house? And wouldn't it be nice to have someone else prepare meals and clean up after them? But his cat-green eyes were sending some kind of urgent message, so she looked down at Cheatham and agreed. "I don't see why we need anyone. The two of us can handle our own messes, Irving. Besides, what if Edna's been sick, or was called away on some kind of emergency? She'd want her job when she comes back."

"Then she should have called me about it," was Cheatham's testy reply. "Really! Just walking off and leaving a job this way—that's grounds enough to fire anyone."

"Better to wait until you can hear Edna's side of it," Silas argued.

"Perhaps." The lawyer looked up at the two of them. "I'm trusting the two of you to let me know if you aren't able to keep up with things around here. We can't have the property deteriorating."

"No, of course not," Silas agreed. "Believe me, we'll holler if the dirt starts to build up. But for now . . . well, we just don't make much of a mess, Irving."

The lawyer nodded his agreement. "Well, there was one other thing I wanted to talk over with you two, but I'm getting a crick in my neck looking up at you this way."

"I'm sorry!" Dani was mortified. Somehow it had seemed so natural to lean over the railing and talk down to Irving Cheatham that she hadn't realized how rude they were being. "Let me come down there and make us some coffee." And as usual, she found herself thinking as she trotted down the stairs, the "little woman" gets the burden of entertaining.

But Irving wouldn't allow her to go to any trouble for him. He only needed a few minutes of their time, he said, and then he'd be on his way so he didn't disturb their work.

It was on the tip of Dani's tongue to tell him that she hadn't been working, but had been searching the house for some hidden, unknown treasure. Something caused her to bite the words back, however, though she couldn't have said why she was reluctant to trust Irving Cheatham.

"The main thing I want to know," he said when they were comfortably settled in the library, "is whether you've had any further importunities from Morris's relatives about getting into the house."

"No . . ." Silas shook his head. "Unless we were invaded by Pepita Mayo *after* we talked to you. I can't remember now whether I told you about her."

"You did. The family Bible business."

"That's it. Well, she was the last of the crew that we've seen."

"Hmm." Cheatham nodded thoughtfully. "Well, I've had four of the six in my office with varying tales of woe about some irreplaceable item they left here, or something Morris supposedly promised would be theirs. I'm beginning to wonder if they really think I'm that stupid. Anyway, Roxy Resnick and Ina Jasper are the only ones who haven't shown up yet. I don't know whether that's just coincidental or it's because they aren't interested. Either way, I'm convinced that the rest of them are convinced that Morris hid something of value here. I've put my ear to the ground, but so far I haven't a clue what the item could be—if it even exists. We mustn't forget that this could all be delusional, based on some misunderstanding."

"That's a nice thought," Silas agreed, "but not one I'm prepared to bank on. Especially if they start showing up around here again." He didn't mention the ghost he had seen—the thought stuttered to a halt as he remembered seeing Dani in his doorway just a short time ago. But the Dani in his doorway hadn't been wearing the red shorts, white blouse, and headband that this Dani was wearing right now. Had he really seen Dani, or had he seen . . . that apparition? That vision he had refused to think about since the night when he had seen it because it was just too damned uncomfortable. His mind had neatly stashed the memory in an out-of-the-way location so that he had nearly forgotten it. Until now.

He looked at Dani but didn't say anything about the woman he had seen standing in his doorway. The apparition was just another reason to get to the bottom of this mess.

Nor did he mention Dani's vision of Morris. Cheatham would be likely to have them both Baker Acted—involuntarily committed—to the nearest mental hospital.

"Well," said Cheatham presently, "just be on the lookout. I wouldn't put it past some of this crew to try something underhanded. If they're interested, it's because they think there's money involved, and if there's money involved there's little enough they won't try."

"Why in the hell did Morris marry these women?" Silas wondered.

Cheatham's answer took Dani utterly by surprise. "Because they loved him."

11

---◆◇◆---

"Wasn't that fascinating, what Irving said about Morris?" Dani asked Silas right after the lawyer left.

"What difference does it make," Silas groused. "He threw the damn breaker and I lost everything I wrote today! He's lucky I didn't string him up on one of those palms out front."

"You mean you wrote all that time and didn't save your work?" Dani couldn't imagine it.

"Don't rub it in! But there wasn't even a cloud in the sky! It never occurred to me that the power would go off."

"Don't you have auto backup?"

"Auto what?"

"Automatic backup. You know, where the software saves your work every so many minutes to a backup file."

He shook his head. "I don't think so."

"What software are you using?"

He told her, tossing the words over his shoulder as he headed toward the laundry room to turn the power back on again.

"That performs an automatic backup," she called after him. "I'll go see if it was set to do one."

"Don't bother. I never set it to do anything like that."

He disappeared into the laundry room, and she stared after him, frustrated. He'd been careless, which was bad enough, but now he wanted to be pigheaded besides, and not let her see if the software had saved his work. "You just don't want to be rescued by a woman!"

"Horse manure," he called back.

All of sudden, the *1812 Overture* was blasting at deafening volume from the speakers all around her. She clapped her hands to her ears and wondered if a jury would acquit her on grounds of temporary insanity if she just killed the man right now. Probably. All her lawyer would have to do would be to play this damn music at this volume for three or four hours and the *jury* would be ready to kill Silas.

Turning, she ran for the stairs, taking them two at a time in her hurry to get out of the firing line. She slammed her office door behind her, wondering where she could get a bazooka to blow out those speakers for good.

A minute later, the racket died abruptly. Shortly thereafter, Silas hammered on her door. "Dani? Dani, I'm sorry about that racket. I clean forgot the stereo was still on."

"What difference would it make?" she demanded, glaring at the closed door. "You play that racket all the damn time anyway! I'm going to go nuts if I have to keep listening to it!"

There was a silence that lasted so long that she was sure he had gone away. Just as she was turning to face her computer, the door opened slowly.

"Dani?" Silas poked his head in. "Is it really bothering you?"

"Bothering me? Bothering me? Why in the world would you think it *isn't* bothering me?"

He entered the room and settled his hands on his hips. Why, she wondered desperately, did the sight of him with his hands on those narrow hips always make everything else seem so unimportant? Struggling for focus, she dragged her eyes up to his.

"It doesn't bother *me*," he said.

"Oh, great. So you're stone deaf. I'm not!"

"Actually," he said mildly, "I'm not deaf at all. The music helps me to concentrate. I hardly even hear it, but don't ask me to explain why."

Dani sighed, feeling as if she were being utterly unreasonable, even though she knew perfectly well she was not. Guilt. Why was she always so quick to feel guilty any time she wanted anything? Any time she had an opinion? "Well, it doesn't help me to concentrate, sorry to say," she told him honestly, although she was beginning to wish she could back down from the entire issue.

"I forget not everybody loves the way that piece sounds at full volume. I'll turn it down and play it less often."

"Thank you." Although now she felt guilty for depriving him of what was obviously a great pleasure for him.

"And next time I'm doing something that's bothering you, don't be a wimp about it. Just come right out and tell me."

"I am not a wimp!"

Silas shook his head, grinning. "You trying to tell me this music hasn't been bothering you for weeks now? Come off it, teach. You may have your students cowed, but it's plain to me you're a pussycat."

"I am no such thing!" She nearly spluttered in her frustration. "I'll have you know I regularly stand up to boys who are bigger than you are!"

"But they're not my age, are they, teach? Nope, you can stand up to boys, but you haven't the foggiest idea about how to handle a *man*."

She drew herself up to her full height, wishing she could glare at him eyeball to eyeball. Instead she had to crane her neck, and that rather ruined the effect. "Are you challenging me?"

He shook his head. "Nope. Just pointing out an obvious fact. You're scared to death of me, and I don't think it's because you're afraid I might hit you.

No, that's not it at all. So maybe you ought to think about why it is you're afraid to ask me for a simple thing like having the music turned down."

He headed for the door, then paused and looked quickly back. "By the way, what did you want earlier?"

"Earlier when?"

"Just before Cheatham showed up. When you came into my office but didn't wait until I reached a convenient breaking point."

"I wasn't in your office. Turn your ego down a notch or two, Northrop. I haven't wanted to see you all day!" Which was an out-and-out lie, but it sounded good, and anyway, he would never guess just how much time she was wasting today thinking about a kiss. A stupid kiss!

"I saw you standing there, wearing a white . . ." His voice trailed off as he paused. A white what? Come to think of it, he hadn't seen her all that clearly.

"I've been wearing these clothes all day," Dani told him. "And I haven't been in your office."

"No, I guess not." He dropped the subject swiftly, suddenly utterly convinced that she had indeed not been in his office. "I must have been thinking of something else. I'll keep the music down. And next time you tell me if I'm irritating you with something. I'll sure as hell tell *you*."

"I'm sure you will," was her dry reply as he closed the door behind him.

Out on the gallery he paused, leaning over the railing and looking up to where Dani claimed to have seen Morris. And all of a sudden he was remembering the old movie *Gaslight* where someone had tried to scare someone else out of the way by staging a haunting.

He'd already considered and discarded that possibility, however. My God, the wiring and equipment it would take to have these ghosts pop up in random places . . . Except that it wasn't really random to have an apparition on the gallery, one in Dani's bedroom, and one in his office, which he'd seen nearly a half dozen times now. That would be relatively easy to lay out. Only the one beside his bed when he and Dani had camped out would be difficult to explain. That would have to mean that every room in this place was wired to produce a ghostly apparition, and surely the equipment involved in that should be enough to break someone's bank account.

But he didn't like the alternative at all, even though circumstances kept forcing him to consider it. What if these ghosts were real? Morris he could understand—maybe. It would be just like Morris to come back and annoy the hell out of him this way. The old s.o.b. must be laughing himself silly on a cloud somewhere.

But what about the woman? Who could she possibly be? Why did she look so much like Dani? That fit better with the *Gaslight* theory. Someone wanting to scare them could easily have gotten a photo of Dani thinking it would scare her silly to see her doppelganger haunting this house. Yeah, that made a lot of sense.

Tonight, he promised himself. Tonight he was going to tell Dani about what he had been seeing. The sooner the two of them got to the bottom of this, the better.

"Silas?" Dani opened her office door and looked out. "Do you want me to check for a backup file on your computer? Maybe your work didn't get lost after all."

Coming on the heels of their little spat it was a generous offer and he knew it. He wondered if he was a big enough man to accept it. "No, thanks," he said. "I can check it out myself."

"Fine." She closed the door loudly, leaving him to grin into space.

She was a spitfire, all right. And damned if he didn't like it.

Silas was still trying to work out a way to bring up the subject of his Dani-lookalike ghost that evening when their dinner was interrupted by someone at the door.

"I gave at the office," Silas said when he heard the knocking.

"Do you suppose it's another relative?" Dani asked, looking dismayed.

"Could be. If it is, should I send him on his way or drag him in for questioning?"

"Questioning didn't work too well on Pepita."

"I don't think anything would work well on Pepita except a big bank account. Admittedly, I'm prejudiced and should probably keep my mouth shut, but I think the only language that woman truly understands is the language of dollars and cents."

"Or *centavos*."

Silas gave a bark of laughter and rose from the table. "Guess I'd better answer it."

Dani followed, satisfying her curiosity, which was far more important than satisfying her hunger. At least for the moment.

Silas opened the door to reveal a small woman with short dark hair and enormous dark-rimmed glasses that nearly concealed her face. In her arms she held a large, rectangular white box. "Mr. Northrop?" she asked tentatively.

"Yes?"

"I'm Ina Jasper, your next door neighbor." The woman looked from him to Dani and back with a warm smile. "I've come to welcome you to the neighborhood." She offered Silas the box. "I made a strudel for you, from an old family recipe."

Silas was suddenly all smiles. "Why do come in, Ms. Jasper. We were just in the middle of dinner. You'll join us, won't you? I have enough steak to go around, especially since Dani here doesn't eat anything except bean sprouts and olives . . .''

In one smooth movement, talking all the while, Silas ushered Ina Jasper into the kitchen and got her seated at the island on a stool. Dani was a little astonished by Silas's unusual friendliness but then realized she had never seen him in his normal milieu. Perhaps away from this house and these uncomfortable circumstances he was a gregarious man.

Ina permitted herself to be served a tiny piece of steak and a plate of salad, admitting that she hadn't eaten anything since breakfast that morning. "It was one of those hectic days for me, I'm afraid. My practice is ordinarily well-ordered, but today . . ." She gave an expressive shrug.

"What kind of practice do you have?" Dani asked her.

"I'm a plastic surgeon."

"When did you ever find time to make a strudel?"

"Well, I cheated a little," Ina said with a twinkle. "I made it last night, but don't worry, it's still fresh and good."

"I can hardly wait to try it," Silas assured her. "I love strudel, but I haven't had any that was homemade since I was stationed in Germany years ago."

"My grandmother used to make it all the time when I was a little girl. Of course she was a housewife, so she was home all day and didn't mind that she had to keep coming back to it in the course of the day. It's time-consuming, but not too difficult."

"So which neighbor are you?" he asked. "North or south?"

"South." She pointed. "I'm sorry I didn't get over sooner to welcome you but . . . well, I was a little reluctant to come over. This house is—was—so quintessentially Morris's that . . ." She trailed off, shaking her head, apparently overcome. "Morris must have thought a great deal of the two of you to leave you this house."

Silas looked at Dani with an arched brow. "Well . . . we're not sure exactly what Morris thought of us that made him do this. It may have been a joke."

Ina smiled at that. "He did have a sense of humor, didn't he? And he always loved his little practical jokes. But he was just the *kindest* man."

"Yes, I thought so, too," Dani said. And she always had believed Morris to be kind. Even his peculiar sense of humor had never been hurtful.

"I love him, you know." The woman's smile was teary. "He came along when I was at absolutely the worst point in my life. My husband had walked out and left me with four small children. My job didn't pay enough to keep them all in day care while I worked, not if I was going to feed us all. And welfare . . . well, whatever some people think, it doesn't keep a person in the lap of luxury. No matter how I did it, I was barely scraping by."

"Didn't your husband pay any child support?"

"Oh no! He just vanished. I couldn't even find him to serve divorce papers to him. Anyway, I was working as a legal secretary at the time. My boss tried to help me as much as he could, but he honestly was paying me as much as he was able. I certainly couldn't have found a better salary anywhere else."

"How did you meet Morris?"

"He knew my boss from somewhere. A club of some sort I think. Anyway, he had our firm handle a real estate purchase for him." She smiled again. "I used to love it when he came in. He'd always be early for his appointment and we'd chat . . ." Her voice trailed off as she became lost in memory. "I think I fell in love with him the very first time I set eyes on him. Oh, I knew he was too old for me, but I didn't care. He was *nice*. Do you know how hard it is to find a *nice* man?"

"I have some idea," Dani said, giving Silas a pointed look. He pressed his hand to his heart as if wounded.

"Anyway, one day Morris took me to lunch, and the rest is history. It seemed to happen so fast, but when I look back on it . . . well, I felt as if I had known him all my life. And he was always so good to my children. Always. They just worshiped him. I will never, ever regret marrying him."

Silas finally broke a silence that was growing too long. "How long were you married?"

"Oh, only five years. I don't think . . . well, Morris wasn't really the marrying kind, you know? His heart wasn't really in it. Sometimes I think he was just in love with romance, and when the bloom was off the rose he lost interest. Oh, don't misunderstand me, he saw that we were well cared for. In fact, he sent me to medical school. I never could have done it without his help, not with all my children. No, he didn't abandon us when he and I divorced. That wasn't Morris's way. In fact, the children and I kept on living here until just recently, when I was able to buy the house next door."

She smiled rather tearily. "I did it all on my own, but I can thank Morris for providing the opportunity. In fact, I can thank him for my success. He knew all these Hollywood people, and he sent a great many of them to me for their cosmetic surgery."

"He was a very generous man," Silas agreed. "Is there something *we* can help you with?"

Dani suddenly felt as if she were sitting on pins and needles. If *this* woman said she had left something behind . . .

"Oh, no! Really!" Ina shook her head vehemently. "Certainly not. Morris gave me all the help I will ever need, more than enough for a lifetime. Once when I became rather effusive in my thanks, he cut me off by telling me that he just hoped I would do a kindness for someone else someday. I've been trying to practice that principle ever since, and that's the only reason I came over here. To welcome you."

Dani thought Ina was getting her fluff up just a wee bit much in response to what surely was an innocuous question. Guilt, perhaps? Or had this woman somehow caught wind of what other relatives were up to, and was now reacting to the suggestion she might be party to their actions? Impossible to tell.

Ina leaned forward a little, inviting them to confidentiality. "There is nothing I want. Truly. But the others . . . well, Morris made some bad bargains in his life, and some of his other ex-wives were among the worst. I don't know how he could tolerate their greediness. And some of *their* relatives! Well, it beats me why Morris thought he owed so much to so many. But as you said, Mr. Northrop, he was a generous man. Generous to a fault. His will was generous, too, but you can't tell that by the carping some of them are doing now. Disgusting, that's what it is."

She straightened. "No, I'm not one of them. Morris was more generous than he should have been to all of us, myself included. I have no complaints on that score."

"I'm glad to hear that," Silas said with a positively glowing smile. "We were beginning to feel under siege."

"I can imagine!" Ina looked genuinely indignant. "Well, you needn't worry about *me*."

"Do you have any idea why they think something of value is hidden in the house?"

"Is that what they think?" Ina laughed. "Good God, what imaginations! Morris was no fool. No fool at all. If he had anything of value, it was mentioned in his will. I can't imagine him hiding something for that crew to tear this place apart looking for. No, he liked his little jokes, but they were never of a kind to actually cause any harm to persons or property."

She refused to join them in the strudel, telling them she was awfully tired and really needed to get to bed early so she could be ready for another difficult day at her office.

"But you really must drop over on the weekend and visit me," she insisted as they walked her to the door. "There's a path that leads between our houses. If you haven't walked it yet, do. There is an absolutely *wonderful* banyan tree on the path that you shouldn't miss. It must cover nearly a half acre, and it's the most enchanting place. You can feel the magic when you stand beneath its limbs." She gave a little laugh. "It's on Morris's property, but I keep begging it to grow in my direction. I just hope it's listening."

She paused. "Someday . . . well, when you have a few minutes and wouldn't mind, could you walk me through the house? I have so many memories here . . ."

When Silas closed the door behind her, he looked inquisitively at Dani. "Well? What's your assessment?"

"She talks to trees. That sounds like someone Morris would marry."

Silas nearly doubled over as a whoop of laughter escaped. "True," he gasped a moment later. "Too true!"

"Actually, I can't figure her. She didn't press us to let her get something from the house. Maybe she's really on the up-and-up."

"I doubt it, but then I'm just a suspicious cuss by nature. Come on, I want a piece of that strudel. There is nothing like a homemade strudel."

"If it's not poisoned."

He laughed again. "I'll eat it all. If it kills me, you'll know she poisoned it."

"Funny, funny." She wasn't hungry though, and the strudel didn't appeal to her at all, so she joined Silas in a cup of coffee while he ate a healthy portion. Odd, she thought, how far they'd come in such a short time. Instead of carefully dividing everything, and cooking separate meals, they were doing most things together as comfortably as old roommates.

"So," Silas said, after smacking his lips appreciatively, "do you think this was just a friendly visit, a Trojan horse, or a warning?"

"Probably a Trojan horse. She was too quick to warn us and distance herself from the others."

"My feeling exactly—although I may just be getting paranoid because of all this crap. She had a definite point about Morris not leaving behind something he considered valuable without mentioning it in his will. I think his sense of humor was far weirder than Ina gives him credit for, but I still don't think he would have set this up consciously."

"Which means Morris didn't consider the item to be of any particular value—at least until after he died, to judge by his ghostly visits."

"So we're back to the theory of papers again. A manuscript? Could he have been writing a book? I know if he finished one it would be worth a pretty penny, but only to the charities he left his copyrights to. I can't imagine how *that* would benefit these relatives."

Dani leaned back in her chair and shoved a lettuce leaf across her plate with her index finger. "I give up. I can't imagine what this thing could possibly be. We're never going to find it."

"Now, now," Silas said bracingly. "If we take that attitude we can be sure we'll never solve this mystery."

Her head snapped up. "You know what I think? I think Morris ought to just make it clear what we're supposed to look for. If he wants to scare me out of my wits by showing up at the foot of my bed, the least he could do is tell me what the hell he wants!"

Silas hesitated the merest instant before rising and coming round the table to drop into the chair beside her and slip his powerful arm around her shoulders. "It's awful, isn't it?"

"It stinks! I never know from what direction the next threat is going to come! For heaven's sake, Silas, someone locked us in the hurricane room. The more

I think about it, the uneasier I get. What if we hadn't been able to get out? Did he intend to leave us there until we starved to death? As hot as it was in that room, we might have died from heat exhaustion in relatively short order. I can't escape the feeling that these people might actually mean us harm!"

His arm tightened around her. "It's been crossing my mind, too."

She tilted her head so she could look up at him. "What can we do about it?"

"Assuming you don't want to throw in the towel and abandon this entire project, the only thing we *can* do is be alert and keep looking for whatever may be causing all this brouhaha."

Dani looked down at her hands and wondered if she really *did* want to keep pressing forward. How much did she really want to write this novel? At home there simply hadn't been time. Much as people believed teachers had an easy life with long vacations, the truth was she only had four weeks to herself in the summer, between meetings, training sessions, and all of the preparations needed to begin each year. As for the school year—well, that was something else altogether. She taught English, and her students wrote volumes and volumes of essays and research papers, all of which she had to grade. In an average week she could easily spend eighty or ninety hours on her job, the vast majority of it at home during evenings and weekends, reading and grading all that writing. There simply wasn't time left to do her own.

That was the primary reason this chance had been such a godsend. Was she prepared to give up what might well be her only opportunity to write her novel?

That was inconceivable. She needed to do this for herself, so that someday she wouldn't be sitting in a rocking chair in some nursing home regretting that she had not seized this opportunity. Regretting that she had never done the one thing she wanted to do above everything else in this life: write her novel.

It didn't even matter if it got published. Well, it mattered, of course, but she would still write it anyway, even if she knew for a fact that no one would ever read it. She would write it because she needed to write it.

Her chin lifted and she looked at Silas. "No, I don't want to give up. So we just have to come up with some idea of how to make ourselves safe."

"Easier said than done," he replied bluntly. "That'll mostly depend on how determined these people are."

Dani shook her head. "I know. But I'm not going to quit anyway, unless one of these characters turns out to have a violent criminal record. Is there some way we can find out?"

"I'll give Cheatham a call. He'll probably know how to do it."

"And if he doesn't?"

"Then I'll call in a few favors in some less savory quarters. That's a good idea, Dani. A really good idea. It might give us some idea what we're up against."

Deep inside her something unfurled, basking in the warmth of his approval. Don't be a goose, she told herself. Don't let him affect you this way.

But she might as well have tried to halt the planets in their courses.

There was a strong offshore breeze that night. Warm and soft, it felt like a caress. As she stood on the dune watching moonlight dapple the dark waters, Dani could see the flare of lightning on the western horizon. Clouds that were invisible would suddenly appear, lit from within and turned pink by the lightning. They were still so far away she could hear no thunder, which somehow made the sight eerie, and even more beautiful than it would have been otherwise.

The cicadas were loud tonight, a constant screech that would have utterly drowned out the cacophony of the crickets in Ohio. The thought made her feel homesick, and she stood as if glued on the dune, staring out over the water, trying to hold in an ache as big as the Gulf of Mexico.

She was lonely. Not just lonely for her friends and her cat and her snug little cottage. She was lonely in a deeper, greater way, as if something she had forgotten had been taken away from her, leaving a gaping hole in her soul as the only reminder of its existence.

The feeling was a familiar one, a touch of melancholy yearning that seemed to have no cure. When she felt this way, she needed to stand alone outside at night, beneath the stars, surrounded by the vastness of the universe. Somehow the mystery of the heavens seemed to help put her yearning in perspective and keep it from overwhelming her.

Tonight, though, she wanted company. She wanted Silas to get a sudden urge for a walk on the beach. She wanted him to appear beside her and reach out to her. Somehow deep inside she knew that if he would just take her hand and walk with her for a little while, the ache would leave her.

Silly.

Sighing, she wrapped her arms around herself and tried to pay attention to the stars, the moon, the restless waters. The wind tossed the sea oats and stirred the palm fronds, and the cicadas abruptly fell silent.

She allowed herself a moment of hope, just the merest instant between one heartbeat and the next, that the cicadas had been startled into silence by Silas's appearance outside. But another heartbeat later the cicadas resumed their song, and Silas never materialized beside her.

She didn't care that she was acting like a foolish girl instead of an adult woman. Who would ever know? Silas made her feel things she had always believed were the outrageous fantasies of novelists. Just thinking about him made her insides go soft and weak, and even when she was feeling an urge to hit him with the nearest sofa cushion her body was betraying her by wanting to just melt into his arms.

Wasn't she a case? She'd watched enough girls in her high school classes to know that she was showing all the signs of a crush. And crushes didn't last long. In a few days she'd regain her senses. In the meantime, she ought to give thanks that Silas seemed to be avoiding her ever since dinner, because she was in serious danger of throwing her principles to the wind and indulging herself in a casual affair.

Because casual was all it could ever be. Heavens, he didn't particularly seem to like her. In fact, she was quite sure he could barely tolerate her. Then, their lives were over a thousand miles apart. Whether or not she published her book, she would have to go back to her job in Ohio. Very few published writers earned an adequate living from their writing.

But nothing in her life before had prepared her for the things that Silas Northrop made her feel. For the very first time she understood what sexual attraction was. Good grief, the man could turn her into a puddle merely by looking at her. Embarrassing portions of her anatomy seemed to grow heavy and throb whenever he was around. Never, ever had she imagined such feelings could be real.

Did she really want to pass up what might be the only chance she would ever have to discover what all the hoopla was about? Thomas had certainly never ignited her this way. Had never even come close.

But it was more than sexual yearning that kept her out here in the night. It was more than an ill-defined wish that Silas would join her and wrap her in his arms. Loneliness was a soul-deep ache that no mere hug would ever satisfy.

Was there such a thing as a soul mate? Standing

alone with only the companionship of the night, the wind and the cicadas, she stared up into the star-strewn heavens and wondered.

Wake up!

The command interrupted Dani's dreams, out of place. Wrong. She stirred a little, woke just enough to remember she was sleeping, then drifted away into a new dream.

Wake up!

The voice seemed to be right behind her as she stood on a stream bank, watching a golden fish swim lazily. She thought of turning around, then decided against it. Whoever it was could just leave her alone.

Dani, wake up now!

The urgency of the command this time compelled her. She was as instantly awake as if someone had dashed her with cold water. Around her the night seemed silent and still. Even the air conditioning was off, so the air was motionless. Her digital clock was the only source of illumination, a red glow that told her it was 2:57 a.m.

The command was still loud inside her head, almost an echo of what she had heard. Had she dreamt it? Or had a strangely familiar voice really barked at her to wake her?

She waited, feeling as if there wasn't enough air in the entire universe while her heart thudded uncomfortably in her chest. Then, slowly, drawing on every ounce of courage she possessed, she rolled over to look behind her.

At first she saw nothing at all. In the dim red glow from her clock she could make out familiar shapes of furniture. If anyone was there, he was hiding behind something.

But then, so slowly she thought it must be a trick of her eyes, a silvery shimmer began to appear in the air. As if a light shone on dust motes—only there was no light. Dani blinked rapidly, trying to clear her vision, but the silvery glow stubbornly brightened a little more.

It grew slowly, holding her gaze in an inexorable grip. To save her life, she couldn't have looked away. The glowing spot, still dim, expanded upward and downward, and after a span of time it vaguely resembled the shape of a man.

Oh, God, she was watching Morris materialize. Surety tightened around her throat like an iron noose. Gasping for air, she eased back in her bed until she was as far away as she could get.

The luminescence seemed not to care. It brightened some more, and one corner of Dani's mind noted that bright as it was, it illuminated nothing around it. It cast no light at all. She was imagining it. She *had* to be imagining it.

But it didn't go away. Slowly, steadily, it appeared to solidify until, beyond any shadow of a doubt, Morris Feldman stood at the foot of her bed.

He wasn't smiling. Instead he looked very concerned, and lifted an arm, pointing directly to her window.

"Look!" he said.

Then the darkness swallowed him whole.

12

Minutes passed in stark terror. Dani didn't even dare blink, and her heart was beating so hard she thought it was going to burst from her chest. Only when she was sure that nothing else was going to happen did she dare ease from her bed. Keeping her back to the wall, she inched around the room toward the window.

Although fear nearly paralyzed her, her mind registered one very important fact: Morris had wakened her to tell her something. Well, she had wanted him to tell her something, hadn't she? Hadn't she been complaining this very night that if he had something to communicate he could at least just come right out and say it?

Well, he had said it. *Look*, he had said, and pointed to her window. So she was going to look.

Problem was, in order to look she would have to turn her back on the room. She honestly didn't think Morris wanted to hurt her, but that didn't make her any more eager to turn her back on a ghost. Heavens, she thought with a shiver, she'd be happy if she never saw another one! It was just too creepy!

That was when she realized she hadn't screamed. She had seen Morris and hadn't even let out a peep. Maybe she was developing some real backbone at last. Or maybe she was just getting used to sharing accommodations with a ghost.

She reached the window at last, then hesitated there, reluctant to discover what lay beyond. Her heart was galloping so hard that she was gulping air like a sprinter at the end of a race. Every instinct shouted at her to keep her back to the wall. The effort required to turn to the window was nearly superhuman, but somehow she managed it.

From up here, she could see over the dune to the beach and water beyond. The moon was in the west, and the gulf waters beyond the dune were dappled dull silver and black. The sand of the dune and the beach glowed whitely, while the sea oats shifted from gray to black.

Her gaze wandered over the scene, wondering what Morris could have considered so important.

Then she caught sight of movement on the beach, near the water's edge, and her blood turned to ice.

"Silas!" Trying to keep her voice to a loud whisper, Dani shook Silas's shoulder desperately. "Silas, wake up!"

With a speed that seemed humanly impossible, Silas was suddenly on the far side of the bed, kneeling, with a pistol leveled straight at her.

"Silas . . ."

He released an audible breath and lowered the gun. "Good God, woman, I could have killed you! Next time call me from across the room!"

"You stupid oaf! If you didn't have that horrible gun there wouldn't have been any danger at all!"

"Wanna bet?" Standing, with his left hand he tugged his boxer shorts up and ran his fingers through his hair. the Browning never left his right hand. "What the hell's going on?"

"There's something on the beach! Two of them. They look like creatures from the Black Lagoon."

"You're dreaming."

"Damn it, Silas, I am not! I saw them. Morris

woke me up and told me to look out the window, and there they were! Whatever they are. You have to come look!"

"*Morris* told you to look?" His voice couldn't have been thicker with disbelief if she'd just told him the *Titanic* had docked out back.

"I swear it! Silas, will you just come look? There are two monsters out there, and they can't possibly be up to any good!"

"Monsters seldom are."

She wanted to bean him. All that held her back, apart from a naturally civilized nature, was the fact that she needed him. Besides, sarcastic or not, he was swiftly tugging on some camouflage pants over his shorts, and shoving his feet into boots.

Moments later he was striding to the door. "Let's go."

She had to run to keep up with his long, rapid strides as they hurried toward her room. Only then did she realize she was running around in a thin cotton nightgown and bare feet. Goosebumps covered her chilly arms. All she could do at this point, however, was give a mental shrug.

When they reached her window, there was nothing at all on the beach. The creatures she had seen were evidently gone.

"But I saw them," she whispered vehemently. "Believe me, I didn't imagine them. I was wide awake by the time Morris vanished. Good heavens, my heart was galloping like a stampeding horse! There is no way I was dreaming at that point, even if I *did* imagine Morris. I worked my way around the room with my back to the wall I was so frightened."

He looked down at her. She could feel his gaze almost as if it were a physical touch. Then, surprising her, he reached out an arm and drew her up against his side. His skin felt so warm and smooth against her chilled arm, and his hand on her shoulder felt protective.

To her surprise, he didn't pull away from the window and dismiss her completely. Instead he remained still and watchful, keeping his attention fixed out back.

And then, little by little, the monstrous black shapes began to rise above the dune as they climbed the far side.

"Damn," Silas muttered.

Dani felt vindicated. "You see? You see? I didn't imagine them. What in the world are they?"

Completely black from head to toe, they were only vaguely human in shape, with bulging eyes and enormous webbed feet . . .

Silas gave a quiet laugh. "My God, I don't believe it. I don't believe it!"

"Don't believe what?"

"Frogmen! Only the idiots haven't taken off their flippers! Their combined IQ must be all of ten points! Do you have any idea how hard it is to walk and climb in those damn things?"

"Uh, no . . . You mean they're not monsters? Their eyes—"

He cut her off. "Those are night vision goggles."

She would have felt like a perfect fool except that two men arriving in that kind of getup were probably as dangerous as any monsters would be.

"Oh, this is rich," Silas said. He sounded absolutely delighted. "You stay right here, Dani. Don't turn on the light. I don't want them to know they've been spotted. I'm going to go downstairs and throw on the flood lamps. With those night goggles on, they'll be blinded and I ought to be able to capture both of them. Then maybe we can get to the bottom of this mess!"

"We should call the police."

He looked down at her. "Again? And tell them what? Dani, after the last visit we don't have any credibility with the local gendarmerie. Of course, if you want to call and tell them Morris woke you . . ."

"Forget it."

"I knew you'd see reason. This won't be hard at all. Just keep clear until I tell you otherwise, okay?"

Before she could reply, he tightened his arm around her and stole a breathtaking kiss from her mouth. She was still sagging against the window embrasure after he was gone.

Stay in this room in the dark? Alone? Fear swiftly replaced dazed passion as she realized what Silas had done to her. How could he have left her here with Morris and all the other things that might go bump in the night? Damn him!

She was freezing, but couldn't even stir up the nerve to go to her closet and get a robe. Nor did she want to miss whatever happened below. Silas might believe he was indestructible, but she knew better. These men might be armed and could seriously hurt him.

They *were* armed. As she watched the two of them struggle across the dune in those ridiculous flippers, she saw that they were carrying something that looked like a very thin rifle. No . . . more like a spear. Oh, no, not a spear gun!

It was almost like watching an old episode of "Sea Hunt," she found herself thinking. Or a Jerry Lewis comedy. The two men were having an inordinately difficult time walking, and kept bumping into one another. One of them kept turning on the other as if he wanted to brain him. In spite of everything, Dani found herself smiling in genuine amusement.

Just as the two men reached the bottom of the hill, the backyard flood lamps switched on. Dani could only imagine the blast of light the men had gotten through their goggles, but there was no doubt they were blinded as they stumbled into one another. Silas appeared, trotting across the backyard toward them. When he got close, he adopted a marksman's stance, his legs splayed and his gun held in a two-handed grip.

By this time, both men had ripped off their goggles

and were stumbling back up the dune, scrambling on hands and knees as fast as they could go. Suddenly one of them rolled onto his back and aimed his spear gun at Silas.

Silas took a quick step then froze, lowering his gun and bending over. Dani saw a spear sticking out of his leg, saw him reach out to grasp the shaft in one hand. The men were scrambling over the top of the dune.

Turning, Dani gathered up the hem of her nightgown and took off at a dead run. Silas was hurt and needed help immediately.

She fairly flew down the stairs and out the back door. Over the sussuration of the trees and the quiet thunder of the surf, she heard him uttering a stream of invectives that she was sure no one but a marine could know. Apparently her students back home were singularly unimaginative.

Well, if he was cursing that creatively he couldn't be at death's door, she assured herself, but that didn't keep her heart from climbing into her throat as she approached him.

"Silas?"

He was still bent over, tugging on the shaft, but he looked over his shoulder at her to growl, "I thought I told you to stay put!"

"I don't take orders from you! Anyway, they're running away, and you're hurt. You might at least admit you need help."

"I *don't* need help!"

"You're hurt!"

"I am not. Damn diapers . . ."

Diapers? She hesitated a moment, then decided he must be even more seriously injured than she had feared if he was already delirious. "Silas," she said, squaring her shoulders and coming around to face him, "you must have a terrible wound."

"I don't have any wound at all, damn it!" He tugged viciously on the spear.

"Don't do that. You'll make it worse! And of

course, you're wounded. Why else would you be delusional?"

"I'm not delusional!" He glared at her. A lesser man or woman would have shut up. Dani merely wagged her finger at him.

"Of course you are. You're muttering about diapers—"

"Oh for Pete's sake," he said in utter disgust, letting go of the spear and straightening. He poked a finger at her. "Listen to me. I am *not* wounded. The thing is stuck in my pants. I *am* wearing diapers. That's what we call these damn cammie pants, ever since they put the extra layer of material in the seat. I'm muttering about diapers because the damn spear is stuck in the material, right beneath my *cojones*, and I can't take a step without getting poked. Are we clear?"

He was roaring at her by the time he finished, but she was more embarrassed than annoyed. Right beneath his, er, unmentionables? Her cheeks flamed.

"They're getting away," she said inanely, because she suddenly could think of nothing else.

"Of course they're getting away!" he roared. "If I could get this damn spear out of this material I'd go after them, damn it!"

He reached for the spear again and gave it a savage jerk.

"You're going to hurt yourself," Dani scolded.

"Do you have a better idea?"

"Take your pants off."

It was a statement of the obvious, and she had the distinct feeling that it wasn't very well received— probably because it *was* so obvious. To her surprise, however, he didn't say a word.

Instead he popped the buttons on the fly, then sat down on the grass, tugging first at his boots and then pulling the pants down.

"You could have been hurt," Dani said as she watched him strip to his shorts.

"No kidding." His words were heavy with sarcasm.

"Well, excuse me for caring."

"I don't remember asking you to."

"Fine then." She folded her arms across her breasts as she watched him clamber to his feet.

"Now get into the house before you get hurt," he commanded her, then took off barefoot up the side of the dune with his Browning in hand.

Almost immediately she realized she was standing alone outside in the dead of night in her thin cotton gown. Barefoot on grass that might well be swarming with icky bugs. Looking down instinctively, she gasped at what she saw. She was standing in the bright light from the flood lamps, and her gown was so thin that every detail of what lay beneath it was visible. Her nipples, her areolas, her . . .

She wanted to sink. At once she turned for the house, but remembered Morris. She didn't know what to do. She didn't want to stay out here in the glare of the lights where anyone at all might see her, nor did she want to go back into the house alone, nor could she climb the dune because she might only distract Silas, and besides, who knew what might be crawling among all those sea oats?

So, hating herself for her timidity, she crept back to the archway and hovered in the shadows, wondering if Silas was all right or if those two men had somehow managed to ambush him.

It was like a damn Keystone Kops adventure, Silas thought angrily as he ducked low and worked his way cautiously across the dune. Shot in the crotch with a spear gun by two dimwits who didn't even have the sense to take their flippers off, arguing like a child with Dani . . . Damn.

Before he had switched on the lights, he had heard the two men grumbling at one another, neither of them very happy about their mission. It had sounded like Abbott and Costello on a bad day. By now, even hampered as they had been with their flippers, they were probably long gone. If only he hadn't found himself unable to chase right after them.

Sure enough, the beach was empty, a silvery expanse of white sand in the moonlight. The two men were undoubtedly swimming away, or riding a rubber raft into the night. He sure wouldn't be able to pick them out on the dappled waters, and even if he could, what could he do about it now? He'd never catch up.

Imagine those two lamebrains coming ashore in the dead of night like something out of a bad James Bond movie. Hell, that was probably where they'd gotten the idea for it.

The humor of it struck him forcibly, and he sat back on the sand, laughing quietly. Damn, it took all kinds. If he hadn't seen for himself that they were full-grown men, he would have thought they were a couple of thirteen-year-olds acting out a fantasy.

He chuckled again and pushed himself to his feet, heading back toward the house. It shouldn't be funny, he supposed, but the more he thought about it, the more hilarious it seemed.

As soon as he came over the dune, he spied Dani standing in the archway. Moonlight gave her white nightgown an ethereal glow, and for a moment he indulged a fantasy that she was some faerie come to tempt him. No, he decided after a moment. He didn't want her to be a faerie whose wiles were nothing but magic. He wanted her to be a real woman with a tart tongue and a maddening defensiveness.

What *had* made her so defensive? Well, he was the last person on earth she'd talk to about things like that. As near as he could tell, she could barely stand him. Except for brief flares of sexual interest, of course. More than once he'd caught sight of the curiosity and hunger in her eyes. But you didn't have to like someone to want them, and despite all that women said about love, he was willing to bet that was as true for them as it was for men.

Maybe.

Lately it wasn't all that true of him. It was getting so he couldn't look at a woman without seeing everything that was wrong with her, and when he thought about having sex with one, she suddenly became downright repulsive. He didn't know what was making him so finicky, but it was kind of a relief that Dani didn't make him feel that way. At least he could be sure there wasn't something wrong with him.

Unless, of course, you counted the fact that he was interested in a prickly-pear cactus of a woman who could barely stand to be around him. That was grounds for getting his head examined.

She waited for him in the entryway, looking small, fragile, and frightened as she stood there barefoot, with her arms tightly folded. A protective urge almost overwhelmed him, but he smothered it.

"They're gone," he said.

"Do you have any idea who they were?"

"Nope. Thanks to that damn spear, they got away." He started to turn to go get his cammies and his boots, but he somehow never made the pivot. Perhaps she moved, perhaps an errant beam of moonlight was just playing a wicked trick, but something suddenly dragged his gaze down to her breasts. Her arms were folded beneath them, and the cotton of her gown concealed surprisingly little in the silver light. He could see her rosy areolas. More, he could see her pointed little nipples pressing against the cloth.

She drew a sharp breath, realizing where his gaze had strayed, but she made no move to cover herself. Instead she looked down and saw what he was seeing. A shuddery breath escaped her, a breath that spoke volumes to him about her sudden awareness.

He was lost. He was lost and didn't give a damn if

he went to hell for it. This woman in that gown in the moonlight was the most irresistible temptation he had ever faced. In an instant she had him as hot and as hard as a young stud.

Passion pounded in his veins and it was exhilarating. Damn, it was sweet to feel this way again after so long. His blood was singing with desire, and he felt so incredibly alive. In thrall to forces as old as time, he reached out for Dani.

She drew back, looking up at him as if he terrified her. "No . . ." The sound was a whisper, the merest breath, lost in the crash of the surf.

But he saw the syllable her lips formed, and felt the denial in his heart. He should have backed away, but instead he stepped even closer. "Dani . . ." Somehow he needed to reassure her because, by God, he needed to hold her.

"Silas, please don't . . ."

"Just a hug. Just let me hug you."

He saw her resistance start to crumble. For an instant she remained frozen as if ready to flee, then she swayed toward him. Reaching out, he wrapped her in his arms and drew her against him. She was soft and warm, and her fragrance was so exquisitely feminine. So female. A shudder passed through him as need triumphed over restraint. He wanted her. Now.

All the mental games he'd been playing with himself to avoid facing up to his desire for her vanished like puffs of smoke. There was no place left to hide from himself.

One last wisp of sanity caused him to sweep her up into his arms and carry her into the house, closing the door on the night and all its threats. Now there was just the two of them in the dark stillness of the house.

Dani shivered, cold and hot at once, and clung to Silas as he carried her through the dark house. She felt ensorcelled, as if the web of a wizard's spell had been cast over her, depriving her of will and speech. Every muscle in her body had turned soft and heavy, ready to yield in the confrontation ahead. A deep throbbing had begun between her legs, a hypnotic pulse that steadily drove every thought from her head.

He set her on her feet and she swayed a little. Her legs weren't strong enough to hold her. The craving to lie down had never been so strong. But he supported her with his powerful arms, hugging her snugly to him so that she was aware of every one of his hard contours. His arousal pressed firmly against her belly, and awareness of it sent shimmering thrills straight to her womb. He wanted her. Oh, yes, he truly wanted her. Fierce joy filled her.

"Easy," he whispered roughly. "Easy, Dani . . . I won't hurt you . . ."

She shivered in response to his words. It had never occurred to her that he might hurt her. Strange . . .

Electric sparks shattered the night as he bent to press soft kisses on her lips, her cheeks, her throat. Behind her closed eyelids she saw brilliant whorls of light, as if she were seeing his touches as well as feeling them. Liquid heat poured through her veins, melting her even more.

"Don't do a thing," he murmured. "Not a thing. Just let me . . ."

Let him? How could she not? She simply didn't have the will to deny him something she wanted so very much. Her head sagged backward in silent surrender. In silent entreaty. *More*, her body pleaded. Oh, please, let there be more.

Slowly, as if savoring every moment, his hands slipped down her back and cupped her bottom. Until that very moment she would have denied that was an erogenous zone, but the instant he touched her, she knew differently. A soft gasp escaped her, then another as he lifted her toward him, pressing the hard length of his arousal against her. Swirling tides of desire lifted her and carried her away.

Slowly, oh so excruciatingly slowly, he lowered her once again to her feet, allowing her length to drag sensuously against him. He groaned, and an answering sound came from the back of her throat. Desperately needing support, she reached out blindly and clutched at his upper arms.

Skin. Warm, hot, male skin met her palms, filling her with a restless need to stroke, knead, explore. As she dragged her palms across his chest, he groaned again and her womb pulsed with a deep, tight ache.

His hands were clutching at her nightgown right over her bottom, but not until he had gathered all the material up did she realized what he was doing. When his hot, calloused palms met her bare, soft curves, the heat within her exploded into a conflagration.

"Easy, Dani. Easy."

His voice was a rough whisper against a background of intense sensations. Her entire universe centered around the caress of his palms, around the sheer intensity of the feelings he was giving her. Part of her was afraid, part was exhilarated, and part of her was terrified that he would suddenly stop and leave her hanging on the edge of this aching precipice of need.

"Please . . ." she whispered hoarsely. "Please . . ."

"You want me." It wasn't a question. "Say it. Dani just say it . . ."

It should have been easy but it was somehow hard, and the difficulty of it started to draw her back from the ragged edge to which he had swept her. The pounding in her veins receded a little, clearing the sensual fog from her mind.

But almost as if he sensed he was losing her, he brought one of his hands between them and slipped it right between her legs, palm upward, pressing against her in a way that nearly drove her out of her mind right then and right there.

She cried out, a woman's wordless plea.

He answered, pressing his hand against her again with unerring understanding of what she needed.

"You like that, don't you," he whispered. "Have you ever touched yourself here like this? Has anyone else ever done this to you?"

She gasped, digging her nails into his shoulders as she clung for dear life. From somewhere came a helpless shake of her head.

"I figured," he said, his whisper nearly as ragged as her own breathing. "What a damn shame. God, you are so sweet . . ."

His hand shifted and suddenly his fingers were sliding between her velvety folds, growing slick with her moisture. The sensation was so strong it was almost painful. She started to pull away, but his arm tightened around her and his hand never stopped moving between her legs.

"Shh," he murmured. "Shh . . . I won't hurt you. Just relax. Relax and give yourself a moment to enjoy . . ."

Relax? She felt as if she were drawn tight on wires and suspended helplessly above the floor. Part of her was scared to death by what was happening inside her body, and part of her was scared to death she might miss a moment of this incredible experience.

Another cry escaped her as the pleasure-pain he was inflicting with his fingers steadily transformed into the purest pleasure. She ached to clamp her thighs together and deepen the stimulation, yet feared if she did so he would not be able to caress her. Trapped by seemingly opposing needs, she arched her back and undulated her hips, and silently begged him never to stop.

"That's it," he murmured. "That's the way, honey. Ride me to the top . . ."

She was riding a roller coaster, the wildest ride she had ever taken, only this one seemed to keep climbing and climbing. A kind of fear gripped her that she would never attain the pinnacle that seemed so close . . . yet so far . . . so close . . . so far . . .

Watching her, Silas forgot his own hammering need in the exquisite beauty of watching Dani approach her apex. He could have taken her right then, but something held him back. Something that wanted to make these precious moments Dani's and Dani's alone.

"Come on, honey," he crooned to her. "Come on . . . you'll make it . . ."

Only the dim bulbs of the night lighting were on in the atrium, and her face was in shadows. But not so shadowed he couldn't see the furrow of concentration that creased her brows, or the way she bit her lip as she struggled toward release.

And she *was* struggling. Dimly, it began to occur to him that he was trying to take her somewhere she had never been, along a path she didn't know. She was locked in the grip of the passion that buffeted her, but had no idea where it was taking her. No idea how to help herself along.

Some part of him was shocked that a woman of her age could be so inexperienced, and some part of him was thrilled. To be the first man she had trusted herself to in this manner was at once exhilarating and terrifying. He wasn't sure he wanted that responsibility. Not sure at all.

But he couldn't leave her like this. Somehow he had to coax her to culmination, but he didn't have a foggy idea how to do that. The women in his past had been considerably more experienced in such matters, and the last thing they had needed was a coach. What could he say or do to help her?

Cradling her as close as he could, he ignored his own throbbing body to trail soft kisses along her cheek and throat, murmuring reassurances as he did so. Trying to get her to relax enough that her body would follow that path by instinct.

"Easy does it, honey. That's the way, Dani . . ."

And finally, daringly, he slipped his finger into her moist depths. The sensation seemed to electrify her, for she arched sharply and let out a low keening that excited him as much as the soft undulations of her body.

That one touch had been all the answer she needed.

At the self-same instant came a loud hammering at the front door. Startled, Silas looked toward it, then down at the woman in his arms. No way could he put her aside while he went to see who could be pounding on the door at four in the morning. No way.

Dani sagged against him, soft and warm and liquid with satiation. All he wanted in the world right now was to join her in that exquisite feeling.

The pounding came again, louder this time. Silas considered picking up his gun and shooting the asshole.

Again, three loud bangs, this time followed by a demanding voice. "Police! Open up!"

Dani shivered, and her eyes snapped open. "What—?" She sounded breathless, lost.

"It's okay. I'll take care of whatever it is. You just run upstairs and get something on."

Her eyes darkened. "I don't want to go up there. Silas . . . Morris!"

He wanted to shout his frustration. To hell with Morris and ghosts and relatives and cops. What he ought to be doing right now was climbing under the blankets in bed with Dani and cuddling her close. What he ought to be doing was filling her body with his until he reached the stars.

The hammering sounded again, and he knew the cop's patience was wearing thin. "It might be important," he told Dani. "I have to answer the door, but you don't want him to see you in that nightgown."

She looked down at herself. "No," she said in a smothered voice. "I guess not." She looked deliciously rumpled, and very much like a woman who had just been well loved. "I'll hide in the laundry room, then." She sent him a beseeching look. "Silas, I know it's silly, but I don't want to see Morris ever again!"

"I can understand that. Dani, I have to get the door before he breaks it down."

Nodding, she darted toward the laundry room. He gave her just enough time to reach it, then he headed for the front entrance. The cop hammered and shouted again, and this time Silas shouted back.

"Keep your shirt on! I'm coming."

Maybe someday he'd even be able to appreciate the irony of that statement.

The officer at the door was, thankfully, not the same one who had answered Dani's call the other day. Nor was he alone. Clearly visible near the patrol car was another policeman, hand casually resting on the butt of his gun. What had these guys all worked up?

"Are you the property owner, sir?"

"No, I'm the tenant. Is something wrong?"

"We've had reports of persons acting oddly on the beach tonight. Have you noticed anything?"

"You were going to wake me up to ask that?"

"Your back floodlights are on, sir. They weren't on earlier. It's a good indication that someone here was up and about."

Silas had to give this guy points for that one. "Well, we did see two figures come across the dune, but when I turned on the lights they ran away." No way was he going to tell this guy about the spear that had kept him from chasing the intruders.

"Do you think they were planning to break into your house?"

Silas shrugged. "How would I know? They never got close enough." Nor was he going to say a word about what he and Dani suspected was going on. Word might get back to the relatives, and the last thing he wanted them to know was that he and Dani were on to them. It was much better to have them bumbling around in plain sight where he could keep an eye on them.

"Can you think of why anyone might have come by way of the beach to break into the house?"

Silas couldn't help it; a snort escaped him. "Look, I don't read minds. Maybe they just saw too many action-adventure movies."

The officer cracked a smile at that, and snapped his notebook shut. "Thank you for your time. If you notice anything unusual, give us a call."

Silas watched him walk down to the car and climb in. Just before he closed the car door, however, the officer looked up at him and called, "Have the ghosts settled down yet?"

With a roar, the patrol car tore down the drive, leaving Silas to seethe on the step. Those officers suspected *him* of being involved in the antics on the beach. They had come here to leave a not-so-subtle warning: "We know you're weird, but you'd better not let it bother the neighbors."

Muttering a string of oaths, Silas stormed back into the house to tell Dani she could come out of the laundry room.

Offended as he was, though, with each step he took he found himself remembering more and more vividly the minutes just passed with Dani in his arms. How soft she had felt pressed to him. How warm and velvety her depths were. Step by step he slipped back into the mood of passion that had nearly deserted him. He was going to sweep that woman right off her feet and carry her away to bed with him. Nor would the arrival of an army of cops or a flotilla of thieves deter him. Nothing, absolutely *nothing*, was going to keep him from making love to Danika Hilliard.

Except Dani herself.

He knew he was in trouble the minute he flung

open the laundry room door and found her standing with her arms folded across her breasts and her lips drawn into a thin line.

He halted on the threshold, wishing she hadn't turned the light on. Not only did it hurt his eyes after the dimness of the atrium, but it prevented him from misinterpreting the look in her eye. Instead of desire, he found anger.

"Dani? What's wrong?"

"How could you?" she demanded in a low voice.

"How could I what?"

"Take advantage of me that way!"

He was definitely missing a critical link in the line of reasoning here. Since when was giving a woman an orgasm considered taking advantage of her? Hell, he hadn't even achieved one of his own! "I didn't take advantage of you. What are you talking about?"

"You used me. Humiliated me! From now on you keep your dirty paws to yourself!"

With that she fled past him and ran up the stairs, making a sound very much like a sob.

Between the frogmen, the cops and Dani, he was batting oh-for-three tonight. He should never have gotten out of bed. And damn it, the next time Dani saw monsters, he was going to tug the blanket over his head and hide!

13

❦

The atmosphere was so icy in the house that Dani half expected to be able to skate along the gallery. Silas was freezing her even more effectively than she was freezing him . . . which was fine except for the thunder of the *1812 Overture* which was once again filling the atrium in defiance of their agreement.

The racket wasn't any easier to bear even though she had already finished her writing for the day and was merely doing her part to search the house for the treasure. Nothing would make that repetitious noise easier to take. In desperation, she grabbed her sun visor and left the house, deciding to take a walk toward Ina Jasper's place and see the banyan tree.

Besides, she was edgy. Having Morris wake her up and talk to her the other night had left her almost too nervous to bear. It was bad enough to *see* Morris, but to actually have him wake her up and warn her of events beyond her window . . .

Though it was still early afternoon, the storm clouds were already building for the daily deluge. In a couple of hours lightning would crackle and thunder would roar, but for now the day was perfect. Well, except for the mugginess. At least there was a nice breeze to keep her from sweltering.

A great egret strolled slowly across the lawn, its

stride wonderfully regal. It paused a moment to look at her, then resumed its unhurried walk. Little, she had learned since arriving here, unduly disturbed these birds.

The air was a lot hotter and muggier once she stepped from the lawn into the woods. The palmettoes and other undergrowth, as well as the trees, killed the breeze. The air here hung heavy, and smelled of mulch.

The path was easy enough to find, though, which surprised her. She wouldn't have imagined that there'd be a beaten path between these two homes. Adults in estates like these didn't commonly run back and forth to borrow sugar, did they? And no young children had been in residence at Morris's place in a long time, as far as she knew.

As she wandered through the woods, however, the oddity of the path seemed unimportant. What mattered was that it was here and she could wander beneath the green canopy of palms and coastal pines. The lush vegetation was like another world, and the heat sapped the nervousness from her even as it leached her energy. She was beginning to feel more relaxed than she had in days, perhaps weeks.

The banyan tree was even more impressive than she had imagined it might be. Had she not known about banyans from her reading, she would never have realized that these dozens of trunks were a single tree. Awed, she stepped within the embrace of the ancient limbs and turned slowly, feeling the same kind of reverence she felt in a cathedral. What an absolutely wonderful work of nature!

Content, she sat at the base of one of the trunks and leaned backward so that she could stare up into the branches. Now she understood the beaten path she had trod. While this was her home, she would probably want to come here every day, just to touch the magic of nature and the peace of this place.

Unfortunately, the peace gave her more opportunity to think, and she found her mind roaming over the events of the other night when Silas had, um, touched her. Intimately. In a way no one had ever quite touched her before. Afterward she had over-reacted, and she knew it, but she couldn't bring herself to apologize for it. She was so *embarrassed*.

Not just embarrassed by the way he had touched her, although that had been shattering enough, but embarrassed by the way she had reacted. Humiliated, actually, by the ease with which she had succumbed. She had felt so exposed, as if some dirty secret of hers had been revealed. It was worse than being stripped naked in broad daylight, to have those parts of oneself exposed to someone who apparently wasn't feeling the very same thing. She didn't know Silas well enough, or yet trust him enough, to feel comfortable with all that she had let him see.

But that was her own fault. For all she had acted as if he had done something wrong, the bottom line was that she had fully cooperated in what had happened. Perhaps even instigated some of it. It had been so very wrong of her to claim he had taken advantage of her.

Her cheeks colored even now as she remembered his scalding touches and found her body responding again, almost as strongly as it had to the real thing. Worse than her folly in letting him do those things was her folly now in wanting to experience them once more. If Silas had come upon her this very instant and reached out for her, she would have flung herself into his arms.

And that was a very difficult thing for her to accept because it went against her very strict rules of conduct. While she didn't deplore premarital sex—what was the point in this day and age?—she definitely was opposed to casual sex, and sex between her and Silas couldn't be anything else, could it?

But oh how wonderful it had been . . . She sighed, feeling her eyelids growing heavy. Nerves had been making it difficult for her to sleep, and it was so peaceful here. Her eyelids drooped until she could see the tree only through a fringe of eyelashes.

Thinking of soft, knowing touches that had set her nerve endings afire, she drifted away into deep sleep.

Silas was about as p.o.'d as he'd ever been. He still couldn't believe Dani had accused him of taking advantage of her. He'd been around the block enough times to know when a woman was falling into his arms, and he'd never yet been so desperate that he'd even considered seducing a woman against her will.

And Dani knew that. He was convinced of it. Her reaction had been born of embarrassment . . . which, actually, he could understand considering how they had been interrupted at a very delicate point of affairs. He might have overlooked the entire thing if only she hadn't been acting like a wounded doe the past couple of days, darting him frightened looks as if he might spring on her again.

He wasn't apt to spring on anything in her present state. Dani might unfortunately be one of the sexiest women he had ever met, but there was nothing sexy about hurt looks. Nope, they shriveled him right up.

He kept waiting for her to settle down, but she didn't. The wounded looks just kept flying his way, and finally he had enough of it. Out came the *1812 Overture*, at full blast, as pointed as he could get without bloodshed in his attempt to drive her from his mind.

It was a relief when he glanced out his window and saw her walking off into the woods. At least for a little while he could roam the house freely and forget that she equated him with the reincarnation of Genghis Khan. He cut the volume by half and went back to work.

But he couldn't concentrate. Even with Dani out of the house, his own conscience insisted on reminding him that he had hurt her. His mind's eye made up for her absence with a slide show of her wounded looks, springing a new one on him every time he tried to completely banish all thought of her.

Damn! He wasn't going to be able to put it from his mind and let time take the edge off this mess. Apparently he was going to have to take the bull by the horns—in short, have it out with Dani. He was damned if he was going to feel like a criminal simply because she was embarrassed.

Muttering a string of oaths, he saved his document, switched off his computer, and headed out to find her. He noted a string of thunderheads in the distance as he crossed the yard, but figured they wouldn't get here for a while yet. At this time of year in Florida, scarcely a day went by without a thunderstorm but he could always hope.

A couple of years ago Morris had taken him out to the banyan tree, so he found the path without any difficulty. The air was still and sultry beneath the branches of the coastal pines, as if the trees were holding their breath in anticipation. A squirrel scurried away, dashing up a tree trunk and chattering down at him from safety in a high branch.

Then he stepped into the sheltering arms of the banyan. It was almost eerie the way the atmosphere changed, as if he had stepped within the heart of a living being. This tree, with its many trunks and its parasol of oval leaves, was a world unto itself, a place of magic where he expected at any moment to see a nymph or an elf.

Dani slept against one of the trunks, reclining against an ancient tangle of roots that had grown together into a seamless whole, leaving only an impression of their earlier form.

It was as if he had stepped into a fairy tale. The peaceful aura of the banyan seemed to permeate him, driving away cares and irritations, and leaving him to simply stare in awe at Sleeping Beauty as she slumbered beneath the sheltering boughs of an enchanted tree.

God, she was cute. Her skin was dewy and pink from the heat, and her mouth had fallen into a gentle curve as some pleasant dream entertained her. He had the strongest urge to stand here like some knight of yore and guard her sleep. He even wanted to sweep her up in his arms and carry her off to his own castle, claiming her as his.

But mostly, fairytale-like, he wanted simply to kiss her awake and see the soft smile come to her eyes and mouth.

It was as if all the air suddenly drained from the universe. His mouth went dry and his heart began to pound. In a moment of sheer insanity he wondered if the reason she had been so frosty for these last several days was because she was disappointed that their lovemaking had gone no further.

As if bewitched, he stepped toward her. Slowly, slowly, he dropped to his knees beside her. Oh, God, he shouldn't do this! But he did it anyway, bending to press a kiss upon her sleeping lips.

She sighed and stirred, her eyes fluttering open. For an instant she appeared alarmed, but then she recognized him. "Silas . . ." A sleepy whisper of wonderment, not protest. Heartened, he kissed her again, just as gently.

"I'm sorry," he murmured against her mouth. "I'm sorry I hurt you. I don't want to hurt you . . ."

He forgot what he was trying to say when her mouth moved against his, kissing him back, when her hands lifted to his shoulders and held him. Oh, God, she was sweet, so sweet. Heat sizzled along his nerve endings, blood pounded in his brain as his heart hammered in his chest, and he didn't think he'd ever wanted a woman as much as he wanted this one . . .

Then, out of nowhere, a familiar voice said, "I thought this was where you were headed. Y'all better come in before the storm hits."

Ernie Hazlett was still dressed all in black, and his greasy little ponytail was still pulled straight back from his face. He was also within seconds of being a dead man, but Silas didn't bother to tell him that.

"What the hell are you doing here?" he bellowed at the man as he leapt to his feet.

Ernie held up placating hands. "Don't holler at me, man. Look, I just came by to see if you had changed your mind about letting my Aunt Gert come get her things."

"No." Silas's answer was as uncompromising as ever. Allowing his definitive response to sink in, he took the opportunity to help Dani to her feet.

"That's what I told her," Ernie said, once they were both standing, "but she insisted I ask again."

Silas tipped his head back and looked suspiciously down his nose at Ernie. He couldn't believe it was going to be this easy. "What is it you *really* want, Hazlett?"

"I told you. Aunt Gert left some of her stuff here. Her diary, she said. And a perfume bottle that Morris gave her a long, long time ago."

"Describe the diary to me. If I come across it, I'll let you know."

Ernie hesitated, chewing on his lower lip. "Nah," he said finally. "If I tell you what it looks like, you might read it."

"An old woman's diary?" Silas snorted. "Not bloody likely." He turned toward Dani and, with a hand at her back, ushered her toward the path to the house. Ernie followed close behind. "You might as well tell me what this diary looks like, Hazlett, because if I run across any little books, I'm going to open them to see what they are unless I already know."

Ernie hesitated another ten or fifteen seconds before answering. "Just promise you won't open them."

"Them?"

"She has a stack of them, I guess, from all her life long."

"Well, I promise not to open your aunt's diaries."

"Okay, then. They're in those black marbled composition books, like they used to use in school ages ago."

"I remember them. What do they say on the front?"

Ernie shrugged. "Probably just 'Diary.' She said she never put her name on them, though, in case someone found them." He gave a little grin. "I guess a circus performer could have a scandalous past. It might make fun reading—after she's gone."

Silas nodded. "If I find them, I'll give you a shout. What's your number?"

Two minutes later Ernie was driving away in a downpour, while Dani looked around at the world and wondered how a lovely day could have turned so dreary. Together she and Silas walked into the house.

"What do you think Ernie was up to?" she asked.

Ruining my sex life. But he couldn't say that to her. No way. "A new tack for getting what he wants. I'm surprised he didn't search the house instead of talking to us. After all, he found the door open, and the two of us nowhere in sight."

"Maybe that's what he did before he found us."

"Bingo." He smiled and resisted an urge to smooth her wind-tossed hair. "Good thinking, Watson."

"I'd rather be Sherlock." She moved past him and back into the atrium.

"Nobody wants to be Sherlock. He was nuts."

"He was drugged."

"Nah, those were the later books. He was just nuts."

Dani stopped in the middle of the atrium, near the statue of Chacmool, and slowly turned around while looking up at the galleries. "Okay, Morris, we know what it looks like now. A stack of composition books."

"That was my immediate thought when Ernie described them," Silas agreed, deciding not to comment on the way she was talking to Morris. "Morris always carried one of those things for scribbling in. Hell, in Beirut we had to crawl back into a bomb crater to rescue one of them because he dropped it when he was running from an incoming round. Damn near turned my hair white."

Dani looked disbelievingly at Silas's hair.

"I said *nearly*."

She gave him another one of those faint smiles that told him she was still feeling emotionally bruised, but was trying to overcome it. The woman had backbone, he decided. It was a trait he valued highly. "Do you think he was keeping a diary?" she asked him.

"I don't know. I just know he was always carrying one of those notebooks and scribbling in it. I kind of assumed he was working on a novel, or keeping track of ideas for one."

"But he could have been keeping a diary. Good heavens, Silas, do you know what his diary would be worth?"

"Well, that kind of depends on whether it's interesting or boring."

"Knowing Morris's writing, can you doubt that it's fascinating? And if it is . . ." She shrugged expressively.

He nodded. "It's not covered by the will, either. So whoever finds it . . ."

Dani nodded, her brown eyes big. "That's it, Silas. That's got to be it. But why would it be so hard to find? Why isn't it stored on a bookshelf or a filing cabinet somewhere?"

"Because he considered it intensely private? But

before we get carried away here, why would Ernie give us such an important piece of information?"

Dani bit her lower lip, reflecting. "I don't know. Maybe because he doesn't know we're on to what's going on around here, and thinks we'll really give it to him if we find it?"

Silas's brow puckered. "Do you really think he's that stupid?"

They studied one another for a long moment, then said in unison, "Yes!"

Now all they had to do was find the damn things.

14

Max Fuller called the next morning to ask how they were getting along on their books. After all the crazy relatives they had met, Dani felt she was talking to a friend when she talked to Max. Silas asked her about the possibility of a diary.

"Hell, yes," Max said. "I believe he *did* keep one. I never really thought about it, but I know he told me once that he had a driving compulsion to write everything down, and that he hated to think someone might ever read all those personal thoughts. I suggested he just burn everything as soon as he wrote it, but he said he liked to go back over old entries. It was a way, he said, to keep experience and feelings fresh. It helped his writing."

"So he probably would have hidden it?"

"Absolutely. In fact, considering how much he loathed the idea of anyone reading it, he probably squirreled it away where no one would *ever* think to look for it."

"That's it then," Silas said.

"It appears so," Dani agreed. "Would it be worth anything, Max? I mean, would this diary justify all these relatives trying to get back in the house to hunt for it?"

"I'd bet my desk on it. Morris wasn't one to hide his flaws from his friends, so it's not as if he had some icon of an image to maintain. But I'd guess he was very honest in his private thoughts—hell, that's part of what makes a good writer—and I imagine his diary could stir more of an uproar than *Peyton Place* did when it first came out. It's exactly the kind of thing a publisher might well be willing to pay very big bucks for, especially given Morris's stature as a popular novelist, and given that he probably recorded his thoughts about a great many celebrities. He moved in some exalted circles, did our Morris."

"Considering just the people he mentioned to me," Dani said, "I can say you're probably right."

"So when you find it, send it straight to me," Max said. "This could get interesting."

"We need to check with Morris's lawyer first, though."

"Why?" asked Silas. "Dani, the contents of this house will be ours at the end of six months."

"Irving can hold onto it until we get that part of it settled. I just don't want to get accused of stealing something."

Silas sighed. "Okay. You're right. We might as well play by all the rules until this is done. I just don't want to see that jerk Ernie Hazlett get the thing. God knows what he'd do with it."

"Probably just what *I* will," Max said humorously. "Auction it to the highest bidder. Keep me posted, guys."

But Dani had some objections and voiced them forcefully after they hung up. "Silas, I don't think Morris would like having his diary published. That's the whole reason he hid it. If we can find it, we should see that it's protected from publication."

"I agree." He smiled at her astonishment. "Didn't think I was going to be a pushover, huh? Truth is, if Morris wanted it hidden, then I'll do my best to keep it that way. But we have to find it, Dani, so someone else doesn't find it first."

Feeling glum, she sat on Chacmool's bowl and looked up at the gallery. "Do you really think Ernie was dumb enough to believe we'd just hand it over to him?"

"Assuming there's no identification on it, yes. If we didn't know he was up to something, would we be suspicious of his request?"

"I guess not." She shook her head. "But he should have considered the possibility we might find it and discover it's not Gert Plum's after all."

"He did. I promised not to open her diaries, remember?"

Dani cocked her head, giving him a speculative look. "Do you often make promises you don't intend to keep?"

Silas had the unsettling feeling that this conversation had just moved to a different level. "Actually, I have every intention of keeping the promise. I said I wouldn't open his *aunt's* diary." He stepped closer to her, suddenly remembering those moments under the banyan tree when he had felt as if he was hovering on the brink of discovery. Apparently she remembered, too, because she licked her lips. "I never make a promise I don't fully intend to keep, Dani. Never."

Her heart was racing like a tom-tom out of control. She now knew what this man's touch could do to her, how with a few caresses he could set her body on fire. And now she also knew that she could succumb to that passion, that once she was in its grip, common sense fled. She, who had always been sensible, could in the flash of an instant, become a creature ruled by her feelings and needs.

The whole idea scared her to death. As Silas stepped toward her, it was as if she observed herself and her life from afar with distressing clarity. All she had ever wanted was to be safe. She had spent her entire life trying to build a storm shelter for herself against the vicissitudes of life. It was why she taught English rather than writing her novel. It was why she had dated Thomas Rivett for more than ten years while there was not a single spark of passion between them. It was why she had pretended to scorn Thomas when he had taken a sudden fall for a luscious brunette with a wild streak.

Thomas had made a bid for life. She, on the other hand, had simply drawn deeper into her cocoon, only allowing herself to be tugged out a tiny bit by Morris's bequest to her.

Now there was Silas, looking at her with a wild fire in his cat-green eyes, a fire banked behind a suddenly slumberous expression. She felt as if she were being stalked.

"Silas . . . really . . . we shouldn't."

"Why not?"

"Damn it, Silas . . ."

He smiled wickedly. "Tsk. You almost never swear."

"You make me want to swear."

"I know." His smile widened.

She could hardly breathe. With each step he took toward her, there seemed to be less air in the room. Her body wanted him every bit as much as her mind wanted to flee him. Desire was a warm syrup in her veins, holding her where she was in breathless anticipation, even as her mind screamed warnings.

She was terrified of this man's control over her. Terrified that he could seduce her with nothing more than a look and the merest intimation of his touch. Horrified that once before she had turned to putty in his hands and allowed him such liberties. Appalled that she had lost herself so quickly and so easily in the raging river of passion.

The threat of losing control terrified her. The thought of being so vulnerable nearly petrified her. Thomas had never threatened her this way. No one ever had. She had no idea how to handle it, except to turn and run.

She rose from Chacmool's bowl and stepped sideways around the statue, never taking her eyes from

Silas, putting the reclining god between them. "Silas, no."

"Dani, yes." His smile was almost gentle and he took yet another step in her direction. "You want this as much as I do."

His arrogance registered even through the hazy heat of her rising desire. "You don't have a big head or anything, do you?"

"I've got something even bigger than my head."

That did it. As simply as that, something inside her snapped and laughter tumbled out of her. "Good grief, Silas, my ninth graders would come up with a line like that!"

He had the decency to look embarrassed. "It was stupid, wasn't it?"

"Grotesquely so." She giggled again, fear forgotten as Silas looked sheepish. The threat was gone. "I know you can do better than that."

"I'm out of practice."

"Not for the last twenty years, surely. You must have developed a better line since you were fourteen."

He tilted his head thoughtfully, moving another step or so in her direction. "Hmm. It's been a lo-o-ong time since I needed a line."

"Oh, come on. You're not going to tell me women just tumble into your bed without any effort on your part!" She had come darn close to doing just that, but she'd go to the stake before she'd ever admit it to him.

"Actually," he said apologetically, "I don't *let* very many women tumble into my bed. It's too dangerous these days. Besides, it's messy."

"Well, you don't know very much about me, so you should be wise and stay away."

"Actually, I know a hell of a lot about you." He stepped toward her and she stepped back. "I know you've never let a man touch you the way I touched you the other day."

Her cheeks turned cherry red and her voice

sounded stifled. "That's not true! I've had experience!"

"Really. No *truly* experienced woman would give me that crap about taking advantage of her when she'd just had an orgasm."

She couldn't believe he was saying these things to her. That he was being so blunt. That he would even *dare* to hint at such things, never mind just say them out loud so frankly. Since the floor wouldn't open up to swallow her, she took the other alternative: flight.

Turning sharply, she stumbled . . . and fell right into the fountain. When she surfaced, blowing bubbles, Silas was laughing heartily. Before she could catch her breath enough to tell him he was a disgusting, loathsome, subhuman slug, he kicked off his shoes and climbed in right beside her. An instant later she was reclining in the lukewarm water, cradled by his arm as he stretched out beside her and leaned over her.

"A water nymph," he said, with a gleam in his eye. "I've caught me a nymph."

"Silas—" Her protest was weak, and died when he placed a gentle finger over her wet lips.

"I won't hurt you, you know." His voice was rough, husky, sending a shiver down her spine. "I won't touch you in any way you don't want. You're safe with me. I'm an honorable man."

He then proceeded to prove he was utterly without scruples. His finger trailed slowly down from her lips, across the hammering pulse in her throat and up the gentle rise of her breast.

"Such a pretty breast," he murmured, running his finger slowly—oh, so slowly!—around her hardening nipple. Teasing. Taunting. Driving the breath from her body. Making her throb helplessly at her very center.

"We won't do anything you don't want," he whispered again. "Not a thing. We're just playing, Dani. Just playing a wicked and delightful game. Relax and let me make you feel good."

It was impossible to imagine feeling any better than she did right at this moment. Anticipation held her suspended between the hope and the fear that his finger would stop making its taunting little circles and touch her nipple. She wanted him to. She wanted him not to. Never in her life had she imagined it could be possible to both want and fear the same thing, or that two such opposite outcomes could seem both desirable and dreadful. Until Silas had touched her, everything in her life had been crystal clear. Now confusion reigned, and there seemed to be no good answers to anything.

She ached for more, and fought herself, not wanting to give in to the impulses that were trying to take command of her. Tension between opposing desires drew her taut until her self-control was the thinnest veneer over hungers that were as old as time.

It felt so good, the slow, teasing circling of his finger. The throbbing between her legs seemed to be draining all the strength from her, making her heavy and compliant. Little by little the resistance was seeping out of her. She wanted this. She wanted this desperately, and for once in her life she was going to take what she wanted, consequences be damned.

His finger brushed across her nipple, and sent a shaft of pleasure straight to her core. She arched toward him, pride and vulnerability and all those other worries forgotten as her body begged for more and more and more . . .

"Sweet thing," he said hoarsely. "So sweet . . ."

Her mind, succumbing to the red haze of passion, couldn't make sense of his words, but she was past caring anyway. The water lapped gently at her, so close to her body temperature that only the slight tickle of its surface tension told her it was there. It buoyed her, making her feel as if she floated in a place out of time and space. His arm steadied her, keeping her from falling, and the light brush of his finger back and forth over her nipple enthralled her.

When he reached for the button of her blouse, she never would have thought to tell him no. Instead she lay in his embrace with delightful anticipation of mysteries yet to come. His lips feathered hers, warm and dry, feeling so good. She arched her neck and begged for a deeper kiss, and quivered with delight when his tongue found hers. Then the last button gave way on her blouse and she felt his warm hand on the soft skin of her midriff.

"You feel like silk," he whispered roughly against her mouth. "Softer than satin . . ."

The world turned suddenly topsy-turvy as he lifted her and settled her on his lap, straddling him. She blinked in astonishment at the swift change, then met the heat of his bright green eyes and felt everything inside her soften and melt. He was sitting against the rim of the fountain pool with his legs stretched out straight. The cascading water from the higher levels was behind her, a soft, seductive rush of sound. The air chilled her wet back, but she forgot that when Silas reached up, and with a quick twist released her bra.

Her breasts spilled free, damp, rosy and puckered with both the chill and passion. Dani watched in helpless fascination as Silas cupped her with hands that felt hot by contrast.

"You don't mind, do you?" he whispered.

She couldn't have made a sound nor could she even bring herself to shake her head. Helplessly in thrall, she could only stare at the wonder of a man's powerful, tanned hands on the soft whiteness of her breasts, could only draw a sharp breath as he gently squeezed her.

Fresh rivers of passion surged through her, and her hips began a gentle, helpless rocking, trying to find the answer to the ache that was blossoming ever larger at her center.

"That's it," he encouraged her in a ragged whisper. "Give in to it. Enjoy it . . ."

Giving in was all she could do at this point. There was no way now she could halt the internal firestorm. But she felt safe, so wonderfully safe. Even in these intimate moments his hands were gentle, his eyes were tender . . . he wrapped her in his surety and strength and carried her away with him.

His hands on her back urged her forward, then his hot mouth closed on her breast. A cry escaped her as he sucked strongly on her, sending pulses of pleasure racing through her. Not in her wildest imaginings had she thought such a touch could make her feel this way. Another cry escaped her, and she pressed her hips more strongly to him, needing deeper, harder touches to satisfy the building ache.

But he wanted to torment her. His gift to her would not be given so swiftly and easily this time. He wanted to draw out each and every moment until she was utterly lost in the building excitement.

Nor was she going to arrive at the pinnacle alone this time.

His own body was throbbing in time to the gentle rocking of her hips. No way was he going to let her make this journey alone. There was a limit to gallantry and gentlemanliness, and this was it. He needed to be inside this woman as desperately as he needed to breathe.

He sucked strongly on her breast, taking as much pleasure in her enjoyment as he would soon take in his own. His hands, on her hips, steadied her as she rocked against him, tightened as he heard a groan rise from deep within her. She was incredible, giving herself to him with complete abandon.

The demands of his own body were building, the throbbing of his loins deep and insistent. He had to get them out of the fountain if he was ever to have what he needed. Holding her with his hands around her waist, he gathered his legs beneath him and lifted them both from the water.

The air-conditioned air felt like ice against his wet

skin, and chilled his wet clothes almost immediately. He hardly noticed, nor did Dani seem to as he set her on her feet on the tile floor, and steadied her.

They needed to strip off these clothes, he realized dimly. Water was puddling rapidly around their feet, making the tile treacherous. Nor did he want to make love to her for the first time on a hard floor.

Make love. Why the hell was he doing this? The woman was half crazy—she talked to Morris, after all—and not even remotely his type. She was too small, too smart, too sharp-tongued, and too firmly rooted in a state half a continent away. He was crazy . . . crazy . . . crazy . . .

And he kept right on peeling her soaked shirt off. When he reached for her shorts, he heard her quickly indrawn breath. Hesitating, he looked straight into her hazy brown eyes, waiting. If she had changed her mind, she'd better tell him now.

She bit her lip, closed her eyes, held her breath . . . then whispered, "Don't stop. Oh, please . . . don't stop . . . no matter what . . ."

No matter if the cops hammered on the door, or a relative walked in . . . Damn, he had to get her upstairs before Dawn Moonglow arrived to report another vision, or Lester Carmichael decided to wander in, or Pepita Mayo . . . or Ina Jasper . . . or . . . With a tug he yanked Dani's wet shorts down to her ankles. The movement brought his eyes level with the dark curls at the juncture of her thighs, and his entire body responded with a thrill that reached every nerve ending.

He closed his eyes, steadying himself a moment before straightening. He held Dani's shoulders while she stepped out of her shorts, bent again to help her out of her sandals, all the while refusing to look at her because if he looked at her naked body he was going to lose it right here and now on the puddle-covered tiles.

With eyes closed, he stripped off his own clothes, flinging them away without a thought to where they landed. Then, nude at last, he bent and scooped Dani up into his arms.

She had begun to shiver in the chilly air, and he cuddled her as close as he could, trying to warm her as he loped up the stairs with her in his arms. When she looped her arms trustingly around his neck, he felt as if he'd just won the Pulitzer prize. He tucked her beneath the blankets on his bed and started to slip in beside her, when he remembered himself.

Protection. He had to find protection. Safe sex wasn't just an expression with him, it was a credo. No way would it be fair to either of them to proceed without a condom.

He must have one somewhere. While Dani watched with a sleepy but perplexed look on her face, he tore his room apart, searching for it. Damn it, why hadn't he gone out the other day and bought a box, the way he had been tempted to after their first close encounter? No, he'd been sure he had some. Jerk. It appeared he didn't have any at all.

But he did. He found them at the back of the bottom dresser drawer along with the spare clip for his Browning. A huge sigh of relief escaped him.

"Silas?"

He turned. She was watching him wide-eyed from the bed, no longer looking passion-drunk. Instead she looked worried, and clutched the covers to her throat.

"It's okay," he told her, waggling the condoms at her. "I wasn't going to take a chance with you."

The corners of her mouth curved upward, into a soft, faint smile, telling him it was okay. He could have jumped for joy. Tossing the packet on the bedside table, he slipped beneath the covers beside her.

"It's okay," he said again.

"Yes."

"Come here, Dani. Come closer."

After an almost imperceptible hesitation, she slid closer. His passion was rising again, a steady drumbeat in his blood, driving him to take her, but something—he never knew what—made him pause.

Then he said, very quietly, "Are you sure? Are you very, very sure?"

She nodded, her wide eyes fixed on his. "I'm sure," she said on a broken breath. "But Silas, I'm not very experienced . . ."

"I know." He touched her lips with a gentle fingertip. "I know." She was as close to a virgin as it was possible to be these days. He'd known it from her reactions to him. "Tell me about it, Dani."

"I . . . um . . . when I was in college I had sex with my boyfriend, a couple of times. I hated it, and I never wanted to do it again. Thomas—" She cleared her throat and tried again. "Thomas was never . . . interested and I was grateful for that. We dated for over ten years . . . Silas, I'm awful at this!"

"What about you? Were you ever interested?"

"Not until . . . you."

The breathless admission humbled him, and filled him with an amazing tenderness. Drawing her close, so that they were touching head to toe, he gave her a gentle kiss. "You're safe with me," he said. "I swear it."

A kind of relief trickled through Dani, now that she'd admitted what she felt was her deepest, darkest secret and he hadn't pulled away. She had always thought that it must be something wrong with her that she hadn't enjoyed sex her first few times. Painful and messy were the words that came to mind to describe it, and although she was scared that this time would be no better, it was still a relief not to be rejected as a failure. After all, sex was supposed to come naturally, wasn't it?

After his almost absurd hurry earlier, Silas now seemed to have all the time in the world. Dani felt herself sinking into the warmth of his body, enjoying the way his skin felt against hers. Enjoying the hair-roughened texture of his legs as they tangled with hers. A position that should have felt embarrassingly intimate simply felt right—as right as anything she had ever known.

His hand smoothed over her back and hip gently, as if he were stroking a kitten. "Promise me one thing," he rumbled in her ear.

"What's that?"

"That if you see Morris you won't scream in my ear."

She might have taken offense, but instead some little devil promptly took charge of her tongue. "Oh. Are you afraid you might wilt?" She couldn't believe she had said that, but the words were out before she could catch them.

He lifted his head sharply, glaring at her. "You little vixen," he growled. "I was worried about my *eardrums!*"

The next thing she knew, he was tickling her in the ribs, causing her to squeal with laughter and roll away. He caught her, though, and gently brought her back into his embrace. "That kind of remark deserves appropriate punishment."

"What's appropriate about punishment?" The real miracle, she thought, was that their banter had driven away her awkwardness.

"That depends on the punishment, doesn't it?" He wiggled his eyebrows, and drew another laugh from her.

As they looked at one another, smiling, the atmosphere in the room began to change. Dani felt her breath accelerating, and her lips parted as she stared at Silas. His lips parted, too, and his eyes dilated, sending an unmistakable signal.

"Punishment," he whispered. "I could nibble your earlobe until you beg for mercy."

She couldn't have spoken to save her life, not with her breath locked in her throat in the agony of anticipation. A nod was all she could manage.

His eyes darkened even more. "I could bite your neck . . ."

Her throat opened enough to allow her to draw a deep, ragged breath. Every nerve inside her was pulsing in time to her womb as Silas at last bent and pressed his hot, wet mouth to the hollow of her throat. In that instant everything inside her let go, relinquishing her last resistance. She wanted this. She wanted every bit of this enough to ignore her fears of disappointment. Silas wasn't that long-ago, nearly forgotten lover. Silas was older, more experienced, more patient. She *had* to believe that there was nothing wrong with her. Refuse, for now at least, to admit the possibility that she might be flawed.

Silas felt the tension leave her, and with it he let his own go, giving himself up to the sheer joy of making love. In his youth he had been driven by a need for physical satisfaction, but now he was older and wiser. Now, for him, the closeness and sharing were far more important than the actual gratification. Consequently, he savored each and every step of the journey.

And Dani made it a wonderful journey to savor. Whatever she believed of herself, she was incredibly responsive to his slightest touch. Her skin quivered beneath each caress, and as he grew bolder she made gasping little moans and began to writhe. The blossoming of her passion fueled his until at last he couldn't bear another moment of anticipation.

Rolling onto his back, he tugged her over him so that she straddled him. Her eyes flew open, growing huge as she felt him between her legs.

"It's okay," he reassured her, his voice husky. "It's okay . . . take me . . . take me as slow or as fast . . . as you . . . want."

Reaching down, he guided himself to her entrance. Then, as he felt his shaft begin to sink into her moist depths, he touched the little knot of nerves that would bring her the greatest pleasure.

The touch electrified her. She gasped, arching her back and cried out. It was too much, so much it was painful, so much it was unbearable. So much it was exquisite. She had to stop, but couldn't bear to stop, needing to be filled with him, needing his maddening touch to go on and on. Needing the pleasure-pain he was giving her with every fiber of her being.

He crooned soft words to her, soothing her even as he drove her to the brink of madness. Little by little she settled on him, her slowness and tightness nearly crazing him. It was almost impossible to keep from thrusting himself deep into her, almost impossible to battle down a need that was engraved on his very cells. With gritted teeth, he held himself still, allowing her to take her time and come to him in a way that would not harm her.

Dani's world had become a musk-scented place of pleasure that bordered on agony, of needs that would not be denied. The drumbeat in her blood deafened her to anything at all beyond Silas and his gift. And when at last she encompassed him fully, she experienced a thrill of excitement unlike any she had ever known.

In an instant she became both conqueror and conquered, victor and vanquished. In an instant they became one.

She never clearly remembered what happened then. Only that a rhythm built, carrying her ever onward in search of a place she feared she would never find. His hands on her hips, steadying her, guiding her, his growls of satisfaction, her own moans of delight . . . the surprising sensation when he reached up and pinched her swollen nipples, sending a heightened shaft of excitement through her.

The final moments when everything was out of her control, when there was nothing to do except let the miracle happen.

It felt as if she came apart one nerve ending at a time, in a cataclysm so intense it defied description. An instant later he joined her.

* * *

Dani lay drowsily on Silas's damp chest, feeling replete and almost too happy to be believed. Silas's hands stroked her back soothingly, bringing her down gently from the heights she had reached.

Wrapped in the warm glow of having been well-loved, Dani could have stayed there forever. The feeling of skin on skin was surely the most exquisite thing she had ever felt. And what a relief to be free of all the hesitancy and fear that had been plaguing her since the first time he had touched her. She was free in a way she had never been free before, and she exulted in it.

"That was beautiful," Silas said softly. "*You* were beautiful."

The praise warmed her, making her heart swell. She could love this man, she thought hazily. It wouldn't be hard at all . . .

That was when she felt the first tendril of fear, along with the dawning realization that she had never been so vulnerable in her life. A little shiver of dread began at the back of her mind, but she tried to suppress it. Right now, nothing on earth seemed to matter except that Silas was holding her . . .

But the fear wouldn't entirely go away. She wanted these moments, wanted them desperately, but was afraid of the inevitable consequence. She sighed, knowing this couldn't go on forever. Nothing this good could.

Then her stomach growled. Loudly. She blushed, embarrassed. "I guess I need to eat something."

"How about me?"

"Silas!" Her cheeks flamed bright red, and when she saw him laughing she grew annoyed. "Shame on you. That's the kind of remark I would expect from a thirteen-year-old!"

"Aw, come on, teach! Lighten up."

"Don't you tell me to lighten up!" Leaping up from the bed, she grabbed the afghan that lay across the back of a chair, and threw it around herself. Where did he get off telling her to lighten up?

Especially when he was acting juvenile! "And don't you call me teach!"

"What the hell is it with you? You're always scolding me and telling me to behave as if I were in one of your classes! Hell! If I *had* been in one of your classes when I was a kid I wouldn't have let you get away with talking to me like this!"

"Do you think it surprises me that you were incorrigible?"

"Incorrigible!" He rose to his feet and stood glaring at her in all his nude magnificence. "I was *never* incorrigible. But then I never had an uptight, self-righteous prude like you!"

Dani gasped, unable to find breath on which to speak. Finally, through quivering lips, she was able to say, "Intimacy with you was ill-considered."

"Ill-considered! What a namby-pamby, pallid way to say what you really mean. Come on, lady, be human! Say what you really think."

"That you are an ill-mannered, uncouth, arrogant slug? Is that what you want to hear?"

Silas bared his teeth. "Is that the best you can do?"

Furious, she clutched the afghan to her breast with one hand and with a dramatically outflung arm used the other to point to the door. "Get out of here. Get out of my room *now!*"

Silas obliged. Head high, he stalked to the door. When he slammed it behind him, it rattled every window in the house.

~~~~~

15

Silas stalked down the gallery toward his room—
then abruptly realized that he *had* been in his room.
Dani had thrown him out of his own room! The
realization made him feel stupid, which only made
him angrier. He hated to feel stupid.

Ill-considered. Ill-mannered. God! The woman
talked like a walking dictionary! Why couldn't she
come down out of her ivory tower and talk like a
normal person. Why couldn't she just say this had
been a mistake.

And it had been a mistake. A big mistake. Something told him he was going to regret this one for a
long, long time. Damn, hadn't he learned his lesson
about tangling with women? Celibacy was better
than a wrestling match with an angry virago!

Glancing up, he saw Morris standing on the other
side of the gallery. "Morris, you son of a bitch!" he
shouted. "What the hell is the matter with you,
leaving us with this damn mess and all these stupid
relatives of yours? And now you come back and
won't even tell us what to do about it? *Get lost!*"

Turning, he reentered his room and slammed the
door. Dani was still standing where he had left her,
the afghan held around her. She looked shell-

shocked, pale and shivering, her eyes as huge as saucers.

"This is *my* room," he growled at her. "Get the hell to your own room. And on the way, tell Morris to get lost! He's standing out there on the gallery again! Cripes. I can't think of anything more useless than a ghost!"

Then two things struck him at once: that he had actually seen Morris's ghost, and that Dani was standing there frozen as if something truly horrifying had happened. He was instantly torn by competing desires . . . on the one hand he wanted to run out and see if Morris was still there. On the other, he wanted to find out what was wrong with Dani.

Dani was the more pressing issue, he decided. Morris could go hang.

"Dani?" He approached her cautiously, not wanting to frighten her further. "Dani, what's wrong?"

She turned her head stiffly and looked at him. "I just saw a ghost."

He stifled an exasperated sigh. "You've been seeing a ghost ever since I got here."

"But it wasn't Morris."

"Of course not. He's out on the gallery. I don't think that even a ghost can be in two places at once."

"Silas, please! I saw a woman standing right here! A young woman. And . . . and she looked just like me!"

Dani was shivering so hard now that her teeth chattered. Without a word, Silas crossed to his bureau and yanked out a pair of gray sweatpants with a drawstring waist, and a short-sleeve gray sweatshirt. "Here," he said, tossing them to her. "Put these on before you freeze to death."

When she didn't move, he smothered another sigh and went to do the job himself. It was just like dressing a porcelain doll, he thought. Move the arms, move the legs . . .

Reaching for a pair of jogging shorts, he shoved

his legs into them. Something about being naked
made a guy feel too damn vulnerable. The shorts
weren't any protection, not really, but they made
him feel better.

He took Dani gently by her upper arms and
waited until she turned her frightened brown eyes up
to him. "Dani," he said. "I've seen her, too."

She blinked, and her jaw dropped. "You've seen
the ghost?"

He nodded. "That's why I thought you were
creeping up on me, remember? When I yelled at you
for hovering in my office?"

She nodded slowly.

"It wasn't until the night we shared a room that I
realized it wasn't you at all. She was standing over
my bed when I woke up, but you were sound asleep
in your bed."

Her eyes couldn't have gotten any bigger. "Why
didn't you *say* something?"

He shrugged almost sheepishly. "I didn't want to
believe it was real. Sounds stupid, doesn't it? But I
pushed it right out of my mind, more than once."

Silas looked so embarrassed that Dani took pity
on him. "Just human nature," she assured him.
"I've done it, too, from time to time."

He slipped his arms around her, and to his relief
she leaned willingly against him. Their spat of the
moments past appeared to be forgotten. "We've got
to do something about this."

"What can we do about ghosts? I don't think
there's a yellow pages listing for ghost extermina-
tors."

"We don't need to exterminate them." Her hair
felt soft and silky beneath his chin, and her curves
felt so nice pressed to him. Why couldn't the world
just leave them alone? What they needed to do right
now was tumble back into that bed and reaffirm the
joy they had taken in each other. Instead they had
quarreled and then been invaded by two ghosts.

Two! "Maybe we can get Roxy Resnick to come up here and check things out. Maybe she could find out what's going on."

Dani tilted her head up and looked at him. "Are you suggesting a séance?"

His head lifted sharply. "Séance?" The mere sound of the word put his hackles up. "Of course not! I won't have any truck with that kind of stuff. Phony ectoplasm, tipping tables—all a bunch of hogwash designed to scam the gullible. I am *not* gullible."

Dani leaned back against his arms. "Did I say you were? But just what do you expect Roxy Resnick to do? Walk through the house and give us a thirty-page report? Mediums hold *séances*. It's what they do."

He shifted uneasily, unhappy with all the images his brain was conjuring. "Dawn said her mother is a channeler. Trance channelers are different."

"It's just a new name for the same old thing, Silas. Whether she calls herself a medium or a channeler, she goes into a trance and spirits speak through her."

He could have groaned. "Do you believe in that crap? That spirits speak through them?"

"Who, me? Not until I started seeing ghosts."

Silas eyed her grimly. "Let's think about this for a while before we take any action."

"It wasn't *my* idea. I can wait as long as you want."

He'd have preferred a more supportive answer. Dani, he guessed, wasn't any happier about calling on Roxy Resnick than he was. But what else were they supposed to do?

"So you saw Morris?" Dani asked him.

"On the gallery, plain as day. Enough to make me wonder if he really is dead, or if they dumped somebody else's ashes in the gulf."

"He's dead, Silas." Dani felt again a wave of sorrow over Morris's absence. "I wish he wasn't, but he is."

"Well, I yelled at him."

"Yelled at him?" Dani's eyes widened again. "You didn't!"

"I did. I was just so damn mad. Well, we had that quarrel, and then I realized you'd thrown me out of my own room, and I was stomping back here to give you a piece of my mind, and there he was." Silas shook his head. "It made me furious. How could he do this to us? How could he give us this place to write our books, then leave us at the mercy of all these wacko relatives of his?"

"I don't think that part was deliberate."

"Oh, no? Think about it, Dani. Think about Morris's warped sense of humor. He sure as hell could have conceived of idiocy like this."

"Too true," she admitted and sighed.

"So I yelled at him for handing us this mess, then coming back to stand around and not even tell us what to do about it. You'd think he could at least tell us where the damn diary is!"

"You would, wouldn't you. Especially since he warned us about those guys on the beach that night."

"It just doesn't add up, Dani."

She stepped out of his embrace, not really wanting to, but needing to move and work off some of the nervous tension that was building up in her. His sweat suit was far too big for her, and only the gathered cuffs on the pants kept her from tripping over it. It was warm and snuggly, though, and a corner of her mind wished she could keep it.

"It seems rather odd," she said after a moment, "that we both saw one of them at the same time . . . and that this time you saw Morris and I saw the woman."

"Yeah, it was a switch. You're right about the time thing, though. That hasn't happened before."

"At least not as far as we know." Reaching up, she combed her fingers through her hair. "Say it hasn't happened before. Why should it change now? Why should we suddenly see the other one's ghost—"

"Hey, it's not *my* ghost."

He was grinning, but she scowled at him for the interruption anyway. Impatiently, she shook her head. "Silas, this is important. There must be a reason the apparitions would switch like this."

"There're a lot of assumptions inherent in that statement, Dani." He wasn't grinning now, but was deadly serious. "For instance, that the ghosts are conscious."

"Instead of vibrational imprints on the house, you mean?" A shiver rippled through her. "The truth is, since Morris warned me about the men coming across the beach, I haven't been able to believe anything except that Morris *is* conscious. That this really *is* Morris. The woman I don't know about."

Silas nodded in grim agreement. "The woman really does look like you, though. It's incredible."

More ice water seemed to run down Dani's spine. "I was hoping you'd say it was my imagination."

"It wasn't. I saw her, too, and always thought it was you. Except that you never dress that way."

"What way?"

"All in white."

Another shiver trickled along Dani's nerves. It was extremely unnerving to have a ghostly duplicate. As for wearing all white—she wouldn't even dream of it. White made her look pasty.

Just then, the phone rang, echoed through the house by an assortment of other phones, some chirping, some beeping, some buzzing. Silas eyed the instrument on the bedside table warily. "It can't be good news."

"Why not? Maybe you just won the lottery."

"I didn't buy a ticket." He snatched for the receiver and lifted it to his ear with patent reluctance. "Yeah?"

Dani watched with increasing trepidation as Silas's face grew grimmer and grimmer. When he finally hung up, she wished she didn't have to hear what he was about to say.

"Get dressed. We've got to get out to my boat-yard."

"Why?"

"Somebody tried to burn the place down."

"Are you sure you want me to go with you?" Dani asked as they were pulling out of the driveway thirty minutes later.

"Why not? I don't want to leave you here alone."

"But . . . should we leave the house unoccupied? What if somebody breaks in?"

"I don't give a flying crap if anyone does," Silas said through clenched teeth. He looked just about ready to chew nails. His grip was so tight that Dani wouldn't have been surprised if he left permanent fingerprints in the steering wheel.

"But Morris's diary—"

"Morris should have thought of that before he kicked off! Leaving us with this mess—I swear, Dani, if he weren't already dead, I'd shake the living daylights out of him. At this point I don't give a damn what happens to that diary! If some relative finds it and publishes it, it'll be no less than Morris deserves!"

She was almost inclined to agree with him, although she wasn't quite as angry with Morris as he appeared to be. Of course, he had his boatyard to think about, too. Why would somebody have tried to burn it down? "Was the fire bad?"

"Dale says they caught it before it did much more than destroy the paint locker. It pays to have a night watchman."

"Could it have been an accident? I mean . . . paints are flammable, aren't they?"

"Yup. Except that Dale says the arson investigator says it was deliberately set . . . on the outside of the building."

"Why would anyone want to do that?"

He turned his head and looked at her. "Thrills and chills. Or insurance money."

"But you . . ." She trailed off.

"Exactly. I'm going to be a prime suspect."

Dani didn't like the sound of that at all. "But you were at our place all night."

"Can you prove it? Did you spend the night with me?"

Her cheeks pinkened. "I guess not."

He shook his head. "I've got my business heavily insured, largely because people leave their boats with me, and boats are expensive. So are all the tools and supplies I have for doing repairs. When something like this happens and there's a lot of insurance, the business owner is always the first suspect."

"Well, they can't believe you did it. After all, you have a night watchman. Why would you pay someone to keep watch on the place the night you wanted to burn it down?"

Silas flashed her a quick smile. "Makes sense to me. Let's hope it makes sense to the investigators."

When they pulled up in front of the boatyard offices, Dale was waiting for them. At the moment he was looking singularly unhappy.

"The damage is minimal, Si," he said quickly, giving Dani only a quick nod of recognition. "We could replace all the stuff that was lost for a couple of thousand, and a new paint locker . . . hell, we could knock one together in a day, maybe a day and a half. No big deal. Problem is . . ."

"Problem is it's arson," Silas said.

"The arson investigator and the insurance company want to nail somebody on this."

"Yeah, I'd like to nail somebody myself. I don't like the idea that the jerk who did this might try it again."

They walked through the boatyard to the paint locker. The smell of burned paints, oils, and wood lingered heavily, and a layer of soot had settled over everything. A few firemen wearing protective overalls wandered around with a kind of purposeful aimlessness. Boatyard employees stopped to talk briefly with Silas, all of them expressing perplexity as to why anyone would want to do such a thing.

"Why the locker?" one of them asked. "I mean, it's almost in the middle of the compound. It'd be easier to torch something near the fence."

Silas nodded, giving Dani a look as if to say, there's another reason they'll be suspicious of me.

The fire department's arson inspector was poking around in the blackened skeleton of the building that had been the boatyard's paint locker. Dani had imagined a small storage cabinet, or even a tiny shed, not something of quite this size. "You must have had a lot of paint stored here," she commented—inanely, she thought as soon as the words were out.

"Yeah," Silas said. "All kinds of marine varnishes, paints, strippers, thinners—" He broke off and shook his head. "More than a couple of thousands of dollars worth of stuff." He glanced at Dani. "I didn't want any jobs to get delayed because we didn't have the right materials on hand, so we had pretty much everything we might need."

She nodded and wondered how the fire department had ever managed to put the blaze out with that kind of fuel. Probably most every marine paint was oil-based.

"It was some fire," Dale remarked. "Ted called me right after he called the fire department, and I got here just after them. You shoulda seen it. Flames must have been shooting thirty feet in the air. It's a wonder the whole damn place didn't burn to the ground."

"Yes, it is, isn't it?" said a new voice. All three of them turned to find a man wearing a three-piece suit and holding a clipboard had come up behind them. "I'm Avery Wittles, the insurance adjuster. You must be Mr. Northrop?"

"Yes."

"Well, it is indeed a wonder that the entire place

didn't burn to the ground." He peered at Silas over the tops of his glasses. "You carry a rather large amount of insurance on this property."

Dani felt herself bristle at the implication, but Silas seemed to take it in stride. "Of course I do. If something happened, I'd want to be able to reopen the business."

"Hmm." Wittles studied his clipboard. "You'd receive a rather large sum of cash to compensate for interrupted cash flow, though, wouldn't you?"

"The idea is not to have to file bankruptcy while I rebuild," Silas answered levelly. "I won't need any money to get through this, though. I'm sure we can restock the paint locker pretty quickly. No more than a few days for most of it."

"I see. And where were you when all this happened?"

Silas explained, but that only seemed to make the adjuster more suspicious. "You're thinking about changing careers?" he demanded.

Silas shook his head. "No. I already have a writing career. I'm just working on a novel. It's sort of a vacation."

"It sounds to me as if you can't do both at once."

The muscle in Silas's cheek worked visibly. "If I can't, it'll be the writing I give up, not my boatyard."

Wittles nodded and scribbled something on his clipboard. Dani suddenly realized that her hands were clenched so tightly that her nails were digging into her palms. How she wanted to sock that adjuster! Every word out of his mouth was an implied insult.

Wittles looked up at Silas. "Is there anyone who can testify as to your whereabouts last night?"

Silas opened his mouth, but before a sound could emerge, Dani stepped in front of him. "He was with me, Mr. Wittles. All night. And all day yesterday, too, for that matter." Her cheeks burned with embarrassment. Never in a million years would she

have imagined herself declaring to the world at large
that she was a scarlet woman . . . and certainly not
when she had to lie to do so.

"Dani . . ." Silas's tone was admonishing, but she
ignored him. Nothing he said would be believed
anyway, not when she stood there, red-cheeked,
insisting that he had been with her.

Wittles looked positively disappointed, but only
for an instant before he regained his balance and
turned his baleful gaze on Dani. "Who are you?"

Silas had had enough. He stepped around Dani,
inserting himself between her and Wittles. The
space between them was now only inches, and he
had to look down at the adjuster. "I don't like your
tone of voice, Wittles. I don't like your insinuations.
Hell, I don't like the color of your tie or the way you
comb your hair! I'll be damned if I'm going to let
you give this woman a hard time. Someone tried to
burn my business down last night. Why don't you
figure out who it really was?"

"Mr. Northrop—"

Silas waved him to silence. "In the meantime, I'll
just rebuild on my own and then get me a lawyer to
sue the hell out of you and your company." Turning,
he tucked Dani's arm through his and marched her
away.

"Are you sure that was wise?" Dani asked.

"I don't really give a damn. I can repair the
damage without any help from the insurance."

"What's the point of having insurance if they
don't pay for the things they're supposed to be
covering?"

"I've often wondered about that. Don't worry
about it, Dani. They'll pay. One way or another,
they'll pay."

But of course, nothing was as simple as that. The
arson investigator from the fire department couldn't
be brushed off because he was investigating a criminal act. On the other hand, he was a whole lot more
polite about it than Wittles. At no point did he

insinuate that Silas was behind the fire, even though it was clear he hadn't dismissed the possibility.

Then Silas put his head together with Dale, ordering the repair and replenishment of the paint locker, and deciding to hire additional security guards from a local firm. One night watchman, they concluded, apparently wasn't enough protection. At least not right now.

It was well past dark when Silas and Dani at last headed back to Morris's villa. Silas was glummer than Dani had ever seen him—not that she'd known him that long, she reminded herself—and she wished she could figure out how to cheer him up. Everything that occurred to her, however, sounded like a silly Pollyanna-ism in the face of the threat to his business. The best she could offer was "It probably won't happen again, Silas. It was probably a couple of kids with a stupid idea about how to have fun."

"Yeah. Probably." He continued to glare down the road as if he might find a solution somewhere in the tunnel of light cast by his headlamps. "Where do you come off lying to them about being with me last night?"

"I didn't like the way that man was talking to you." Once again her cheeks heated as she remembered her boldness.

"It was a lie, Dani. You don't want to commit perjury."

"No, I guess I don't, but they didn't ask me to swear to anything, and anyway, who's going to tell them any different? Morris?"

That drew a half smile from him. "Well, if they ask you again, especially if they ask you to swear to it, tell them the truth, huh? I appreciate your wanting to protect me, but the simple fact is, you *don't* know where I was last night."

She blushed again and was grateful for the dark. "Actually, I do know."

"How could you? You were asleep."

"I woke up and heard something so I came to get you. Only what I heard was you. You were working on your book."

"Why didn't you say anything?"

"Because you, um . . . you weren't . . ."

"Dressed?"

"That was it."

This time he actually guffawed. "Naked as a jaybird, that's what I was. It wouldn't scare you off now, though, would it? Not after this morning."

She pressed her hot cheek to the cool window beside her. "I don't know," she said in a smothered voice. "That was . . . well . . . I don't really know you that well . . ."

"Ha." The syllable was sharp, and very much to the point. "You had your hands all over me this morning, sweetheart. The blushing maiden bit isn't going to make it."

"Silas!"

"Oh, relax, Dani. Enjoy it! You're a fallen woman, m'dear. Hell, you just announced it to half the known universe!"

"I knew it was mistake!"

"A mistake. Now, you know, I like that a whole lot better. I'd much rather be a mistake than be 'ill-considered.' The latter sounds so—oh, I don't know. Like a disease, I guess. I don't consider myself to be a disease. A mistake, yes. I've been a mistake any number of times in my life, but never, ever, have I been *ill-considered*."

It would have been easy to think he was angry, except that Dani could see that he was enjoying himself hugely. Part of her was glad he had, for the moment at least, put aside the fire. The rest of her was goaded by his teasing.

"Damn it, Silas, don't mock my feelings."

"I wouldn't, if I thought they were your real feelings. The truth of the matter is, we had a great time this morning, you enjoyed every minute of it as much as I did, and the only problem now is that your puritanical background is giving a few twitches to your conscience. Instead of thinking about how *you* feel about what we did, you're wondering what everyone back in Idaho would think."

"Ohio," she said automatically.

"Ohio, Idaho, Nebraska, or Montana, the point is the same. They *don't* know and there's no reason they should ever know—unless, of course, you're planning to make another bald announcement to anyone who cares to listen."

"The point is *I* know."

"Exactly. So the only opinion that matters is your own. Dust off your brain, teach, and consider whether you're measuring your conduct by your own standard, or by some mythical idea of what's proper for a schoolteacher. I'm not planning to tell the school board. Are you?"

She didn't answer. Instead, twisting her fingers together she looked away, allowing her gaze to follow the shadows of trees as they drove through the night. Was he right?

Thinking back over the person she had been before she climbed into her car to drive to Florida, she saw a pinched, colorless woman with little vitality and personality. When she thought of herself now, she saw a riot of colors. A rainbow.

If nothing else, the change in her self-perception had been beneficial.

But what about Silas's accusation that she was letting the anticipated opinions of others color her experience of their lovemaking? Was she really that concerned about the censure of people she hardly knew? Because certainly her friends wouldn't condemn her. But what about the school board? Was she concerned about them?

No. The answer was unequivocal, leaving not a doubt in her mind. So, if she wasn't afraid of censure, then what *was* she afraid of? Because there wasn't a doubt in her mind that she had been acting out of fear this morning when she had gotten so angry at Silas. He had hit the nail right on the head with that one.

But of course, once she faced up to the fact that she was afraid, she could see the answer that was staring her right in the face: she was afraid of being vulnerable. Afraid of being hurt. Afraid of not being totally in control. Picking a fight had been an easy way to restore the distance between them and raise her emotional guard.

And it was *so* easy to pick a fight with Silas.

She looked at Silas, wondering if she should confide in him. But wouldn't that make her even more vulnerable? Was she prepared to trust him that much? Could she trust *anyone* that much?

She shifted in her seat and returned her attention to the garish neon display that lined the highway here. Maybe her inability to trust was the root of a great many of her problems. Maybe she had endured her tepid relationship with Thomas for so many years simply because she hadn't needed to commit anything important to it. He certainly hadn't asked for anything—such as her heart—that would have required her to trust him.

He hadn't even wanted a sexual relationship with her, which had left her feeling . . . bruised? Inadequate? At the time she had told herself that she was relieved not to be troubled with those repugnant matters, but the bitter truth was Thomas's indifference had left her scarred with the belief that there was something intrinsically wrong with her.

Then this morning with Silas . . . well, it had been fabulous. For the first time in her life she believed that sex was quite wonderful. But that had scared her because she knew she wasn't the kind of woman a man truly wanted. Thomas has proved that adequately. Silas, she thought deep inside, had merely been taking advantage of her availability, which was something men were wont to do, she had heard. Now that they had been intimate, he would surely lose his interest and go hunting elsewhere. After all, there was nothing about Danika Hilliard that would hold a man like Silas.

So, she was frightened because he had the ability to hurt her by rejecting her.

And she was frightened because he was so earthy and she was not. She could only disappoint him, and in doing so would wound herself afresh, proving once again that she was not an adequate lover.

And she was frightened because he made her feel out of control. Because something about him made her act in ways that weren't normal for her. Because he made her want him enough to do something abysmally stupid—such as lie to an arson investigator.

With a start, she realized they were pulling up in front of Morris's house. The outside lights were on, having come on at dusk as usual. Inside, the atrium would be full of light and the soothing gurgle of the fountain. Surrounding that one oasis, however, would be all those dark, deserted rooms.

"I don't want to go in there," she blurted as Silas turned off the ignition.

"I don't blame you. As roommates, ghosts leave something to be desired."

Neither of them moved to get out of the Jeep; they just sat staring at the house. Presently, Dani spoke. "Do you suppose the woman has something to do with Morris?"

"It wouldn't surprise me. Morris never lacked for women in his life."

"All his wives are still living though, right?"

"That's my understanding."

"Mm." Still she didn't move, and was relieved when Silas didn't either. "The more I hear about Morris from other sources, the more curious I get about him."

"What do you mean?"

"Well, he was such a mix. Everyone seems to have a different take on him. Getting all these glimpses from different angles has made me start wondering why I ever thought I knew him. I mean . . . have you ever wondered why a war correspondent would devote himself to writing family sagas? Doesn't that seem like an odd combination?"

"Morris was an odd combination," Silas shrugged. "If you expect him to add up, you can forget it. I learned a long time ago that when it came to Morris Feldman, two and two did not make four. If there was any way he could swing it, he'd make them add up to five. Or seven-and-a-half. Sometimes I think he deliberately refused to fit into anyone's mold. At various times I thought he was a true Renaissance man, and at others I concluded he was just a pigheaded nonconformist. Take your pick."

Dani would have chuckled except that her insides were still in knots over everything that had happened that day. "I wonder if it's ever going to get peaceful around here."

"Finding the diary would probably help a whole hell of a lot. Once that's out of our hair, the relatives will vanish, too."

"You hope."

"C'mon. There's nothing else they can hope to get from the house. Or us. Everything is on an inventory."

"Except the ghosts."

He gave a bark of laughter. "True. I wonder if we can get Dracula to remove them, since they aren't listed in the will?"

She felt her lips curving into a smile. "Let's ask him and see what he says."

"He'd probably have us committed." Silas sighed and tapped the steering wheel with his fingers. "I've had it with all this crap. I'm going to find that damn diary if I have to take this place apart stone by stone and board by board. And I'm going to do it before another week is gone!"

16

By dawn they were both exhausted and filthy. It was amazing, Dani thought, how dirty unused rooms could get in the absence of someone to dust from time to time. Even turning off the air conditioning on the third floor didn't seem to have cut down on the layers of dust.

"Maybe Edna never cleaned up here," Silas suggested. "Maybe these rooms have been closed off for a long time."

"Not that long." She pointed to dusty handprints on the top of one of the tables. "Someone's been up here."

"Someone's been in a lot of places up here. Possibly when they took inventory."

"And possibly it was the relatives. Come on, Silas, you know how hard they've been trying to get in here."

"Yeah. So somebody has already checked the place out." He ran his fingers impatiently through his hair. "Are you getting tired of striking out?"

"Yes. But I console myself by remembering that *they* haven't found it either."

Silas shook his head. "How about a shower and some breakfast? Followed by a nap. A long nap."

Dani didn't answer immediately. A ray of morning sunlight had come through the window at a sharp angle to the wall next to it, and she could see the faint shadow of a straight horizontal line about six feet above the floor. It was right at a seam in the wallpaper and was probably nothing but poor workmanship, but she nevertheless crossed to it and reached up to feel it with her fingers.

When she touched it, Silas saw it, too. At once he was beside her, tracing the crease with his fingers. "It's a cut," he said. "See if you can find any vertical ones on that end of it while I check this end."

In no time at all they had traced the outline of a narrow rectangle that might well have been a doorway. The edges were cunningly concealed behind an unglued overlap of the wallpaper, making them invisible.

"Somebody could have just cut out the wall for some reason," Dani suggested. "I imagine there's all kinds of wiring and plumbing that need work from time to time."

"Yeah, but that's an awfully big hole for something like that. And why would they leave the wallpaper unglued around the top and one side?"

"I guess that doesn't make any sense." She watched as Silas pushed on the panel and hunted for some kind of latch mechanism, afraid to hope they'd found something, but hoping anyway.

He tossed her a grin over his shoulder. "This is the part where you're supposed to move something somewhere in the room and make the panel spring open, isn't it?"

"Yes. And then you disappear behind it." All her weariness was forgotten as she watched impatiently and wished the damn panel would just open. "You know, we could always get a crowbar and pry it open."

"Naw. That lacks finesse."

"How long are you going to finesse this?"

"Another five or ten minutes. Then I'll vote for brute strength."

As it turned out, he didn't need any strength at all. Moments later, as he pressed the top right corner and the left side at the same time, the door released and swung silently open.

Dani stepped back instinctively, as if some part of her expected a ghost to leap out. Instead, all that was visible was a landing and a deep, dark hole. Silas leaned in, feeling around the edge of the door, and gave a satisfied grunt as he found a light switch.

"All the comforts of home," he remarked as yellow light filled a stairwell. He stepped in and looked down. "I'll bet this goes all the way down to the ground floor. You stay here and keep this door open while I check it out."

"Do I have to?" The thought of staying up here all alone made her skin crawl with dread.

Silas stepped back into the room and slipped his arm around her shoulder. "No, you don't have to. You can go down the stairwell if you want, and I'll wait here. I just don't want to risk the door swinging shut with both of us in there."

"Sorry. I'll be okay."

He studied her a moment, then nodded and let go of her. "Okay. I'll be as quick as I can."

The third floor of the mansion was eerie in its silence. Here, not even the *whoosh* of air-conditioning alleviated the oppressiveness. The air was motionless, warm, and stale, and there was a faint, unpleasant odor of mildew.

Silas made surprisingly little noise as he disappeared down the stairwell. Dani stood leaning against the open door, afraid that Morris might choose this moment to reappear. Her nerves, stretched by fatigue and a total unwillingness to be alone anywhere in this house, felt like guitar strings that were on the edge of snapping. One little thing would probably send her into total collapse.

Drawing a deep breath, she scolded herself sternly for being such a wimp. There was absolutely nothing here to be frightened of except her own hyperactive imagination. The ghosts were just ghosts, and neither of them had done a single thing to indicate they intended any harm—unless, of course, they were trying to scare someone to death.

Silas called up to her from below. "This is very interesting, Dani. I think you ought to come down here."

"But what about the door?"

"I've got the one down here open. Come on."

Stepping into the stairwell was surprisingly difficult. She actually had to give herself a stern lecture about being a fraidy-cat. Maybe she was developing a slight touch of claustrophobia?

When she stepped onto the landing, however, she couldn't see Silas on the landing below. Nervous, she called out to him.

"There's a switchback on the stairs," Silas called up to her. "When you reach the next landing you'll be able to see me."

"Okay." She hesitated just a moment longer, then headed down. After all, she could hear him.

There were only a dozen stairs to the next landing but the risers were so narrow that she had to move cautiously. Keeping her hand on the wall for added balance, she felt for each step before she put her weight down on it. "It would be easy to break your neck on these things," she called.

"It sure would. Take your time, Dani. I'm holding this door open, otherwise I'd come help you."

The suggestion that she needed help getting down these steps, however narrow, stiffened her spine somewhat. "I'm all right. I can manage a few silly stairs, Silas."

But even as she spoke, the fine hairs on the back of her neck stood up, and she looked swiftly behind her, certain that someone was there. The staircase behind her was empty.

She must have heard some little sound, she told herself, and in her heightened state of nerves, she had misinterpreted it.

"Dani?" Silas called her name from below. "Is something wrong?"

"I—no. Nothing's wrong. I'm coming." She took another step down and then froze in stark terror as the lights went out and the door upstairs closed with an audible thud.

"Dani?"

She couldn't move. Every muscle in her body had turned to stone the instant the darkness settled over her. The air felt as if it had solidified around her, a heavy weight that held her in place and wouldn't allow her to breathe. The blackness before her eyes appeared to swirl wildly, causing her to feel as if she were falling.

"Dani? Are you all right?"

A scream tried to rise from the pit of her stomach, but she couldn't find air on which to give voice to it.

"Dani!"

From a distance she could hear Silas curse savagely, but he was so far away, and he couldn't save her anyway.

"Dani . . ."

Strong arms seized her, and suddenly not even her feet touched the floor. Anchored now only by arms that held her, she felt herself falling . . .

"Dani! Damn it, woman, open your eyes! You're safe!"

A heavy shudder passed through her, causing his arms to tighten around her, and then she opened her eyes.

They were in her room. She blinked, scarcely daring to believe it.

"Can you stand?" Silas asked her. When she gave him a jerky nod, he set her on her feet. "Doesn't this beat all?"

What beat all as she looked at the door through which they had come was the fact that there was a secret entry to her bedroom. She looked from the door to Silas. "My God," she whispered hoarsely. She still felt stunned, hardly able to absorb it all. The memory of being in the dark on those stairs was every bit as terrifying as realizing they led directly to her bedroom.

"Well, it sure explains the man we saw standing behind you in your doorway the night Max was here." He looked grim. "It might also explain Morris's apparition."

Another chill shook her. "Silas, I don't like this at all."

"Me either. From now on you're sleeping with me. I'll be damned if I'm going to have these goons terrorizing you any time they get the urge. This is over the line."

"Did you—did you switch off the lights?"

He shook his head. "The bulb on the landing just burned out. There isn't any light switch down here, though I can't imagine why."

She shivered again. "It's strange that the door should slam and the light burn out at the same time."

"Yeah." His expression darkened even more. "Do you want to wait here while I go upstairs and check it out?"

"You think . . . you think someone's up there?"

"If they are, I'm going to find them! Why don't you wait in the car?"

But the last thought she could stand right now was being alone. If someone had closed that door behind her . . . No, she wouldn't feel safe alone, even in the car with the engine running. Besides, after the way she froze on the stairs, some irrepressible kernel of pride made her want to face whatever had caused her that fright.

"I'm coming with you," she told Silas. She needed to prove to herself that she could. Needed to see that what had frightened her was no more than a draft-slammed door. Needed to prove to herself that bogeymen weren't populating the empty third floor. Left to its own devices, her imagination would fill all those rooms with horrors even Hollywood hadn't yet invented.

He hesitated. "Promise me you won't get in my way if someone's up there?"

"Why would I want to get in the way? I'll even stay behind you." Except that she'd much rather precede him so her back would be guarded. But that was a fear she could handle easily.

She hoped.

"First I'm getting my pistol. And I don't want to hear one little peep out of you about it."

Right now, a pistol sounded good even to her. Feeling a little stupid for acting like a faithful puppy, she trotted after Silas to his room, watching with trepidation as he retrieved his Browning 9mm and checked the clip.

"If there's someone up there," Silas told her, "he's gone back into hiding. It may be impossible to find him unless we work as a team."

"How do you mean?"

"You'll need to watch the gallery so that he can't run from room to room while I'm busy searching individual ones. Do you think you can do that?"

Dani didn't even hesitate. "Of course I can. I'm really not a cowering wimp, you know."

All of a sudden, his face gentled and his voice softened. "If you hadn't needed me, nothing on earth could have made me go up those stairs when the light was out. I have a few old terrors of my own. Believe me, I know you're not a wimp. Are you ready?"

She followed him up the stairs, feeling warmed by his tenderness. He had a way of surprising her with it when she least expected him to, catching her utterly off-guard. With just a tone of voice he could sidle past her defenses and catch her straight in the heart.

By the time they reached the top of the stairs, however, the only thought on her mind was the lurking threat behind whoever had closed the door.

"Stay right behind me," Silas whispered. "I'm going to check out the room with the secret stair first."

"Okay." She wanted to cling to his belt buckle and stumble blindly behind him as she hid her face against his back. Like a kid, she instinctively longed to believe that what she didn't see couldn't hurt her.

"All right, you stay right here and watch the gallery while I check it out."

She pressed her back to the wall, making sure that no one could come up behind her. Silas patted her shoulder reassuringly and stepped across the threshold into the room.

An instant later, sounding rather odd, he said, "Dani? Could you come in here?"

Something about the way he said that had her bracing for just about anything, up to and including a decapitated corpse. What she never expected to see was Morris.

She screamed. Or rather squeaked, something akin to "Eeps!" Her heart was suddenly locked in her throat as she found herself staring directly into an all-too-well-remembered pair of blue eyes. Morris was looking straight at her, smiling, and he most definitely saw her. That scared her as much as anything, the awareness in those blue eyes.

"You stand right there and watch," Silas told her. "I'm going to walk around him."

"Why?" Lord, the room felt cold. Her teeth began to chatter.

"If it's some kind of projection, I should cross the beam and block it out."

"Oh."

"And if it's some kind of projection, he should look the same from every angle."

"Okay." But it was no projection. She looked into those blue eyes and knew for a fact that Morris was looking at *her*. He even looked amused as if he knew they doubted his reality. Could a projection look amused like that? Not very likely.

Moving cautiously, as if he wasn't quite sure what he was getting into—or as if he felt like a jerk for what he was about to do—Silas stepped forward and began to circle the apparition. Morris actually turned his head to watch.

To Dani, Silas disappeared behind Morris, as if Morris were as solid as any other human being. "I'd be able to see you through a projection, wouldn't I?" she asked Silas.

"Yep."

"Well, I can't see you. Not at all."

Silas emerged on the other side of Morris, while Morris watched with exaggerated interest. "I couldn't see you either and I was looking at Morris's backside."

"Really?" Dani felt another chill run down her spine, and shivered.

Silas looked at Morris. "He's looking at me."

Dani nodded, clenching her chattering teeth. "Actually, he looks as if he thinks you're very funny."

"Well, I don't think he's funny at all. The image hasn't flickered?"

"Nope. I'm telling you, Silas, he's there. For real."

Silas reached out and passed his hand through the apparition, watching it disappear and then reappear on the other side of Morris. Morris looked as if he were about to break into hearty laughter. "That's no projection," Silas said reluctantly.

"I told you! What good does this do us?"

"Well, we know it's really a ghost." He shook his hand. "And that you don't need a freezer when a ghost is around. Damn, I feel like I have frostbite."

Morris shook his head as if sympathizing.

"Darn it, M-morris," Dani said through chattering teeth, "if you can get up all this energy to come laugh at us, why the heck don't you tell us what you want!"

"*Find it*." The words seemed to come out of the air everywhere, as if Morris surrounded them. It was a startling effect, and Morris looked as if he was thoroughly delighted with it.

"Find what?" Dani demanded, refusing to be cowed again. "Your diary?"

"*Find it*." Morris started to fade.

"Damn you, Morris!" Dani nearly shouted in her frustration. "Don't you dare go away without telling us where it is!"

But Morris was gone before the last word emerged from her mouth, and the room temperature soared instantly back up to a stifling eighty-five.

Silas stood looking at her, and she at him. "Wasn't that illuminating?" he finally said.

"Illuminating? What was illuminating about that? Who the hell does he think he is?"

"A ghost. He seems to be enjoying it, too."

"Morris enjoys everything, especially if it's driving someone else nuts."

Silas flashed a smile. "Now you understand him. I think his mission in life was making people crazy."

"Well, it's not amusing. How can you stand there looking as if you're enjoying this?"

"Because I am."

Dani glared at him, wondering how she could have ever softened toward him. Couldn't he take anything seriously?

"Aw, come off it, Dani! It's just a great big treasure hunt. If you make a game out of it, it won't seem half so bad."

But she didn't want to admit he was right, nor did she feel like revising her attitude. She was grumpy, and annoyed past bearing with Morris who, if she could get her hands on him, would join Silas in that pot of boiling oil she was once again considering.

Silas wiggled his eyebrows at her, but she refused to smile. "Morris did this deliberately," she said.

"So it would seem. Which means we'll find the diary eventually."

"How do you come to that conclusion?"

"If he really didn't want anyone in the world to find it, he would have burned it. He wouldn't be standing here in this stupid room telling us to find it."

"Obviously. But that doesn't mean we'll eventually find it. It could be hidden anywhere."

"It could be, but I doubt it."

Dani bit back an exasperated sigh. "Are you being deliberately obscure, or do you enjoy watching me try to pry every little bit of information out of you?"

"The latter actually." He ducked when she made as if to swing at him, but she never followed through on the gesture. "Come on, Dani, this is a game. Morris's *final* game, most likely. Let's get into the spirit of the damn thing and make it fun."

"Just how are you proposing we get any more into the spirit of it than we already are? Good grief, Silas, we've had strange people creeping in and out of this place, the unknown man who was standing right behind me in my bedroom that night, the person who locked us in the hurricane room, frogmen coming at us in the dead of night with spear guns—just how would you feel about all this right now if that spear had hit you in some vital spot? Have you thought about that?"

He closed the distance between them and took her gently by the shoulders. The humor had evaporated from his face. "I've thought about it, believe me. And if I ever find out who did that, they're going to wish they'd never been born."

Dani felt another shiver pass through her, this time at the hard expression in Silas's eyes. He might appear to skim the surface and make light of most things, but it remained that he was a man who was perfectly capable of carrying out the threat. She wouldn't want to cross Silas Northrop. No way.

"But as for the rest of it . . ." He shook his head and his expression lightened. "The rest of it is Morris's cockamamie idea of a joke. He probably never thought of spear guns or other things like that, but he probably had a great time imagining us overrun by his lunatic relatives, all of us looking for a diary that, when all is said and done, is probably more boring than anything else."

"I would imagine the diary is *fascinating*."

"Parts of it could be. But most of it is probably a tedious listing of daily events that would be boring to anyone not involved. What would *your* diary look like?"

"I'm not Morris."

"Thank God for that."

Before she could decide how to interpret that, he had stolen her mouth in a kiss that left her breathless. Lifting his head, he scanned her face to judge the effect of his kiss, and nodded in apparent satisfaction. "*We* can have fun," he told her. "Whether or not we find the diary, we can make this fun."

"How can we do that?" Not that she cared. Right now all she cared about was that he keep holding her and go on kissing her. Talking to her was a very poor substitute.

"By having a séance."

The word pierced the fog of desire that was beginning to swamp her and brought her briefly to her senses. "Silas, Morris is perfectly capable of talking to us himself. What more could a séance do—assuming Roxy Resnick is for real."

"Morris doesn't seem to be capable of saying more than a few words at a time. Roxy might get more information through her guide."

"Assuming Morris wants to share any more information."

Silas shrugged. "Have you got a better idea?"

She hated to admit it, but she didn't. "No."

"So, I'll call Roxy. And maybe we ought to ask all these damn relatives to join us. This could get interesting. Sort of like Agatha Christie."

"People die in Agatha Christie books. I'll pass, thank you."

"Actually, given the caliber of people we're dealing with, it's apt to be more like a Peter Sellers movie. See? It could be fun."

"Yeah, right." She refused to be cajoled into a better mood. Besides, he'd frustrated her by kissing her and holding her but going no further. It nearly stunned her to discover that she had suddenly become a sensual woman. And Silas was purely to blame for that. She didn't know if she liked that. Life had been so uncomplicated before, when it had no sexual overtones or undertones.

"Of course," he continued, "there's another way we could have fun."

"What's that?" As if she wanted to know.

"We could make love."

She gasped at the bluntness of his suggestion, and felt her heart slam into high gear. Tell him to get lost, said the voice of the old Dani. But the new Dani had a mind of her own. Lifting her arms, she looped them around Silas's neck and drew his mouth down for a hot, wet kiss.

This, she thought blissfully, was exactly where she wanted to be. Why had she ever thought she was annoyed with him?

Silas scooped her up and carried her away.

There was a ferocity to Silas this time that thrilled Dani in a way she had only dreamed of. As if he were out of patience, he nearly tore her clothes away, and cast off his own as if they singed his skin. Moments later she was stretched out on the bed and he was atop her, penetrating her with his shaft in one long, swift thrust that left her feeling taken and possessed in the most wonderful way.

His impatience fueled her own, driving her desire to peaks she had never imagined. He murmured hot words in her ear, words that made no sense but conveyed his hunger. The sounds sent new thrills spiraling through her, until she felt as if wave after wave of ever-increasing pleasure washed through her. She was lost in a sea of sensation so intense that it defied her conscious mind's ability to comprehend.

She became a creature of pure passion, a burning flame of womanly need. With Silas, she scaled the top of the most beautiful mountain in the universe.

And together they crested, then drifted down the other side, as gently as if they were made of down.

"This time," Silas rumbled, "we're not going to fight. Don't even consider it."

Dani, lying curled against his side with her head on his shoulder, wiggled closer. "I wasn't considering it."

"Good. It'd be a crime to ruin this mood with a quarrel."

"I agree." She smiled into his shoulder as he ran his palm down her back and a ripple of sheer enjoyment raced through her.

"I, um . . ." He hesitated. "I'm not quite sure how to say this, but I don't usually . . . come on quite so rough."

"I don't recall complaining."

"You didn't. It's just that . . . I should have taken more time with you."

"Why?"

He lifted his head, and two cat-green eyes scowled at her. "Are you being deliberately obtuse?"

"Probably."

"That's what I figured. Sometimes, sweetheart, you can be a royal pain in the butt. You're just naturally contrary."

He was teasing; it was evident in the way his eyes twinkled. Nevertheless, she knew he was right. There were times—too many times—when the thought of agreeing with him made her feel irritable, so she gave him a hard time. That was not, however, her usual mode of conduct. Something about Silas seemed to ruffle her fur, as it were.

"Hey," he said quietly. "It's okay." He brushed a

soft kiss on her cheek. "I don't mind it at all. In fact, I kind of like the way you get all prickly."

No one had ever before made her feel as accepted as Silas did. Everything inside her softened and she turned her head to press a kiss on his shoulder. "I guess I *do* get difficult sometimes."

"It's no big deal." He gave her a quick, hard squeeze. "Now what about this séance idea? I was half angry and half joking when I said it, but the more I think about it, the better I like it." He shifted a little against his pillow, and looked rueful. "Well, I don't really *like* it. That's not the right word. But at this point it's the best possibility I can see for getting to the bottom of this mess. If Roxy could come up with something useful, it might cut months off these shenanigans so that we can get on with writing our books."

Dani didn't answer immediately. It was illogical, but even after seeing Morris's ghost repeatedly, she had an instinctive aversion to the entire idea of spirit channeling. The notion that anyone could go into a trance and allow the dead to speak through them set off all kinds of internal alarms about fakery and charlatanism. "I'm having a problem with this," she said finally.

"Me too. I've never believed in all that stuff. Never. I always believed that the dead were dead and stayed buried, and even if there was an afterlife why would they care about us anymore? You could say my preconceptions are running up hard against the brick wall of reality in the form of ghosts."

Dani stirred uneasily, feeling as if agreeing to hold a séance would somehow violate some deep-rooted principle.

Silas spoke. "I wonder who the female ghost is?"

Temporarily distracted from her internal conflict over the idea of a séance, she looked up at him. "I was wondering about that, too. What do you think her connection is to Morris?"

"I don't know . . . although, given the age of this

place, there could be a dozen ghosts running around, none of them related."

Dani shook her head. "Don't even suggest it. Two are enough. In fact, two are more than enough."

"You know, if a channeling really works—or worked in this one case—we might be able to find out not only where the diary is, but who the woman is."

That sparked Dani's interest. She sat up, clutching the sheet to her breasts and tossing her hair back. "Now *that* would be interesting."

"Yeah, that's what I thought. Funny, but I'm more comfortable with the idea of a medium getting information from a ghost I don't know than with her getting information from Morris."

Dani nodded. "I am, too. I think that's because anything a medium claims to say on behalf of the woman would be unverifiable, whereas anything she says on behalf of Morris *could* be verified. One I could ignore, the other I'd have to take very seriously indeed."

"And there goes everything you've believed all your life."

"Exactly. Not a pleasant thought."

"Nor a comfortable one." He put his hands behind his head and wiggled his eyebrows at her. "Do you know how fetching you look sitting there wrapped in nothing but my sheet?"

She felt her cheeks color brightly. "Don't change the subject." But it was too late, he had already succeeded in doing just that. Helplessly her eyes trailed over his broad chest and down toward his manhood, which had somehow remained modestly covered in a corner of the sheet.

"Go ahead," he said huskily. "Look all you want. Feel free to touch."

Just like that she was all on fire again, ready, willing, and able to do things that once had been the stuff of her most private fantasies. Ready to be loved again.

"Do you know how you look when you get in the mood?" Silas asked hoarsely. "Your eyes get all sleepy and your lips open just a little until all I can think about is getting inside you."

And all she could think about was getting him inside her. In an instant she was caught in passion's spell and surrounded by the heavy heat of need. Her limbs felt warm and weighty, as if they were filled with syrup. Her womanhood was throbbing in a slow, steady beat that pulsed throughout her body. Everything else in the world drifted away, seeming insignificant beside the tension that was building between her and Silas.

"Come on, Dani," he coaxed in a rough whisper. "Come on, sweetheart. Explore me . . ."

Her heart racing, she reached out and tugged the sheet away from him, baring him completely. He was a beautiful man, perfect in every line. There wasn't a thing about him she would have changed, from the top of his head to the tip of his toes.

Ignoring for now the most intimate part of him, she leaned forward and began to run her palms over his chest, enjoying the wonderful texture of his skin and the way his nipples hardened at her very first touch. He drew a sharp breath, letting her know how sensitive he was there, and she paused to play, teasing him gently at first and then with hard little pinches that caused him to moan.

The feeling of power was a heady one, and she bent down to kiss and tease one of his nipples. One of his hands clutched at her, holding her close, letting her know that he didn't want her to stop. Finally, though, in a whimsical mood to dominate, she pulled away and went exploring further.

It was as if the last of her inhibitions evaporated in the heat of passion. The sheet fell away from her, and she didn't at all mind that she was completely naked, or that Silas could see as much of her as she could of him. Nor did it ever occur to her to be embarrassed as she dropped kisses across his hard, flat belly and right into the thick nest of curls at the apex of his thighs.

Nor did it occur to her to do anything except take his hardening shaft deep into her mouth. Never had she done that before, and she was enthralled by Silas's nearly wild response. His hands clutched at the sheets, and a long, low moan escaped his lips.

He was hers, utterly. Delighted by her newfound power, she settled in to enjoy herself, like a cat with a delicious bowl of cream.

"Don't stop," he pleaded hoarsely.

She wouldn't have dreamed of it.

17

Silas groaned. "You did it on purpose."

Dani propped her cheek on her hand and arched an inquisitive eyebrow. "Did what on purpose?"

"Wore me out. Turned me into limp spaghetti."

"Now why in the world would I do that?"

"So I'd forget everything else and spend the rest of my life being your happy love slave."

Dani felt her cheeks heat and she looked quickly away. *The rest of his life!* She wished he wouldn't joke about that. Those words evoked yearnings she'd buried a long time ago, a deep-rooted ache to have someone be part of her life forever. As for his being her love slave—it was amazing how good that sounded to her now, when only a few weeks ago the mere thought would have made her howl with laughter. Or die of embarrassment.

It was horrifying, actually. Here she was getting involved with a man who had no long-term interest in her whatsoever. He, manlike, was simply having a fling. If she allowed herself to care too much, she was going to suffer a wound that no amount of time would heal.

Emotionally, she was in danger of stepping into quicksand. Time to call a halt before the muck was over her head. Time to call a halt while she could still reach for safety.

Rolling smoothly away, she leapt to her feet and grabbed for her clothes. "Let's go set up that séance now." The sooner they got to the bottom of this mystery, the sooner she could get back to her novel, and the sooner she could start avoiding Silas for most of the day.

Silas sat up, a perplexed frown on his face. "Dani? What's wrong?"

She barely glanced at him as she pulled on her shorts. "Not a thing. I just want to get this diary taken care of so we can get back to work."

"Agreed. But even if I call Roxy Resnick right now, it'll be days before we can pull this thing together. What difference will another five or ten minutes make?"

"Five or ten won't make any difference. But if you keep taking five or ten it adds up, and then it *does* make a difference." She headed for the door, still buttoning her blouse. "Let's just get the ball rolling."

He stared after her, wondering what the hell had gone wrong.

Dani was exhausted. They'd been up all night, then with the discovery of the secret passage, adrenaline had given her a renewed burst of energy. But now it was midafternoon and her eyes were burning like hot coals.

"I need sleep," she muttered into the silence of the kitchen as she waited for the coffee to finish brewing. "Lots and lots of sleep."

Silas's voice from the doorway startled her. "That was the next thing on my agenda. You shouldn't have popped out of bed so fast. I figure sixteen hours should about do it, and then we can call Roxy in the morning."

It galled her that just because they had made love twice he seemed to think she ought to *sleep* with him. Having sex with her didn't give him any rights, certainly not the right to demand she sleep in his bed. "I'll go to bed when I'm good and ready."

"You look good and ready. Hell, you look well past ready and on the edge of crashing and burning. Why don't we just cancel the rest of the day and call Roxy in the morning?"

"Are you weaseling out of this, Northrop?"

"Are you looking for a fight, Hilliard?" He shook his head. "Okay, I'll call Roxy now, if it'll calm you down. She's probably in the middle of mumbo-jumboing to some blue-haired old lady who misses Ralph, her favorite Pekingese, and she won't be able to come to the phone."

Despite her rotten mood, Dani was amused. "Nobody calls a Pekingese Ralph."

"Hey, we're talking about someone who would go to a channeler. All bets are off."

Dani studied him suspiciously, hearing more in that comment than was superficially apparent. "You've got cold feet!"

He glared at her. "So? Don't you?"

"I'm too exhausted to have cold feet. They could be frozen solid and I wouldn't know. What I want is an end to this mess!" Her voice had risen, and only with great effort did she stop before she began a tirade.

Silas felt a twinge of sympathy for her, but reined it in. Sympathy wasn't going to help either one of them right now. If irritation could keep them going a little longer, then irritation it would be. "Take it out on Morris, not me."

"If I could get my hands on him, he'd rue the day he was born."

Silas tilted his head. "I haven't heard that expression in years. I wonder why."

"Which expression?"

" 'He'd rue the day.' I always kind of liked it, but we seem to have switched to stronger expressions these days, like 'I'm gonna kill him.' "

"I like it because it leaves so much to the imagination."

He perched on a stool and faced her across the island. "Does your imagination run that way?"

She scowled at him. "I've boiled you in oil a dozen times."

A crack of genuinely amused laughter escaped him. "Only a dozen times? I'm wounded. I thought I was more annoying than that."

"You *know* you're annoying but you keep right on doing it?"

"Actually, you're the only person I seem to annoy seriously. I wonder why that is."

Dani closed her burning eyes and wondered why she was even attempting to have a conversation in her present state. Her mind was beginning to act like a grasshopper, jumping away from the current subject to strange places that bordered on dreams. "Just call Roxy, Silas. And take it from me—you're annoying."

"I'm wounded."

"Yeah, right."

They didn't have Roxy's phone number, but directory information had no difficulty finding it. A psychic, in order to keep herself fed, had to let people know where to find her.

Silas punched in Roxy's number on the phone, then drummed his fingers on the countertop while waiting for an answer. "Dawn? Hi. This is Silas Northrop. Remember me?"

Apparently she did because Silas gave Dani an "okay" sign.

"Well, it's kind of hard to explain, actually," he continued in answer to whatever Dawn had said, "but we're having a little problem with ghosts. Morris's ghost to be precise." He looked embarrassed to be saying such a thing out loud, but Dani gave him credit for plunging manfully ahead. "Yes, both Dani and I have seen him, and he's getting downright persistent about us finding something.

Frankly, we've had enough. We wonder if your mother would consider holding a séance for us. As soon as possible."

He nodded and listened, said, "Okay," and hung up.

"Well?" Dani demanded impatiently.

"Roxy's in a session right now. Dawn says she can't speak for her mother on this, so Roxy'll call us back later."

"How much later?"

"She didn't say."

"And you didn't ask?"

His brows lowered. "It's too soon to get pushy. We want the woman's cooperation, remember?"

"It wouldn't have hurt to ask. Maybe you'd have gotten some kind of time frame."

"But I didn't ask!" He threw up a hand. "The most annoying thing about you is that you know what everyone else ought to do, teach. If you don't like the way I handle things, do them yourself next time!"

It would have been the perfect time for Silas to stalk out in high dudgeon, but Dani was between him and the door. The detour would have deprived the gesture of its dramatic impact. Instead, he contented himself with scowling at her. The woman was impossible! He must be nuts to feel so attracted to her.

But then she surprised him.

"I'm sorry, Silas. You're right. I'm just frustrated with all of this. It seems like we spend all our time waiting for someone else to act because we don't know what the devil is going on. Sometimes I want to scream."

He mellowed immediately. Dani had the ability to utterly disarm him with nothing more than her own softening. "I sympathize," he told her honestly. "I'm as frustrated as you are. But we *have* been doing something, Dani—searching the house."

"With no luck whatsoever."

"I don't know that I'd say that. After all, Morris took the trouble to tell us to find it."

"Yeah. Some help."

In spite of himself, Silas felt his lips twitching. "Actually, it's kind of funny, when you think about it. Do you suppose there are rules a ghost has to follow? Like he can only appear for so long and so often, and if he says anything it has to be enigmatic and leave out all the important stuff?"

The last thing on earth Dani felt like doing just then was smiling, but the image Silas painted was so ludicrous she couldn't help it. From what she knew of Morris, he wasn't very obedient when he didn't like the rules.

"That's better," Silas said gently. "Now go take a nap. When Roxy calls, every phone in the place will ring off the wall. No way we can miss it."

But the thought of trying to sleep in her room nearly curdled her blood. "I can't," she blurted.

"Can't what?"

"Sleep in that room." Embarrassed and scared all at once, she looked up beseechingly at Silas. "I mean . . . that secret passage. I don't like the idea that someone could get into my room that way. The idea that someone probably has."

"But we can block the doorway with a piece of heavy furniture."

But even that couldn't ease Dani's discomfort. "And then there's Morris . . ."

Silas sighed and nodded. "Okay. I agree. Your room is off-limits. We'll just move your stuff somewhere else. *After* we check for more secret passages. In the meantime, go lie down in my room. I'll be along just as soon as this coffee is done." He reached out and squeezed her shoulder gently. "You're not alone, Dani. You don't have to be alone unless you want to be."

All of a sudden there was a lump clogging her throat, and her eyes prickled with tears. She was just overtired, she told herself, choosing to ignore the seductive promise of his words—a promise, she told herself, he didn't mean. "Thanks," she said huskily, and turned swiftly away so he wouldn't see the moisture in her eyes.

She eased past him, glancing out the window over the sink as she did so. Suddenly she froze and whispered, "Silas? Silas, someone is creeping under the window."

He was instantly beside her, looking out over her shoulder. There was no mistaking the hunched form of a man clad in black creeping toward the rear of the house. "You stay here, Dani. I'll check it out."

Oh, it figured, Dani thought in disgust. Left behind to wait while he "checked it out." Just because he used to be a marine, just because he was a man, he thought he could handle it better than she could. Never mind that it was true. She was past caring about anything so rudimentary as logic. Emotionally she was tired of feeling helpless, useless and frightened. She was tired of the *assumption* that she was incapable.

Turning, she followed Silas out of the kitchen.

When he reached the back door, he looked at her. "I want you to stay here."

"I want to go with you. I want to know what's going on." As she spoke, she thrust out her chin.

"Dani, don't be ridiculous."

"I'm not being ridiculous."

"Yes, you are! There's no need for both of us to get into trouble. You stay here in case something happens and the police need to be called, okay? Somebody has to be able to do that."

This time she let him go without argument. Even her sleep-deprived brain couldn't deny that she was being stubbornly foolhardy. Being fed up was no excuse for idiocy.

The realization didn't improve her mood, however. It was never pleasant to admit one was acting like a fool. Grumpily she sat on Chacmool's bowl, folded her arms, and waited impatiently. At this point she was past feeling even a twinge of apprehension. All she wanted was to throttle anyone responsible for the current state of affairs.

Just when she thought she was going to explode with impatience, there was a loud knock at the front door.

She hesitated, looking from the front to the back door, wondering why Silas would be knocking to come in the front right after he'd gone out the back. Wouldn't he have gone all the way around if he couldn't find the man who'd been creeping under the window?

Of course he would have, her groggy mind decided. Therefore it had to be someone else at the door. Who?

The knock sounded again. Pushing herself reluctantly to her feet, Dani went to answer it.

Ina Jasper stood in the entryway, a big smile on her pleasant face and a heaping plate of homemade chocolate chip cookies in her hands. Dani's mouth watered at the sight.

"I hope I didn't come at a bad time," Ina said cheerfully. "If I did, just tell me to go, but I wanted you to have these while they were still warm from the oven."

"They look wonderful!" Dani told her sincerely.

"Well, have one then," Ina said with a friendly laugh. "Have two."

But it would have been incredibly rude to snatch a cookie and send Ina on her way—with or without an explanation about the man outside the window, so Dani invited her in. "I just made some coffee. Join me?"

"I'd love to."

It was easy to see why Morris had fallen in love with Ina, Dani thought as she and the other woman walked to the kitchen. That smile was infectious, warm and inviting.

"I've had such a week," Ina confided as she slid

onto a stool at the island and accepted a cup of coffee. "Most of my practice is cosmetic surgery, which at least is convenient in terms of scheduling, but occasionally I take a serious burn or accident victim who doesn't have any insurance. For those patients, some things have to be done early, so that natural healing processes won't cause additional problems that'll have to be corrected. This week there were a couple of small children and I just couldn't turn them away. I'm exhausted."

Dani felt herself warming even more to the woman. "That's very generous of you."

Ina shook her head. "None of us has a right to take unless we're willing to give something back. Morris taught me that."

This woman couldn't possibly be involved in the lunacy surrounding Morris's diary. No way. And where in the world was Silas? This was taking too long. Had he gotten into some kind of trouble? Wondering if she should call for the police, Dani kept a smile plastered to her face and reached for a cookie. Five minutes. She'd give him five more minutes, then she'd call.

And make a fool of herself with the cops again, probably. By now everybody on the force must have heard about the batty tenants at the Feldman place who thought they had a ghost.

"Where's Silas?" Ina asked.

"Silas?" How was she supposed to answer that? For all she didn't think Ina could be part of the diary fiasco, she wasn't prepared to confide in her, at least not yet. "He's . . . around somewhere. Went out for a walk. He'll be back soon . . ."

As if on cue, Ernie Hazlett slouched through the door . . . or at least he tried to. It was a little difficult when Silas, a much larger man, was holding him by the back of his collar and pushing him along.

"Look what I found in the garden digging a hole behind an azalea plant."

Ernie shoved his hands into his pockets and tried to look nonchalant. He failed, largely because Silas kept a tight grip on his collar. "I wasn't doing nothin'."

"He wasn't doing nothin'," Silas repeated sarcastically. Then his gaze fell on Ina. "What the hell is *she* doing here?"

Ina, startled by his angry question, stiffened. "I just brought some cookies over."

"Yeah, right. Just like Ern here was digging in the garden for brontosaurus bones."

"Hey," Ernie protested, trying to twist free of Silas's grip. "I *hate* to be called Ern."

"What makes you think I give a damn what you hate?" Silas demanded. With an emphatic flick of his wrist, he released the younger man and backed him up against the wall. "What you were doing out there was trespassing, plain and simple, and so far you haven't given me a good reason for why you'd want to be digging a hole among the azaleas."

"I told you, man. I buried my dog there. I got to thinkin' I didn't like having him somewhere I couldn't get to him, so I decided to bring him to my new place."

"Yeah." Silas snorted in disgust. "If that's true why didn't you just knock on the door and ask if it was okay?"

"Because I figured you'd tell me I couldn't dig any holes unless I checked with Dracula. Only I ain't gonna ask him, because he hates me."

"I can't imagine why."

Dani, who was beginning to think that perhaps Silas was being a little harsh, said, "Silas, these cookies are really very good. Ina is a wonderful cook."

"Actually," Ina interjected, "I had my housekeeper make them. I haven't had time to fool around in the kitchen. By the way, whatever happened to Edna?"

"I don't want a cookie right now," Silas said.

Ernie was of a different mind. "Can I have one?"

"Of course, Ernie," Ina said, leaning over to offer him the plate.

"This isn't a tea party," Silas growled. "Put the damn cookies away."

But with a defiant look, Ernie took two anyway, and bit into one of them. "I don't know what you're being such a bastard about, Northrop. It's just a little hole, and I think I'm entitled to get Sparky's remains."

"Sparky? You had a dog named Sparky?" Silas looked revolted.

"What's wrong with that?" Dani asked. "It's a cute name."

"It was a cute dog," Ina confided to her. "Little black thing with a white star on its chest."

"There really was a Sparky?" Silas looked stunned.

"Yes!" Ina and Ernie spoke in emphatic unison.

"And you really buried it under the azalea?"

Ernie nodded. "You bet."

But Ina shook her head. "Really? I wonder why I thought you buried it under the banyan tree."

"The banyan!" Dani was startled. "I saw a hole out near that tree, like somebody was digging a deep pit."

"Why didn't you mention that before?" Silas demanded.

"I don't know!" She threw up her hands. "It didn't seem important at the time."

But Silas had already turned on Ernie. "What are you up to, digging holes all over the place?"

"Who said I dug the other hole?"

"Who the hell else would be digging holes around here?"

Ernie, getting every bit as irate as Silas, stood on tiptoes and glared up at the larger man. "*Anybody* else could be digging holes around here! A kid. The telephone guy. A sea turtle that got confused and traveled too far to lay its eggs. How the hell should *I* know who else might be digging holes around here?"

"Well it won't do you a damn bit of good," Silas said hotly, jabbing his index finger at the smaller man. "You can't tunnel through all this sand! It'll just collapse on you."

"Who said I was tunneling?"

"What the hell else could you be doing?"

"Oh, I don't know," Ernie said, each word dripping with sarcasm. "Burying a treasure? Planting another azalea bush? Oh, no, that's not dastardly enough to suit Mr. Suspicious Northrop. How about . . . let's see . . . Oh! I know! I was burying a Claymore mine so that next time you go crawling through the azaleas it'll blow you into teensy-weensy, itty-bitty little smithereens. No? Then how about I wanted Sparky's body so I could bury him close to me?"

"Then why didn't you just ask?"

The two men looked ridiculous, Dani thought. The difference in their sizes as they squared off reminded her of a Chihuahua and a mastiff. "Why don't you two just stop it?" she suggested tartly. "You're acting like a couple of four-year-olds."

They both turned on her as one. "Stay out of this!"

Ina started laughing and, helplessly, Dani joined in. The laughter had a strange effect on the men, who suddenly looked self-conscious.

Silas made a muffled sound deep in his throat, and for a moment Dani thought he was going to burst into laughter, too. But an instant later, his brows lowered in a scowl and he looked at Ernie. "Get out of here, and don't show your damn face again without an invitation or I'll—" Silas broke off, letting the implied threat dangle.

Ernie tugged down the sleeves of his black suit jacket and replied in a rather miffed tone. "What about Sparky?"

For the first time, it struck Dani as odd that the man had come out here to dig a hole wearing a suit. Didn't he own any overalls? And why was he dressed like that in this heat anyway?

"Tell me where the damn dog is and *I'll* dig him up."

"Never mind. I don't want you touching my dog." Head high, Ernie stalked out of the kitchen. Silas followed to make sure he did indeed leave but wasn't gone long.

"There was no dog," he said flatly to Dani as he returned to the kitchen. "He was after something else as sure as I'm standing here."

Ina spoke, still looking vastly amused. "I was sure he buried that dog out by the banyan. We all had a deep fondness for that tree when we were living here. There's something absolutely magical about it."

Dani was liking Ina more and more. It was nice to know Morris hadn't been mistaken in all his wives. "I was out there the other day and just loved it. You're right, there's something very special about it."

"But I wonder what he could have been looking for under the azalea," Ina mused. "Even if Sparky *had* been buried out there, I doubt Ernie could have found much in the way of remains. Things rot very fast in this climate, and as I recall he didn't wrap either the dog or the box in any plastic. He'd have found a few bones is all."

"Trust me, he wasn't looking for the dog." Silas turned to Dani. "Babysit the phone while I go check it out some more?"

"Sure."

Ina sipped her coffee and nibbled at a cookie. "I get the feeling things have been a little exciting for y'all around here."

Dani looked at her, wondering how to interpret that. Had the last few minutes with Ernie really been enough to give Ina that impression, or had she heard from someone else about all the things that had been going on? Or was she herself getting just a wee bit paranoid?

Dani's sense of frustration was suddenly acute, enough to make her want to have a minor temper tantrum. Which, of course, she would not do. Not at her age. Behaving like a child would only leave her feeling embarrassed, so she chose to behave like an adult, keeping her outward cool while her blood pressure rose through the roof. "Not really."

Ina looked faintly surprised, then shrugged. "None of my business."

Now Dani felt embarrassed, as if she had been impolite. "Really, I wasn't trying to be rude. It's just no big deal."

The other woman smiled. "That's all right. It's really none of my business."

It was time to change the subject. "You've known Ernie for a long time?"

"Forever. He played with my children when we all lived here with Morris. He was always a tough little shit."

Startled, Dani let out a laugh. Ina shrugged, smiling. "I always thought he was going to grow up to be one of those awful street punks. Maybe he has. I don't see him all that often anymore. Anyway, he never told the truth if a lie would do as well, and he drove my poor kids nuts by playing nasty pranks on them. Although to be fair, he could be nice enough for long periods at a time. I decided finally that his rotten spells had to do with whatever was going on at home. His mother was—well, Ernie used to come stay for long periods with Gert when his mother fell off the wagon. Sometimes he'd arrive here looking like he'd been through a cement mixer. Just an old sad story sung to an old sad tune. I'm sure you've seen it countless times, being a teacher."

Dani nodded.

"So, Ernie was a problem. Shifty. Slick. Basically untrustworthy. If he'd been able to stay permanently with Gert, that might have changed, but sooner or later he always went back home. I can hardly imagine how all that has affected him."

"And Lester Carmichael. Do you know him?"

Ina smiled. "Indeed I do. He was just starting college when I married Morris. His mother was Tilly. Have you met her? Absolutely a blast. She was an aspiring actress who never quite made it and was definitely over the hill when I knew her. Apparently Morris met her shortly after Lester was born. Lester, I gather, was the seed of some producer who used the casting couch to seduce Tilly with promises of leading roles. The only role she ever got was a nonrepeating character on a soap."

"How sad!"

"Tilly was pretty much at the end of her rope when Morris ran into her—I think it was at a casting call for an off-Broadway play. Anyway, Morris did his usual knight-to-the-rescue thing. By the time I met her, Tilly was a real character, with a wisecrack a minute. She told me that Morris gave her back her self-respect and her sense of humor. Well, heck, you couldn't be serious around Morris for too long. He hated glum faces."

"So you think Morris liked to rescue people? I was wondering that myself."

"That's my impression." Ina took another sip of her coffee. "The way I see it, Morris left you and Silas this house to save you both from something. Now I wouldn't presume to say exactly *what* he thought you needed rescuing from, but it would be my guess that he thought you two needed rescuing."

Dani didn't like the sound of that at all.

"Ina thinks Morris believed we needed rescuing," she told Silas after Ina left. "She says that's why he left us the house."

"I don't need any rescuing, except from Morris's relatives," Silas pointed out. "Do you?"

"I would have said no, but we're not talking about

what you and I think. What matters is what Morris
thought. I wonder if Ina is right."

Silas shrugged one powerful shoulder. "I don't
know that it makes any difference why Morris did
this. As far as I can see, all he did was leave us a
mess. Damn, I wish Roxy would call so I could stop
waiting for the phone to ring. And I wish I could
figure out just what Ernie thought he could dig up in
the garden. There's not a damn thing out there
except a lot of dirt and sand."

"Maybe he really *was* looking for his dog's remains."

Silas gave her a look as if to say, "Yeah, right, and
cows fly."

Dani sighed and folded a paper napkin in half,
running her nail along the edge to give it a sharp
crease. All she wanted to do was sleep, but she didn't
want to lie down alone, and Silas was determined to
wait for Roxy's call. "Ernie must have been digging
for a reason."

"Exactly, and I don't think it was his dog's bones.
Not after all this time. Think about it, Dani. That
dog must have died quite a few years ago."

"Maybe. But if he wasn't looking for that, he was
looking for something else, only there isn't anything
else."

"So it appears. Unless he got some cockamamie
notion that Morris would have buried his diary
under a bush."

"Somehow I can't see Morris doing that."

"Me neither." Silas stomped over to the coffee pot
and refilled his mug. "Come on, let's go into the
library. You can stretch out on the couch and I can at
least be comfortable while we wait for Roxy to call. I
can't imagine what's taking her so long."

"I don't think we're high on her list of priorities."

"Why not? We have Morris's ghost."

The couch felt wonderful as she stretched out on
it, and Silas insisted she put her head in his lap. That
felt good, too. Amazing, she thought sleepily, just

how wonderful it could feel to be close to another human being. How had she missed feeling this all her life? Why was it that only Silas could make her feel this way?

And what the dickens had Morris thought she needed rescuing from? The question revolved in her mind like a whirlpool, sucking her down into sleep.

18

─◦◦◦─

The shrill shriek of the telephone woke Dani with a start. Apparently night had fallen outside; the room was dimly lit by a single lamp. She blinked hard, trying to remember why she was sleeping on the couch. Reality returned with a thud as she heard Silas speak.

"Hi, Roxy. Thanks for calling. Yes, we met about two years ago, remember? At Morris's book signing for *The Avedon Inheritance.* That's right. Look, before we get into that, could you hold on a minute while I get Dani Hilliard on the phone with us? She's as involved in this as I am, and she's seen Morris more frequently."

Silas thrust the receiver into Dani's hand. "Here, you say hi to Roxy while I get on the kitchen phone."

Dani stared blankly at the receiver, wondering what the hell she was supposed to say to this woman. Hi, how are your crystals? Yeah, that'd be one heck of a start. But aware that Roxy was waiting for her to say something, she put the phone to her ear. "Hi. This is Dani Hilliard."

Roxy's greeting was warm and friendly, as if she were absolutely delighted to be talking to her at last. "Dawn had such nice things to say about you! I sincerely hope we have an opportunity to meet."

Her voice could have melted glaciers, it was so warm, soothing, and friendly. Dani wasn't exactly certain what she had expected, but not someone who sounded like everybody's fantasy of the perfect grandmother.

"I think it's absolutely marvelous that you're seeing Morris," Roxy continued. "Morris always gave me such a hard time about my channeling—until Mustafa showed up. But Dawn told you about Mustafa, didn't she?"

"Yes, she did," Dani assured her. "That—well, frankly, I'm still having trouble believing that."

"That's quite all right," Roxy assured her comfortably. "Most people have a great deal of difficulty with the idea of channeling. When you think about it, it's really strange that it's so hard to believe."

"How do you figure?" Silas asked from whichever phone he had picked up.

"Because most of us believe absolutely in a hereafter. If we believe our loved ones live on after death, then it should hardly require a huge leap of faith to believe they might be attempting to communicate with us." Roxy laughed almost gently. "Be that as it may, channeling sticks in most people's craws."

"I won't deny I'm skeptical," Silas said flatly. "But I saw Morris with my own two eyes, and I'm not the kind to hallucinate. And Dani's seen him . . . what, three times?"

"More than that," Dani said. "And don't forget the woman ghost."

"There's another ghost, too?" Roxy sounded fascinated. "This is going to be a wonderful session! We might learn so much!"

"All I want to know is what Morris is after."

"Be that as it may," Roxy said firmly, "this is a marvelous opportunity to learn something about the spirit world. Morris will probably have a million things to tell us."

"There's only one thing I want him to tell me, and

that's why he's been haunting this place. When can we do this séance?"

"Well, that's a bit more difficult," Roxy said hesitantly. "I have so many sittings scheduled, and I'll need a whole day to drive up there, hold the sitting, and then drive home . . . let me think. I'll have to rearrange a few things . . . Tell you what. I'll see what I can do with my schedule and have Dawn call you back with the time and date. Is there any day that isn't good for the two of you? Oh, this is exciting! I can hardly wait to hear what Morris has to say!"

Moments after they said goodbye to Roxy, Silas was back in the library. "This is getting to be more than a little frustrating," he told Dani. "We have a ghost who can't seem to get his message across, and a channeler who can't fit us into her schedule. If we ever do find the damn diary, it'll probably turn out to be written in invisible ink."

"None of this makes any sense," Dani agreed. "Morris wants us to find a diary he was hell-bent on keeping private, but we're just as likely to turn it over to Max as any of his relatives."

"But maybe Morris doesn't believe we'd hand it to Max. Maybe he's concerned that it not be published, and he instinctively knew you and I would see that it wasn't."

"So now Morris is reading everyone's minds? Maybe Ernie doesn't want it to be published either. Maybe he knows some really wealthy person who just wants to put it in their collection."

Silas arched a brow at her. "Do you really believe that?"

Dani grimaced. "It *does* sound farfetched, but everything about this is farfetched. I mean, maybe Ernie just wants to line his dog's pen with the paper."

Silas snorted, then wagged a finger at her. "His dog is dead, remember?"

In spite of herself, Dani laughed. "I give up!

Nothing makes any sense. Well, whether Morris likes it or not, I'm going to read the darn thing when we find it. I want to know what's so important that he's hanging around this place when he could have moved on to something better."

"Are you so sure it's better?"

Startled by his sudden seriousness, she looked closely at him. He wasn't kidding, she realized. He wanted an honest answer. "Yes, I'm sure it's better. Aren't you?"

In some subtle way, his eyes seemed to darken. "Not really." He looked away, as if seeking privacy for whatever might show on his face.

"Silas?"

He shook his head slightly, then sighed. "When you said that about Morris moving on to a better place, it shook me a little. Made on remember."

"What did you remember?"

"Beirut." Again he shook his head, as if trying to shake loose of memory. "Sorry. I didn't mean to go all grim on you. It's just that I laid there in the dark a long time, thinking I was going to die, and all I could think about was how badly I wanted to live. And I found it nearly impossible to believe there was a better place waiting."

Dani rose and went to stand in front of him, slipping her arms around his waist. After the briefest hesitation, he wrapped his arms around her shoulders. "Anybody would have found it hard to believe," she told him.

"Yeah." He gave a short laugh. "Now here's Morris who's already over there, and he keeps hanging around. It really makes me wonder."

"So ask him. When Roxy channels him, just ask him."

"*If* Roxy ever channels him. If she can squeeze us into her schedule."

"She will." Dani tilted her head back and looked up at him. It terrified her to realize how deeply she was coming to care for this man. Nothing brought that home any more clearly than her reaction to his present mood. She wanted him always to feel good, and wished desperately that there was something she could do to brighten his spirits.

And that was dangerous; she knew that. It was engraved on her soul. She had allowed herself to care about her boyfriend in college, but he had deserted her almost the instant he had taken her virginity. Then she had cared for Thomas, a much deeper, more mature feeling that had grown steadily over their long association, only to have her heart broken when he deserted her for another woman. It was appalling to realize that she had been foolish enough to get herself in the same fix again.

Just then the phone rang, saving her from having to retreat from the emotional intimacy. Silas let go of her and snatched the receiver. "Northrop."

His shoulders sagged visibly and Dani wanted to reach out and tug on him, to make him tell her what was going on. Had Roxy said she couldn't hold the séance any time soon?

Finally Silas spoke. "Look, Wittles, I don't care what any damn informant told you. I didn't set fire to my boatyard, and I didn't pay anyone to set fire to my boatyard. My people are already rebuilding and resupplying the place, and we'll still be in business whether or not you and your damn company ever pay a dime on the insurance. But I can promise you one thing. If you folks don't hold up your end of the deal, you're going to be talking to my lawyer." He slammed the receiver down and swore under his breath.

Dani approached, touching his forearm gently. "What happened?"

"Some damn anonymous tipster called the cops and said they'd seen me enter the boatyard the night of the fire. Never mind that the night watchman never saw me. Never mind that you told Wittles I was with you. He's going to believe some anonymous slimeball."

"What a jerk!"

Silas shrugged one shoulder. "Just doing his job. Insurance companies don't get rich by handing out money without a fight."

Dani had a feeling that the money didn't concern Silas nearly as much as the accusation. "What are you going to do?"

"Exactly what I've been doing. My people are putting it back together at the yard, and when I finish out this damn six months I'm going back there to pick up where I left off."

Dani turned away and pretended to have a sudden fascination for the books on the floor-to-ceiling shelves. "I always wanted to have a library like this."

"Yeah. Me, too. It's my favorite room in this mausoleum."

She shivered. "Don't call it that."

"Why not? The only permanent residents seem to be a pair of ghosts."

"What about us?"

"We're not permanent. And we never will be."

Dani felt as if a vise were squeezing her chest. The pain and the pressure were so intense for a moment that she couldn't even draw a breath. Did he mean that the way it sounded? But why should she take it so hard if he did? He hadn't promised anything at all, and certainly not any kind of permanence. "Aren't you—aren't you going to finish your book?"

"You know, I'm beginning to wish I'd never started the damn thing. That I'd never agreed to this. Why should anyone else want to read about me spilling my guts over Beirut?"

"I thought it was a novel."

"It is. At least it's supposed to be. In the tradition of the worst novels, it's autobiographical."

"Oh." She wondered what she could say that wouldn't sound like a platitude. Nothing came to mind and she felt miserably helpless.

"Anyway, it doesn't matter. I'm great at fixing

boats, and I even write a damn good column. I don't need to write a novel in order to feel like a success."

She turned from her scrutiny of the bookshelves to look at him. He had flopped into the easy chair, and had his long legs stretched out before him. His hands were folded on his abdomen. She would have expected him to look depressed, but he didn't. In fact, the only thing reflected on his face was serious annoyance.

"I don't know why I let Morris rope me into this," he said. "Dead or alive, I should never have let him run my life."

"Is that what he's doing?"

"What do *you* think? When he was alive he was always running other people's lives. Look at his wives. He decided to rescue them, according to Ina. Isn't rescue the same thing as running someone else's life? What if they didn't want to be saved?"

"Now you're getting morbid."

"Am I? I think not. Morris stepped in to rescue persons who might, just might, not have needed rescuing. People who, if left alone, might have actually solved their own dilemmas in their own ways. In which case they wouldn't have wound up so dependent on him that they all ended up living with him."

Dani had never before looked at it that way. Astonished, she sat on the arm of the couch and stared at Silas. "Is that how you see it?"

"I don't know. I'm beginning to, but I don't like it."

"Ina doesn't seem to have turned into a dependent. Or Roxy."

"True enough. But I still think it's significant that all these women lived with him after their divorces."

"Maybe they just liked him. He was a very likeable guy." Even she knew it was thin. "Is that what you think Morris was trying to do with us? Rescue us, like Ina said?"

"It would fit, wouldn't it?"

"I liked it better when you didn't think that was what was going on," she told him frankly.

He smiled crookedly. "I had a little while to think about it. The more I think about it, us writing novels is probably the least likely reason for Morris to have set this up."

Dani liked the idea even less upon renewed consideration. "I was happy with my life the way it was . . . other than that I never seemed to have time to write my book."

Silas sighed and allowed his eyes to close. "I was happy, too. Why do I get the feeling that Morris didn't see it that way?"

The phone rang again. Silas stayed right where he was, merely stretching out one long arm to reach the receiver. "H'lo?" he said almost warily. "Oh, hi, Dawn. Yeah. Okay. We'll be ready. Oh, by the way. Does Roxy mind if we have a whole bunch of people? We were thinking about inviting all of Morris's ex-wives. Okay. Talk to you soon."

He hung the phone up and looked at Dani with a big grin. "It's a go for next Wednesday evening. And we can invite as many people as we want. What a shindig this is going to be!"

Before the day was out, Silas helped Dani move all her things into the suite next to his. He seemed to be every bit as determined as she that she not spend any more time close to the secret stairway.

"You know," Dani reminded him as they stashed the last few items in her new suite, "we never did figure out who was in my bedroom doorway the night that Max was here."

"I know. It keeps nagging at me. Although, given the number of Morris's relatives I guess it could just be someone we haven't caught *in flagrante* yet."

"Oh, I imagine it must be. I was just wondering why we never glimpsed him again. If he was taking an active part in all this, you'd think he'd be hanging around somewhere."

"Probably upside down under the rafters."

It took Dani a moment to catch the pun, but when she did she cracked up. Silas caught her up in his arms and swung her around. "I love to see you laugh."

As soon as he spoke, he seemed to regret the words. His expression became suddenly wooden, and he released her. "Sorry," he said gruffly. "I got carried away."

Feeling somehow wounded, Dani watched him turn away. It hurt, she thought. It hurt to be held at a distance.

And it appalled her to realize that was precisely what she had been doing to him.

"I'm going to call Dracula and tell him what's coming down," Silas said, heading for the door.

"It's after hours," she reminded him.

He didn't reply, just disappeared down the gallery toward his room. It was an excuse, she thought, just an excuse to get away from her. How many times had she done the same to him?

Well, she should know better, she told herself sternly. Getting involved meant getting hurt. Keeping a distance was a good thing.

But some determined little voice in the back of her brain wouldn't fall silent. Instead it wanted to know how two people could ever get closer if both of them were so determined to keep a safe distance.

Irving Cheatham was initially dubious about the idea of a séance, particularly one which involved all of Morris's ex-wives.

"I don't see why," he told Silas, "you need that whole mob. Actually, I don't see why you want to have a séance in the first place, but inviting all those women would be insane. Morris was the only person who could make them be civil to one another, and in my experience, entering a room with all of them is akin to entering a hive full of angry bees."

"For a minute there I thought you were going to liken them to sharks."

Irving snorted. "They're not *that* deadly. No, they just don't like one another and they take every opportunity to sting. Pity the poor unfortunate soul who walks into the midst of that group and gets caught in the crossfire."

"It's only for one evening, Irving. The important thing is to try to get to the bottom of what's been going on. Neither Dani nor I can work productively if we're being driven crazy by ghosts and lunatics. I don't care to be locked in the hurricane room again, nor do I want to have to hunt in the shrubbery for strange individuals. If all this séance yields is a big confrontation, it might be enough to put an end to all this bullshit."

"That may be, but I still have grave qualms about bringing all those women together." He sighed audibly. "Very well. I'll have my secretary call all of them in the morning. This promises to be a nightmare!"

On the appointed evening, Roxy Resnick arrived on waves of lavender perfume, wearing flowing robes of purple. Her feet were clad in matching satin slippers, and her head was swathed in a turban made of amethyst satin. A lock of brilliant red hair had escaped just over her forehead, a startling contrast. Her lipstick was far too bright and too orangey, but her unusual lavender eyes more than made up for her other defects of appearance. Warm and full of laughter, they seemed to dance. She hugged both Silas and Dani effusively, as if she had known them for many years.

Dawn Moonglow was more reserved than her mother, but her greeting was friendly. She wore a slacks suit that made her chunky body look mannish, and a new pair of tortoise-shell eyeglasses with round lenses that reminded Dani of a racoon. She wondered if Dawn was trying to make a statement of some kind.

"I know I'm way too early," Roxy said, "but I absolutely *must* have time to get into the proper frame of mind. I need quiet and time to meditate. But first I want to go through the house and see what I can pick up on."

Dani exchanged glances with Silas and saw that he had the same concern: Roxy wanted to go through the house. Was she just after the diary, too?

"I'll have to accompany you," Silas told her politely enough. He didn't want to make this woman hostile unless it was necessary because he wanted her to perform this séance. How else were they going to get to the bottom of all of this?

"Of course you will," Roxy said, as if surprised he felt it necessary to say so. "And Dani, too. I wouldn't expect *anyone* to let me wander unsupervised through their home. My goodness, it's as much in my best interest as it is in yours. If something turned up missing, I would *hate* to be thought responsible!"

Dani relaxed. For some reason she didn't want to believe Roxy was involved in these shenanigans.

The tour of the house, at Roxy's direction, started at the top, where Dani had first seen Morris. Climbing the stairs proved to be difficult for the older woman, who became breathless and flushed.

"Good Lord," she panted when they at last reached the top floor, "I can't believe how fast I've gotten out of shape. I used to charge up and down those stairs as if they were nothing." She pointed across the gallery to the suite in the northwest corner. "Those used to be my rooms over there. I loved being up so high. At times I fancied it was like being a seagull." She glanced fondly at her daughter. "Dawn's rooms were right next to mine, when she came to visit. Which wasn't nearly often enough back then."

Dawn smiled faintly.

"Well, it wasn't," Roxy chided her gently, "but you were young and you needed the room to try your wings. I understood." She turned to Silas and Dani.

"It's been years since I lived here, but Morris kept my rooms for me so that I could visit whenever I wanted. He did that for all his ex-wives."

"A bit unusual," Silas remarked.

"Morris was an unusual man. I loved him desperately while we were married, but . . ." She shrugged. "I was never quite what he wanted. I always felt as if I were failing to measure up to some invisible icon that only he could see. Oh, he wasn't critical of me. Never that! But I never felt I was . . . oh, it's so difficult to explain! I just felt, somehow, that I was a substitute. It's the primary reason we parted ways. I've wondered ever since if it was my own insecurity that made me feel that way. It very well could have been. He was such a sweetheart and never did or said anything to make me feel that way."

She sighed, and for a brief moment looked melancholy. "He was a wonderful, intoxicating man. He went to my head like champagne. Ah, well." She sighed, then shook off the mood. "But that's neither here nor there, and it was a long time ago." She turned and began walking slowly along the gallery. "I may or may not pick up on anything, but it's worth an effort."

Dani wasn't sure what kind of mumbo jumbo she had expected, but all Roxy did was stroll around the gallery as if she were thinking about buying the house, occasionally pausing in the open doorway to glance into a room.

What made the hair on the back of her neck stand up, though, was that completely without prompting, Roxy suddenly stopped on the exact spot where Morris had made his first appearance. Roxy turned slowly in a full circle, an almost perplexed look on her face.

"I sense . . . anguish," she said finally. "Great loss."

Silas spoke. "Someone died here?" His tone was laced with enough skepticism that Dani felt embarrassed.

Roxy shook her head slowly. "No . . . no, nothing like that. I just feel that someone who stood here felt a deep grief. And a great yearning for . . . something lost." Roxy tipped her head back a little and closed her eyes, drawing a deep breath. "So sad," she murmured finally. "So very sad."

Dani was dying to tell them that this was the spot where she first saw Morris, but caution silenced her. It was best not to tell Roxy anything that she might be able, either consciously or unconsciously, to build the rest of the evening's events around.

Roxy sighed again and shook her head. "I always wondered why Morris bought this house to begin with, and why he kept it when it must have been eating him alive in expenses."

Silas and Dani were both waiting for an explanation, but Roxy said nothing more, merely resumed her stroll around the gallery.

She came to an abrupt halt in front of the room that contained the door to the secret stairway, the room where Dani and Silas had most recently seen Morris.

"What a confusion of feelings here," the medium said. She spread her arms as if trying to encompass them all, and purple chiffon flowed softly, theatrically. "Fear. Someone was afraid in here. Just recently. I sense frustration, anger, controlled passion. Doubt. And something . . . darker. An older feeling. Harmful."

She backed up, as if the room were distasteful to her. "Someone with bad intentions was here not too long ago. Have you had any prowlers?" Before anyone could answer—not that either Dani or Silas was going to volunteer anything at this point—she plunged on. "I don't like this feeling at all. It may be tied into the threat Mustafa was trying to warn you about, the message I had Dawn bring to you. Do you remember, Dawn?"

"Yes, Mother."

Roxy swung about and looked sternly at Dani and

Silas. "If I were you, I'd keep a sharp watch for mischief. I don't like this feeling at all."

"We're hoping we can settle this all tonight," Silas reminded her. "Or at least glean enough information to settle it soon."

"Just be careful. Someone wants something, and you two are in the way."

"Not one of our spirits?"

"No, this person is very much alive. The spirits . . ." She cocked her head to one side as if listening. "An old, wistful sadness fills this place. Something beyond price was lost, but never forgotten."

She wandered on, pausing in the west alcove to remark that happiness had filled it once upon a time, then she moved on again.

"Didn't you feel all of this when you lived here?" Silas asked her.

"There were too many people living here. The living are like a stereo turned up to full volume, drowning out the quieter whispers of the dead."

"Oh."

"Besides," Roxy said prosaically, "I didn't want to. I lived here. I spent most of my time trying to *block* impressions. Good God, I could have *drowned* in them if I hadn't exercised control."

Silas slipped his arm around Dani's shoulders as they followed Roxy on her journey through the house. Dani's initial reaction was one of uncertain embarrassment—public displays of affection left her feeling awkward—but then it struck her how good it felt to have Silas's arm around her. And more, how good it felt that he didn't mind being seen with his arm around her. Thomas would never have done such a thing.

Of course, at the time, she had been in agreement with Thomas about such things. There was a time and a place for displays of affection . . . only there had never been a time or a place for them in her relationship with the lawyer. Silas, on the other hand, seemed to think just about any time was a good time . . . and she was discovering that she liked that.

Roxy became pretty quiet after that, but Dani noticed that she was looking more and more dazed as time wore on.

Dawn leaned over, whispering an explanation. "She's concentrating very strongly on the vibrations. Her state right now is meditational. I doubt she'd hear us if we said anything."

Dani nodded, stifling an instinctive reaction to the mention of "vibrations."

Silas merely looked even more wooden, as if he were restraining something stronger than mere discomfort. Well, neither of them were exactly into this kind of thing.

Roxy didn't speak again until they were in the library, gathered around the long oak reading table where the séance would later be held. In preparation for anything her mother might say, Dawn set up the steno machine she had brought along and fed paper in. Her equipment seemed somehow jarringly out of place.

When Roxy started talking slowly, Dawn's fingers began to dance quietly on the keys.

"There is so much sorrow in this house. A terrible, terrible amount of sorrow, some of it very old and some of it recent. All of it . . . I get that all of it has to do with Morris. It's his sorrow . . ." Her voice trailed away into a sigh, and a tear rolled slowly down her cheek. "I never knew he was so sad. He never let anyone know . . ."

Silas shifted uncomfortably as if he found himself unexpectedly eavesdropping, and Dani herself was unsure what to make of this. Morris sad? That was the last description she would ever have thought of applying. Silas looked as dubious as she felt.

"Oh, this is too much," Roxy said finally. Sniffling quietly, she tugged a lavender handkerchief from within the voluminous folds of her caftan. "I don't think I can bear to do this."

Dani's heart sank to her shoes. Not until that moment had she realized just how much hope she was pinning on this evening. Somewhere at the back of her mind, she had apparently concocted a belief that tonight everything would be resolved. What if nothing happened at all?

"Why not?" Silas asked Roxy. "What's wrong?"

"The sorrow!" She dabbed at her eyes again. "Really, Silas, I had no idea that Morris was so *sad*!"

"What's he sad about?"

"I have no idea!"

"Can't you find out?"

"I don't want to!" Roxy sniffled again and scrubbed at her nose with her hanky. "I can't bear the thought that he's feeling this way."

"But maybe—"

With a shake of her head, she cut him off. "No! No, really, I can't. The vibrations . . . the vibrations are atrocious. The atmosphere is jangling with them."

"What does that have to do with anything?" Silas sounded faintly exasperated, but Dani gave him credit for not letting it show more than that. Roxy probably didn't realize that she wasn't explaining very well . . . so it was probably a good thing that at this point Dawn intervened.

"Mother needs a peaceful atmosphere in which to go into a trance. Trancing requires a high level of sustained concentration that she won't be able to achieve if the vibrational field is uncomfortable."

"Oh." Silas appeared to be left speechless, so Dani leapt into the breach.

"But Morris might need your help, Roxy. Maybe you're the *only* one who can help him."

She shook her head sadly. "I can't help him if I can't get into a trance."

Dani sat next to her and took her hand. "But surely you've dealt with unhappy ghosts before."

"They weren't people I loved!"

Silas spoke. "I'm sure that your feelings for Morris

make it a lot harder to handle his sadness but . . . Roxy, if we care about him we'll do everything in our power to help him with this. If something has distressed him so much that he needed to come back from the grave to tell us, we owe it to him to listen."

"I know . . . I know . . ." She fell silent for a while, dabbing absently at her eyes, even though the tears had stopped falling. "It's horrifying to think he may have lived with this sorrow his entire life. Awful to think that no one around him even guessed it."

"Well, this is our chance to make amends."

She nodded reluctantly. "Yes. It is. All right, I'll try, but it'll be difficult and probably take a lot of time."

"We'll be patient."

Irving Cheatham was the first of the guests to arrive. He looked as if he wished he could have come incognito, so that no one in the world would have the least idea that he was involved in such things.

"This is absurd," he said as he sat at the far end of the table from Roxy. "Utterly absurd! I can't believe I'm allowing myself to be dragged into all this folderol!"

"Then why are you here, Irving?" Roxy asked mildly enough.

"Because I'm going to get to the bottom of this nonsense, whatever it takes."

"What nonsense?"

Silas jumped in quickly. "The ghosts. Seeing Morris's ghost."

Irving was nothing if not quick on his feet. He took the hint immediately. "Stuff and nonsense. Ghosts! But if my late client has anything at all to say, he's going to say it to me! I have to protect his interests, you know."

Roxy laughed, evidently getting past her sorrow of moments ago. "Bless you, Irving," she said. "You were always good for a chuckle."

"I don't see anything in the least amusing about what I just said. This psychic nonsense is precisely that: nonsense! The entire profession ought to be outlawed. It preys on the gullible and the weak."

"I don't prey on anyone any more than you do, Irving Cheatham!" Roxy replied calmly enough. "Admittedly, some of my so-called colleagues are fakes, but some lawyers are shysters. Does that mean *you* are, too?"

Irving harumphed. "My wife visits one of your ilk every week. And every week she comes home with some new hare-brained notion about how I should run my practice, or how we should change the living room carpeting to create better vibrations in the house. That psychic is the bane of my existence, and if she ever once steps a hair over the line of what's legal, I'll run her out of business so fast she won't know what happened."

"My!" Roxy sat back in her chair. "You really are put out. But let me assure you, your wife's psychic is not of my 'ilk.' I've never tried to tell anyone how to run their business!"

"So you say." Irving sniffed and pulled a legal pad from his omnipresent briefcase, and set it squarely on the table, lining up its edges so that it was perfectly straight. Next he took a pen from his inside pocket and placed it next to the pad, adjusting it until it was perfectly even. Only then did he look at Roxy again.

"My problems with my wife and her psychic reader are of no consequence to the matter at hand. Assuming *arguendo* that you *are* different, I need to be here to protect my late client's interests."

Silas spoke. "Do you know how many are coming this evening?"

"Everyone, I should imagine. Curiosity is a powerful motivator."

"Good. Then we'll have a full house."

"I don't know that that's good," Roxy remarked. "The six of us never got along very well."

"How did you all manage to share a roof?"

"It wasn't easy sometimes."

The next person to arrive was Gert Plum. Leaning on the arm of her nephew, Ernie Hazlett, she tottered into the room and took a seat midway between Roxy and Irving. Apparently she used the same bottle of dye that Roxy did, because her hair was the same shrieking orange of the lock that poked from beneath Roxy's turban. She was a petite, lean woman, with small, very dark eyes.

"You'll have to excuse Aunt Gert," Ernie said. "She has an inner-ear problem that makes her dizzy."

"That must be awful," Dani said sincerely. "How do you stand it?"

"What?" Gert demanded. "What?"

Taken aback, Dani didn't have any idea how to respond. Had she been too personal?

Ernie leaned over to his aunt and shouted, "Damn it, Gert, put in your hearing aid!"

"I don't want to put the damn thing in," she shouted back. "Makes every noise so loud all I'll be able to hear is people breathing and papers shuffling."

"Well, you won't hear anything else if you don't put the damn thing in your ear!"

Gert glared at him, then pulled a small velvet pouch out of her pocket and popped a small hearing aid into her right ear. "Damn thing," she muttered. "Makes *everything* louder."

"That's the general idea," Ernie said.

Gert ignored him, turning again to Dani. "What did you say, young lady?"

"I just commented that it must be awful to be dizzy all the time. I don't know how you can stand it."

"Some days are better than others. Today's a pretty good one. Ernie here takes care of me." She patted her nephew's arm as fondly as if she had not just glared at him. Then she turned her attention to Roxy.

"So you're still conning the stupid old women, huh?"

"I don't con anybody."

"Yeah. Right. And cows can fly. If you're so all-fired psychic, what do you need those crystals for?"

"She needs them," said a new voice from the doorway, "the same way a radio needs them. Every crystal has a specific harmonic frequency."

All heads turned to see a stunning woman of approximately thirty-five standing in the doorway. Wearing an emerald-green jacket dress and black pumps, she looked like a successful professional. "I thought you might need me. After all, I tune the crystals better than you ever will."

19

~

"Rainbow!" Roxy said, clapping her hands in delight. "Everyone, this is my daughter, Rainbow Moonglow."

Rainbow Moonglow? Dani felt utter sympathy for anyone who had had to go through life with that name.

"Rainy for short," the woman said as she walked into the room. Her smile was pleasant and her unusual green eyes seemed to dance with merriment. "You must be Dani and Silas. I'm delighted to meet you at last. Have you figured out what Morris was up to with his will yet?"

Dani shook her head, while Silas rose swiftly to his feet to greet the other woman. She suppressed a quick pang of jealousy, but before she could answer Rainbow, Silas was speaking.

"If we could figure out what's going on, we'd be thrilled."

"Something *is* going on," Rainbow said firmly. "With Uncle Morris, something was *always* going on."

"I don't doubt it for a minute," Silas said wryly.

Rainbow greeted Irving, Ernie, and Gert, then sat near her mother, across the table from Dawn. No one would ever have guessed that the two women were sisters.

"So, Mother," Rainbow said, "will you be able to trance?"

"I'm not sure. The vibrations here are so . . . so overpowering! You feel them, don't you?"

Rainy nodded. "Morris left a very strong imprint. But . . . Mother, unless I'm mistaken, this aura of sadness wasn't as pronounced when we lived here."

"No . . . no, I didn't think so either. I wonder why it's grown?"

The younger woman looked down at her lap for several moments, then lifted her head. "Perhaps all the people living here simply masked it. Maybe that's why Morris wanted everyone here."

The older woman looked surprised and then thoughtful. "That would certainly explain something *I've* never understood," Roxy finally said.

The next arrival was a tall, boyishly built woman wearing jeans and a jacket that was covered with the logos and names of various companies that dealt in automotive products. She was Chloris Fletcher, Morris's third wife.

"Hey, gang," she said easily to the assembled group. "Jeez, Irving, I never expected to see you again after the reading of the will. What the hell are you doing at a shindig like this?"

"Protecting the interests of my client."

"Your client is *dead*, Irving." Chloris's voice was dry. She pulled another chair up to the table and took out a pack of cigarettes. "Anybody mind?"

"I do," said Roxy. "I've never been able to trance around that noxious stuff, and I don't intend to try. Step outside if you need to."

Chloris shrugged as if it were of no importance and put the pack away. "So what the hell are we *all* doing here?"

"Waiting for everybody else," Irving said. "And they're late."

As if conjured by his words, the doorbell rang again. This time it was Tilly Carmichael in the company of her son Lester. Tilly was a fragile-looking woman who, in her day, must have been stunning. The years hadn't been kind, leaving her a lackluster dishwater blond. She wore far too much makeup, perhaps because she had learned to make up her face for the camera, or perhaps because she was trying to hide the ravages of her advancing years. Either way, she simply looked pathetic to Dani.

She nodded to everyone, but didn't say a word. No one seemed to find that unusual. Lester's greeting to Silas and Dani was surprisingly warm, considering the circumstances of their meeting.

Pepita Mayo wasn't far behind. She arrived wearing a pink tube dress that barely covered her from her nipples to the tops of her thighs. If she breathed wrong, Dani thought, she was going to fall right out of that dress. The men all seemed to have their eyes attached to Pepita's bustline by Super Glue. Dani considered kicking Silas beneath the table, then thought better of it.

He surprised her though, suddenly looking her way and giving her a wide smile, as if to say: I know, isn't she ridiculous? Personally, Dani thought a dress like that bordered on an invitation to an assault.

Finally there was Ina Jasper, looking as if she had barely gotten home from the office, and was still feeling rushed and frazzled.

"Well," said Gert, "it looks like we're all here. Christ, Pepita, why didn't you just wear a coat of pink paint?"

Pepita looked down at herself approvingly. "Is eyecatching, no?"

"It certainly is that," Gert agreed. "How's racing, Chloris? Did you ever win anything?"

Chloris didn't catch the sarcasm. "Fantastic. I've

got this new car that corners like she was glued to the road. I can hardly wait to try her out at Daytona."

Gert just sighed, as if she couldn't believe how stupid some people were. "And Ina's still making the rich and beautiful more beautiful, I suppose."

"Absolutely," Ina said flatly. "And getting richer all the time."

"Can we get down to business?" Silas asked with deceptive politeness. "Whatever you ladies think of each other, this isn't a good time to indulge yourselves."

Gert looked up at him, the light of challenge in her eyes. "Okay, Mr. Big. Tell us what this is all about. Dracula here called and said it had to do with Morris, but Morris is dead, and the last I heard, the dead can't change their wills even if they *do* speak through some charlatan."

"I am *not* a charlatan," Roxy said icily. "Gert, just shut your mouth before I put my fist in it."

"Mother . . ." both Moonglow daughters said at once.

"Hush, girls. Gert's mouth has always been too damn big, and it's time somebody closed it." Roxy started to rise, but Dawn stopped her.

"Let me," Dawn said. "I'll wipe the floor with her if she says another word."

"Don't take it personally, Roxy," Ina said. "Morris gave all of us the same chances and opportunities. Some of us wasted them and don't particularly like those who didn't."

"Are you talking about me?" Gert asked.

"I wouldn't dream of it," Ina assured her sweetly.

"Just because Morris sent you to medical school—"

"He'd have sent you to medical school, too," Ina told her. "If you had wanted to go."

"I didn't want to go!"

"Precisely."

Gert looked confused, as if she wasn't quite sure what had happened.

Chloris spoke. "He never offered to send *me* to medical school."

"That isn't exactly what I meant, Chloris. But he did something for you, didn't he?"

She nodded, a big smile spreading across her face. "He gave me my first Formula One car."

"You see? And now you race for a living, right?"

"Yeah. And despite what Gert thinks, I do pretty good. I pay my bills."

Irving cleared his throat. "This is all very interesting, ladies, but I'd like to get to the point of this meeting."

"Dress it up however you want, Dracula," Gert grumbled, "but it's still a séance. Are you going to tip the table, Rox?"

Roxy rolled her eyes but didn't reply. Silas took the floor again, rapping his knuckle on the table to get everyone's attention.

"As I was trying to say, we called this meeting because Dani and I have been seeing Morris's ghost."

For an instant it was so quiet in the room that it was possible to hear the clatter of palm fronds through the closed windows. Then everybody started talking at once, all their animosity forgotten. Silas finally had to bang on the table with his fist to quiet them.

"Now, folks . . . let's just settle down here. If there's a reason Morris is coming back, something he wants to tell us . . ."

"I can't deal with this," Tilly said, the first word she had spoken. Her voice had a feathery, die-away sound. "I can't . . . no. I have to leave . . ."

"Mom, I'm not going to take you home right now," Lester told her firmly. "I want to see what's going to happen. If you aren't up to this, you'll have to wait in the atrium."

"No!" Silas and Irving said at the same instant. Apparently the same thought occurred to them as occurred to Dani—that Tilly would have the run of the house while they conducted the séance. What if she went looking for the diary?

"No," said Irving again. "As executor of the estate, I have to insist that everyone stay here in this room throughout the evening. Anyone who wants to leave will have to leave these premises."

Tilly covered her mouth with her hand, looking as if she wanted to cry. "Really, Lester, I don't think I can . . . if Morris is actually here . . . I'd be so terrified to see a ghost . . ."

"Actually," Irving intervened, "I've been reading up on this—"

"Lawyers read up on *everything*," said Gert sarcastically.

"Cut it out," Ernie told her. "You're just holding up the show."

Irving nodded to him before continuing. "As I was saying," he paused to clear his throat, "I've been reading about this. I'm not at all sure that Silas and Dani have been seeing a ghost. There's apparently a phenomenon that occurs in the survivors of the recently deceased . . ."

Heads around the table obediently nodded.

"Well, it seems it's not at all uncommon for people to see their friends and loved ones who have recently died. There's a school of thought that thinks the visions are brought on by grief, and another school that thinks they mean something much more. In any event, it is not *unusual* for Silas and Dani to have seen Morris."

"And your vote lies with hallucination," Roxy remarked.

"Certainly it does," Irving said. "Having people come back after dying would make everything so . . . disorderly. It would break all the rules."

"Maybe there's a rule you don't know about," Rainbow remarked gently. "Maybe there's a rule that we don't stop caring about our loved ones after we die, and perhaps we're permitted to come back a few times to look after them."

"At this point, I'm willing to admit any possibility into consideration, Miss Moonglow. Shall we then at least get on with it?"

Roxy drew forth a velvet pouch from within the folds of her voluminous caftan and spilled sparkling colored crystals from it. "I think it would be best to use the clear crystal."

"Oh, no," Rainbow said, leaning toward her mother. "Morris always had an affinity for red, remember? Use the large red crystal. It has a lower frequency and a higher amplitude. It'll work better for a first contact."

Roxy shook her head. "I wasn't planning to contact Morris directly. It might be a whole lot easier to have one of my guides speak for him."

"But, Mother, Morris is *manifesting*. Knowing him, he probably wants to speak for himself."

"He probably does, but Mustafa could certainly do it better."

"Not really. Mustafa will just be another interpreter between Morris and us. He could very well garble things even more. We ought to let Morris speak."

"It's hardly a matter of *letting*, as well you know," her mother told her sternly. "Good heavens, child, channeling is *difficult* even when both sides of the process know exactly what they're doing. And Morris will probably bollix everything up with one of his ridiculous jokes!"

"Be that as it may, it would be best to let Morris speak for himself."

"Then *you* channel him!" Roxy said in exasperation.

"I think," Silas interrupted, "that if Morris wants to speak for himself, he'll manage to get Mustafa out of the way. If he can't, well Mustafa is better than nothing, right?"

"Mustafa might feel differently about that," Roxy said. "Be careful how you speak of the spirits. You most definitely do *not* want them to be annoyed with you."

Silas looked up at the air over their heads. "Sorry, Mustafa. I didn't mean that the way it sounded."

Dani bit her lower lip, wondering how he managed to say that with a straight face.

He turned back to Roxy. "Just go into a trance," he said encouragingly. "Do it however is most comfortable for you, and we'll talk with whoever comes out."

"Comes through," Roxy corrected. She nodded, but then looked at Rainbow again. "You really think the red one?"

"Positively. It has a much broader band." She lifted it and held it in her palm. "It's warm already. It's tuned to something in this room."

Roxy nodded and took the crystal from her daughter. "All right." Closing her eyes, she cupped the crystal in both of her hands.

Long minutes ticked by in utter silence. It was one of the most unquiet silences Dani had ever known. The tension in the room was thick enough to feel, and it prevented people from sitting still. Rustlings, throat clearings, faint scrapings as chairs moved over carpet . . . finally someone coughed, and it caught like wildfire, passing around the table until everyone was struggling against a tickle in the throat.

Silas reacted quickly, leaving the room and returning a minute later with a pitcher of water and a tray of glasses. The pitcher passed swiftly around the table and for a few minutes the room grew quiet again.

Not for long. Roxy began to breathe heavily, and everyone looked toward her. Apparently, regardless of what they claimed to think about her, all of them were eager to hear what she might have to say.

Her face began to change, growing impossibly slack, as if there was no Roxy in there any longer.

Her head rolled forward, and for an instant Dani feared the woman had died.

That was when the air in the room began to grow cold.

"I don't like this," Tilly wailed, and closed her eyes as tightly as she could. "I won't look! I won't!"

"Hush," said Ina. "Don't disturb Roxy."

But Ina, Dani noted, looked as uneasy as any of them. None of them had ever been to a séance before and they had no idea what to expect. The way Roxy's face had changed was scary.

But neither Dawn nor Rainbow seemed concerned, so they all sat glued to their chairs and waited for whatever would happen next.

When Roxy finally lifted her head, her eyes were open, but she no longer looked like Roxy. Dani couldn't imagine how it could be explained to someone who hadn't seen it, but something about the way Roxy's face muscles were positioned made her look like an entirely different person.

"Holy shit," whispered Chloris, and Pepita made a squeaking sound, something like a mouse in distress. Irving remained stone-faced, and Gert looked uneasy. Tilly kept her eyes closed.

Roxy drew a couple of long, noisy breaths and then shuddered from head to foot. An impossibly deep voice boomed out of her. "I'm here."

"Hello," Dawn said. "How are you this evening, Red Feather?"

Oh, my God, Dani thought. *Not* an Indian guide. The worst of all possible clichés. All of a sudden she wished she were anywhere but here. She could just imagine what her principal would say if he ever found out she had attended a séance.

"My spirit is strong," said the deep voice. Slowly Roxy's head turned and her eyes surveyed the group scattered around the table. "A gathering of nonbelievers?"

"You could say that." It was Rainbow who answered him. "Actually, Red Feather, we're trying to get in touch with Morris Feldman, who died recently."

"Morris is eating buffalo burgers at the great powwow in the sky."

Dani looked uncertainly around the table, unsure whether to release the giggle that wanted to bubble up from her stomach. No one else looked as if they found this amusing.

"We know that already," Dawn told Red Feather. "But we need to speak to him."

"Do I look like white man's errand boy?"

"Actually, you look like my mother."

A loud laugh rolled forth from Roxy's mouth, a sound both deeper and louder than the woman herself could possibly have made. "Okay, okay, I'll tell Morris you're looking for him, but he already knows that. He'll show up when he feels like it."

Roxy's head drooped, and Dani had the unmistakable feeling that someone had left the room.

"He's not usually this obstreperous," Dawn said to her sister. Before Rainbow could reply, Roxy's head snapped up and her eyes opened.

"Not yet," she said, in the deep booming voice of Red Feather.

"Not yet what?" Dawn asked.

"Not yet time." Roxy looked around the table. "The vibrations are bad."

Behind Dani, Silas sighed impatiently.

"Why are the vibrations bad?"

"Someone who is ill of spirit is here. Do you have any idea how difficult it is to speak from beyond the grave?"

"Uh, no, not really," Dawn said.

"It takes great energy, great patience, and great understanding. *Practice.* Morris hasn't practiced enough. He can only speak when the vibrations are right."

"Can you speak for him?"

"I'm thinking about it. There are other difficulties."

"Such as?"

"We're not supposed to interfere too much."

"Oh, yeah, right," said Irving sarcastically from his end of the table. "My wife's psychic reader does nothing except interfere."

"Your wife is a fool," Red Feather answered.

"Very likely," the lawyer agreed.

"Her psychic is not a psychic. This woman I speak through *is* a psychic. She creates a channel through which I can hear you and you can hear me."

"What about Morris," Irving said.

"Morris is . . . not ready. He has manifested a number of times to some of the persons here, but that isn't so difficult. We all do that for a time after we die, appearing to those we love. Sometimes they see us, sometimes they don't, but we *all* do that. Talking is something else again."

Dani, her heart pounding, dared to say, "Morris spoke to me twice. Once he woke me up from a sound sleep and warned me of something that was about to happen. The other time he told me to find something."

"Really?" said Red Feather. "But can he do *this*?"

The lights in the room flickered and went out, casting them all into utter darkness. An uneasy murmur passed around the table. Somebody— probably Ernie—swore.

"Does anyone have a flashlight?" Irving asked.

"No," Dawn said. "No light. Wait a minute."

"Wait for what?" Silas demanded.

Before his words had quite faded from the air, a small globe of blue light appeared over the table, winking into existence as if a switch had been thrown. It cast enough illumination to make the faces of everyone in the room dimly visible. Everyone was staring in horrified fascination.

The ball grew in size, though not in brightness, and moved slowly from one end of the table to the other, finally coming to rest again in the middle. Something was beginning to swirl inside it, as if it were filled with luminous steam. Dani battled an urge to back away, torn between a desire to seek safety, and wanting to see what happened next.

Slowly, as if the ball were an amoeba, a small pseudopod extended outward. When it reached about eight inches in length, it began to stretch and thicken in different places, as if seeking a particular formation.

A hand! Dani gasped, and from around the table came various sounds of fright or astonishment.

"A hand!" Lester Carmichael said. "Look, Mom, a hand!" Tilly refused to remove her hands from her eyes. "You're missing everything!"

It did indeed look as if the ball had grown a hand with clenched fingers. As they watched, the detail grew clearer, and finally the hand moved, extending the fingers until it offered an open palm.

"You see?" said the deep voice of Red Feather, less loud now as if the image he had created cost him energy. "Morris can't do that."

"Who cares?" Silas said impatiently. "We didn't come here to see a sideshow, we came to hear what Morris has been trying to tell us!"

"Silas!" Dawn and Rainbow said simultaneously.

But it was already too late. The ball began to dribble down the table like a basketball being bounced by the ghostly blue hand that grew out of it. Back and forth it rapidly bounced in complete silence under control of the hand. Everyone's eyes followed the motion in horrified fascination.

"Follow the bouncing ball," Red Feather said cheerfully.

All of a sudden, the ball started darting around the room, dive-bombing people as it went. Shrieks erupted, and in the dark people scrambled to hide beneath the table and behind chairs.

"Stop it," someone screamed. "Dawn, make him stop it!"

"I can't." Dawn was crouched beneath a corner of the table.

As suddenly as it had begun, it was over. The ball of blue light winked out, the lights flickered back on, casting their warm, reassuring glow over the room. It was a shambles. In their haste to hide, people had knocked over chairs and small tables. One of the lamps that had switched on was lying on its side on the floor.

Dani looked at Silas. "I don't think you should have said that."

"Apparently not."

Rainbow Moonglow got up from the floor and brushed her hair back out of her face. "I think it's time to change frequency."

Amazingly, Roxy was apparently still in a trance, her chin resting on her chest, her eyes closed. While everyone else straightened chairs, and Tilly Carmichael threatened to leave immediately, Rainbow pried open her mother's hands and replaced the ruby crystal with a sapphire one. "Try this one, Mother," she said softly.

"Boy, *he* was some character," Silas said as he righted the last table.

Dawn shrugged. "They all seem to be a little like spoiled children, at least the ones who come through channelers. It's as if once they get center stage they don't want to relinquish it."

Rainbow spoke quietly. "Maybe that says something about the type of personalities who want to speak regularly through channelers."

Silas agreed. "Could be. It seems like kind of a strange occupation to me."

"It would bore me to tears," Ina remarked. "After I'm gone, don't anybody look for me to come through a channeler."

"I think I would enjoy eet," Pepita said.

"Why doesn't that surprise me?" Silas muttered to Dani. Raising his voice, he turned to Dawn and Rainbow. "Do we continue or quit?"

"Why don't we just quit?" Gert said irritably. "This is going nowhere. If Morris has something to say, he can just come out and say it. Otherwise we're wasting our time. What *was* that thing we saw?"

"Some kind of manifestation," Dawn said briskly. "I imagine it was ectoplasm."

"Ectoplasm?" Silas choked on the word. "Oh, spare me! That stuff doesn't exist. It was trickery cooked up by mediums in the past. Whatever we saw, it *wasn't* ectoplasm . . . unless the three of you are up to some kind of scam."

Dani didn't like the direction this conversation was taking. In a minute people were going to start arguing, and that would accomplish nothing at all. "Silas, really . . ."

"It's okay," Dawn said. "We know we're not scamming, and I suspect Silas does, too. As for ectoplasm, I don't think Mother's ever materialized it before." She looked at her sister for confirmation.

"Not to my knowledge," Rainbow said.

Everyone at the table looked tense and unhappy, and followed the conversation as intently as if their lives depended on it.

"Look," said Irving, "can we get going? I haven't got all night. I have an early court appearance in the morning, and I'd like to get to bed before it gets much later. What do we need to do now?"

Just then, Roxy's head lifted. "What happened?" she demanded querulously. "Why am I holding the blue crystal?"

"We've had a rather interesting interlude, Mother," Dawn said. "Red Feather was on a tear and terrified us all with some sort of manifestation."

"Manifestation?" Roxy's eyes grew huge and her hand settled on her bosom. "What kind of manifestation? I don't do that!"

"You did this time," Irving said sharply.

"It was quite a show, all right," Lester said. "Super cool! I didn't know you could do stuff like that!"

"Neither did I," Roxy said faintly.

Silas stood with his arms folded, watching Roxy

with narrowed eyes. Dani would have given considerably more than a penny just then to have had access to his thoughts. "I think it was my fault," he said slowly. "I think I made Red Feather mad."

Dani could hardly believe her ears. She didn't think Silas believed a bit of this spirit nonsense, other than the possibility that he had actually seen Morris.

"I'd say so," Dawn agreed. "He's always been easy to offend. Anyway, Mother, he was just showing off, having a minor temper tantrum."

"Just who are you trying to impress with this crap?" Gert demanded sourly. "It was some kind of damn trickery, and all your moaning about how you didn't do it isn't convincing me that this was anything but a good carnival trick."

Roxy looked wounded. "This is beyond enough! I should never have agreed to do this session! I should have known these women couldn't remain civilized even for a couple of hours. The vibrations in this room are positively hostile. I'm leaving. Now."

She returned her crystals to their pouch even as she rose to her feet.

"But what about Morris?" Dani asked. Roxy didn't deign to answer.

Silas, however, intercepted the woman at the door. "You can't leave," he told her, barring the way.

"I'd like to see you try to keep me. I could charge you with kidnapping."

"In a roomful of people? Come off it, Roxy. Let's talk about this before you go storming out of here."

"I'll storm if I want to!"

"I suppose so. But what about Morris? How is that going to sit with your conscience?"

Irving snorted. "If she has one."

Roxy rounded on the lawyer. "I have a conscience, a very strong one. Probably a lot stronger than any thieving lawyer has!"

"I resent that, madam!"

"Then watch how you talk to other people," Silas

snapped at Irving. "Just zip your lip and let *me* deal with this."

"There's nothing to deal with," Roxy said frostily. "In fact, I won't be *dealt* with. I don't like the implication."

"All right, so I'm not dealing with you. Will you at least let me talk to you?" Silas's voice was rising, and he was clearly restraining his own temper with difficulty. Not that Dani could blame him. Everyone here tonight was acting like some kind of lunatic.

"Roxy," Silas said persuasively, "we've got to consider Morris. There has to be a reason he's been haunting this place, and we owe it to him to find out what's wrong."

"I don't owe Morris a damn thing," Gert said flatly. "None of us do, if you want the truth. He spent his entire life masquerading as a do-gooder, but he was using us to forget something. And as soon as he discovered we couldn't make him forget, he dumped us. No, I don't owe that man a damned thing."

"Now, Gert," Ina said, "that's unfair. He did a lot for all of us. I think we need to admit that we probably used him every bit as much as he used us."

"How did *we* use *him*?" Gert demanded.

"Every one of us needed a white knight. Every one of us was in an untenable situation when he found us. He got us out of our messes."

"That's true," Chloris agreed. She took a tin of chewing tobacco from her back pocket and stuffed a wad way back in her cheek. "It's not like we all had perfectly happy lives that he interfered with."

"No, it's not," Tilly said, joining the conversation at last. "I was pregnant and unwanted when he found me. I had nothing, nothing at all, and even less to look forward to. I'd been used like . . . like a piece of tissue and tossed aside. I didn't even have a career left. Morris rescued me. I'll never forget that. Never."

Chloris looked at Roxy. "What did he do for you?"

Roxy shook her head. "Took me away from the small town where I was living. Probably saved me from being stoned as a witch, actually."

"You see?"

But Roxy had stubbornly made up her mind. "Morris isn't the issue here. I won't continue to wear myself down for a room full of ingrates."

"Ingrates? If I wasn't grateful for this opportunity, why would I be begging a medium to continue a seance?" Silas's voice rose until the last words came out on a near-shout. He threw up his hands, expressing his exasperation as clearly as he possibly could. "Roxy, the issue *is* Morris. I don't hold with all this hocus-pocus, but if there's a chance in hell we can find out what's got him all stirred up, then by God we're going to do it!"

20

~~~

Roxy claimed she needed something to soothe her nerves before she could continue. Dani offered to make some tea, but Dawn shook her head. "I have what she needs."

From her purse, Dawn pulled a gold flask. Roxy drank from it as unselfconsciously as a sailor on Friday night. It smelled unmistakably like brandy.

"Why don't I get a drink for everyone," Dani suggested. "I'm afraid I don't have any liquor, but I have tea, coffee, soft drinks . . ."

While Dani was in the kitchen getting beverages for everyone, someone knocked at the front door. She stepped out in the atrium in time to see Silas open the door and give voice to one sharp oath.

"I don't have time to talk to you now, Wittles. I've got a houseful of company."

"Well, you'll just have to take a few moments. As you can see, I have the fire department's arson investigator with me."

Dani's heart slammed hard and her hands curled into fists. Their suspicions were unjust, and little made her as angry as injustice. They had absolutely no right and no reason to suspect Silas of trying to burn down his own boatyard.

She stepped forward, wanting to avert any more

trouble. If Silas threw them out, as appeared to be his intention to judge by his posture, they would only become more convinced that he had something to hide.

"Why don't you ask the gentlemen to join us, Silas," she suggested. "Maybe they should ask their questions of Roxy."

Silas looked at her, at first blankly, then with an unholy grin. "That's sounds like a great idea to me. Come in, gentlemen. Come in and join us."

The change in Avery Wittles's expression was almost comical. In a flash it went from accusatory to doubtful. "I just need a few minutes . . ."

"I think you ought to join us. Really. Both of you. Roxy may be able to give you some useful information about the fire."

Roxy, considerably more relaxed after several swigs of brandy, was glad enough to welcome them to the session. Two more chairs were pulled up to the table while Silas explained that Wittles and Johansen, the fire department's investigator, were trying to find out who had set fire to the boatyard.

"Oh, my word," exclaimed Roxy. "Tell me the fire wasn't bad. Morris once mentioned that you've put almost your whole life into that business, Silas."

"It wasn't bad, Roxy, not at all. We're already replacing everything that was damaged. But I was wondering if you might be able to get some information for these gentlemen about who might have started the fire."

"I'll certainly be glad to try."

"Who's she?" demanded Wittles. "Why should she know anything about the fire?"

"My mother is a trance channeler, Mr. Wittles," Dawn told him levelly. "One of the best. You ought to listen to what she says."

"My God, a medium!" Wittles looked utterly disgusted. "I can't believe you expect me to sit here and listen to this hokum, Northrop! Just answer my questions!"

"After the séance. I'm not going to keep all these people waiting just to indulge your sense of self-importance!"

"Hear, hear," said Gert, clapping her hands. "Some people have no manners!"

"Now sit!" Silas barked in his best military command voice. They sat.

"Are you ready, Roxy?"

The brandy had relaxed her considerably. She smiled and nodded quite happily, not at all the tense, nervous woman she had been earlier. Accepting the sapphire-blue crystal from Rainbow, she cupped it in her hands and stared intently into it.

Avery Wittles looked as if he were about to erupt and was barely restraining himself. Johansen, the fireman, was at once interested and embarrassed. Everyone else, having so recently been treated to the bouncing ball, appeared tense and very much focused on Roxy.

She went into the trance much more swiftly this time. Dani found herself on the edge of her seat in anticipation. Whatever that blue ball of light had been, she didn't think it had been very friendly.

"Good evening."

The voice that issued from Roxy this time was neither as loud nor as deep as Red Feather's had been. Her head lifted slowly, and her eyes opened, seeming like dark windows on eternity.

"Good evening, Mustafa," Dawn answered. "We're trying to reach Morris. Is he there?"

"It is . . . possible."

"God," muttered Gert, "can't these spooks give a straight answer?"

Roxy's eyes focused on her. "You have no understanding of my reality, and thus you have no understanding of what is a straight answer." He had a distinctly British accent, not at all what Dani had expected from someone named Mustafa. "Morris will speak when he chooses. For now *I* am speaking. Have you any questions for me?"

"Do you have any messages for anyone here?"

Roxy's head cocked. Nearly a half minute passed before she spoke again. "Someone is outside the window trying to hear what is happening. Why don't you invite him to join us?"

Silas was instantly on his feet, and when he threw open the curtain at the window behind Roxy, he revealed the startled face of the gardener, Rosario. Although it was pitch black outside, the man was holding huge shears and was trimming the hedge beneath the window.

"Son of a bitch!" Silas swore. Releasing the latch, he opened the window and said, "Get your butt in here, Rosario. Now."

Rosario promptly disappeared. Irving, who had come to the window to stand beside Silas, looked down at the hedge and shook his head disapprovingly. "I pay that man to trim the hedges, not massacre them!"

"I wonder what he's so interested in?" Silas turned to Roxy. "How did you know he was out there?"

"I saw him," the spirit answered.

The back of Dani's neck began to prickle seriously.

"Oh, this is ridiculous," Wittles said. "Nothing but a waste of time!"

"I would have said so at the beginning of the evening," Gert told him. "Stick around. You'll change your mind."

"Could we at least come to the point?" Irving asked, resuming his seat. "We seem to be wandering all over the place and accomplishing nothing."

Rosario, hat in hand, entered the room and looked around uncertainly.

"What the hell were you doing out there?" Silas asked him. "And don't tell me you were trimming the hedge. Not at this time of night."

"Not into *that* condition," Irving interjected.

Rosario darted a nervous glance at the lawyer,

then looked at Silas. "I saw all the cars. I was . . . curious."

It was possible. Dani didn't want to think Rosario was a part of this mess, and apparently neither did Silas, as he let the subject drop. "Pull up a chair and join us."

"The more the merrier," agreed Lester, speaking for the first time in a while. Tilly was still hunched nervously at his side with her eyes screwed tightly shut.

Mustafa cleared his throat loudly, drawing everyone's attention back in Roxy's direction. "I have some messages."

"We're listening," Dawn assured her, and indeed they all were, even Wittles, who had been made very uneasy by the announcement that someone was outside the window.

"First," said Mustafa's very cultured, very British voice, "Rainbow, you must not take the job you are considering. You will be very unhappy."

"Thank you, Mustafa," the woman replied.

"Silas . . ." Roxy's dark gaze scanned the room, coming to rest finally on Silas. "I am to tell you to get your head out of your ass and see what is right under your nose." There was a pause, then, "That was a mixture of metaphors. If your head is in your ass, I don't imagine you would *want* to see what is right under your nose."

Silas chuckled. "I don't think so."

"Well, you get the idea. Apparently you're overlooking something. Now . . . Lester. Lester, you're skirting the edge of something very dangerous. Flirting with disaster can be stimulating, but are you prepared to pay the price?"

Lester looked startled, then settled back in his chair. "I guess not."

"Then refrain."

Irving snorted loudly. "This is all pointless babble that could have been dished out for the general masses by any two-bit astrologer. Or printed on a fortune cookie message. Why don't you tell someone they're going on a long journey and will meet a tall, dark stranger?"

"I already did," Mustafa replied. "She'll be meeting you tomorrow at noon."

Irving shook his head in disbelief and settled back into his chair.

"To continue . . . someone has a question about a fire, and several people have a question about a diary."

In an instant, the atmosphere in the room became electric. Tilly whimpered that she wanted to leave *now* and Lester stood up. "All right," he said. "I'll take you."

"Stay where you are," Silas said.

"But my mother wants to leave!"

"She wanted to leave all along but you ignored her until you were given a warning and the fire and the diary were mentioned. I find that just a little strange."

Lester sank slowly back into his seat. "We'll leave in just a little while, Mom."

"That's better," Silas said approvingly. He took up station in front of the library door with his arms folded across his chest. The message was unmistakable.

Mustafa had been quiet through all this, but now he asked, "May we continue?"

"Yes, of course," said Silas. "By all means. This is the part I've been waiting for."

"With regard to the diary everyone has been looking for—"

Silas interrupted. "*Everyone*?"

"Everyone," Mustafa repeated. "As well as another not here present."

Silas looked around. "Who's missing?"

Mustafa didn't answer.

"Dammit," Silas groused, "I hate this crap. Just come out and say it, Mustafa. It's pointless to hint and leave us dangling. If you know, just say it."

"It's not that simple."

"Why the hell not?"

"There are rules."

"Ha!" Silas slapped his hand against his thigh and settled his hands on his hips. "Didn't I tell you, Dani? Rules! Morris must be ready to bust."

"Rules or no rules," Dani said, "there has to be a way around them or this entire exercise is pointless."

"It's beginning to look that way."

Irving sighed. "I knew I was wasting my time."

"Who said we're wasting our time?" Silas asked. "For God's sake, Irving, haven't you ever had to pry information out of a reluctant witness?"

"Well . . . yes . . ."

"And haven't you had to draw conclusions by running in rings around them without ever stating them outright?"

"All the time."

"Then that's what we'll do here. Mustafa is willing to talk, right?"

Mustafa's reply was prompt. "Certainly. As much as I can. In fact, it matters a great deal to Morris."

"What *can* you tell us?"

"Oh, goody," said Gert sarcastically. "A game of twenty questions. Or maybe charades. Excuse me, but I'm out of here."

Silas barked at her like a drill sergeant. "Not likely, lady. Keep your butt right in that chair. Mustafa, talk."

Mustafa sniffed audibly. "It would be very easy to take your tone amiss."

Silas impatiently ran his fingers through his hair. "Look, *you* may have all of eternity to waste getting around to things, but *we* don't. Then you won't have any audience at all to play the prima donna for. And I can't believe I'm talking to a ghost this way! How about we just get on with it?"

A silence greeted his words, as if no one knew precisely how to react, least of all Mustafa. But finally Roxy stirred in her chair. "All right," she said in Mustafa's cultured voice. "Let's get on with it then, shall we? Oh, by the way, I was educated at Oxford."

"What does that have to do with the price of potatoes?" This from Silas who was looking more frazzled by the moment.

"Nothing, really, except that you were wondering about my accent. My mother was British, and I was educated in British public schools, then went up to Oxford. I am, however, Lebanese."

"Thank you," Silas replied with heavy courtesy.

"Or rather, I *was* Lebanese. I still haven't worked through all the lessons from my Mustafa existence, so I tend to identify rather strongly with him still."

Silas leaned back against the door and folded his arms across his chest. "I give up. Dawn? Can you get him back on track?"

"I *am* on track," Mustafa said stiffly. "Just listen. We'll get to the damned point!"

"So get on with it!"

"The point I am trying to make here, is that after we die we go to school, so to speak. We don't immediately shuffle off our earthly identities, but instead review the lessons we have learned—or should have learned as the case may be. There is a lesson—you might say Morris has learned something, and it has made him very persistent in trying to get your attention. He cares for you, you know."

"We care for him," Dani said promptly. If nothing more came out of this evening, she hoped Morris at least would hear that.

"He knows who does—and who doesn't. Be that as it may, he cannot simply tell you the lesson he has learned, because that would be against the rules. We can mention the diary to you now because you already know about it, but we can't tell you where to find it."

"This is absurd," Wittles said aside to Silas. "I am not going to sit still for this. I came on business, and

I want to get my business taken care of. You don't help your case very much when you refuse to answer my questions."

"I haven't refused to answer anything," Silas said calmly. "I'll answer all your damn questions later. Now sit still and shut up."

"As for the fire," Mustafa continued, sounding vaguely amused, "I can tell you who set it, and who paid him to set it."

He might as well have thrown a flaming bomb into the room. Ernie Hazlett leapt to his feet, shouting, "You can't prove a damned thing, and no ghost can testify in court!"

Gert shrieked, "I told you it was a stupid idea! You stupid schmuck!"

"I didn't know anytheeng about eet until later," Pepita said, looking frightened and tearful. "They didn't tell me till after they done eet."

"Good God," said Ina. "I can't believe this. *They* did it?"

"Who didn't tell you?" Silas asked Pepita.

She raised her hand and pointed straight at Ernie at the same instant he shouted, "You stupid bitch, don't tell them anything!"

"She's not the stupid one," Gert told her nephew. "Do me a favor and don't get any more bright ideas!"

Ernie ignored her and turned to Wittles. "You can't prove a damn thing. Her say-so isn't enough, and there's no evidence to tie me to anything."

"That remains to be seen," said the arson investigator who had accompanied Wittles.

"He did eet to make Silas leave the house," Pepita told Ina. "He say he have to get Silas and Dani out of the house so he can search. He was mad because the fire wasn't any worse, so Silas, he gone only a short time."

"You bastard," said Silas. "You wanted to burn down my whole boatyard!"

"Prove it! You can't prove a damn thing!"

"I don't *need* to prove a damn thing!" Silas clapped his hand to Ernie's shoulder and forced the younger man down into his seat. "Don't move or I'll rip your arms off!"

"I'm satisfied," said Wittles. "I apologize, Mr. Northrop, for believing you to be responsible for the fire. Now, if I may have the necessary information regarding the man who was apparently the—er—brain behind this operation, I'll be on my way."

The fireman evidently agreed. "I'm gonna get you, sucker," he told Ernie. "I'll find a way to nail you, and I'll nail you good."

Ernie for once didn't have anything to say.

After the two investigators were gone, Silas leaned over Ernie and looked him square in the eye. "You're going to tell me exactly what's been going on."

"I'm not telling you a damn thing."

"That's what you think." Silas loomed menacingly. "But I happen to know a dozen infallible methods of persuasion, and they're all excruciatingly painful."

Ernie winced. "You wouldn't."

"You wanna bet?"

The two men clashed silently for ten or fifteen seconds, but finally Ernie caved in. "Oh, hell, it was no big deal. Morris had a diary and we thought if we could get it and sell it, we'd make some money."

"What's wrong with the money you were left in the will?"

"Come off it, Northrop. There's always a use for more. We figured that diary must be worth millions, and we could split it."

"Who's *we*?"

"Me, Gert, Pepita, and Lester."

Tilly shrieked. "Lester! Lester, tell me that's not true! You wouldn't. Oh, my God, if it hadn't been for Morris I'd have had to leave you in an orphanage!" She slapped his shoulder and he twisted away.

"Mom, you're overreacting—"

"Overreacting?" She hit him again. "I am not overreacting. For God's sake, Lester, *arson*! Arson and who knows what else! Oh, I am so ashamed of you!"

"Look, I didn't have anything to do with setting fire to the boatyard. I didn't even know about it until tonight. Mom, I swear I'd never have anything to do with arson."

"You shouldn't have anything to do with this at all! If Morris had wanted us to have his diary, he would have left it to us. The fact that he didn't means he doesn't want *anyone* to see it. I can't believe you'd betray him this way, and for nothing more important than money. My God, Lester, the man was the only father you ever had!"

Lester had the grace to look ashamed.

"If you *had* found that diary and gotten any money for it," his mother continued sternly, "I'd have made you give it all to one of Morris's favorite charities. Good God, you couldn't possibly believe I would have let you keep such ill-gotten gains! This is hardly better than thievery!"

"Oh, don't be ridiculous, Tilly," Gert said impatiently. "The diary is up for grabs!"

"It is *not*!" Irving said sharply. "If that diary is within the walls of this house, it is already covered by the will, and will transfer with the house when the terms of the will are carried out."

"I figured it would transfer with his other copyrighted material," Silas remarked.

"Well, I suppose that could be argued legally, but in my opinion, the diary is personal property. He never intended to publish it, nor did he ever register a copyright on it . . . as I should know since I verified all his registered copyrights. No, it will transfer with the house."

"Unless someone was given it as a gift before he died," Ernie said.

Irving turned a dark look his way. "If anyone were silly enough to claim such a thing, they'd have to prove that it was a gift. It's far too valuable an item to have been given as if it were no more than a sweater or a wristwatch."

"Oh." Looking completely deflated, Ernie slumped back in his chair.

"I told you this was stupid," Gert said to him. "I told you from the very beginning. It was bound to backfire one way or another!"

"That's enough," Silas said. "What I want to know is who locked us in the hurricane room. Who was standing in the doorway of Dani's bedroom that night that Maxine Fuller was here? Why were you digging in the flower beds, Ernie? And who were the two frogmen who shot at me with a spear gun?"

Tilly gasped. "Lester, no!"

He looked shamefaced.

"A spear gun," Tilly said, aghast. "Oh, tell me you weren't injured, Silas."

"I was lucky."

"His diapers protected him," Dani chimed in. By the time she realized how that sounded, it was too late to correct it. Her cheeks flamed.

Tilly turned on her son. "Just wait until I get you home!"

"What about the rest of it?" Silas demanded of Ernie. "Who locked us in the hurricane room?"

"It sure as hell wasn't me."

Silas scowled menacingly. "I don't believe you."

"I'm telling you the truth, man. I didn't do it and I don't know who did."

"It wasn't me," Lester said.

"I didn't do a theeng except come here and try to see the house," Pepita said. "I didn't lock anyone in anytheeng."

Mustafa spoke for the first time since the uproar began. "Look in the garden. The answer is in the garden."

Silas rounded on Ernie. "Is that why you were digging in the azaleas?"

"I told you—"

"And I don't believe you! That dog died so long ago you'd be lucky to find a couple of bones. What were you *really* doing out there?"

Ernie threw up a hand. "All right, dammit. I wanted to see if Rosario had found it."

"Rosario?" Silas swung around in time to see the gardener easing toward the door. "Rosario? What the hell have you been up to?"

The smaller man froze, gripping his hat tightly in both hands. "Nothing. I haven't found nothing."

"Were you looking?"

He half shrugged, half shook his head. "I wasn't doing nothing."

"It was you who locked us in the hurricane room, wasn't it?" Dani asked him. She felt so terribly disappointed. She had liked Rosario a whole lot.

The man nodded reluctantly, looking miserable. "I didn't want to. It was gonna be for only a short time. Edna wanted to look in your rooms."

"Edna? *Edna*? What the hell does she have to do with all this? I thought she was gone!"

Rosario twisted his hat and shook his head.

"Where is she now?"

"Prob'ly upstairs somewhere. She been stayin' in the attic."

"Good Lord," Silas said. "What a circus!" He looked at Dani. "That probably explains the person Max and I saw behind you that night. I'll bet she's been using the secret stairway."

Rosario nodded. "There's a couple of them stairways. You can get all over this house without nobody seein' you."

"Great. Just great. And who the hell else is involved in this?"

Rosario shrugged; Ernie did likewise.

Silas scowled at Ernie. "What made you think digging in the azaleas would tell you if Rosario had found the diary?"

"Because that's where he used to hide his Cuban cigars."

Rosario looked stricken. "You knew that?"

"Of course. We used to pretend you were a pirate, and we'd follow you around to see where you buried the treasure."

"Did you find the diary?" Silas asked Rosario.

He shook his head. "Edna's still lookin'."

"Edna's still looking." Silas repeated the words flatly. "Isn't that nice."

"Well, you won't have to worry about Lester, Silas," Tilly said firmly. "We're leaving right now, and Lester *won't* be back." She took her son firmly by the arm and dragged him toward the door.

"Hold it," Silas said. "Nobody leaves until everyone leaves."

Tilly frowned. "Why ever not?"

"Because I want to know where everyone is until this mess is settled."

"What difference can it possibly make? You don't know where Edna is, and apparently she's still looking. For all anyone knows, she may be looking for the diary right now!"

"Could be. Then again, as long as all of you are right here, there's only one other person I need to wonder about. I like it better that way."

Tilly sat with a thump and glared at him. "Sit down, Lester, and keep your mouth shut."

"Yes, Mom."

"Now let me see if I've got this all straight," Silas said. He clasped his hands behind his back and spread his legs into the classic military parade rest posture. "The idea here was to find Morris's diary and sell it to a publisher in the hopes of getting millions of dollars?"

Ernie nodded. "That's about it."

"Never mind, of course, that Morris considered his diary extremely private and never wanted another soul to see it."

Ernie groaned. "What difference does it make now, man? He's *dead*!"

"Apparently not so dead that he doesn't care. Why else does he keep appearing around here?"

"Oh, come off it. You don't expect us to believe you've actually seen Morris! And if you think you have, then you're just crazy. There is no such thing as a ghost!"

Which of course, Morris being Morris, was exactly the wrong thing to say.

"Oh, my God . . ." groaned Tilly. Ina gave a squeak, and Chloris swore sharply.

There beside Roxy, as plain as day and as solid-looking as the people around him, stood Morris Feldman.

Tilly fainted. With a soft whisper of sound, she slid from her chair and hit the floor with a thud. Lester, gaping at Morris, didn't even notice. Gert was silenced completely, unable to do anything but stare in horror. Ernie looked as if he'd just been caught with his hand in the cookie jar. Pepita burst into a whining string of rapid-fire Spanish that might have been a prayer. Chloris and Ina looked stunned.

Irving spoke for them all in a hoarse whisper. "I don't believe this."

Morris smiled as if he heard, but he didn't say anything.

"What now?" Ina whispered.

"I don't know," Silas said. "Morris, are you going to tell us where the diary is?"

Mustafa spoke. "He says it can be found where Dani sits. More than that he cannot say. And this woman grows exhausted with the effort of channeling, so I will leave you now, too. Farewell."

Roxy's head slumped forward onto her chest, then Morris vanished. Moments later a soft snore escaped Roxy.

"It's over," said Dawn. "Mother has done all she can tonight. We need to get her home."

But no one was paying attention to her. Dani suddenly found herself the cynosure of all eyes. Too many people were staring at her with a hungry, calculating look, as if she were a morsel of meat and they were hungry wolves.

"It must be in the chair," Ernie said. "In the stuffing of the chair."

"Or under eet," suggested Pepita.

"Are you nuts?" Ina asked. "Even if you find it you can't keep it, so forget about it!"

"That's right," said Irving. "It doesn't concern you."

That didn't keep Pepita from yanking Dani to her feet. The next thing she knew, Ernie and Lester were pulling the stuffed chair apart and Irving was ordering them to stop this very instant.

Silas's arm closed around Dani, and all of a sudden she felt warm and safe. Tilting her head, she looked up at him.

"Are you okay, honey?" he asked.

Honey. The endearment dribbled through her like warm syrup, filling her with the most wonderful feeling. "I'm fine. Really."

He searched her face, then released her. "Just give me a minute here."

Chair stuffing was flying everywhere, and nearly everyone seemed to be shouting something at someone. Pepita, Lester, Ernie, and even Gert were tearing at the chair while Ina and Chloris tried to stop them. Irving was bellowing at everyone. Tilly was beginning to stir on the floor, and Rainbow leaned over her solicitously. Roxy slumbered on while Dawn packed up her steno machine.

"That will be enough!" Silas's voice cracked like thunder through the room and seemed to strike everyone dumb. Ernie and Lester even stopped tearing the chair apart—not that there was much left to tear.

"Everybody out of here now!" It was the voice of a man accustomed to giving orders and accustomed to being obeyed. And the truly amazing thing was that no one argued. Not even Ernie. In less than five minutes, everyone was out of the house except Roxy and her daughters, and Irving.

"I'll have someone come out to remove that chair," the lawyer said, pointing at the skeletal remains. "I can't believe they did that, especially when they know now that they don't stand to make a dime off that diary."

"They probably don't believe that," Silas said. "Some publisher could conceivably be willing to pay a fortune for the diary and agree never to reveal where it came from."

Irving shook his head. "They'd be sued by the estate and they know it. No, it's not marketable."

"Maybe not to a legitimate publisher," Dani said slowly. "But what about a collector? There must be a number of people who would pay large sums of money for that diary even if they could never show it to a soul."

"Hmm." Irving nodded reluctantly.

"Great," sighed Silas. "I guess we'd better find the damn thing or they'll never leave us alone."

"I should think they'll have to be a lot more careful now," Irving remarked. "They've been unmasked."

Roxy startled them by speaking sleepily. "That's assuming Ernie uses the brain that God blessed him with. I'm sorry, I'm exhausted. Did it go all right?"

"You were wonderful," Dani said sincerely.

"I don't think I said very much."

"You didn't, but what you did say was quite useful. And Morris appeared."

Roxy perked up. "Did he? Did he really? And I missed it!" She astonished them by tilting her head back and looking upward. "Morris, you jerk! Couldn't you have waited until I was around to see you?"

Dani glanced quickly around, half expecting to see Morris suddenly appear, but he didn't. Only silence answered Roxy's complaint.

"I give up," Roxy said to her daughters. "I'm

doomed to spend the rest of my life channeling for other people and never experiencing a damn thing for myself. I'd like to see a ghost once in a while, you know. Or hear what one of my guides has to say firsthand, instead of having to read it from a transcript. You'd think I'd be allowed, wouldn't you?"

"I don't think it works that way, Mother," Rainbow said gently. "Come on. We need to get you home."

A few minutes later, Silas and Dani were alone once again in the big, echoing, empty house.

21

—◈—

Well . . . almost alone, Dani amended as she looked around at the shambles of the library.

Almost. Except for Edna, the missing housekeeper, who was apparently haunting this place even more efficiently than Morris. The thought made her skin crawl.

Besides, while she felt exhausted after the turmoil of the last several hours, she didn't feel at all sleepy. Somehow she suspected she was going to spend all night wide awake, replaying this evening's event *ad nauseam*.

Silas slipped his arm around her shoulders and surveyed the room. "What a mess. Could you believe those idiots, tearing that chair apart like that?"

"Incredible, wasn't it? I hope Irving bills them for the damages."

Silas chuckled quietly. "Yeah. Maybe that would get their attention. In the meantime . . ."

Turning, he scooped her up into his arms and headed for the stairway.

"Silas?"

"I vote we leave the diary until morning. I vote we leave Edna until morning. If she wants to spend another night skulking in the walls, let her. In the meantime . . . in the meantime I want to make love to you until you're so exhausted you can't lift a finger, and then I'll make love to you all over again."

How could simple words have such a powerful effect? All at once she felt deliciously weak, soft and warm, and a slow pulsing began at her very center. All at once she was aware of little except a growing hunger deep within her, and the hard muscular chest against which she lay. He carried her so easily, and while under other circumstances that might have been a threat, now it seemed reassuring. Comforting. Exciting.

She let her eyes close, allowed her head to fall against his shoulder, gave herself up to the wondrous feelings. With her nose she nuzzled his neck, loving the soapy, masculine smell of him. A deep rumble, like a purr, rose in his chest. How could she ever have thought she disliked this man?

He carried her to his bed, an assertion of possession she accepted willingly. All she wanted now was to surrender to him, to give all of herself, to claim him through being claimed by him.

The world seemed to spin dizzily as he laid her down. He switched on a small lamp on the lowboy beside the door, casting a hazy golden glow through the room. She noticed that he locked the door, closing out Edna and all the other threats. This room was to be their sanctuary for the night, inviolate.

"You're beautiful, you know," Silas said. He stretched out beside her. His finger trailed across her cheeks to her lips. "I just about go out of my mind wanting you."

A thrill pierced her, causing her womb to clench deliciously. Before she could find her breath or her wits enough to answer, Silas captured her mouth with his, plunging his tongue deep into her warm depths, making a promise she could not mistake.

Her arms lifted, twining around his neck, pulling him closer until his weight crushed her breasts, easing their growing ache. She wanted this. She wanted him. But even more than the undeniable sexual excitement she felt a need to be near him. To be held close by him. To be surrounded in his arms and by his love.

A pang of fear and impending loss penetrated her yearnings and jerked her back from the precipice of desire. To be surrounded by his love. His *love*. That was never going to happen. When this all was over, he was going to walk away without even a backward glance, and her heart was going to be a shambles. She was going to be left alone with an aching loss beyond any she had ever known.

The premonition of grief gripped her until she found it difficult to breathe.

"Dani? What's wrong?"

She looked deep into his green eyes and remained silent, unable to give voice to her fears, or to admit to the yearning ache that filled her. He didn't return her feelings, and if she let him know how involved she had become he would probably back away right this instant, rather than lead her any deeper into a doomed relationship. Because if there was one thing she had learned about Silas Northrop, it was that he was a kind man. He might bark and he might growl, and he might be totally impossible when someone was being a nuisance, but he was essentially the kindest of men.

"Nothing," she told him, her voice husky. "Nothing at all is wrong. Love me, Silas. Please." *Love me with your heart and soul, Silas. Love me for the rest of our days.*

He flashed a wicked grin. "Love you, huh? Do you know how many wild and wonderful ways there are to love you? I've thought about them all."

She felt a blush rise to her cheeks as he reached for the top button of her blouse.

"I could tie you up, you know," he said throatily as he freed the buttons and began to tug the blouse from her shoulders. "I could find soft, silky ropes and tie your wrists to the head of the bed. Then you wouldn't have to do anything at all except enjoy yourself. And you know what I'd do?"

She was now so breathless she could barely talk. "What?"

The blouse was gone, and now so was her bra. His palm brushed gently back and forth against one of her hardening, aching nipples. "I could lick you from head to foot," he told her. "Think how it would tickle in some places, but you couldn't stop me. Think how good it would feel in other places. Maybe I'd lick you for hours and hours . . ."

Her breath was coming in deep gasps now, and when he tugged her shorts off her, there was only relief to be free of the barrier. The sheets felt exquisite against her back, and the vision he was conjuring was unbearably delicious.

"Of course, once I had you helpless, I could take a feather and draw soft patterns all over you, finding every exquisitely sensitive nerve ending . . ."

She gasped as his fingers touched tender flesh, and she arched toward him, holding her wrists up beside her head as if she were already bound, afraid to move in any way that would break the spell.

"That's it, darlin'," he murmured. "Enjoy yourself."

His finger slipped between her moist folds, feeling rough as if she could feel every whorl of his fingerprints. She licked her lips as he stroked her gently, igniting sparks that plunged deep within her.

Helplessly in thrall to the waves of need that were pouring through her, her body took over, rocking against his hand hungrily. When his mouth closed on her breast it was as if an arc of exquisite, nearly painful, sensation leapt from his mouth to his hand, leaving her suspended in a sea of desire.

"So sweet . . . so responsive . . ."

The musk of desire filled the air, a heady scent, and his hands and mouth were relentless, driving her higher and higher. She wanted to linger as long as possible in this wonderful place, but other needs took precedence, sweeping her toward the very pinnacle.

Then, everything within her hushed as his mouth left her breast and journeyed slowly downward. She wavered on the knife edge of anticipation, frustrated at his slowness yet enjoying the suspense. Would he . . . oh, please . . . let him . . .

The rough texture of his finger was replaced at last by the wet lash of his tongue, a slick, cool sensation so intense it bordered on pain.

Helpless now as no silken bonds of rope could ever have made her, she reached down with both hands and pressed him closer and closer, as if she would draw him completely inside herself. Her hips arched hungrily, small whimpers escaped her, and her entire universe shrank to the small point where his tongue and lips touched her.

When she crested she felt as if she would never return to earth.

Silas had the most beautiful body. Lamplight fell across him, turning his tawny skin a deeper bronze, highlighting the hills of his muscles, the flat plane of his abdomen, the power of his thighs. She ran her palm over him slowly, reveling in the changes of texture as she passed from smooth skin to body hair and back again. If she lived to be a hundred, no one would ever look as beautiful to her.

Everything about him intrigued her. She touched the hair of his armpit, marveling at its silky softness. She buried her nose in the crisp hair at his groin, loving its springiness and musky scent. She played awhile with his small nipples, delighting in their responsiveness, thrilling at the way a groan escaped him. He was as much a captive to their passion as she had been, and she loved it.

He watched her from sleepy-looking eyes, giving her silent permission to use him as a playground.

Nor did he try to conceal the strength of his arousal. It was as if he wanted her to know the power she had over him.

But finally, as if she had taunted him just a bit too long, he drew her up over him and with the touch of his hands drew her into the spell of passion with him. When every nerve ending was alive and singing with joyous need, he slipped himself into her, mooring them both in safe harbor.

Then together they departed on a star-strewn journey through the mysterious sea of love.

A loud crash came from somewhere in the house. Silas stirred and swore softly, as if he hadn't the energy to work up any real indignation. His sex was still nestled within Dani, reluctant to relinquish a single moment of bliss.

"Silas . . ." Dani's mood evaporated instantly. Perhaps because she hadn't been toughened by years in the marines the way Silas had been, anxiety about the source of the noise gripped her immediately.

"It could be a shutter," he mumbled against her throat. "It could be Edna. Maybe she fell off the balcony. Or maybe the whole damn family is breaking in. Not that it'll do them any good."

"Silas . . ." It could be other things, too. A small explosion from a fire. A burglar who *wasn't* related to Morris. Her imagination had no trouble providing possibilities.

But Silas was already moving. In an eye blink he had become fully alert, no vestige of his grogginess left. Swiftly he slipped on a pair of shorts and retrieved his gun from the shelf in the closet.

"You stay here," he told her. "Lock the door behind me."

For once she didn't argue. Instead, as soon as she locked the door she dressed hurriedly in her wrinkled clothing. No threat could be adequately met stark naked.

She was getting awfully tired of this. Tired of

living on tenterhooks, wondering when the next thing was going to happen. Tired of seeing ghosts at unexpected moments, tired of Morris's relatives traipsing in and out, tired of not getting her writing done when that was the one thing she had promised herself she was going to do during this six months.

And being tired of all this was beginning to make her truly angry. If some burglar came through that door right now, he was going to have his hands full of irate female.

But nobody came through that door, giving her no opportunity to vent her anger. Minutes ticked by while the house remained as silent as a tomb. How did Silas think he was ever going to find anyone in this mausoleum? Good heavens, the place was big enough to easily conceal a half dozen people. All Edna—or whoever it was—had to do was keep a step ahead of his search.

Frustrated, she tossed a pillow at the door. Just as she threw it, Silas stepped in. He ducked the pillow and looked at her strangely. "Did you think that was going to scare someone off? I thought I told you to lock this door."

"I did. Something must be wrong with the lock."

Silas closed the door and locked it. When he attempted to open it, it didn't give.

Dani stood beside him, watching with confusion. "Silas, I swear I locked it."

"I'm sure you did. Maybe it just didn't catch right. It doesn't matter anyway. Come on downstairs and meet Edna before the ambulance arrives."

"Ambulance! What happened?"

"She tripped on the stairs. I think her leg is broken."

"How awful!"

He shrugged. "I'm having trouble rustling up sympathy for her. After all, she locked us in the hurricane room."

"Or maybe Rosario did at her behest."

"Behest? People still use words like that?"

"I do." He was beginning to irritate her again. "So you called the ambulance?"

"Didn't I just say so? Come on, let's go down. She says she was trying to leave. She eavesdropped on the séance and decided to clear out because we found out about her. Or at least that's what she says."

"It's probably true." As they walked down the gallery, she could see Edna down below in the atrium at the foot of the opposite stairway. She was stretched out on the tile with a sofa cushion beneath her head. From this distance, Dani would not have guessed the housekeeper was female. The woman had short dark hair and wore slacks and a dark shirt, and simply looked like a stocky man. "Was she the person you saw behind me that night?"

Silas nodded. "I'm pretty sure she was."

For some reason that relieved Dani immensely. Maybe it was just having the mystery solved, having all the villains out in plain view that made her feel as if a tremendous weight had been lifted from her shoulders.

Edna didn't look any too happy about her predicament when they joined her, but she wasn't exactly hostile, either. More like resigned.

"Why did you do this?" Dani asked her. "Didn't Morris leave you something?"

"Yeah, he left me some money. But that diary was worth a lot more money, maybe millions. I figured I could retire the way I always wanted to. Who was it going to hurt?" Looking tired and disgusted, she let her head fall back on the sofa pillow. "I kept house for Morris for nearly twenty years. I figured I'd earned it."

Looking for something to say that wouldn't stir up more trouble, Dani remarked, "I don't see how you kept up with this house all by yourself."

"When no one was here it wasn't any problem. When the place was full I always had some extra help. Mostly what I did then was cook. I'm a damn good cook."

"I'm sure you are. I wish I had tasted some of it."

Edna looked bitterly amused. "If I'd kept my place and cooked for you the way Mr. Cheatham expected me to, I wouldn't be in this mess now. Are you going to turn me in?"

"For what?" Silas asked her. "I don't have any proof you did anything wrong."

Dani thought that was a very magnanimous statement, especially since they could have had the woman arrested for trespassing at the very least. But then Silas had proven himself to be a very generous man.

The ambulance arrived a few minutes later and carted Edna away to the hospital. All alone in the echoing atrium, Dani and Silas looked at one another. It was three in the morning.

"I don't know about you," Silas said, "but I'm too keyed up to sleep. How about we look for that damn diary now?"

Goose bumps rose on Dani's arm, and a shiver passed through her, as if a cold breeze had just blown over her. There was nothing frightening in the sensation, nothing threatening. It was almost like a chilly but gentle nudge. Morris, she thought. Morris wants us to find it. "We might as well. I couldn't sleep either."

"So where do we start? If Mustafa wasn't just blowing hot air, then it's where you sit. That could mean a lot of things."

"It could be the chair in my office."

"Or your entire office. After all, it's *where* you sit."

"True, I hadn't thought of that."

"So why don't we just start with your office."

"Again." It wouldn't be the first time they'd searched the room.

"It's kind of depressing, isn't it?" He leaned over her and kissed her gently on the lips. "We don't have to search tonight if you don't want. In fact, you can go back to bed and I'll do it by myself."

She gave him a tiny smile. "I don't think so. I'd just lie there in bed wishing you were beside me and I wouldn't sleep a wink. Besides, I don't think we're going to have any peace until we find the darn thing."

Together they climbed the stairs and went to her office. With all the lights turned on it was possible to forget that it was the middle of the night outside, but with so many different light sources, shadows bounced crazily around the walls every time one of them moved.

They took all the books off the shelves. Morris's house was chock full of books. Dani suspected the library must have run out of room years ago, and more recent acquisitions had found their way onto the shelves in most of the guest rooms. These were novels for the most part, as if Morris had left them for his guests to read.

But there was nothing behind them, nothing hidden behind a false cover, no little cubbyhole uncovered where something could be stashed. When Silas tapped on the walls behind the shelves, they sounded solid.

Next they explored the sofa. Unlike Ernie, Pepita, and Lester, they didn't rip the stuffing out of the pillows, but they checked for loose or uneven stitching in the fabric that might have indicated a hole had been sewn up. Silas even wedged his head beneath and checked to make sure nothing had been tucked into the frame or springs from below. No luck.

None of the other chairs had been tampered with either, and a couple of hours later they sat dejectedly on the couch and surveyed the room one last time.

"It's not here," Silas said. "It couldn't be. We'd have found anything bigger than a hairpin."

"Maybe."

"Maybe what we ought to do is invite all of the relatives over for a search party."

Dani almost laughed at the image that sprang to her mind. "Irving would have a conniption. And *we'd* get billed for all the furniture they tore apart."

"And for the cleaning crew afterward."

"And I bet they still wouldn't find it. Silas, it's hopeless. We've been searching this house for weeks and we haven't found a damn thing. How many places are left to look?"

"Under all the bathtubs? At the bottom of the fountain? The kitchen? We haven't really searched that room yet."

"It doesn't seem like a very likely hiding place."

"Which is why Morris would think of it," Silas reminded her with a crooked grin. "*And* the laundry room."

"Max said he spent a lot of time in the laundry room. That sometimes he used to lock himself in."

Without another word, they both rose and headed for the laundry room.

"I wonder why he spent so much time in here," Silas said as he removed bottles of bleach and soap and stain remover from high shelves and checked to be sure there was nothing behind them.

"Probably to get away from his wives," Dani said. "Why else?"

"Or maybe it just appealed to his twisted sense of humor." Silas looked up at the ceiling. "Do you hear me, Morris? You had a twisted sense of humor!"

A box of fabric softener sheets tumbled from the shelf to the floor. Neither of them had been near it.

"Did you see that?" Dani asked in a hushed voice.

"I saw that." Silas stared at the box as if it had suddenly sprouted a head. "I must have accidentally shoved it right to the edge when I was pulling this other stuff down."

"Yeah. Right."

"Right." He looked at her, and there was a funny smile in his eyes. "I guess Morris didn't like my description of his sense of humor."

"Too bad." Dani's chin thrust forward stubbornly. "How else could you describe it? He set this whole mess up! He never for a minute thought we'd write our books while we were here. No, he knew we'd spend all our damn time hunting for this stupid diary of his, and he's laughing his head off over it!"

A towel fell from the folding table onto the floor. Neither of them were within three feet of it.

"So he's not laughing his head off," Silas said. "Big hairy deal. We're still spending all our time looking for the damn diary, aren't we?"

"You know what really makes me mad?" Dani asked, hoping Morris really *could* hear her. "The way he can shove things off shelves to get our attention but he can't find the damn diary for us! He scares us half out of our wits by appearing here and there, but does he do anything useful? Does he *point* to where it's at? Oh, no! That would be too helpful!"

"Mustafa said there were rules."

"Damn the rules!"

Silas chuckled. "Actually, I agree with you, but Morris probably can't get away with it."

She stared sourly at the fallen towel and the dryer sheets. "It occurs to me that while Morris may have sat in here, I never have."

"Hell." Silas looked around. "I guess we're wasting our time in here. Better move on to the kitchen."

"Assuming Mustafa was right."

"At this point I'll assume it because it makes the search easier. If we don't turn up anything in all the places you sit, then I'll discard it."

"Fair enough."

The kitchen was a far worse place to search. Every cabinet was full of something, whether it was dishes or cans or boxes. The sun rose while they worked, painting the sky with a tangerine brush. From the windows, Dani glimpsed birds pecking their industrious way across the lawn and squirrels scampering up and down the live oaks.

"We're going to crash sooner or later," Silas

remarked. His voice was muffled as he stuck his head in a lower cabinet.

"When it happens, it happens." Her eyes felt gritty, but she was still too energized to slow down. She wanted to be *done* with this.

The sound of the front door knocker interrupted them. Hollow-eyed, they looked at one another.

"I think we're supposed to answer that," Dani said presently, when the banging came again.

"That's the idea. I'm just trying to decide whether to oblige."

"Oh." After all this time living with Silas, it no longer surprised her that he might ponder such a thing. For him such things were choices. He never did anything simply because it was expected.

"I guess I'll answer it," he said finally. "Maybe Morris decided to send a registered letter. Or maybe some other psychic's had a message from him."

It was a measure of how tired Silas was that it took him so long to make a decision. It was a sign of how tired Dani was that she didn't laugh at the absurdity of his suggestion.

Hollow-eyed, looking like a couple of zombies, they went to the door. Silas opened it and swore.

"Look, I'm sorry," Lester Carmichael said. "I swear. I had to tell you that I honestly didn't have anything to do with the fire at your boatyard. It really kills me that Ernie did that. I mean . . . it's one thing to try to get the diary but it's another to go destroying somebody's property. Aw, hell, I shouldn't have done either one."

"No, you shouldn't have. I'm not in a very forgiving mood at the moment, so maybe you'd better just clear out before I start thinking of all the things I have to be angry about."

Lester nodded. "I can see where you're coming from, Silas, but I gotta tell you one more thing or Mom's gonna skin me alive."

Silas assumed an attentive expression, but his

fingers were clenching and unclenching on the door-knob in a way that told Dani he couldn't have cared less what Lester might have to say.

"Look, I'm gonna make it up to you. Every week I'll pay you some money toward the damages the fire caused. Say a hundred dollars?"

Silas froze, as if he couldn't believe his ears. "You're offering to pay for the damages?"

"Isn't that what I said?" Lester shifted uneasily. "I shouldn't have listened to Ernie and all his bright ideas, but that's no excuse for me being such a jerk. So I should pay for the damage, right?"

"That would be very much appreciated, actually."

"I kind of figured it would. A hundred a week is all I can manage, though. Will that be okay?"

"That'll be just fine."

"Great." He hesitated a moment more, giving them a crooked smile. "You two look like hell, ya know?"

"We know. We've been up all night."

Lester laughed and turned to his car. "I think everybody was up all night. Mom never stopped yelling at me from the time we got into the car until I left this morning. And we saw _Morris_! Can you beat that?" Shaking his head, he walked to his car, climbed in, and drove away.

"I get the feeling," Silas said, "that Morris's appearance had some interesting consequences."

"Well, it might make one take the afterlife a little more seriously, and taking that more seriously might cause one to take a close look at one's conduct."

"Yeah. I guess it would."

"Of course, I'm just speculating."

"So?" He closed the door and locked it before turning to look at her. "Who cares? It's as good an explanation as any for that young man offering to pay for the damage to my boatyard. Hell, he claims he didn't even know about it until afterward. I'd expect him to be bellowing that he wasn't responsible for any of it."

"I suspect Tilly can be persuasive."

Silas shook his head, remembering. "And didn't she turn out to be something? The way she was quivering and quailing when she first got here, I never would have guessed she had so much fire in her."

"She's one wife I wouldn't mind getting to know better." Exhausted, Dani plopped down on Chacmool's bowl. "If I thought I could sleep, I'd fall into bed right this instant."

"Me too."

"I don't think I can face that kitchen again."

Silas perched beside her on Chacmool's knees and draped his arm around her shoulders. "It's been a beach of a night."

"So I hear tell."

"From where?"

"Every cell in my body."

"Mm. The kitchen can wait, sweetie."

"So can the damn diary."

Turning a little, he pressed a kiss to the top of her head and then let his mouth rest there against the silky strands. "Maybe if we curl up together real close we can relax enough to doze off."

That sounded absolutely wonderful to her. "Let's go try."

She slid off Chacmool's bowl, swaying just a little from fatigue. Just as Silas rose beside her, the door knocker sounded again.

"Good God," grumbled Silas. "I thought we finished all this stuff last night."

Dani sat down again, wincing when she misjudged and hit the edge of the bowl. Maybe what she ought to do was curl up right here, just recline on Chacmool and pretend he was made of feathers instead of stone.

Rosario was at the door this time. He stood there wringing his cap and looking about as abject as a man could possibly look. "I . . . just want to know if I still have a job. I guess you probably don't want

me, but . . . what I did was wrong. It's just that I
been friends with Edna for damn near twenty years
and the diary didn't seem like such an important
thing . . ."

Silas shook his head. "Rosario, as far as I'm
concerned, you still have your job. But that isn't up
to me. You'll have to talk to Irving Cheatham. He's
the one who's paying you."

"But you don't care if I cut the grass and fix the
hedge I chopped last night?"

"I don't care at all. Help yourself."

Looking relieved, Rosario headed for the tool
shed.

Silas shook his head again as he turned back to
Dani. "You know, I don't think most of the folks
involved in this are bad people. Like Rosario. Or
even Lester. Ernie—well, him I'm not sure about.
Five to ten in the pen might be just what he needs."

He was looking at her, smiling kind of sadly at the
foolishness of people, when a thought struck him.
"Dani?"

"Hm?" The room was beginning to look as if it
were on a merry-go-round, spinning slowly. Or maybe she was the one on the carousel . . .

"What exactly did Mustafa say about where to
look for the diary?"

"He said, 'Look where Dani sits.' That's all I
remember."

"What are you doing right now?"

Perplexed, she looked down at herself. "Nothing.
Am I? What do you mean?"

And then it dawned on her. "I'm sitting."

"That's right."

Slowly, hardly daring to believe it, she rose from
Chacmool and stepped back to look at the stone
statue. She'd been plopping down on the darn thing
almost since the instant she arrived. Even after all
this time she thought the statue was ridiculously out
of place in the atrium, but that was Morris.

That was Morris. He wouldn't even be subtle

about it. No, his hiding place would be in plain sight, so out of place as to be ugly.

"It can't be," she said. But already she believed it was. Hadn't they looked in every other possible place?

Silas was already prowling around the statue, peering at it, testing every chink and crease in the stone for looseness. "This has to be it," he muttered as he tested and pushed. "It's got to be."

Dani started helping him, pushing and pulling on the statue every way she could think of. "It could be underneath."

"Too heavy. Morris couldn't have moved it easily enough to make it a practical hiding place."

But nothing appeared to be loose—until Dani, frustrated, twisted the bowl on which she always sat. The effect was immediate. It came loose in her hands. Gripping the heavy piece tightly, she lifted it from the statue.

And there in a tidy little hollow lay a small stack of marbleized composition books.

22

━━◦◦◦◦━━

All thought of sleeping was gone. They took the books with them to the kitchen and made a big pot of coffee. Outside, the lawnmower started up, a sound that Dani always found somehow lazy and reassuring. It was going to be a beautiful Florida day.

"These can't be all his diaries," Silas said. "The man scribbled in these notebooks nearly every day for seventy-odd years."

"He probably had the good sense to burn all the ones he didn't want found. After all, Mustafa had warned him he was about to die."

Silas nodded, looking at her ruefully. "You're beginning to believe in Mustafa, too."

"I'm beginning to believe in a lot more than Mustafa." Dani touched the cover of one of the books. They were numbered in sequence. "I'm afraid to open them."

"He *did* want them kept private."

"Except for these," she said, lifting her gaze to his. "These he didn't destroy. And he told us to find them, remember?"

"We're assuming he meant the diaries."

"What else could it be?"

"Nothing, I guess." He passed his hand over his eyes and sighed wearily. "Hell, Morris, why didn't you just mail these damn books to us? It would have saved a lot of trouble, you know."

But it wouldn't have been as much fun.

Dani could have sworn she heard Morris speak the words, as if he were right in the room with them. "Fun?" she said. "Maybe it was fun for you, Morris, but it's been awful for *us*."

"You tell him," Silas said encouragingly. "Let him know what we really think."

"What I really think?" Dani was getting wound up now. With the diaries in hand, the whole situation seemed even more ridiculous than it had at the outset. "What I think is that you were a kind, loving, generous-to-a-fault type of man, Morris, but you had the brain of a twit when it came to some things! As practical jokes go, this one ceased to be funny about the third time one of your relatives invaded this place. It got downright grim when we got locked in the hurricane room! And what about Lester and Ernie playing frogmen and shooting a spear gun at Silas? Morris, he could have been seriously hurt and it would have been *your* fault!"

Silas propped his chin on his hand and regarded her from sleepy eyes. "Never to late to learn, huh?"

Dani shrugged. "It doesn't matter whether he heard or not, I just feel better for having said it."

The coffee finished brewing. They filled large mugs and sat side by side at the island.

"Who reads and who listens?" Silas asked.

"Why don't we just read silently together?"

"Good enough."

Morris's handwriting was surprisingly graceful for a man's, but as he had once said to Dani when she commented on it, "I was raised in an era where good penmanship was an important asset."

The first page was addressed to the two of them, making it clear that they were meant to read further.

"I know you two will probably be a little annoyed with me for leading you on this chase, but it's important that you spend time together before I share this with you. I believe you'll understand why after you read these pages.

"This is a record I've made over many months, ever since the lady started to appear with regularity and a great deal of persistence. Have you seen her? I somehow think you will have by the time you read this."

Dani and Silas exchanged looks, then hunched closer over the diary.

"That lady is Tricia Younger. There's a photograph of her taped to the inside back cover of this book—"

As one, Dani and Silas flipped right to the back cover of the book.

"Oh my," Dani whispered as shock slammed through her. She stared dumbly, trying to deny what her eyes were telling her. "Does it—" She broke off, unable to say it out loud.

Silas had no such problem. "It does," he said, sounding a little unnerved himself. "It's the spitting image of you. *Is* it you?"

"No . . . no . . ."

The woman wore the white dress of another era, the simple saque of the 1920's. Her smile was sweet, full of the innocence of someone too young to have met the darker side of life. Behind her the gulf waters looked placid and the sky was cloudless. It had been a perfect Florida day.

And now Dani understood why Morris had pursued a correspondence with her. It was a little disappointing to realize that it hadn't been her sparkling wit, or the brilliance of any question she had asked him at the seminar. It had been, simply, her resemblance to someone who must have meant a great deal to him. Oh, well, she told herself philosophically, regardless of why their friendship had begun, it had been a wonderful friendship.

"It's uncanny," Silas said. "Unreal. Damn. No wonder I thought it was you standing in the doorway all those times. The damn ghost is your spitting image."

"I have a feeling this is going to be a sad story."

"Yeah." He flipped back to the beginning of the diary. "I get that feeling, too."

Tricia Younger, Morris wrote, had been the niece of Julio Riveras, the wealthy Tampa cigar manufacturer who had owned the house in which they were currently staying. Morris had been the son of a small-town doctor, nowhere near her social equal. They had met when she was eighteen and he was barely twenty-two and fresh out of college. At the time he had been working as a stringer for the newspaper, assigned to cover social events. He had been covering a black-tie affair at one of the grand St. Petersburg beach resorts when he had met her.

It had been love at first sight. Not an hour into the evening they had escaped from the hotel's stuffy ballroom out onto the fresh white sand of the beach where they had strolled in the moonlight, leaving behind all their responsibilities.

For a while they had continued to meet in this fashion, at social events where he was reporting. When her uncle, who was also her guardian, learned of their relationship, he wasn't disapproving. "Not the domineering guardian of the popular myth at all," Morris wrote. "He told me that I was a fine young man with apparent potential, but that Tricia was accustomed to a comfortable life. He asked how I proposed to support her in her accustomed style on a stringer's pay.

"Well, of course I couldn't," Morris wrote. "I could barely support *myself* on my income, and a wife—of any class—was economically beyond my reach at that time. Tricia professed herself willing to live on beans in a shanty, but I couldn't bear the thought. Nor was I certain I could even provide the beans."

Dani could almost hear Morris speak those words in that incredibly wry tone of his.

That, Morris continued, was his first mistake. "I should have done anything and everything within my means to make her my wife. I loved her, you see. And she loved me. Together we could somehow have surmounted everything. I truly believe that, and the greatest sorrow of my life has been that I didn't have the sense to believe that when it actually mattered."

Julio Riveras had offered Morris a position in his cigar factory, promising him that if he showed aptitude, he would advance quickly. It was a sincere offer of assistance for which Morris was grateful, and marked Riveras forever in Morris's mind as a true gentleman, but Riveras had three sons who were rising in the business, and Morris felt he would be intruding on their hopes for the future. Besides, he admitted frankly, he didn't want to be dependent on anyone else for his success. He didn't want to win Tricia through the efforts of her uncle; he wanted to win her through his own. He wanted to be *worthy* of her—and that meant making his own success.

"Pride," he wrote these many years later, "is the worst sin of all, because it leads a man—or a woman—to do truly foolish things. I could have had Tricia had I been willing to swallow my pride just a little. Instead I chose to leave her behind in my quest to become a worthy husband for her. Fool!"

"*Romantic* fool," Silas said quietly. Somehow it softened the epithet.

"I think I would have done the same thing," Dani said.

Silas nodded. "Yeah, the inclination is there."

Tricia had vowed to wait for Morris, and wait she did. The stock market crash of 1929 and the ensuing depression made Morris's dreams of success even more difficult to achieve. He wandered the globe, eventually reporting on the Spanish Civil War and the rise of German military might. The success that he sought eluded him until 1938, when a book he had written about the Spanish Civil War was published and called a "triumph of journalism."

"But," Morris wrote, "it came too late. Tricia waited faithfully, although as the years passed I began to urge her to find a good husband before it was too late. We saw one another only once a year, and then only briefly. It was enough to keep the spark alive and make the separations nearly unbearable. We tortured ourselves in the hope of a future together, but it was in vain.

"The last time I came home to see her, I was something of a literary lion. I wasn't wealthy, but I was comfortable, and felt that I could offer her a decent life of reasonable comfort. She was so beautiful that day. Her cheeks were as rosy as I had ever seen them, her eyes as bright as if they glowed from within. When I told her how lovely I found her, she gave me a smile that I have carried within my heart ever since.

"I was blinded by my own excitement and success. I should have noticed she was markedly thinner, but I didn't. It should have struck me that this time we didn't walk on the beach as we always had before, but instead sat on the patio and talked. I should have realized that she didn't run to greet me as she always had, but had waited for me to come to her chair and bend down to kiss her."

"Oh dear," Dani breathed as she read. An ache was already filling her heart for what was to come. When Silas reached for her hand and squeezed it, she clung gratefully. Together they turned the page.

"She refused my proposal," Morris wrote. "I was stunned. She had waited for me for ten years, and now she was refusing me. Was there another man? No. No, she said she simply didn't feel ready to marry. She had discovered that she enjoyed her life of spinsterhood, and that she didn't want to dash madly around the globe after me.

"I was crushed. All along she had appeared to share my dreams of traveling the world, and now she was telling me that she wanted no part of it. When at last I was convinced she couldn't be swayed, I ran. I ran as far as I could go, to Europe on the brink of war. I took the most dangerous assignments my wire service offered, determined to get myself killed somehow. But luck was against me.

"Silas, do you remember Beirut? You thought I was so foolhardy, but the truth of it is, I had learned a long time ago that when your time comes it comes, and until that moment your existence is charmed. Mine was charmed for fifty years too long! How glad I am at last to be at the end."

Tears squeezed out of Dani's eyes and clung to her lower lashes. She blinked uselessly a couple of times, trying to clear her vision, but finally had to dash the tears away with the back of her hand. "Why did she do that to him, Silas? Why, after she waited so long?"

"I have my suspicions." He turned the page and they began to read.

"I spent the war years in both Europe and the South Pacific," Morris wrote. "My parents had died—I was an only child—and I no longer had any reason to return home. The whole time I kept waiting for a shell to fall on my head and put an end to my emotional misery. In retrospect I think I was being a self-indulgent young ass. The loss hurt and hurt deeply. Hell, it still hurts today! But the suicidal *angst* was an expression of immaturity. I blush to remember it."

"I've had those moods," Silas remarked.

"Me too." Morris had always seemed so self-assured and in charge, she found this image of him to be . . . charming. It was surprisingly easy to imagine him as a young man dashing from war zone to war zone, risking his neck wildly while nursing his sorrow. A dark, Byronic image. Yes, that would have appealed to Morris. It was the writer in him that had led him to be so dramatic. Not that she was minimizing his pain. Now that she had come to feel so deeply for Silas, she could easily imagine how the loss of Tricia must have wounded him.

Sighing, she snuggled against Silas's shoulder and read on.

"When the war was over, I had earned a name in print journalism on a par with Walter Cronkite and Lowell Thomas in radio journalism. It allowed me stay overseas longer, to report on the progress of the Marshall Plan. Then in '47 I got involved in the Palestinian situation and spent a lot of time in Jerusalem and Tel Aviv. I managed not to set foot again in the state of Florida until just about the time the Korean situation blew up. I was all set to head that way when for some reason I'll never know I decided to stop over here.

"I guess in some way I needed to believe it was truly over. Maybe I thought that seeing her with several children and a doting husband would make me let go of it all.

"I never dreamed! When I came up the driveway to the house, I was appalled by the way things had deteriorated. Most people had made sacrifices during the war, but the war had been over for nearly five years, and I would have thought the Riveras household would be back to normal. Instead I found near dilapidation. Their business must have fallen on hard times. I remember hoping that whoever Tricia had married was doing considerably better.

"Imagine my astonishment when I discovered the house was empty and for sale. Perhaps, I thought, the beachfront home had become too expensive and too rarely used, and the family had chosen to get rid of it. They did, after all, have a beautiful home in Tampa. And that's where I next went. Even as I was doing this, I wondered that I was spending so much time on it. Why didn't I just get a phone book and call the factory. All my curiosity could have been settled that easily.

"Instead I drove into Tampa. What I learned there broke my heart forever."

"I knew it," whispered Silas.

Dani nodded against his shoulder, bracing herself for what they would read next.

"I found one of her cousins living in the house that had once been filled to the rafters with Riverases. Jorge Riveras invited me inside and we shared a bottle of wine as he told me all that had happened.

"The brothers had sold the cigar factory to a competitor during the war after their father died. The family was all still in the area, but everyone had separate lives now and they got together only for holidays and special family events. The old patriarchy had passed away with Julio.

"As for Tricia . . . I sensed he didn't want to get around to telling me about her, so finally I asked him point blank. When he swallowed hard and his eyes began to sparkle with tears, I knew the worst. Tricia had never had the happy, contented life I had tortured myself by imagining for her. She had never married, and had never had those beautiful children I was so sure she must have conceived.

"No, she had died of consumption in 1944. That was why she had sent me away and told me she didn't want to marry me. That bright color in her cheeks and in her eyes was a symptom of her illness but I hadn't recognized how unnatural it was. I hated myself for that. I don't know what I would have said, how I could have comforted her . . . but at least I would not have left her.

"She had been ill for months before our last meeting, but hadn't wanted me to know. She had prayed, Jorge told me, for a miracle that would make her whole again for me. It didn't happen. The family wanted to tell me how ill she was but she forbade them because she knew I would come back to her immediately. She didn't want me to know, he said, because she knew I would insist on marrying her anyway.

"She was, you see, every bit as much a fool as I was. We both deprived one another of what we most needed in our lives because neither of us was willing to ask the other to make a sacrifice.

"How noble. How sad. How unutterably foolish.

"I bought the house, obviously. Tricia had lived most of her life within these walls, and had died here on the upstairs balcony looking down at the water. If there was any place on earth that she truly loved, it was this house. So I made it mine.

"Over the years I've seen her a few times. At first I thought I was losing my mind, and made sure I was never here alone. Finally—allow me a small grin here—I got myself to the point where I couldn't be alone even if I tried. Which is why I got a reputation for locking myself in the laundry room.

"But I continued to see Tricia on and off in odd moments, sometimes even when the room was crowded with my wives and their children. She's always given me a sad, wistful smile, as if she wished things could be different but knew they couldn't.

"Lately I've been seeing her far more often. Nearly every day in fact. That's why I sat to down to write this, and why I filled the other enclosed notebooks with personal reminiscences about our relationship. She has been close to me, telling me my time is near, asking me to fulfill our relationship in the only way that's left.

"Now you ask yourselves why I've passed these books on to you.

"Silas, you remind me of myself. Oh, in some ways we're very different people, but there's a certain boldness to you with which I feel a kinship. And a certain loneliness I recognize.

"Dani, you remind me so much of Tricia that sometimes my heart aches. Not only in your looks—though that was certainly what initially brought you to my attention—but also in your personality. You have the same tartness, the same directness and the same insecurities. You feel you are unlovable, and so did Tricia. It grieves me that I needed so badly to prove myself that I never gave her what she most needed: my love.

"The two of you will identify with Tricia and me, so it is to you I entrust our story.

"And to you I give one final piece of advice: Seize every moment that comes your way. Take what life offers now, because it may never be offered again.

"I love you both. God bless you."

Dani was in tears, hardly able to read the final words, but her heart heard them as if Morris were standing right beside her speaking them. When she turned toward Silas, his arms were already there to offer comfort.

They finally slept. Vaguely, Dani was aware that the phones rang a couple of times, and that someone hammered on the door, but the disturbances weren't enough to drag her out of her much-needed sleep.

When at last she woke, the sun was setting, painting the evening a deep pink. Silas was gone from the bed, but when she stirred she saw him sitting in the chair watching her.

"Hi," he said.

"Hi," she responded, in a voice husky with sleep.

"Sleep well?"

"Mm."

"Me too." He gave her a small smile. "Do you suppose Morris left those damn diaries to us to make us do some thinking?"

Dani propped herself up on her elbow and looked at him. It was such a luxury to be able to lie naked beneath the sheets and feel so comfortable with him. "I think that was part of it."

"Yeah." His smile deepened another shade. "So I've been sitting here thinking."

Why did that make her heart leap into high gear, as if she were leaning over a precipice and in danger of falling?

"I've been thinking that Morris was right. I've been wasting my life trying to get somewhere. The worst of it is, I'm not even sure where I'm trying to get to. Just some mythical place where I'll feel good enough."

"Why wouldn't you feel good enough?" She couldn't conceive of it.

"My dad was a shrimper. Not exactly high up the social ladder. I guess I still feel like the barefoot kid I used to be. I was lucky to get through high school the way I sometimes had to fill in when Dad couldn't get up a whole crew. I often missed six weeks of school at a time."

"But you made it."

"Yeah, I made it."

"You should be very proud of yourself for that. A lot of people would have given up."

"Actually, I stuck it out because I wanted to get away from the damn shrimping business. Sometimes I wondered if I'd ever get the stink of fish and diesel oil out of my skin. Anyway, I needed that diploma to get away, and the very first thing I did with it was show it to the marine recruiter. Three days later I was outta there."

"So you succeeded again."

He gave her an odd look. "Little Miss Pollyanna."

"I'm just telling it like it is. You accomplished two major goals you set yourself by the time you were eighteen. Not everyone can say that."

Again that faint smile appeared on his lips. "Maybe. And maybe they weren't the right goals. As it happens, along about the time I got the stink of fish out of my skin I started missing it. They say once the sea gets into your blood it never goes away, and I guess that was true of me. After Beirut I was more than happy to hightail it home and take over the business."

"It looks to me as if you've been quite successful at it."

"I have been, I guess. I'm especially pleased by the way the boatyard has prospered."

"But you still feel somehow unworthy?"

"I still feel like that barefoot fisherman's kid who always smelled funny so the other kids didn't want to be around him. Well, hell, what can you expect when you get up every morning before school to work on the boat or the nets or the traps? I put in half a day before the morning bell, and I smelled like it."

"I have kids in my classes who are in the same position. Farmer's kids. But there must have been others at the school who were fishermen's children."

"Oh, sure. But we knew we were being set apart. You can't miss it. Now look, I'm not saying I'm still brooding about things that happened when I was kid. I'm just saying that I guess somewhere inside those feelings still persist. It's dumb, really."

He looked away briefly, his jaw muscle working visibly. Finally he faced her again, his cat-green eyes looking haunted. "There's more, though. You've helped me to realize it isn't true, but I felt . . . inadequate ever since I was drummed out of the corps."

Dani straightened. "Drummed out? What do you mean?"

"Discharged for disability."

"Oh. But . . . Silas, you don't have any disabilities, do you?"

He gave her a humorless smile. "How about a morbid fear of the dark in confined spaces? Ever since the bombing . . . well, hell. I don't know if you can understand, but when we were in the hurricane room . . ." He shrugged. "It doesn't bother me to be outside at night, nothing like that. It's only inside, in an enclosed space. If the light goes out, I get . . . unreasonable."

"Not that I noticed." Dani wanted to reach out to him, but hesitated, feeling somehow that the time wasn't right. A hug was not the answer he needed right now. "Silas, for heaven's sake, look how well you handled yourself in the hurricane room. I don't have claustrophobia, but I was on the edge of panic.

If you hadn't been there . . . well, I don't want to think about it. And on the stairway. My word, you dashed up that stairway to rescue me! Who was the person frozen in the dark? Me, not you!"

His smile grew gentler. "I noticed. It's, well, you make me feel like a man again, Dani. Dumb, huh?"

"I don't know about that. Look at me. I still get scared to death by the wind, and because of a couple of stupid men I feel like the unsexiest thing that ever walked the earth."

"You?" His smile deepened. "Honey pot, you are the *sexiest* thing I've ever seen. I get turned on at the mere sight of you."

A blush flooded her cheeks and spread all the way down to her breasts. "Thank you."

"And what was that Morris meant about you feeling unlovable?"

Her blush deepened and she looked down at her hands. "I guess I do. I mean . . . I don't think my fiancé really loved me. If he had, would he have run off with another woman?"

"Probably not. But how does that add up to you being unlovable?"

"Just that—nobody ever—loved me that way."

Suddenly Silas was there, kneeling beside the bed, clasping her hands and looking earnestly into her eyes. "*I* love you," he said.

She lifted her gaze, wide, wondering eyes that searched his face as if desperately hungry for the sight of him. Her mouth opened on a soft gasp of surprise.

"I do," he insisted. "I love you till I'm half out of my mind with it. But . . . I understand that you don't feel the same way. I mean, how could you? You're educated and refined and I've never been to college and I have the manners of a goat—"

"Oh, stop. Stop!" She pressed her hand to his mouth, unable to bear listening to him say such things. "You're doing just what Morris was warning us against. Do you really think a college degree matters one way or another to me? If it does, then how come I love you so much?"

The faint, wistful smile on his face suddenly blossomed into full-blown joy. "You do? You really do?"

When she nodded, he crushed her to him, squeezing her until she finally protested with a squeak. He looked down at her from glistening green eyes. "What about your job?" he asked huskily. "I'm sorry, but I can't move my boatyard to Kansas."

"Ohio. I can teach here just as well as there, Silas. That's not a real problem. Besides, I'm taking Morris's advice and grabbing every moment that life gives me. Consider yourself grabbed."

Laughing, he tumbled onto the bed with her and pulled her into a bear hug. "I grabbed you first, teach, and don't you ever forget it."

Epilogue

———❦———

"Roxy will be here in just a few minutes," Silas said. He was standing in the atrium, looking up at the gallery.

"What's up?" Dani asked. She came out of the kitchen carrying their six-month-old daughter Shannon. The little girl had just finished a bowl of applesauce and was gurgling contentedly against her mother's shoulder.

"Oh, it's Morris again. He and Tricia are standing up there looking impatient."

Dani glanced up and smiled at their ghostly companions. "They don't look impatient to me. Just eager."

Silas took Shannon from her and bounced the baby gently. "You smell like applesauce, princess. Mmmm, wasn't that good?"

Dani felt her heart swelling as if to burst, a feeling that was all too common since she and Silas had married two years ago. This man made her so incredibly happy.

Neither of them had been able to bear the thought of parting with the house, not once they knew the story behind it. The upkeep wasn't as dreadful as Dani had feared, and Silas's income from the boatyard made it possible for them to keep Rosario and to bring in part-time housekeeping help.

Dani no longer taught. Her first novel had been successful enough for her to decide to make writing her career, and she was even now finishing her fourth book. Silas, too, had been successful with his writing, though with the boatyard to occupy him it remained a hobby.

And Morris and Tricia visited them often. The Northrops had grown quite comfortable with the two ghosts, and Dani suspected that when they moved on she and Silas were going to miss them dreadfully.

And tonight Roxy was coming by, as she did periodically, to see what Morris might have to say. It was always a curious experience.

Silas slipped his arm around Dani, and smiled when he saw Morris do the same with Tricia. "I guess ghosts like to hug, too."

Dani nodded, happily rubbing her cheek against Silas's shoulder. "I guess so." Never had she imagined it could be possible to feel so content.

Shannon Tricia Northrop reached out just then and tugged her mother's hair. Dani squeaked and then giggled. Silas laughed.

Morris and Tricia laughed, too, then slowly faded away.

Their inaudible laughter seemed to linger on the air after them, casting peace and joy over the house and those within.

Discover Contemporary Romances at Their Sizzling Hot Best from Avon Books

JONATHAN'S WIFE   *by Dee Holmes*
78368-1/$5.99 US/$7.99 Can

DANIEL'S GIFT   *by Barbara Freethy*
78189-1/$5.99 US/$7.99 Can

FAIRYTALE   *by Maggie Shayne*
78300-2/$5.99 US/$7.99 Can

WISHES COME TRUE   *by Patti Berg*
78338-X/$5.99 US/$7.99 Can

**ONCE MORE
WITH FEELING**   *by Emilie Richards*
78363-0/$5.99 US/$7.99 Can

HEAVEN COMES HOME   *by Nikki Holiday*
78456-4/$5.99 US/$7.99 Can

RYAN'S RETURN   *by Barbara Freethy*
78531-5/$5.99 US/$7.99 Can

Avon Romantic Treasures

Unforgettable, enthralling love stories,
sparkling with passion and adventure
from Romance's bestselling authors

SUNDANCER'S WOMAN *by Judith E. French*
77706-1/$5.99 US/$7.99 Can

JUST ONE KISS *by Samantha James*
77549-2/$5.99 US/$7.99 Can

HEARTS RUN WILD *by Shelly Thacker*
78119-0/$5.99 US/$7.99 Can

DREAM CATCHER *by Kathleen Harrington*
77835-1/$5.99 US/$7.99 Can

THE MACKINNON'S BRIDE *by Tanya Anne Crosby*
77682-0/$5.99 US/$7.99 Can

PHANTOM IN TIME *by Eugenia Riley*
77158-6/$5.99 US/$7.99 Can

RUNAWAY MAGIC *by Deborah Gordon*
78452-1/$5.99 US/$7.99 Can

YOU AND NO OTHER *by Cathy Maxwell*
78716-4/$5.99 US/$7.99 Can

Avon Romances—
the best in exceptional authors and unforgettable novels!

WICKED AT HEART   **Danelle Harmon**
78004-6/ $5.50 US/ $7.50 Can

SOMEONE LIKE YOU   **Susan Sawyer**
78478-5/ $5.50 US/ $7.50 Can

MIDNIGHT BANDIT   **Marlene Suson**
78429-7/ $5.50 US/ $7.50 Can

PROUD WOLF'S WOMAN   **Karen Kay**
77997-8/ $5.50 US/ $7.50 Can

THE HEART AND THE HOLLY **Nancy Richards-Akers**
78002-X/ $5.50 US/ $7.50 Can

ALICE AND THE GUNFIGHTER **Ann Carberry**
77882-3/ $5.50 US/ $7.50 Can

THE MACKENZIES: LUKE   **Ana Leigh**
78098-4/ $5.50 US/ $7.50 Can

FOREVER BELOVED   **Joan Van Nuys**
78118-2/ $5.50 US/ $7.50 Can

INSIDE PARADISE   **Elizabeth Turner**
77372-4/ $5.50 US/ $7.50 Can

CAPTIVATED   **Colleen Corbet**
78027-5/ $5.50 US/ $7.50 Can

*If you enjoyed this book,
take advantage
of this special offer.
Subscribe now and get a*

FREE
Historical
Romance

No Obligation (a $4.50 value)

Each month the editors of True Value select the four *very best* novels from America's leading publishers of romantic fiction. Preview them in your home *Free* for 10 days. With the first four books you receive, we'll send you a FREE book as our introductory gift. No Obligation!

If for any reason you decide not to keep them, just return them and owe nothing. If you like them as much as we think you will, you'll pay just $4.00 each and save at *least* $.50 each off the cover price. (Your savings are *guaranteed* to be at least $2.00 each month.) There is NO postage and handling – or other hidden charges. There are no minimum number of books to buy and you may cancel at any time.

*Send in
the Coupon
Below*

To get your FREE historical romance fill out the coupon below and mail it today. As soon as we receive it we'll send you your FREE Book along with your first month's selections.

Mail To: **True Value Home Subscription Services, Inc.**, P.O. Box 5235
120 Brighton Road, Clifton, New Jersey 07015-5235

YES! I want to start previewing the very best historical romances being published today. Send me my FREE book along with the first month's selections. I understand that I may look them over FREE for 10 days. If I'm not absolutely delighted I may return them and owe nothing. Otherwise I will pay the low price of just $4.00 each: a total $16.00 (at least an $18.00 value) and save at least $2.00. Then each month I will receive four brand new novels to preview as soon as they are published for the same low price. I can always return a shipment and I may cancel this subscription at any time with no obligation to buy even a single book. In any event the FREE book is mine to keep regardless.

Name _____

Street Address _____ Apt. No. _____

City _____ State _____ Zip _____

Telephone _____

Signature _____
(if under 18 parent or guardian must sign)

Terms and prices subject to change. Orders subject to acceptance by True Value Home Subscription Services, Inc.

0-380-72774-9